I dedicate this book
to my wife, Susan
and to our children

JOSEPH GOODSON

THE KISS

The Kiss
by
Joseph Goodson

Copyright ©2025

Putnam & Smith Publishing Company

Cover Design by: Brian Harris

Distributed by:
Putnam & Smith Publishing Company
15915 Ventura Boulevard, Suite 101
Encino, California 91436

www.putnamandsmithpublishing.com

Library of Congress Number: 2024944811

ISBN: 978-1-939986-49-8
Printed in the USA

ACKNOWLEDGMENTS

A special thanks to my friend, Brian Harris, who created the book cover of The Kiss. Brian can be contacted at behstudio@hotmail.com.

Also, thanks to Gilbert Girion, Sheldom Cohen, Peter Eisneer & Bill Gardner for all their help along the way.

PART ONE

THE LEARNING TREE

THE KISS

CHAPTER 1

OFF TO SCHOOL

I spent the morning loading my car with clothes and all the stuff you need when you go off to college each fall.

"Good morning, Joseph."

"Morning, Mom," I said, taking the last bite of my tuna sandwich while putting the mayo away.

"Were you going to say goodbye?"

"Mom," I said, joining her at the kitchen table, "Of course."

"Joseph, tell me again where it is you're going."

"Rutgers, Mom. I'm going to Rutgers for my sophomore year, class of '56."

"What about Penn State?"

"Mom, we've gone over this a hundred times."

"Tell me again, what is wrong with Penn State?"

"It's too far from Smith College, so Celeste's dad made a phone call to the Dean of Men at Rutgers who expedited my transfer. We did it last week."

"Celeste's dad knows people like that?"

"Celeste's dad knows lots of people. He owns the "41" Club, it's a world-famous restaurant in New York City."

"So, he knows lots of people, that doesn't mean his daughter is good enough for you. He's probably a crook and she's a pick-up!"

"His daughter is my girlfriend, has been for years, and you are talking crazy. It's time for me to go."

I hugged my mother.

"I love you Mom but not when you're talking crazy."

"I'll walk you to the car."

I knew better than to argue and outside I got in my Chevy and rolled down the window.

"Call me when you get there."

"Okay, Mom, I'll call you."

We both knew I wouldn't. I started the car, waved to my mom, backed out of the driveway and headed for Hempstead Avenue.

I hate my mom, I love my mom, she's very unpredictable; sweet or sour, you never know what you're going to get.

When I exited the Lincoln Tunnel it was pouring, welcome to New Jersey, the Garden State. As I approached New Brunswick the rain was letting up and by the time I found and parked in front of 4 Mine Street it had stopped raining. The only thing missing was a rainbow.

I grabbed a light load of stuff and entered the Phi Ep fraternity house and was directed to the second floor, first room on the left where I decided to pile my things on the only unmade bed. When I exited the building to grab my next load there was a girl walking toward campus on the other side of the street; when she saw me she stopped; she just sort of froze watching me. I ducked into the car, grabbed more stuff and headed inside.

Outside for my next load she was still there. I waved and she waved back as I grabbed a suitcase. On the way in I thought she's about five feet three and pretty, very pretty. On the last trip she was gone and in her place was the hoped-for rainbow.

I purposefully arrived at Rutgers four or five days before classes so that I could check in with the registrar, be sure of my schedule, roam the campus and get a chance to meet my fraternity brothers. Even though I was a sophomore I was the new kid and I wanted to fit in. I met Noel and Max and some of the other 30 or so guys as they trickled in and, of course, I met my roommate, Richard. Richard is from South Jersey, maybe five ten, bushy eyebrows, a pleasant demeanor, not too talky and overall a really nice guy. I was starting to feel pretty good about this transfer.

During the first week of classes I noticed the girl who was watching me the day I arrived; she was in my Classical Music elective. Maybe it was the second or third week we were exiting class at the same time and I introduced myself, "I'm Joseph," extending my hand. She took it, "I'm Kate," she said, holding onto my hand for an extra second or two.

"I've got to go," she said, tilting her head in "that" direction. "My next class is way over there." She walked away and I watched her, thinking, she is very pretty.

As roommates Richard and I settled on lights out around eleven and usually we chatted for a while. One night Richard asked about Celeste.

"You love her?"

"She's my girl," I answered, "what about you? Anyone special?"

"Yes", he said, "I'm dating dentistry. That's my goal and along the way, who knows?"

There is only one phone-line coming into the fraternity house and somehow 30 or so guys managed to make and receive all the calls that were needed. One afternoon a voice bellowed from down below, "Hey Joe, Joe Gordon, there's a call for you; it's the Dean of Men."

"Thanks, I'll be right there," I responded, closing my book. On the way out I saw Richard raise an eyebrow.

"And?" asked Richard upon my return.

"He said he wants to meet me and invited me to his house on Sunday at 5 o'clock."

"His house?"

"Yeah, and he mentioned Bourbon, beer and barbecue. Sounds like a party."

I found his street and his house, the last one on the left. The simple, one story home, was at the end of a long driveway and nestled back into the woods. I pulled into the driveway and parked behind the only car there. It was exactly five o'clock when I rang the front doorbell that didn't seem to work.

"Hello, anybody home?" I called through the screen door.

"Come on in; I'm on the back patio."

I entered the house and was immediately overwhelmed by the stench of cigarettes. Everything was neat and clean as I walked to the back, found the kitchen and exited to the patio where Ed Draper, Dean of Men at Rutgers, was stubbing out a cigarette in a huge ashtray.

"Joe, it's a pleasure," as he stuck out his hand.

"Mine as well," I responded a little uncertain. "This is a beautiful setting back here." The patio was slate and edged with bricks where it curved into a beautiful lawn, maybe a half-acre that disappeared into the woods.

"It's my sanctuary." Ed said as he looked around.

"You could have a hell of a touch football game back here, or maybe croquet, or both?"

He smiled but looked a little sad I thought; this 50-ish man with the ruddy cheeks of a heavy drinker, thinning hair, slightly portly, and the tight, dry lips of a chain smoker.

"Where is everyone," I asked.

"Just the two of us; I thought we should get to know one another. Do you like bourbon?"

"I do. Sure." I replied as I wondered, what the hell is this all about?

"Birchbrook okay?"

"Sure." There's a clue; that's the bourbon they serve at "41".

The Dean had a bar and a fridge and a barbecue all built-in on the patio. I watched as he poured us two big tumblers of bourbon. He handed me one, clinked my glass with his, "Here's to you, Joe."

"Thank you, Dean of Men, Ed."

"How about Ed?"

I nodded and took a long pull on the bourbon; it was good. "What does the Dean of Men do at Rutgers?"

"I see to it that all of the men at Rutgers are getting a good education and behaving themselves, more or less, while they're at it."

"Well you can't have each of us over here one at a time, I don't think?"

"You're right; you are special."

"That sounds a little scary."

"Not at all," he said as he stepped off the patio onto the grass, "Come on, let's walk around."

Ed led the way across the lawn towards the woods that seemed quite dense. As we got closer I could see someone had cleared a little area about ten feet into the woods that offered two wicker chairs. We sat and were instantly at one with nature. It was quite lovely and Ed's house, seen through the trees, seemed a mile away.

"Fun, huh?"

"Yeah. Did you do this?"

"A friend, years ago. At first I was pissed but over time I realized it is a marvelous spot to contemplate anything."

"It depends on how friendly the animals are," I offered.

"Small stuff, although there are plenty of deer. In fact that's why I have no flowerbeds; the deer would wipe them out in a minute."

"Okay I'm contemplating and I have a question."

"Go for it."

"You're a chain smoker and yet you haven't smoked a cigarette since I got here. What's with that?"

"It's a game I play, trying to see if I can get through a meeting, or my drive to the office, or how long I can hold off after Joe arrives?"

"You are doing well, sir."

"Another two minutes and I'll explode but first let me tell you why we are here: your future father-in-law asked if I would arrange for a last-minute transfer and here you are. Pretty simple."

"Probably not that simple and I thank you."

"Jerry also asked me to keep an eye on you because he plans to make you part of the "41" family and he wants to know if you're doing okay."

"So you are a spy."

"That's harsh; I would like us to become friends." Ed stood and said, "What do you say we get a couple of rib-eyes on the barbecue? Besides, I left my smokes on the patio."

As we walked across the grass I wondered who mows the lawn. As if he could read my mind Ed said, "I do."

During dinner we talked about Penn State, Rutgers, sports, "41", and Celeste. It was all pretty light, no pressure, no prying and the rib-eye was delicious. Ed hoisted his beer and toasted, "To friendship."

I echoed the thought, "Friendship."

"How about next Sunday," Ed asked.

"No can do, I'm off to visit Celeste for the weekend. I'll be enjoying the very reason for my transfer; half the drive time."

"I wish you a safe and easy trip and, of course, a good time."

Ed walked me out to my car; as we went through the house I held my nose and Ed feigned a smile.

Back at Phi Ep I found Richard typing something.

"Hey," I said, to let him know I was in the room. Richard, loquacious as ever, asked, "And?"

"Good bourbon, good beer, great rib-eye, but it was weird."

"What, weird?"

"No one else was there, just the Dean and me."

"Wow. You just got here and you had dinner with the Dean of Men at his house; are you in trouble or something?"

"I'm not in trouble and the something is that Ed, the Dean, is the one that facilitated my transfer and I quote, he wants us to become friends."

"Ed!"

"And he wants to have dinner again in a couple of weeks."

"You are going to be a campus celebrity; mark my words."

"No, this is between you and me. Are we good on that?"

"Of course."

Celeste looked pretty as ever and was smiling as I got out of my car. We hugged and kissed ever so briefly; lots of onlookers.

"How was your trip?" She asked.

"It was great, really, so much easier."

"That's terrific, I'm so glad. You look wonderful."

"Me? Look at you," I said while thinking I really wanted to do more than put my arms around her. "Do we have plans?"

"Dinner tonight with Judy and her boyfriend. Nothing special, we'll figure out a place to go later."

That's kind of the way visits went with Celeste: she has good friends who have nice boyfriends and we would spend one night with them and Saturday night, just the two of us.

Of course in the evening we always found a place to park and make out like crazy. But it's different now, the college years are the bridge from teenagers to adults and we found ourselves doing a lot more talking about our studies and the future.

We talked and dreamed and kissed and wiped fog from the car windows. The weekend was nice but something was missing; I could feel it.

Back at Rutgers, Richard closed his book, raised both eyebrows, "And," he inquired, as I sat on my bed and leaned against the wall.

"The weekend was good and the trip up and back was a piece of cake."

"That's great, and Celeste? You know I am looking forward to meeting her."

"Well, she's fine and I might have her down for House Party weekend. Maybe."

"I hope she comes but it sounds like there's something else going on?"

"I guess what I'm feeling is I'm not sure about me, my relationship with Celeste, or my going to work at "41". Right now I'm not sure of anything. I'm a work in progress."

Richard had listened bravely and not said a word. "Rutgers has a counselor and you might consider a visit with her."

"A counselor, that's a great idea and this is between us, okay?"

"Absolutely."

I found Pete's Gym in a horrible part of New Brunswick. I locked my car and hoped it would be there when I came back.

Inside there wasn't much going on: there were a bunch of old lockers against one wall, a boxing ring that wasn't raised, a couple of old treadmills, a pommel horse, a complete set of weights near a bench and a heavyweight punching bag hanging near the ring. It was the middle of the afternoon and what I figured to be some locals sitting in a corner talking quietly. They were all looking at me as I headed toward them; about halfway there I said, "I'm looking for Pete."

"Who is looking for Pete?" Said the man who stood and was walking toward me. I'm guessing he's around 50 years old, crew cut trending toward gray, about 5'8", maybe 140 pounds and he had a funny hitch in his step. But at the same time I got the feeling he could be quick.

I was thinking I should have taken boxing lessons before I came here to get boxing lessons. "My name is Joe, I'm looking for Pete."

"You found him. What do you want?"

"I want you to teach me how to box."

"From the looks of things you've never been in the ring in your life; probably never put gloves on even."

"Pete, I've been asking all over town where I could learn how to box. Most people shrugged, they had no clue, but those that did, they all said, go see Pete. I'm a student at Rutgers and I want something that's physically challenging for me to work hard on while I'm working hard on my studies. What do you say?"

Pete put both of his hands up, palms facing me at about shoulder height and said, "Hit one of my hands, either one, go ahead."

I made a fist with my right hand and missed four times in a row and then, on the fifth try, I hit his right hand with my left fist.

"Okay, kid, here's the deal: 25 bucks a month, you pay for all your equipment; that's the face guard, workout gloves, boxing gloves, I got it all in the Everlast catalog. I want you here two times a week and I think you need some running and weight training. You will be physically challenged. Come meet the guys. We're all going to teach you how to box, Joe, that's how it works, this crazy bunch of guys: we have taught each other how to box. So, welcome to the club. Pete put out his hand and I tried to shake it but he pulled away; I should've known.

Pete was still laughing when he introduced me to Art, Boozer and Jimmy. I got a mixture of nods and grunts and then some looks of almost acceptance when Pete told them I really, really wanted to learn how to box.

We talked about what days of the week would work best for everyone and that fit my class schedule and the good thing was they were open from six in the morning until 10 at night; this was going to work out just fine.

Pete and I went into his office, more like a large closet: tiny desk and small upright filing cabinet. We went through the Everlast catalog and I noticed that Everlast had an office in Brooklyn and they were open on Saturdays. Using Pete's phone, that cost me a buck, I ordered what I needed and arranged to pick it up Saturday morning. I asked Pete if he wanted to go to Brooklyn with me and to my surprise he said, "Sure, what about the guys?"

"I'm good with that. Whoever wants to come, Saturday morning, I'll pick you up at 9 o'clock."

I waved to the guys and left Pete's gym. Outside I was smiling, my car was still there but as I thought about what I had just gotten myself into; I was scared shitless.

CHAPTER 2

KATE

Noel and Max and I walked up to the corner; it was Friday night and a good night for a couple of beers and a Sally's cheeseburger. The joint was packed but Max squeezed through the crowd at the bar and got us three beers while Noel and I stood guard by a table that looked like it could be ours in a minute or two. Sure enough, Max arrived with the beer just as the table was being wiped off. We sat, we ordered and we were three happy frat brothers and part of the crowd.

"I'm going to learn how to box," I announced to Noel and Max.

"You are what?" asks Noel.

"I want to learn how to box. I signed up for lessons."

"Boxing lessons? Where?" Asked Max.

"At Pete's Gym on Ninth. Pete and three of his cronies have taught each other to box and they are all going to teach me."

"Why," asked Noel.

"I want to get in shape and I want a physical challenge and there's another reason, sort of."

"It's your face and it's your nose but I think you're crazy," said Noel.

Max looked very skeptical, "What other reason?"

The waiter arrived with our cheeseburgers and while we enjoyed them I told the guys about the kid that lived down the street from me, I was probably eight or nine, who used to taunt me for being Jewish and beat me up until one day I became so enraged I beat him up. So I think learning how to box is sort of a manly thing to do."

"You are nuts," they said in chorus.

I was almost finished with my cheeseburger.

"How come they are always so good?" I asked.

Max and Noel were still eating and just smiled in agreement. That's when I noticed Kate at the bar.

"Hey guys, excuse me for a couple of minutes, I want to say hello to a classmate."

I found Kate and explained that I was here with some friends but I didn't want to pass up a chance to say hello.

"I am so glad because I saw you but didn't want to disturb you."

"New old friends never have to worry about disturbing one another."

"That's good to know," she said.

"Well, old friend, I'm going to head back to the guys."

"Wait a second, it's a Sally's tradition, a good night kiss." And that's what Kate did, she kissed me: warm and soft and sweet; so much more than just a kiss. It was a conversation. Kate was saying, "I want to walk with you, talk with you, laugh with you and hold you with all of my being." There was nothing urgent or desperate about it, and her kiss became our kiss.

My side of the kiss was tentative, then receptive and I became part of the conversation. Suddenly there was no one else in the room, there was a hush except for our heartbeats and breathing. Time was irrelevant, everything went black and then it was over.

"You're a good kisser, I managed, a really good kisser."

"As are you, Joseph, I'd like to do that again sometime?"

"We'll see, I said, I have to go back and join the guys. We'll see."

Back at the table I felt dizzy and gulped some of my beer.

"What was that?" Asked Noel.

"That was someone talking to me in a language I never heard before, yet I understood every word."

"The whole place went dark for about half a minute," Said Max.

"I thought it was just us. I don't know what to say except I think it's time to go."

"That's a good idea," Noel said, "quick, before the lights go out again."

CHAPTER 3

MAKING CHANGES

Saturday morning I was surprised to see Pete and the guys waiting for me in front of the gym. Art and Jimmy were boxing; not landing punches but going through the motions, feet moving and hands blocking fists. I pulled up to them and got out, "Good morning."

They were already piling in on the passenger side, no small feat as my Chevy was a two-door coupe.

First Jimmy, then Boozer and then Art; they were packed in there like happy clams. Then it occurred to me, these men had been in the ring together; they had punched each other, clinched each other: this was nothing.

Pete got in the front with me and we were off; almost. "We're going to Everlast in Brooklyn," and I read off the address. Within seconds I had four different ways of getting there but settled on Pete's because he had been to Everlast before.

"How are you doing, kid," asked Pete.

"I'm excited, this is all brand new to me."

"He's excited, wait 'til we start smacking you around, then you'll be excited," Pete started in.

I checked the rear view mirror and the guys were smiling but content to be quiet.

"How old are you, Boozer," I asked.

"Take a guess."

I looked in the mirror, "I'm not good at this but I'm going to guess, 53."

At first no one said anything and I was afraid I was way off.

"Okay, who told?"

"Nobody told me, I just guessed."

"Well you guessed right. You know what this means, kid?"

"I got lucky."

"You got so lucky you get to buy us all lunch at Nathan's."

"Nah, the guys are busting your chops," Pete piped up.

"What about you, Joe," asked Art.

"I'm 19, just a kid."

"Family?"

It was time to spill the beans, "I'm the youngest of three, two older sisters and just my mom, my dad died three years ago in an accident."

"What kind of accident?"

"Long Island Rail Road."

"The big one in Queens?"

"Yes."

"Oh, my God."

It was quiet in the car, everyone fidgeting.

After a while I switched gears. "We had a neighbor who bought one of the first Dumont televisions and I saw the Billy Conn versus Joe Louis heavyweight fight live at his house."

"That had to be amazing," Jimmy said.

"I was so young the idea of television alone was amazing."

"Boy, I would have loved to have seen that fight," Boozer reflected. "I learned how to fight when I was just a kid and the youngest of five boys. I didn't learn how to box until I met these guys. Now I'm married and we have two boys. I'm glad you are coming on board, kid."

"Thanks Boozer."

"I'm the youngest," said Art. "I'm 43, a year younger than Jimmy; we met in the army and became friends. We live together, nothing queer or anything like that; just good friends."

Pete had been giving me directions throughout; "turn right here and we're there."

I did and we were and we all spilled out of the car and filed into Everlast. None of us had ever been there other than Pete and it was like being in boxing heaven. We wandered around looking at all of the equipment and the pictures. The guys loved being there and I told the salesman I was there to pick up my order.

The guys wanted to know what I was getting so they had everything out on the counter for their approval; which, of course they couldn't agree on: the workout gloves are too heavy, the boxing gloves too light, et cetera.

"Something is missing, kid," said Jimmy.

"What?"

"You know, down there."

"Down there?"

"The cajones, you gotta protect them."

Boozer moved closer and whispered, "A cup, you need a cup," he stepped back to appraise the situation, "Maybe a large?"

"No, no, added Art loudly, "Extra large!"

Pete saved the day, "He doesn't need a cup until we're working in the ring. For now we are all set and that will give us a reason to come back. Let's go have lunch; Nathan's is around the corner."

I put all of the new boxing stuff in the trunk of my car and went to Nathan's where the guys treated me to lunch. On the way home we all laughed a lot mostly over their finally deciding on an extra teeny, weeny cup.

Rutgers has a counselor and I made an appointment to see her. Seven in the morning, I guess it's the early bird catches the worm kind of thing; I was the worm and Carolyn Hopkins, PhD, was the bird. I went through a door marked, "Counselor," and took a seat in what appeared to be a small waiting room. I had gone for a run and was still in sweats with a towel around my neck. After a minute or two the inner door opened and an attractive fortyish woman asked, "Do you prefer Joe or Joseph?"

"Either is fine," and I followed her into her office. We sat, each in a comfortable leather chair, about 5 feet apart. She was wearing a white blouse and a gray skirt and she had nice legs.

"Okay, Joe, why did you choose to come and see me?"

I thought about that for a couple of minutes. Her use of the word "choose" bothered me and I wasn't sure why. I did, after all, choose to make this appointment but I was feeling very uneasy.

"A friend suggested that I see a counselor."

Carolyn Hopkins crossed her legs and sat back, "I've been running twice a week for a couple of decades. Are you a runner?"

"I'm learning to box and they told me that running is an important part of training for boxing. I just started a week ago."

We had something in common and I relaxed a little.

"What brings you here Joseph, a school related matter or something else?"

"It's more personal. It's life stuff."

"Okay, before we go there please tell me a little about your family."

"Mom and dad and three kids. I have two older sisters and my dad died when I was 16."

"I'm sorry. I'm sure that's tough. Are you, were you a close family?"

"Anything but. Growing up my mom was an extremely disruptive force; nothing was ever good enough for her. Today my oldest sister is married to a dentist; they live out on Long Island. My other sister is single, living in New York City. She's a math whiz and works for CBS. My mom is still living in our house in Rockville Centre; she's unpredictable and can be very disruptive. Growing up we were all like separate islands."

"What about your dad, before his death?"

"He started a film and television firm and did business all over the world. It was my dream to one day go to work with him."

"Did you do things with your dad?"

"We visited his siblings, all seven of them, scattered around the city. They were exciting bigger than life characters and I enjoyed them but anything I did with his family carried a burden of guilt because my mom hated them. We drove around Rockville Centre to see his local cronies, visited a Jewish cemetery in Brooklyn where his dad is buried, and he loved deep-sea fishing and I got to go with "the guys". It didn't much matter where we went or what we did, if I was with my dad that made it special."

Doctor Hopkins checked her watch, "Joseph, why are you here?"

I'm here because," I had to force the words, "Because I'm unsure of my commitment to my longtime girlfriend, unsure of her dad's job offer," I let out a breath, "I'm unsure of me."

Carolyn Hopkins, PhD, uncrossed her legs and leaned in toward me, "I want you to think about this; I believe you are exactly sure of what you want to do about your girlfriend, that job offer, school and you." Hopkins stood up and so did I. "Your past is smothering your now! Think about that and come in when you are ready."

That week I attended all of my classes, looking for Kate. She was not at the classical music class we "shared". On Friday evening I went to Sally's and had a couple of beers, killing time, but no Kate. I figured I would see her the following week in class; I was wrong.

As I walked through the Dean's house toward the back patio I was keenly aware of a change. Everything looked the same and then it hit me; the smell of cigarettes was greatly diminished. It was a pleasant surprise.

I pushed through the screen door to the patio and found Dean of Men, Ed, standing at the bar with a bottle of bourbon in one hand and a large tumbler in the other.

"Bourbon?"

"Sure."

I took the tumbler and Ed raised his, "to friendship."

We each took a pull and it looked to me like Ed might have started hours ago. He gestured and we both sat.

"It's been a while, how are you and how was your visit with Celeste?"

"I'm okay and Celeste is okay. What's with the diminished smell of cigarettes in the house?"

"It's a work in progress and I thank you for that."

"It is I who thanks you."

"It's good to see you," Ed said.

I wondered if he was seeing two or three of me.

"It's good to see you, too, Dean of men, Ed."

We both sipped our bourbon and I thought I had better slow down and that would slow Ed but I was late to the party.

"I have missed you, Joe. I have really missed you.".

I didn't know what to say but I offered, "It's peaceful back here. I've been pretty busy in my head, a couple of brain bursts like a summer squall. I've learned a lot in the last month or so, or I have opened my eyes to things I've known for a long time. Wow, that came out sounding pretty heavy."

"Very heavy, what's going on?"

I took a sip of bourbon and blurted it out,

"I'm thinking of going into the Army."

That was a sobering thought to be sure and I thought it damn near sobered up Dean of Men, Ed.

"What the hell are you talking about?"

"The Army."

"I get that, but why?"

"This is where it gets confusing, I think I need it."

"For God's sake, Joe, we are talking nasty with Korea. What you need is to give this some thought, serious thought."

"I know. I didn't come here with the intention of just blurting that out, in fact I kind of surprised myself. I need a couple of minutes to regroup."

"While you regroup I'll do some blurting, I love you, Joe."

"What!"

"I love you. You're a beautiful young man and I am a middle-aged gay man. There are lots of rumors out there about me being gay; they're not sure, but I am."

In my mind Ed's beautiful green lawn turned brown. I was having trouble with the moment.

"It isn't mutual. If you are gay, okay, but I am obsessed with women, I love women, my problem is I don't love myself."

Silence, we sat in silence until Ed said, "I will never act on it with you, we were blurting and I wanted you to know."

I said, "I don't know whether I can share my mishigas with you."

"Mishigas?"

"A wonderful Yiddish word: craziness, a state of mind and/or the state of what's going on in your life. Great word."

"Okay then you can share your mishigas with me; I have your best interests at heart."

"In that case, a little more bourbon."

Ed splashed me some bourbon and we settled into a new place; awkward and honest.

"I don't know who I am. That's why I need to go into the Army; they will help me find my true self. Otherwise I'm going to go through the rest of my life pretending to be something I'm not.'"

The Dean was shaking his head; was he sobering up?

"I could marry Celeste, work hard at "41" and have life handed to me on a golden platter; it's a tough choice but I know what I have to do; I have to find myself."

Ed asked, "Haven't you ever had a dream?"

"What do you mean?"

"A dream of what you wanted to do when you grew up."

"I had two: one was to work with my father and the other was to become an architect. That leaves me with one choice since my dad is now gone."

"That's your ticket, Joseph. Finish school and become an architect. The challenge will be greater than going into the Army, making the results that much sweeter."

"Makes sense, I guess."

Ed was sitting taller, half smiling, half frowning, "You've got it Joseph, you've got that something special; don't give it to the Army, share it with the whole world. Finish school, you will center yourself and earn self- esteem; then go on to design skyscrapers. You can do it."

"Ed, did you bourbon up earlier to have the courage to tell me that you are a homosexual?"

"I did but I still couldn't tell you."

"Was it my blurting?"

"No, it was the courage of your blurting."

"I'm going to need courage now, I need to tell Celeste I want a timeout. I'll need to tell her dad as well, The "41" Club was part of our dream. I'm giving up a lot."

"Giving up a lot to get even more. It seems to me that you are cleaning up, what was that word?"

"Mishigas?"

"You are cleaning up your mishigas, Joseph."

"It's going to be hard."

"I'm here to help, that's what the Dean of Men does. In fact I have some ideas."

"No ideas, not right now; now I need to sleep and think."

"Promise the Army will not be on your list."

"Okay, no Army."

"I can help shuffle your classes. Can you be at my office Friday morning, 10:00 a.m.?"

"Cool, I'll cut my Lit class."

"Give me a hug."

"No way, gay Dean of Men, Ed. Okay, a small one."

I hugged the Dean of Men and went to my car. Walking through the house I shouted, "It still stinks in here!"

I called the hall where Celeste roomed at Smith. She wasn't in and I left a message. She called me back at Phi Ep and I wasn't in. She left a message. When I next called, she was in and I asked her if I could call back in five minutes and she was good with that. I hung up and, armed with a pocket full of quarters, ran up the street to a phone booth.

"Celeste, I love you and this is going to be a tough phone call. This has nothing to do with there being another woman. This call is about me and who I am and/or who I am not. I don't mean to sound confusing but I am kind of lost."

"Joe, I think I . . ."

"Just let me say one more thing. I don't know who I am and I need time to find out so I can bring you a good me. That sort of sounds weird, huh?"

"Joe, when you said goodbye to me a couple of Sundays ago I knew something was wrong, something was different. I don't know what happened but it felt like you were scared."

"I was scared. Can you understand?"

"Yes, I can. Please know that I love you and I have a suggestion."

"I'm open to that."

"Find a counselor, someone who can guide you and help you. I have to hang up now."

By then we were both crying and I could hear the phone click and I hung up as well.

"Good morning; "41" Club, how may I direct your call?"

"May I talk to Jerry Brown please."

"Who may I say is calling?"

"Joe Gordon."

"Oh, hi Joe, let me see if I can find him."

I waited a few minutes and then there he was, "Good morning, Joe, how are you?"

"I'm good Jerry. Have you got a couple of minutes?"

"I do. Take all the time you need."

"That's funny you should say that; that's exactly why I'm calling. I spoke with Celeste and told her I need some time; I'm trying to figure out who I am and what I want or what I need."

"Joe, it's okay. Celeste called me and if you feel you need a timeout it's extremely important that you take it."

"I'm trying to get my legs under me so at the end of the day, each day, I feel good about myself."

"I am here for you in any way that I can be of help and I wish you the best."

"Jerry, thank you and please extend my thanks to Martha, you both have been very gracious and caring; it's been a tough couple of years."

"This does not end our friendship, Joe, the door is open and you know where we are. Don't forget that."

"I won't. Thanks."

"Goodbye, Joe."

"Goodbye, Jerry."

Still in the phone booth I was a little lost, I didn't know what to do. I thought I was going to cry and then I realized that, more than anything, I was scared; I had just jumped from a yacht into a rowboat because I want to pull on the oars.

THE KISS

CHAPTER 4

THE NEW PATH

I entered the office of the Dean of Men only to find myself in a nicely appointed outer office.

"Good morning, is this the Dean of Men's office?"

"It is."

"And you are the Dean?" I inquired of the stylish, fiftyish woman at the desk.

"I am not; I'm the Dean's secretary, Thelma. And you are?"

I'm Joe Gordon; I'm your ten o'clock."

"I am so glad to meet you," she said, and we shook hands. "He's running late; you're welcome to go in and make yourself comfortable."

"I'd prefer to wait here with you, Thelma." I pulled up a chair.

"He's on the campus so he shouldn't be long and I must say I have not seen him this excited, well, maybe ever."

"You have worked together for a long time?"

"Decades."

I smiled and thought Thelma knows stuff, a lot of stuff, and she's loyal.

"It's like you are his long lost son."

"That's very . . ."

"Good morning, Thelma; good morning, Joe."

Ed Draper, Dean of Men, was all business; suit and tie and on point, a man with a mission.

"Come on Joe," Ed led the way into his office, "and Thelma, no calls, no interruptions."

I waved to Thelma and followed Ed, pulling the door shut behind us.

In his office, Dean of Men, Ed had given me a backpack full of books for the classes I was shifting to for my change of major. Each book was marked to indicate where the class was, at the time of my switch. The bottom line; work hard to catch up and then work harder to graduate from Rutgers with a Civil Engineering degree.

I spent hours going through each book to measure where I was at and it wasn't pretty; doable was my optimistic take but the reality was over-whelmingly overwhelming! I would need help; especially with math and math related courses. Yikes! Ed had also given me the name and phone number of a tutor who he was sure could help me; she was a twelve year-old math prodigy.

I was in my room at Phi Ep surrounded by the books when Richard entered.

"What's with all the books?"

"They represent the rest of my life; I have switched my major, I am going to be an architect with a stop at Civil Engineering. Ergo, the books."

"Wait a second, what about Celeste and The "41" Club?"

"Done. Painful, open and honest; it's over and I am moving on."

"Wow. Gordon, I'm not sure if you are a genius or an idiot but I am rooting for you and I'm with you all the way."

"Thank you Richard, I need all the help I can get."

When I opened the door marked, "Counselor," the inner door was ajar and I saw Dr. Hopkins at her desk.

"Good morning, Joseph, you got dressed up for me didn't you?"

I was wearing a white polo shirt and khakis.

"Good morning, Dr. Hopkins and, yes, I did."

She had left her desk and when she sat in her leather chair I sat in mine.

"I guess I wanted to look good for you?"

"You have succeeded and I guess the gleam in your eye says there's more."

I couldn't help but smile, "When we were last together you helped me open a door to my past and the painful memories that were keeping me from being the best me I can be today. I no longer want to run from my past, I want to earn my future."

"What does that look like?"

"It looks like me wanting to be the best me I can be every day. I called Celeste, my long time girl friend and ended the relationship; both of us were crying. And I called her dad who assured me his door will be open forever."

"You called them because?"

"Because they were my future, rich and powerful, but I want to earn my own future like my dad did. It's in my blood, I know it."

"You have a plan?"

"Already under way. I have switched my major to civil engineering; I want to be an architect and that's a perfect stop along the way to graduate school."

Hopkins smiled and said, "I am excited with and for you."

"There's one other thing. There is this girl that watched me unpack my car the day I arrived at Rutgers and then she showed up in one of my classes and we exchanged first names. A couple of Friday nights ago I saw her at the bar at Sally's. I said hello and before I could rejoin my friends she kissed me and it was a kiss unlike any other; it was a conversation that talked about walking, talking, laughing and holding each other forever."

"Will you see her again?"

"She disappeared. I've looked for her and asked about her but she's gone and I will never forget that kiss."

"She touched the most pure spot in you, Joseph."

"It's the kid," said Art as I entered Pete's Gym.

"Good morning gentlemen, the gang's all here."

They were all in the ring shuffling, throwing soft punches, unexpected punches coming from anyone and from everywhere. It was slow-motion chaos.

"Come on Kid, suit up," said Pete, "you find out who your friends are."

"Or aren't," said Jimmy.

"Okay, I'm in. I'll suit up."

When I stepped into the ring Boozer said, "We call this the Merry-go-round: you work on your footwork, your balance and your focus. It's a ball."

I tried to catch on but every time I glanced down I'd catch a punch and as I tried to spread my focus I tripped on someone's foot or got tripped by some one. It was stressful and I was getting popped a lot; not hard but hard enough to get my attention and then they all popped me at once and they were laughing like crazy.

"Okay stop!" Pete said, "Everybody go to the ropes except the kid and me. It's just you and me, you know where I am and where my hands are."

Pete and I were moving, ducking and punching; nice and easy when Pete "invited" Boozer to get on the Merry-go-round.

Boozer joined us and we kept moving but now I had two guys to focus on; it was intense, especially when Art came in and then Jimmy, until all of us were in the ring and they started busting up.

"What's so funny?" I was hot and sweaty; "What's going on?"

"Hey, Kid, it's not you, it's we've never had a fifth guy in there with us. Five guys on the Merry-go-round is impossible. Phew."

We all exited the ring; Art and Jimmy pulled on their jackets and left saying they would be back in a while.

"I need the big bag," I said.

"Lighten up, Kid, we weren't laughing at you."

"It's not that, Pete, I'm all tied up inside; I want to punch it out."

"Have yourself a party."

I had my gloves on and approached the big bag like I was going to break it open. I started slow but I got into it and was bashing the bag with fury.

"You want to work something out, you want to hurt someone, then let's do it the right way."

I dropped my arms in frustration, my gloves were heavy as Pete approached slowly and spoke softly, "You don't want fury, you want focus and balance. You are not on the Merry-go-round, there's one big bag in front of you and you want all of your strength to come up through your legs. Take a deep breath and let it out slowly and now let your body find a power position and tap the bag. Tap it again; you are telling that bag, that person, that you are coming with focused fury and power; tap the bag and hit the bag hard with your left. Another tap and from your feet up a power hit with your right. Focus your fury; you are a boxer not a mad man."

I could feel my body relax into a power position to deliver powerful blows to the bag. I wasn't exhausted, I was exhilarated and I was punishing the bag.

Pete was on the other side of the bag pushing it back to me for the next blow and then I was done.

"You are a powerful man, Joseph. God help who ever that was."

"It was my mom."

"Your mom!"

"She'll be okay and now, so will I; focus! Thanks Pete."

At the end of the week I went up to Sally's convinced Kate would be there but she was not. I asked the bartender after describing Kate and he knew the girl I meant but "no" he had not seen her recently. Poof; she was gone.

THE KISS

PART TWO

THE TUTOR

CHAPTER 5

LEARNING AND SHARING

On a small piece of paper Dean of Men, Ed had written: Tutor, Gabby Evers and her phone number.

I dialed, "Hello."

"Is Gabby Evers there?"

"This is Gabby. Who's calling?"

"Joe Gordon."

"Oh, Joe, Ed told me you were going to call. He told me all about you."

"All?"

"Not that kind of all, just that you have switched your major and I might be able to help you with some math problems."

"I'm hoping that you can."

"How about Saturday morning at my place, 232 Ninth Street; it's a gray and white two story house. Come at eight, I'll make us breakfast, you bring your books and we'll figure this out."

"Gabby, can I call you Gabby?"

"Certainly."

"I'll see you Saturday."

"Great. Park in the driveway."

I was pretty sure I knew the house, just up the street from Pete's Gym and sure enough there it stood, quite lovely actually. I pulled into the driveway, parked and grabbed my backpack of books.

On the front porch I rang the bell and heard bright chimes from within.

I was getting a grand vibe from the place; everything so neat and clean in what is a relatively grubby neighborhood. The door opened and I was face to face with the most beautiful woman I had ever seen.

"Oh, for God's sake, put one foot in front of the other and come in."

"I'm looking for Gabby Evers," I stammered.

"I'm Gabby, you must be Joe."

"I am."

She extended her hand, we shook and in that instant we both became comfortable.

"I am confused; Dean of men, Ed had described a teenage math prodigy."

"I was, but that's for another time. How about you put your book-pack over on that table and I'll push down the toast, the bacon and eggs are ready. The silverware is in one of these drawers and plates up above."

I set us up at the big, old, round table that was bathed in the early morning sun. It could easily seat six and maybe even eight people but the two of us sat side by side.

"Why on earth did you change your major now, it's almost the middle of the semester?"

"This is really good bacon."

"Oh, come on."

"Okay, but you'll owe me the child prodigy explanation."

"Fair enough."

"This is the short version: I didn't like the life path I was on; I didn't like me or my behavior on that path and I didn't want to take the easy way out because it would have been harder in the long run."

"You are a living algorithm and yet you're having problems with math?"

"I am, but first the prodigy thing."

"No, we have work to do."

"Then how about a tour of your house. I love your house."

"You are a procrastinator."

"Notorious."

"First we clear the table, then we tour, then we set the terms of our agreement and then we work."

In an instant we were on our feet and clearing, followed by cleaning and putting away.

"The tour will now begin downstairs." Gabby led the way and I followed this beautiful, slim and trim, math prodigy, thirtyish woman down to the basement to see her top notch gym, adjoining changing and shower area, laundry and storage room before ascending to the second floor: two bedrooms and one bath and Gabby's bedroom and bath suite with a fireplace in the bedroom. Then we returned to the main floor for the living room with fireplace, Gabby's office where a stunning, large photo of her hung on the wall. She was on the cover of Vogue magazine with her light brown face and body shimmering against the ocean and blue sky beyond. We returned to the completely modernized kitchen with its extended dining area where we had breakfast.

Of course I didn't know who she was and of course I needed a glass of water to wet my parched throat; I'm a nineteen year old guy who roots for the New York football Giants and who rarely looks at Vogue magazine.

Gabby was looking through my books. "Saturdays work best for me. Usually I work on weekdays and sometime I travel for work. We'll have to play it by ear. What I want from you is respect, commitment, effort, trust and love. I'll explain: respect is for the math or the subject matter; it is what it is. Commitment and effort speak for themselves; you have to bring it and I will as well. Trust is mutual, too, and it's the bedrock of our relationship. Love means I am not your professor; we are going to argue but don't shoot the messenger."

"I have several things to say. I understand and agree to the terms of our agreement. I love your home; it flows and it's warm, it's a reflection of you, and lastly I think I understand the prodigy thing; not the details but I am the luckier for it."

"I think we are becoming friends."

"I think so too."

"Let's get to work."

"Okay."

"Two plus two?"

"Five."

"Joe, I'm not kidding. We are going to walk into this; we are not running into a burning building. Calculus is tough, it's going to seem overwhelming but we will stick with it until all of a sudden, WHAM; it will hit you upside the head and you will get it. I promise."

"I trust you, Gabby."

For several hours Gabby led me through the haze of my math "history" until I started to growl from fatigue and frustration.

"How about next Saturday, breakfast at eight?"

"Absolutely."

"We can take a break for lunch, then do some more work; we'll make a day of it."

"Thanks, Gabby, you give me hope."

"Joe, I want you to share a hug with me. I am a very physical person and hugs are way better than a hand shake." We stood and we hugged, it was a friendship hug, a give it everything you've got friendship hug that with Gabby was big, very big. I stuffed my books into the backpack and floated out the door.

I threw the book-pack into my car and walked down to Pete's Gym to say hello to the guys.

"Hey, look who's here, it's the kid," said Pete. His announcement was lifeless and Art and Jimmy seemed down in the dumps.

"What's wrong," I wanted to know.

"Boozer had a heart attack," said Art.

"Two days ago," added Jimmy.

"Where? Where is he?"

"He was home," Art said.

"Where is he now? Is he going to be okay?"

"Good Samaritan," said Pete.

"Can I see him?"

"Thought you'd never ask," said Pete. "Let's go."

They were pulling on their sweaters and jackets as we went out the door.

"Where's Good Samaritan Hospital?" I was leading the way toward my car.

"Manhattan," Pete answered.

I stopped walking; they stopped walking.

"I can't drive into Manhattan."

The three of them were chuckling.

"Come on, it's only four or five blocks from here," Art said.

"Guys!"

We started walking.

"That's your car at the Evers' place? You know the Evers broad," Pete pushed.

We all stopped walking. They waited for my answers.

"Yes that's my car. Yes I know the Evers woman, she's my." I couldn't say the word tutor, I would never hear the end of it.

"Are you, you know, like friendly with her,"

Jimmy asked.

"Yes. That's it exactly; we are friends."

We were walking again and the guys are going, "Friends, exx-aact-lee friends."

I stopped walking. They stopped. "You wouldn't be having this much fun unless Boozer is okay. Is Boozer okay?"

"Yeah, he's going home tomorrow."

"That's it, I am going to put you all in the ring at the same time and beat you up."

Saturdays with Gabby were special; we had a relationship developing unlike any I had ever known. She was amazing; smart, beautiful, direct, a gifted math prodigy and tutor, generous and she was opening up to me, and I with her.

"I was born in this house, in fact, in this kitchen; unfortunately my mother died in childbirth. My aunt and my dad raised me here," Gabby shared one Saturday. "Two years ago I came back to New Brunswick from Paris and decided to tear the place apart and put it back together the way I wanted."

"You, they, did a wonderful job. I got a great vibe from this house before I ever entered it. I was standing on the porch and rang the door bell, I heard the chimes and got that "something special is going on here" feeling."

Calculus was also going on, slow and steady; differentials, functions and methods were spinning in my head and Gabby felt I was making progress. I was waiting for the WHAM. We talked and argued about my other subjects that were a mental workout and most helpful; I was thinking more clearly and was more interested in my studies.

"Gabby, you are a miracle worker," I told her.

"No," she insisted, "you are doing the work, I am just your friend."

Over time we extended Saturdays to include a lunch break and we started cooking together. Then we added a workout in the gym before lunch and the fall chill indicated a fire in the living room fireplace would be nice along with some music and a drink. Often we added dinner and then we added most Sundays. We laughed a lot and we touched each other, held hands and hugged.

"Would you ever go out with me," I asked one day.

"No," Gabby responded firmly.

"Is it because. ."

"It is because," she interrupted, "I love us just the way we are, right where we are." I did not push her any further.

As the weeks went by I told Gabby about my dad and my dream of working with him at Commonwealth Film and Television.

"He was a visionary, he believed in television back in the 1930's and had amassed a substantial library of films and cartoons; perfect for television programming. Just when his business was becoming very robust his life ended three years ago on Thanksgiving eve, my dad's train crashed into a stalled train and 87 people died. He was my hero and my future and, 'poof', he was gone."

Gabby hugged me and whispered in my ear, "Dance with me, Joseph." She was on her feet, hand extended. "It's great therapy."

"Dance to Chopin?" I asked as I stood and took her in my arms. We waltzed and danced into the kitchen and back to the fireplace and around the coffee table and then we sat. We were giggling and our hearts were pounding.

"I never thought of dancing as therapy but that was great."

"In many ways," Gabby leaned her head on my shoulder, "I know there is more to share if you are willing?"

I told Gabby about Celeste, her dad, Jerry, and his restaurant and the future that was assured. "But I knew I wasn't ready to make that decision, couldn't make that decision. Other than working with my dad I had one other dream; becoming an architect and I knew if I accomplished that I would have done it on my own. That's the test I'm taking now."

Quickly, Gabby was sitting on my lap, her arms around me and her head buried in my neck.

"Gabby, why are you crying?"

"They are tears of sadness and joy. In many ways we are so alike."

I knew I was catching up with my engineering peers but I thought it was Gabby's buoyancy. One day during the week I was worrying a calculus problem when I got the WHAM; it was exhilarating.

On Saturday morning, barely in the door, I said, "Gabby, give me a hug."

"What's going on?"

"I got the WHAM."

"That's fabulous!"

We hugged a good hug.

"Breakfast, Joe?"

"Yes breakfast, please."

"It's all ready, just waiting for the toast."

"Gabby, my mind shifted, my thinking changed."

The toast popped and we carried our plates to the table.

"Calculus is challenging but I'm up to the task; I belong in the classroom and it's your fault."

"My fault? No way."

"Yes way, you tutored me and, more importantly, you believed in me."

"You don't need me anymore?"

"What are you saying? I want you more than ever."

"I was afraid you would get the WHAM and we would be over."

"Gabby, I don't want us to ever be over."

Gabby put her finger to my lips, "That's my wish, too. Your breakfast is getting cold."

"But not my heart."

After breakfast we celebrated by settling on the sofa, in front of the fire, instead of hitting the books.

"With the WHAM my brain shifted, actually my mind opened up to my being an inquiring student with vibrant curiosity. I have opened the door to me."

"There had better be room for me."

"There is definitely room for you, Gabby Evers, you helped me open the door; a door that has been shut since I was a toddler."

"That wasn't that long ago, young man."

"A lifetime ago, slightly older woman."

"You may sit at my feet and tell me all about it, grasshopper."

"And you, praying mantis, may curl up in my arms and listen attentively."

We adjusted arms and limbs, got settled, we each took a deep breath and I proceeded to tell Gabby how my mother had stolen me from me; how she smothered me. Gabby started to cry. I held Gabby tight and, emotionally exhausted, we fell asleep.

Gabby woke first and she roused me. "Let's go down to the gym and work out?"

"Great idea."

Gabby ran ahead and by the time I got downstairs she had changed into shorts and a tank top. She was jumping rope and, damn, she was good.

"Started when I was a kid," she told me weeks before, when we first worked out together.

"Teach me," I asked and slowly, much to her amusement, I was getting better.

I watched Gabby as I stretched out; her beauty, her body, amazing.

"Showoff!"

"Not bad for an old broad. But enough, I'm going up to shower, I'll meet you in the kitchen."

"Deal."

I jumped rope, showered and when I got Upstairs Gabby was already at the kitchen table looking clean and fresh and beautiful.

"How do you do it?"

"Do what?"

"Change clothes in an instant. Change your beauty in a flash."

"Changing clothes quickly is a model thing," she explained, "part of the job. When I first started modeling I wanted to be the best and I quickly learned that being ready and willing went a long way with the photographer and the crew; they remembered me and over the years we developed a mutual respect. I have never been a prima donna which has helped carry me to the top."

"And your beauty?"

"On the job it's a collaboration: the director and or the photographer talk to me; they tell me what they want and I have learned how to respond."

"I will never forget," I started, "the Saturday morning when you opened the door and I was expecting a teenage math prodigy."

"That's me."

"You are the most beautiful woman child I will ever know and I glimpsed her downstairs; she was jumping rope."

"This has been some big WHAM."

"Gabby, I'm going home for Thanksgiving break; probably the last one at the old house. Both my sisters will be there and, of course, my mom. What are your plans?"

"No plans. Quiet is good, I just started reading a new book. I'll miss you."

"Yeah, me too you. I'm not sure when I'll be back; how about Saturday, the fifth of December, we can give thanks together."

"I would love that; breakfast at eight."

THE KISS

CHAPTER 6

GIVING THANKS…..EVOKING SECRETS

The Phi Ep parking lot was empty and I realized I might have outsmarted myself; I might be locked out. Thanksgiving break started after class on Friday; I needed clothes and stuff for my visit home. I tried the front door and it opened.

It was dark in there, one dim light coming from the back hallway.

"Anybody home? Hello," I shouted. After a moment or two a thin voice responded, "I'm home, who's there?" and Mrs. Brand, our Phi Ep house-mother, appeared in the hallway.

It's me, Joe Gordon, Mrs. Brand."

Mrs. Brand was probably seventy, slight and a very quiet presence. She came closer.

"Oh, the new boy; have you no place to go?"

"I do. I've been visiting a friend and I'm leaving in the morning to go home for Thanksgiving with my family. What about you, are you here alone?"

"Just for the night, that nice young boy, Peter, is coming back tomorrow."

"I'm your roommate for the night Mrs. Brand. I'm going up to Sally's in a while, I'll bring you something for dinner."

"That would be lovely."

"In an hour then?"

"I'll be ready."

Upstairs I gathered some laundry and went down the hall to the multi-sink, multi-shower-bathroom and went to work. When I was done I had undershorts and socks hanging everywhere; they would be dry by morning for sure.

I walked up to Sally's, sat at the bar and ordered two cheeseburgers to go and a beer. It was quiet enough to study for a final exam and I took that opportunity to contemplate what it would be like spending five days with my mom. I had figured all would be well just as my order arrived. I polished off my beer and headed to dinner with Mrs. Brand.

She had set two places at one of the dining room tables and one lit candle; she was waiting for me.

"This is very romantic of you, Mrs. Brand."

"This is very kind of you, Mr. Gordon."

"It is my pleasure."

I unwrapped the cheeseburgers and placed them on the waiting plates. While I was busy Mrs. Brand said, "I understand you have changed your major."

"You seriously know that?"

"I seriously know a lot about my boys."

"You are scaring the hell out of me, Mrs. Brand."

"I don't believe you for one second, Joseph. All you boys are pretty daring, I make it my business to stay out of your business; I know just enough to keep an eye on you to be sure you are well."

"I sold you short Mrs. Brand. Now I understand why we are dining together."

"Why is that?"

"So I can share a secret with you; I think I am falling in love."

"Don't you think I'm a little too old for you, Joseph?"

"Not after tonight, Mrs. Brand, I think you are perfect."

"You are very sweet."

"What else do you know that I should know that you know?"

"This was a very good cheeseburger, Joseph."

"Oh, that right there, was like a 'no kiss goodnight on our first date.'"

"I wish you a happy Thanksgiving and be sure to let me know when you leave in the morning."

"I will. Are you sure Peter is returning?"

"Yes, he's one of the dependables, I won't be alone."

"Okay, happy Thanksgiving."

In the morning I collected my dry laundry, packed my bag, checked out with Mrs. Brand and hit the road. This was going to be a good Thanksgiving.

"Mom," I called from downstairs, "Are you up there?"

"Joseph, is that you?"

"Yes, Mom."

"I'll be right down."

"Okay, I'll be in the kitchen."

I had cheese and crackers on the table when my mom walked in.

"Hello, Joseph."

"Hi, Mom."

We hugged and looked at each other while I was wondering which mom I was going to get. She looked good, she always looked good; maybe a little apprehensive with the family gathering?

"How's school?"

"Good, lots of good things happening; I'll tell everyone at once at dinner Thursday."

"No hint for your mother?"

"Nope. How are you? What's going on in my mother's life?"

I got the "sweet" mother and we small talked 'till the crackers and cheese were gone.

"Mom, how about I take you out for dinner?"

"I'm not dressed for going out."

"Mom, You look great. We'll go out for pizza. What do you say?"

"I've never had pizza."

"Perfect. Tonight's the night. I'll get my stuff from the car while you get ready, okay?"

"Okay. Fifteen minutes."

"Deal."

We went to the Cosmopolitan, or the Cos as we used to call it in high school, where the music was too loud and the pizza too hot; burn the roof of your mouth hot; jump up and down in your chair hot.

My mom ate her first pizza with a knife and fork. All cheese, no topping. Way to go mom, she even had a sip of my beer but didn't care for it.

When we got home I suggested we take a walk. It was a beautiful evening and we strolled until mom wanted to turn back. On the way home we stopped again and out there, under the stars, I told my mother I was very angry with her for the way she smothered me when I was a toddler and that she raised me to be her little man instead of guiding me to be the best me I could be for me, not for her. My mother was disturbed; she didn't remember anything like that. She got teary and I very gently put my hands on her arms in a very kind and loving way.

"Mom, I forgive you."

"You forgive me for what?"

"It doesn't matter what you remember. What matters is I told you and you heard me and I know what I said."

"Oh." My mother was bewildered.

"Come on, Mom, let's get you home, we have a big weekend coming up."

The next morning I picked up my sister, Sylvia, at the train station; it was wonderful to see her. I put her bag on the back seat and we headed for home.

"Good ride?"

"Yes, the usual forty or so minutes from the City. How's mom?"

"So far so good. She seems okay, says she's not dating; 'no one will ever replace your dad' stuff like that."

"Gloria and Harold?"

"Your sister and her husband are not coming until Thanksgiving day."

"Are you seeing Celeste tonight?"

"Would I leave you alone with our mother?"

"Yes."

"No I would not. We are baby sitting together; last night I took her out for her first ever pizza."

"The Cos?"

"Yeah. Maybe tonight Chinese?"

Mom told us Margaret was coming to help cook the Thanksgiving dinner. That pleased me no end; I love Margaret, who worked for us when I was a kid growing up. Margaret was a voice of reason and when mom "lost it" screaming and ranting with little or no cause, Margaret would walk by me and whisper, "Never you mind, Joseph, it's just your mama's way."

Mom had a short shopping list so Sylvia and I set off to get everything; we even extended the trip almost to Long Beach to get our favorite cheesecake. Later we went out for Chinese and came home for cheesecake.

Margaret came Thursday morning and got the entire Thanksgiving meal underway. Before she left I gave her a big hug and she looked me over, "Joseph, you're looking good and happy, I'm glad. You take care."

"I will. You too, Margaret."

Gloria and Harold arrived around one and we all pitched in to get dinner on the table. Harold offered a prayer, blessing family and giving thanks. Mom got very teary, she missed dad. We understood.

We plunged into our meal, which was delicious, and everyone shared what was going on in his or her life. It was all exciting "stuff" and we cheered each other on.

Mom told us she was going to Florida for Christmas and New Years but she would not share if there was a man involved; but it seemed obvious. We were all very happy for her and a little shocked.

I let my family know that I had broken up with Celeste and everyone was surprised.

"I have changed my major, I am going to graduate as a civil engineer and go on to become an architect."

I think I shocked my family; not a word!

"This is my dream and I'm going for it knowing I'm looking at playing catch up and summer school during two years and then three more years of graduate college to become an architect."

There was a lot of looking around the table until Harold spoke.

"Joe, I went to college and then went on to become a dentist; it's a lot of hard work."

"I know and I know you are skeptical but the Dean of Men helped me make the switch and I have a tutor who is helping me and becoming a close friend."

"You can do it, Joseph; what ever it takes, I know you will and you will make your father and me very proud."

"I wasn't sure that you would remember," Gabby said as she opened the door.

"Are you kidding, I've been counting the days; it's December already."

"Hug?"

"Absolutely."

We hugged a hug that needed time to forget the time we were apart and time for our bodies to find the ultimate intimacy a hug allows.

"How are you, Gabby?"

"I have missed you."

"I know, I missed you as well. Lots to share."

"Breakfast first."

"I'll set the table. "

"Put out wine glasses, we are having Mimosas."

"Sounds special."

"It is, we are giving thanks, remember?"

"Yes I remember, this is our Thanksgiving breakfast."

"Champagne is in the fridge; you're the man."

"You are very bossy."

"I am the chef, you are the sommelier and the orange juice is in there too."

Champagne opened, Mimosas made and food on the table; we settled in for our breakfast.

"To my best friend." I raised my glass.

"That's what I was going to say."

"To us."

We gently touched our glasses, and we drank. After a few bites I said, "You first."

"No, please, you."

"Okay. I give thanks for my crazy family; sometimes close, sometimes distant and sometime downright horrific but somehow there's love and caring. I give thanks for my friends and the crazy boxing guys and for good health. Most of all, Gabby, I give thanks for you. You are my dearest friend." I raised my glass and took a sip, "Your turn."

"I am grateful for you Joseph, you have awakened me. I've been a bit of a shut in; yes, I have my career but in other areas of my life I have been very," she paused looking for the word, "cautious. Now my days are so much happier and I'm experiencing feelings that perhaps I never had before."

"Gabby, you're on fire."

"I'm not on fire; I am looking for matches."

"Clever, Miss Gabby, either way I am rooting for you."

"I know, you're one of my matches."

We finished our breakfast, cleaned up, moved to the sofa with our Mimosas and set up in front of the fire.

"Joseph," Gabby said as she took my hand, "tell me about your family Thanksgiving."

"I took my mom out for her first ever pizza; she ate it with a knife and fork." I shrugged, "Go figure. On Thursday my family was full of surprises: my oldest sister is pregnant, my other sister is engaged and moving into an apartment on the upper West side and I told my family I have broken up with Celeste and changed my major; that I am going to become an architect. Then my mom surprised us all; she is going to Florida for Christmas, staying with a cousin, but we think she has a boyfriend."

I was up and headed to the kitchen to refresh our Mimosas.

"Christmas," Gabby called to me, "Joseph, spend Christmas with me?"

"I would love to, absolutely," I said, adding champagne to our drinks.

"That makes me very happy."

"Me too," I said, settling into the sofa. "What about New Year's Eve?"

"I can't."

"Can't?"

"I'm going to Paris, leaving on the 27th and returning on January fourth."

"Why does it feel like I just got punched in the stomach?"

"I don't want to hurt you. I am so sorry. I have to go, it's the right thing to do. I was in a relationship, a long relationship that didn't end well; that's when I came home, two years ago and poured my heart and soul into rebuilding this house and myself. I thought I was doing well, some personal work with a counselor, a new agent, working hard, top of my game."

We were sitting so close I could feel the heat coming from Gabby's body.

"Then you arrived, I liked you and we were easy together, good friends. We kept getting closer emotionally, physically, feelings that I have never experienced before. While you were gone," Gabby looked like she was going to cry, "I was so lonely and along came the demons and the nightmares of what happened years ago." Gabby paused, she was struggling but determined to continue.

"I was seven or eight when my dad crept into my bed; "I miss your mom, you are so beautiful." Then he would be gone for weeks and return, touching me and he took my hand and put it down there and wanted me to put my mouth there. I couldn't scream, I made noise and my brother Frank, big boy at 15, pulled my father off my bed, "Never again old man, next time I come with a knife." Two years later my dad was killed, knifed in this kitchen, police never found the killer. I have worked very hard to put those demons, those memories to rest and move on. This trip is entwined with my demons in a way that I can't explain until I return."

Gabby was crying, she shifted off the sofa on to my lap and put her arms around my neck, "I'm sorry this hurts you, Joseph. I want to be together, I love us."

She kissed me; long and sweet and warm, mixed with her salty tears it was a dizzying kiss.

"Gabby, we will be okay, we will work through this."

"I want you to be patient with me until I come home."

"I can do that."

"There's more, Mr. Gordon, will you stay here while I am gone, so I can call you at Midnight on New Year's Eve?"

"That's asking a lot," I said with a wink, "but yes, of course."

"Will you sleep in my bed and pretend you are in my arms?"

"I sleep in the nude; are you ready for that?"

"One last thing; when I return will you please be here when I walk in the door?"

"Yes."

"Thank you, Joseph."

Gabby hugged me and I hugged her, this smart, complicated, gorgeous woman child that I knew I loved despite the obvious age, color and religious differences. At that very moment I could love her and believe that we would be friends forever no matter what.

I got an idea, "Let's invite Dean of Men, Ed for dinner on Christmas Eve; he brought us together." "That would be wonderful; we can cook together, we have not done that in weeks."

CHAPTER 7

WAITING FOR GABBY

Dean of Men, Ed was arriving at six and we planned cocktails, along with cheese and crackers, in front of the fire with Duke Ellington playing softly from the stereo; Ed loved the Duke.

Gabby and I were busy in the kitchen preparing the mashed potatoes, green beans and rack of lamb for dinner. It would be a holiday feast along with a California cabernet and followed by toasted pound cake with ice cream and chocolate sauce.

There was also a lot of touching and hugging and laughing going on; so dinner would be delicious.

Dean of Men, Ed arrived with a bottle of bourbon and he and I enjoyed a cocktail; Gabby was waiting for wine with dinner.

"Gabby, Ed said, "the house is beautiful, what a wonderful job you did."

"Thank you, I love it and I often wish Frank was here to enjoy it."

"Joe, I loved Gabby's brother, Frank."

"And he loved you," said Gabby, "and you helped him a lot."

Ed directed this at me,

"It was gangs; I pulled him out of a gang. Frank moved in with me, we were lovers and he was going to Rutgers. Someone killed him and I, we, were devastated."

I listened and filled in the blanks; it was obvious that Gabby was surprised that I knew the dean was gay.

"How is the tutoring going," Ed wanted to know. He was prying of course.

"The tutor and the tutoring are amazing," I said.

"We have become very close friends," added Gabby.

Ed looked at us and smiled, "What a grand evening, thank you both for including me."

We moved to the dinner table to enjoy our meal. The conversation was easy and all the pieces fell into place. I learned more about Ed and Frank and over dessert I told Gabby and Ed about my "secret" Thanksgiving dinner with Mrs. Brand.

Dean of Men, Ed didn't linger; he left after dessert, hugs and Merry Christmas wishes.

"It was nice to fill in the blanks," I said to Gabby as we cleaned up.

"I was surprised you knew Ed is gay."

"I met Ed when he facilitated my last minute transfer to Rutgers and then he helped me change my major; we met a couple of times at his house and he shared he was gay. I assured him I'm not."

"The neat thing is," I continued, "he agreed to do everything he could to help me change my major."

"That's when Ed called me," said Gabby, "and asked that I do everything possible to help you."

"And you are; in many ways."

We hugged.

"I love my Gabby hugs."

"We have to set up for Santa," Gabby said, still in my arms.

"Really?"

"Every year."

"Has he ever come?"

"He always comes; you'll see."

We assembled a tray with a plate of cookies and a mug of hot chocolate that we placed on the hearth by the fire.

"Santa is going to love this. Are you ready for bed?"

"I'm waiting for Santa."

"Waiting for Santa? Bed with Gabby? Hmmmmm?"

"Good point."

We brushed our teeth together; we had done that before. I had slept over before, usually on the sofa, occasionally in one of the guest bedrooms. This was different and it was exciting; we had even discussed the rules: overall we were waiting until Gabby returned from Paris, so sleeping together was insane and yet, how could we not? Gabby was wearing a man's pajama top and I was wearing the bottoms. I turned off the bedside light and the room was bathed in the flickering light of the gas log fireplace. I was shivering, even though I was hot, as Gabby unbuttoned the pajama top. My hands immediately found her body and we kissed an endless kiss. We had promised each other we would stop and we settled down; my hands and my skin had finally found Gabby's beautiful body after weeks of desire and it was heaven, everything I expected and for the moment it was enough. We kissed, we said goodnight and we slept and I dreamed.

When I awakened Gabby was fast asleep; I slipped out of bed, brushed, pulled on my jeans and shirt, went down the hall and retrieved Gabby's hidden Christmas present and went downstairs.

Unless Gabby had been awake in the middle of the night Santa had indeed been to the Evers house and enjoyed a few cookies and his mug of hot chocolate. He had also left a nicely wrapped gift by the fire. I added Gabby's gift and stirred the embers and added a log. In the kitchen I got some bacon going, hoping the aroma would rouse Gabby. I remembered the eggnog, poured some, added some bourbon, flipped the bacon and parked in front of the fire. I had never been more content.

Gabby came downstairs looking like a million bucks and all she was wearing was the pajama top with a red belt and tights.

"Merry Christmas, Joseph." She sat next to me and kissed my cheek, "I have never been happier."

"Merry Christmas, Gabby. I raised my glass, "To us; I could not have accomplished what we didn't do last night with anyone else. We made a promise to and with each other and we kept it. And . . ."

"And?"

"And Santa was here last night."

"Of course Santa was here, silly." Gabby jumped up, running to the kitchen, "And the bacon is burning. If you fix me one of what ever you are drinking I will finish fixing breakfast."

We enjoyed breakfast, cleaned up and went to see what Santa brought.

"You first, Joseph."

I opened my present and revealed a book, "Architecture Since Man" that was monstrously thick and coffee table huge and filled with page sized illustrations from the cavemen's caves to the Empire State building. Stunning.

"Thank you, Gabby."

Gabby's present was a Four by four foot scarf depicting the icons of Paris in a pale blend of blues, white and red.

"I love it, Joseph, it is beautiful. Thank you."

"Santa must have known where you are going."

"Yes, and Santa deserves a kiss."

"And so does Mrs. Santa; the book is a treasure."

We spent much of Christmas day turning the pages of my architecture book and thus touring through centuries of man's architectural accomplishments.

We nibbled and rested and worked out in the gym and showered together and fell silent knowing this was our last full day together; I was going to the city to visit my sister, Sylvia, and Al for a few days and Gabby was off to Paris on the 27th. She didn't want me home when she left; she was afraid she would cry too much. We put Handel's "Messiah" on the stereo and held hands and rejoiced.

The next day, the 26th, I put my travel bag in the car and went back inside to find Gabby.

"You better bundle up, it's cold out there,"

"I will, I promise. You be careful in the big city. Do you have the key?"

I took her in my arms,

"Yes, I do have the key. Travel safely and I will be here for your call on New Years and when you come home through that door. I love you Gabby and no matter what we will be friends forever."

We kissed and looked at each other for a very long time; and then I left.

I went straight to the little Italian grocery where we did our shopping.

"Mister Joe, no Miss Gabby?"

"No Orlando, no Miss Gabby, she's flying to Paris tomorrow."

"You gonna miss her."

"You're darn right I'm going to miss her but only a week."

When I first showed up at the store Orlando thought Gabby had some young white boy in tow; he didn't approve. Over time he saw us holding hands, sharing a hug or tossing a loaf of bread along with a loud last second warning, so it could be caught. "Who is this guy, Miss Gabby," Orlando wanted to know. "He's my best friend. His name is Joe." And ever since Orlando calls me, "Mister Joe."

I picked up some crackers, cheese, a half-pound of sliced prosciutto, a loaf of French bread and a basket of fresh flowers all of which would have to serve as my house warming gift for my sister and Al.

"On Miss Gabby's account, Mister Joe?"

"No, Orlando, this is on me, I'm visiting my sister in New York."

"Then it's gonna be $139.40."

"No, can't be?"

"Okay, for you, $39.40."

"That's more like it, Orlando; you scared me." I gave him two twenties, "Merry Christmas, Orlando, I'll see you next year."

In the city a guy on the other side of the street pulled out leaving an open parking spot. I hung a quick U turn and parked. Lucky me, right in front of my sister's building and then, suddenly, there was one of New York's finest standing next to my window.

"Merry Christmas, a day late, Officer," I read his nametag, "Kelly. What can I do for you?"

"You already have; a perfectly illegal U turn."

"Oh, I was consumed with excitement when I saw the spot open up and, I guess I didn't want to miss it. Maybe you could miss it, too?"

"I could, but . . ."

"Can I interrupt you, right there?"

"Why would you want to do that?"

"Because that leaves us right where you said, "You could.""

"I could what?"

"Miss it and make my day after Christmas very merry. I'm going to visit my sister and she's going to ask me how my trip was and I am going to say "fantastic": I parked right in front of your building and Officer Kelly wished me a Merry Christmas. That's the best I've got."

Officer Kelly gave me a big smile, "If that's your best it's good enough for me. Merry Christmas; what's your name?"

"Joe."

"Merry Christmas, Joe."

I watched the officer walk off. I exhaled and resumed normal breathing. Oh, I wish Gabby had been here for that one.

Al opened the door and I liked him right away.

"Joe?"

"Al?"

"Come on in, big guy."

"I have stuff for the refrigerator and these flowers, sort of a quick fix house warming." "Thank you very much. If you put that on the kitchen counter I'll tell your sister you're here."

I left my travel bag by the door and put the cheese and prosciutto in the fridge and the rest on the counter. I went to the living room and I could tell right away that Al had furniture and Syl had furniture and now they had a mix. And if you looked out the window, off to the left, you could see the Hudson River.

"There's my brother."

I turned from the window and there were my sister and Al with the "you came fifteen minutes too soon" look.

"I can come back."

The guilties gave me that "what" look and we all laughed.

"I think it's close enough to five to have a drink and sit and talk and meet."

"I like this guy; welcome to the family and good luck. Have you met our mom?"

Al was in the kitchen getting ice to pop out of the ice tray. "Yes I have."

"Best behavior," said my sister.

"Who?"

"Both of them."

"What do you drink," asked Al.

"Bourbon."

"Jack Daniels?"

"If I have to."

My sister was in the kitchen at the fridge. "Oooh, prosciutto."

"Guilty," I said, joining them in the kitchen, "And there's cheese and bread and crackers. And the flowers."

"Thank you," they said in unison.

We set everything out on the kitchen table and ate and drank, and talked.

"How was your trip," my sister asked and I told them about Officer Kelly.

We talked about family; Al's and ours and I realized I liked, loved my sister; she was the middle child, not ever easy, and she and I shared the same unpredictable mother that Gloria, our older sister, didn't have. Why, we wondered, what happened that changed our mom? Too many possibilities, lots of booze fueled conjecture and no real answer. Oh, well.

I thought of Gabby and her trip to Paris; I missed her and silently wished her safe travels. I told Syl and Al a little bit about my tutor, my friend and then I sort of didn't want to say too much; not yet. I told them about the WHAM and my shift from idle wanderer to curious, competitive student. That was good enough for a nightcap.

The next day, Sunday, we went to the Carnegie Deli for brunch. After which we walked to Riverside Drive for a stroll along the Hudson River until we couldn't take the cold any longer. We went back to the apartment for a nap and then to El Parador for a Mexican comida. I thought they were calling my future brother-in-law, El Stinko until my sister explained, "It's, El Cinco, because of his Margarita prowess; five of them." One cerveza was good enough for me.

Monday morning we all left the apartment early; Syl and Al went off to work and I was going to Gabby's house in New Brunswick, New Jersey. I was gone before Officer Kelly could cite me for parking illegally between 8:00Am and noon on Mondays, Wednesdays and Fridays. I love New York; but!

In New Brunswick I filled up the Chevy, checked and added a quart of oil and decided to visit Pete and the guys.

"Hey, Pete. Merry Christmas, a little late."

"Hey, look who's here; Merry Christmas and Happy Hanukah."

"Thanks. Where are the guys?"

"They saw you coming and ran out the back."

"Very funny, Peter."

"They're all doing post Christmas stuff. Where you been, Kid?"

"School. Punched in the stomach by calculus and some other subjects; but I've got them in a clinch, I'm winning."

"How's your tutor?"

"How do you know about my tutor?"

"I've been around this town for a long time, Kid; that and your car is up there every weekend. So?

"She is in Paris."

"Paris! Damn. Work?"

"No. Some personal matter," I shrugged, "I don't know."

"Kid, I know the holidays are demanding but we miss you, we want you to get back into a training routine. Wadda you say?"

"Me too, that's why I came by, a couple of weeks; middle of January."

"Good. Don't make me go up to the Evers' place."

"That's not funny, Pete."

"Just kidding. Come on, you wanna go a couple of rounds?"

"No, I'm hungry, I'm ready for lunch. And I need a liquor store?"

"Okay, let's go, we'll do a double header; lunch and the liquor store."

Pete was pulling on his jacket, "Come on Kid, I thought you'd never ask."

"Ask what?"

"Ask me out for lunch and it's a good thing you did."

"Why, Pete, is it a good thing?"

"Mostly it's because we are friends and you are a minor, which means you walk out of the liquor store with nada, nuthin!"

We are in the car and Pete is giving me directions.

"Okay, park anywhere you can."

I do and we are in front of Orlando's Italian Grocery and next- door is a sub/hero sandwich shop.

"Pete, this place looks like it's been here forever?"

"As long as I've been around."

The shop has only five tables and we got one.

"Get the meatball sub, Kid; you order and pay at the counter. One would be big enough for both of us and I'll have a Coke."

I placed the order and in no time they brought it to our table along with Pete's Coke and water for me. Lunch was surprising; each half had a large meatball cut in half, side by side, and boy, was it tasty.

The liquor store was two blocks away and before we got out of the car I gave Pete eighty dollars.

"I'll pick the champagne and you pay. I'm not even sure they will have champagne, Pete?"

"Don't worry they'll have it. What's it for?"

"It's for Gabby and me; for New Year's, belated. You know, when she gets home."

"Are you trying to get lucky, Kid?"

I didn't answer, my look, as we got out of the car, said it all. Inside I was shocked; they had Dom Perignon, Louis Roederer and more, but I went for the Roederer and Pete paid for it: $54.80.

"That's some store, they have it all. Thanks, Pete."

"My pleasure. The guys and me, there's a lot we can teach you."

"I need a couple of weeks; I'll be back."

I pulled in front of the gym and Pete offered his hand; will he pull it away? I went for the shake and it was there, warm and strong.

"Thanks Pete, great lunch."

"Any time," he said while getting out of the car, "Any time."

"Pete."

He was walking away but he turned, "Yeah, Kid?"

"One other thing."

"Yeah."

"My change."

"Oh, yeah," he said, handing me my change, "Oh, yeah."

I watched him turn and walk toward the gym. He reached up with his right hand and scratched the back of his head or did he just flip me off?

On Gabby's porch, I rang the bell just to hear the chimes like that first Saturday. I fumbled for the key; this was so weird, going into the house with no Gabby.

Inside I realized I was on an adventure: I knew the house but I didn't know the specifics; thermostat, light switches, wood for the fireplace, stuff like that. I got the kitchen light on and put the champagne in the fridge. On the table was a basket of fresh flowers and an envelope for me. I imagined it would say everything I would say to Gabby and sure enough; she loves me, she will miss me, she will call on New Year's eve, she will come home to me and please, please be there when I walk through the door: yes, yes, yes and yes!

I bumped up the thermostat, found a pile of old newspapers and cleaned out the fireplace and got a fire going; this called for a bourbon on the rocks and cheese and crackers. Attached to the cheese wrap was a note from Gabby; "I love you, Joseph. You are a cheese whore!" I shook my head, the woman knows me. I turned on soft music and settled on the sofa with my drink and my cheese and crackers. I tried to relax but couldn't; I had Gabby on my mind, but her presence, her energy were missing. I reached for my Christmas present and got lost in the architectural world; I turned the page and came upon the Taj Mahal and a note from Gabby; "This is my favorite, serene beauty exerting max power." I just leaned back and smiled; I loved loving Gabby.

On New Years Eve day I got ready for Gabby's call. I had a fire going, soft music playing and bourbon on the rocks in my hand when the phone rang.

"Gabby?"

"Joseph, I love you and I wish I was in your arms this very moment."

"You are and in my heart. I love you."

"This trip was the right thing to do and I will be coming home to you on Monday."

"I am here for you, for us."

"I am going to cry, I have to say goodbye, with love."

And she was gone; I could hear the click echoing in my ear. What did I say and Gabby? It was all so fast. Could Monday come quickly enough?

The next morning I made breakfast and while enjoying it I realized how much Gabby and I talked together; constantly sharing with complete trust. It all started with calculus and Gabby's guidelines: respect, commitment, effort, trust and love. These were the guidelines for learning that had become our guidelines for friendship and love.

During the past few days I read, I studied, I did laundry and I worked out and it still felt like Monday would never come. So Sunday, after the Rose Bowl game, I drove over to Phi Ep to see if Richard was back from break. Indeed, as usual, Richard was at his typewriter.

"Do you ever write notes by hand?"

"I know the voice, I think?"

"Richard how was break?"

"Cold, family, traffic. Who are you and how was yours?"

"I am your occasional room-mate and my break is truncated."

"Truncated?"

"Gabby is in Paris, some personal matter; she left a week ago and will be home tomorrow afternoon. I've been staying at her place; she called at midnight, she loves me."

"And you?"

"I love loving her and I think I love her."

"That sounds like an English version of a math problem."

"We talk, we share, we confide, we argue, we reason things out, we laugh, we cook and we work out together."

"She's famous; no one knows her name and everyone knows her face and her body."

"She's my tutor and my friend."

"What are you doing when she gets home?"

"Probably celebrating New Year's eve. I'm not sure but I can tell you what we did on Christmas Eve; we had the Dean of Men over for dinner. If you remember, the Dean put me in touch with Gabby, she was once a child math prodigy."

"Is he on to the two of you?"

"Yeah, sort of. The crazy thing is we are not sure what we are up to; we are sort of scared, there are, as you know, differences."

"Then tomorrow evening will be big. I wish you well, Mr. Gordon."

"Thank you, Richard."

Monday I went to my classes and it felt good to be "post break" and challenged; a concept that brought a smile to my face. I also sought out the two professors of my Tuesday classes explaining I wouldn't be in class the next day; a pressing personal matter. I got the green light and the assignments.

Back at Gabby's I got a fire going, turned on some soft music and waited. Shortly before five the door opened and in an instant Gabby was in my arms. We hugged and hugged oblivious to the cold air rushing in through the wide open door. I felt Gabby shivering and sent her to the fireplace while I got her bag from the porch and shut the door.

Gabby, out of her coat and flushed from the fire, took my hand and led me to the sofa where I sat and she straddled me. She was going to say something but she started to cry and buried her face in my neck.

"You are very beautiful when you cry and I am so glad you are home."

"On the flight I tried to put together everything I want to tell you but all I can say now is, I love you and I'm glad to be home and I am glad I went."

"It was good to be apart; to miss you and value you. Time to think."

"And?"

"I think I love you and I thought we might celebrate the New Year together tonight; I have champagne in the fridge?"

"Great idea. Hot shower for me and would you take my bag upstairs, please?"

"Done. Are you hungry?"

"Just a snack." Gabby gave me a quick kiss and was half way up the stairs before I reached her bag.

After her shower Gabby came down wearing jeans and a white shirt; she looked great. I opened the Louis Roederer champagne and we toasted the New Year and then we shared a hungry kiss, a kiss that said, "I missed you." We were on the sofa sipping champagne and eating prosciutto and melon and cheese and bread. We were hungry and for the moment we chose food.

"Joseph, I want to tell you about my trip. I am scared, but I have to tell you now."

"I promise to hear you; you don't have to be scared."

"Irene. I went to Paris to see Irene but I have to go back to when my dad was killed. My aunt Florence and my dad raised me after my mom died in childbirth. My aunt, I called her Flo, took over after my dad's death. Everything was fine; I was smart, especially math, good grades but we were running out of money. Flo took me to a modeling audition, maybe I was 15 and we lied about my age. I was very pretty, pretty enough for them to look past our lie and I got the job. It led to many more and I was making good money. Then I got a location job and they wouldn't let Flo go along. That's when Irene, another model, told Flo she would look after me. She took me under her wing and then took me to her bed and taught me all the pleasures of a woman's body and all the toys that helped."

Gabby was fighting tears but would not give in. "When Flo learned of my relationship with Irene she condemned me, moved to Arizona and Irene became my agent. I was a hot commodity and, after a year or so, Irene moved us to London and then to Paris where we lived for years.

Girls in the business and other agents told me that Irene was using me to her advantage, stealing, and promoting wild parties; but I was vain and stubborn. Quite by accident I found bank statements and contracts that opened my eyes and when Irene was in Italy for two weeks I took everything that was mine or that I had paid for and had it all shipped to this house and I came home to rebuild my house and myself and I have been celibate ever since."

I thought Gabby was done, I was wrong. She straddled me and leaned into me, so close.

"Then you came into my life; we became friends and I felt something new; falling in love along with physical and sexual feelings that became very persistent and I started to think of us. I wondered if we could overcome our differences along with almost 15 years with a woman lover; it's all I have ever known. I am emotional and sexual; I love touching, hugging, teasing, pleasing and being pleased. When we kissed our first kiss I was crying and it was a sweet, salty magnificent kiss; that was the first time I kissed a man and it stirred my love for you.

I wanted to see Irene to measure my feelings and end that relationship in a wise and healthy way for me."

This time she was done, relieved that she had shared her story and anxious about what was coming.

"Gabby, we are friends, I am sure of that. If we choose to be lovers, and I think we are about to, then we go ahead one day at a time. I love you."

"I was afraid you would leave me, unsure of our future."

"I am unsure of our future but I think we would be crazy if we didn't give "us" a chance."

I could see Gabby let go of her fear and relax into her beautiful, playful self.

"Are you trying to take advantage of me; you know I'm exhausted from my trip?"

"I want you at max power, Miss Taj Mahal. We're going to bed, we can sleep in and fall in love all day tomorrow."

Gabby stood, took my hand and helped me off the sofa. I kissed her neck and unbuttoned her shirt that fell to the floor; I kissed her breast.

"Harder, Joseph."

She held me to her with her hands behind my neck.

"God, Gabby, you taste good."

I kissed her mouth and led her upstairs.

In bed, exhaustion overtook desire and Gabby was asleep after one little kiss and a contented purr. I stole away and put our snacks and champagne in the fridge and returned to the warmth of Gabby. We slept until noon.

When we woke we hugged and the heat we generated could have warmed the entire house; we were on fire. The feelings that went beyond friendship and that had been building for weeks, perhaps months, were at the breaking point yet neither one of us went for the "unchartered territory" that we each, until that moment, had only imagined.

"Gabby, I am going to," and that was as far as I got; Gabby's mouth covered mine and our hands found every exciting inch of each other's body. Soon our mouths followed and then Gabby took me to her and we were one, each of us arriving at joy simultaneously.

"I love you, Gabby. You are beyond beautiful."

"And you, Joseph, just took me, several times, to a place I've never been."

After we made love it was a little awkward, I was waiting for Gabby to suggest we go downstairs and she was waiting for me.

"We need to find a comfort zone so we don't break into a thousand pieces," I said.

"I know, I was thinking how easy and how wonderful it would be to stay in bed all day."

"I like that idea, I like it a lot."

"I have," Gabby said, "a new suggestion; let's shower together."

In the shower we brushed our teeth, we would, afterwards, always brush our teeth together; it was sort of childlike and sexy, especially in the shower. Gabby's shower is four by four with two showerheads; and in that hot shower we washed each other: rubbing and scrubbing and touching and kissing. We toweled each other dry and, filled with lust, took each other to bed where we lingered and teased and then feasted and loved all the way to the joy and laughter that follows climax.

When I woke Gabby was asleep next to me; I gently turned her so I could lie nestled next to her. I put my arms around her and cupped her breasts. She was so warm it was intoxicating.

"Nice move, Joseph."

"Nice breasts, Gabby."

"I am so happy."

"Me too. But!"

Gabby turned quickly; we were nose to nose, "But what?"

"I have school tomorrow."

Gabby kissed my lips, "I know, I know you cut class today and I am very grateful; I love you."

"This has been a very special day: home on the fourth and celebrating us on the fifth; a day to remember."

"Can you sleep with me tonight?"

"Only if you feed me dinner."

"Way ahead of you; while you slept I was downstairs slaving in the kitchen."

"You are a masterpiece."

"I will take that as a naughty pun and a lovely compliment; let's go down for dinner."

"I remember doing that earlier."

Gabby tried to slap me but I was too quick; we kissed instead.

Over dinner, we started our debate about "stuff": Contraception: "I am not touching your stunning body until. ."

Gabby smiled, "Way ahead of you, got us covered."

My moving into Gabby's house: "You can't afford the rent."

Going out in public to the movies and/or theater in New York: "This would test our age differences and our color differences."

Fraternity events: "Really; do you, Gabby, want to hang out with young boys?"

Family: "My sisters would love you; my Mom, not so much."

Travel: "The age and color thing, again."

My student responsibilities: "Studying instead of fornicating."

Gabby's responsibilities as a recognizable model: "Gabby Evers, world famous fashion model seen with young white man." And goals: "It's too early in our relationship to have joint goals."

We decided to leave our living configuration the same; I would sleep at/ with Gabby on Fridays, Saturdays and Sundays with an occasional weekday night added on the spur of the moment. We thought ahead to the summer and living together while I continued my summer courses.

I maintained my fraternity friendships including a couple of visits each month to Sally's with the guys for a cheeseburger, a beer and, I confess, a quick glance around for Kate.

At the fraternity house Richard and I kept each other up to date and Mrs. Brand one day asked me, "How is Gabby?"

"Is there anything you don't know?" I responded and I was not surprised at all when she winked and said, "I'm jealous."

Gabby was often in New York for lunch with her agent, Eileen Ford, with whom Gabby was working on a couple of long term "spokes woman" deals with an auto manufacturer and a perfume company. It was big stuff.

Together, Gabby shared her work and I shared my schooling. Gabby was a huge part of my learning as we talked and argued over each of my classes; it was beyond helpful and fun and she is so smart. Gabby said she was finishing her education that she had given up years before.

Often studying opened the door to likes and dislikes and other stuff.

Getting out of the house we went to Orlando's to shop and a couple of times to the sub shop next door to share a meatball sub for lunch, everything else we did at home.

"Let's go to the movies," I suggested often enough, or out to dinner or to the city to see a Broadway show.

"No, Joseph, home; we have every thing we want and need at home."

"Okay, Gabby," and I figured patience, Joe, and when we are living together it will be different.

"What's your favorite food?" I asked Gabby.

"Easy question, easy answer; caviar."

"Caviar? I'm surprised; I don't know why, I'm just surprised."

"What would you have guessed?"

"Chocolate soufflé; I know you love chocolate."

"Mmmm, true. What about you, Mr. Joe?"

"What about me? Hmmm?"

"I love it that Orlando calls you, Mr. Joe."

"Yeah, me too. It's like an acceptance thing. He's very protective of you and he certainly wasn't sure about me at first."

"He's very paternal in how he loves me."

"My favorite food is Gabby."

"Joseph!"

"Okay, okay. My favorite foods are; oysters, beef Wellington, any soufflé and caviar."

"Top dog?"

"Caviar; beluga caviar."

"Aha, something we both enjoy."

"Something? My God, Gabby, there are so many things we both like and enjoy, and I'm not just talking about food."

"True. Calculus, we both love calculus."

"It's an acquired taste. Music; classical, show tunes, Sinatra, Tony Bennett and even a tinge of Duke Ellington," I said.

"Working out and for some of us, jumping rope," Gabby said with a wink.

"I am starting to hold my own. Cooking together; we cut, we slice, we dice, we touch, we create and we eat and enjoy food together."

"We do, we touch and we hug."

"Gabby hugs, the best, since the very first day we met."

CHAPTER 8

EPIPHANY

I called "41" and asked for Jerry Brown; Grace Dwyer, the head operator, asked who was calling and I told her.

"Let me see if I can find him, Joe."

"Thank you." I was in a phone booth all bundled up for the cold weather.

"Good morning, Joe, how are you?"

"I'm good, how about you and the family?"

"We are fine, what can I do for you?"

"I want to buy some caviar, enough for two."

"A quarter of a pound should be perfect; is this for your tutor?"

"How is it that everyone knows about my tutor?"

"Your tutor was here for lunch a few days ago with Eileen Ford, her agent."

"Oh."

"She told me that you are doing very well; that you are smart and a hard working student; I'm proud of you, Joe."

"Wow, thank you. Jerry, can I afford this, you know, the caviar?"

"Of course you can, I'll put it on your tab."

"Jerry, I don't have a tab."

"One day, when you are a high flying architect here in the city, you will have a tab and that's when you can take care of it."

"Thank you. Her birthday is next week, on Valentine's day." "Here's how this works: starting tomorrow you can come to "41" any morning after six, go through the side door, down the steps and ask for Gus; he will have your package."

"Thank y . . ."

"There's more; something else will be in the package, it's for Gabby and make sure you tell her it's from me."

"I will, Jerry, thank you. Thank you for everything."

At 6:30, Friday morning, February 12th I parked in front of "41". I had figured since the winter temperatures were in the high thirties and mid forties, my car trunk would work as a refrigerator for the caviar and a hiding place so Gabby could truly be surprised.

I locked the car, went in the side door, down the steps and asked a short, bald man in a white work jacket for Gus.

"I'm Gus, what can I do for you?"

"Jerry Brown said you would have a package for me; I'm Joe Gordon."

Gus held out his hand, "It's nice meeting you, Joe. It will be about ten minutes."

"I'm parked on the street."

"Go upstairs and drive around the block. Get going."

I started up the steps as Gus said, "I'll be upstairs with your package when you come around. If I'm not there, go around one more time."

"Thanks, Gus," I called back, "Thanks."

I got in my car and did a slow trip around the block. Sure enough, there was Gus with my package that we put in the trunk.

"Wish Gabby a Happy Birthday," Gus said, and I figured the whole world was in on the surprise.

I headed back to Rutgers, hoping to make my ten o'clock class.

On February 14th I wanted Gabby to wake up to fresh flowers; she loves fresh flowers. I asked Orlando to make two special arrangements and to put them on the front porch at seven. I snuck out of bed to bring them indoors; then I returned to Gabby.

"My God, you are freezing. Go away."

"You are my love, my life and my heater; turn it up to high." I reached for her but she fought like a tiger; finally I pinned her, "Happy birthday Gabby." She purred and welcomed me to her and then rolled over and I nested behind her with my hands touching everywhere.

"Not bad for an old broad."

"That wasn't nice, Joseph. It's a good thing I know that you love me."

"I do and probably have since our first breakfast at eight on that first of many wonderful Saturdays; you are an amazing woman, Gabby."

We had discussed this double day; her birthday and Valentine's Day, and we decided to keep it simple; enjoy the day, enjoy each other.

When we went downstairs for breakfast wearing comfortable "grubbies" Gabby noticed the flowers in the living room and read the card aloud, "With love, Joseph."

"Thank you my dear man." We hugged and proceeded to the kitchen where Gabby noticed the flowers on the table and read the card, "Happy Birthday Gabby, I wish you a wonderful, happy and healthy year. Signed, Joseph."

"They are beautiful. Thank you."

"You are welcome. How about I get a fire going and you get breakfast started; I am starving."

"Me too. Kiss?"

We kissed and I said, "It's kisses like that that make me even more hungry."

At the fireplace there were just enough embers for me to catch a fire; a little bit of blowing and a few available twigs and I was in business. That gave me time to get some soft music going and by then the fire was ready for a few logs. And by then I smelled the bacon.

"I love my flowers, thank you."

"I'm glad you like them," I said as we both had bites of bacon.

"Where did you hide the flowers?"

"Trade secret."

"I will withhold sex for a month."

"You can't, I am irresistible."

"Two months."

"Nope."

"Starting now."

"I give you fifteen minutes and you will be asking for a hug and a Gabby hug is better than sex."

"I hate you."

"That is not true and your completely delicious breakfast is getting cold."

Gabby takes a bite, "Mmmm!"

"You want me to warm it up?"

"No! Where?"

"What where?"

Gabby was chewing and trying to look very angry, "Where did you," she had a moment of thought, "that's why you were so cold; the flowers were on the porch?"

I shrugged.

"But they could not have been out there all night, they would have been dead and they are not, they're gorgeous. Some one delivered them at a certain time and you left our bed and brought them in."

"Calculus, Gabby; maybe you don't get it right away and then, WHAM."

"You did that for me; I love you, love you, love you."

"I love you, too."

We cleaned up the kitchen and shifted to the sofa to enjoy the fire, the music, the flowers, the newspaper, the books and the magazines that we had gathered on and around the coffee table. We both loved to read and we talked a lot about my college courses, education, President Eisenhower, the Cold War with the Soviet Union, politics, fashion, food, cooking and sports. We had a full plate and often we would thumb through Life or Time or Vogue, even, clashing or both liking this or that. Gabby was smart and open to confrontation; actually I think she thrived on confrontation ending in a good workout down in the gym.

On this day, her birthday, we read and listened to music and occasionally Gabby would roll over and straddle me and hug me and kiss me and we danced and we napped on the sofa. Eventually Gabby decided, "I'm going down for a workout; come with?"

I'll be down in a couple of minutes, I want to finish this chapter."

"Hmmph!" And she was gone.

When I went down stairs Gabby was jumping rope and sweating; she glistened. Gabby wasn't tall and skinny, perhaps five seven or eight and curvy though she carried no fat; she was alluring.

I changed into a pair of gym shorts and we worked out for a half hour before going upstairs to shower.

We brushed our teeth together in the shower; why is that always such fun and so refreshing? The hot water soothed us as we washed ourselves and didn't want it to end. Finally we dried each other and I quickly put on fresh, comfortable clothes.

"I'll see you down stairs, Gabby, I want to check on the fire."

Downstairs I went straight to the car and retrieved the package from "41". I had to work fast: I put the tin of caviar in the center of a nice blue platter and spread dry crackers around the tin, along with two spoons and two champagne glasses. I was ready; the fire was good, the music was soft.

Gabby, coming down the steps, looked comfortable in jeans, a blue work shirt, red lipstick and a red eye mask; my Valentine.

I took her hand and led her to the sofa, "Your table, my dear."

"No!" exclaimed Gabby noticing the Caviar.

"Yes, and there's more," I said heading to the fridge.

"Joseph! That's two in one day; how did you do this?"

"This, Gabby," opening the champagne, "is Louis Roederer Crystal and it is for you from Jerry Brown at "41". I poured the champagne and we lifted our glasses, "You are the most beautiful Valentine I will ever know."

"And you, Mr. Handsome provide the most wonderful surprising things. Who delivered this?"

"First some caviar."

"Damn Joseph, this is the best caviar ever. Thank you."

"You are very welcome."

Tell me who delivered the caviar?"

"I did. I picked it up at "41" Friday morning a little after six. I kept it in the trunk of my car. Now you know all my secrets."

"I am very grateful."

"Behind that mask are you the woman I know and love?"

"Yes, and I am the woman who loves you back."

"Caviar, Crystal and soft music, let's dance."

We danced, we ate, we drank and we kissed. We were having a wonderful day.

We put away the caviar, plenty left, and the other stuff and we went to bed. We kissed and spoke of the long, wonderful day. Gabby fell asleep, I was lying next to her and, intoxicated by her beauty and warmth, I had an epiphany. Oh, how I wanted to run from that epiphany, but I could not: I want a wife and a family; Oh, my God. This woman is my friend and my lover and, no doubt, she has brought me to this awakening, this moment, and I can feel the pain. Oh, my God.

"You're back now; what, three weeks, and you're doing great in the ring."

"Thanks, Pete. My arms got tired and my gloves dropped a little."

"Nah, you did good. I don't know what you've been doing but for the most part you sure have stayed in good shape."

"Yeah, things are going good: I've turned my studies around, I'm in a strong relationship and I've been working out, she has a gym at her house. It feels good to be back here with you guys."

"You been taking jump rope lessons from somebody?"

"You figured me out. Yeah, somebody that jumped rope almost as good as you, Jimmy."

"I am so glad you are back," said Boozer, "I like punching a fresh face."

"Thanks Boozer, I like going around in the ring with you too."

"I know."

"Do you guys think I'm ready to move up the ladder?"

"Cool your jets, Kid," said Art,

"Boxing isn't something that you rush; you get to a certain level and you sharpen that level. When you get real comfortable there that's when you can go up the ladder. Don't try to rush it, Kid."

"I trust you guys and it feels terrific to be back. I'm going to be here through the summer."

"New Brunswick, for the summer? You got to be kidding."

"Not kidding, I'm taking three summer class courses; I'm working to get ahead, I'm going to be an architect."

"And a damn good boxer," said Pete.

"You really have it in you Kid," said Art.

"I'm going to wrap it up, I have a lot of studying to do but I'll see you guys next Tuesday."

When I walked out to my car I couldn't help but flash back to the very first time I went to Pete's gym; I was just a scared little kid who, for whatever reason, wanted to learn how to box. That scared little kid was right on the money.

THE KISS

CHAPTER 9

SUKI

My epiphany was more empowering than sorrowful and as the months passed I realized I was growing up and assessing my goals and my options.

I was startling to understand that Gabby was an option. She had come into my life as my tutor just as I had made a decision of self- determination; she was a treasure who became my friend and my lover. We talked and argued about everything, made some important discoveries and after Gabby came home from Paris we agreed, as lovers, to go forward one day at a time. Now I wondered how Gabby felt?

We were well into spring and with the warmer weather I was running three times a week and boxing with Pete and the guys on Tuesdays and Thursdays. It all felt great and at Rutgers I was actually excelling and had a good rapport with my professors.

Two of them, with Dean of Men, Ed's urging, allowed me to take two Junior year course finals; I aced them both and I had not only caught up with my classmates but I was leading the field with the possibility of early graduation if I did well during the summer classes. The other thing that Dean of Men, Ed pointed out was my professors would favorably endorse me at one or two of the best Architecture schools.

A big part of my success was due to Gabby: every book that I read to prepare, especially for the two Junior course finals, Gabby also read and we talked and argued our way through them until we were numb. After those sessions we always went downstairs for a workout and we always went upstairs to shower together. And then, but not always, had great sex. Gabby was the one that insisted on the workouts because our study sessions would fuel us up to the max and she didn't want our energy to turn to misdirected anger; smart woman.

Gabby had landed a two- year deal with the Lincoln division of the Ford Motor Car Company as their Spokesperson. She was a very busy woman; traveling across the country and abroad and away on two-week shoots. I was thrilled for her and I was lucky to get that study time with her.

Gabby was away and I was spending a little more time with the Phi Ep guys at Sally's; always with a glance for Kate.

On Friday I couldn't find a book that I needed to read and study for an upcoming exam; I figured it must be at Gabby's and drove to her place and let myself in. Just coming down the stairs was a beautiful, young, perky Japanese girl, maybe 18 and wearing only black panties. The hair on the back of my neck stood up; I knew.

"Oh, sorry surprise. You Joseph?"

"Yes," my lips said as my mind conveyed, "whoa!"

"Me Suki," and she hugged me. My arms went around her, this wisp of beauty, and she pressed herself against me.

"Gabby say apology for you and make you happy; anything you want. Gabby away week more."

We ended the hug and Suki was talking but my mind was talking louder.

"This is Gabby's new girl friend; she's in, I'm out: it's over; it hurts even though I knew, we knew, this could happen. I was moving in next week for the summer; now what?"

Suki was standing, hands on hips, cute as a button.

"What," I asked; "Sorry, I didn't hear you."

"Gabby insist you move in, sleep in her bed. I give you pleasure, handsome Joseph."

In that instant the fear and the pain evaporated; all of this would work out fine.

"Suki, I am looking for a book and . ."

"I have book." She ran up stairs and I watched her.

"I'm coming," she shouted and damned if she didn't return with my book.

"How did you?"

"Gabby say book on her bed, you need."

"Thank you Suki, what can I do for you?"

"Shopping, need food for house and for dinner tonight. List on table."

"Suki, put on some clothes, we are going shopping."

"No leave house; Gabby say."

"Put on clothes and shoes, Joseph say."

Suki flashed a big smile and ran upstairs; I watched her. "Orlando, I want you to meet Suki."

Suki smiled and Orlando beamed at this adorable Munchkin and his eyes shifted to me, asking what's going on?

"Suki is a friend of Gabby and me; we have shopping to do, any specials?"

"For how many?"

"Two! Week next three," Suki said with a smile.

"I'll cut a beef filet and sea bass and some shrimp while you shop."

Orlando, shaking his head, went off to do his thing and we each picked up a basket to fill.

"He very nice."

"He is and he loves Gabby like she is his daughter. He's Italian, very protective and he thinks you and I are cheating on Gabby."

When we checked out Suki said, "Mister Orlando, I love Gabby, never hurt her, not ever."

Suki bowed and Orlando bowed back; all was well and Orlando helped us out to the car where Suki kissed him on the cheek before we drove off.

It took two trips from the car into the house with everything including a basket of fresh flowers that Suki placed on the kitchen table after leaving her shoes at the door.

When we had everything put away Suki said, "I cook, you read. We eat together."

"Okay. One other thing; you are very beautiful."

"Thank you, Joseph."

I called Phi Ep and left a message for Richard that I was fine and I would see him tomorrow, probably. I had found more than my book; it was a whole new world.

Dinner was delicious; Suki cooked the sea bass with onions, mushrooms and a hint of garlic. I had a beer and Suki had a few sips but wasn't sure.

"Japanese beer better," she assured me.

"Where did you grow up?"

"Tokyo. Two brothers, younger; I was mama, real mama busy. Crowded, Tokyo big."

It seemed like Suki was answering questions often asked of her.

"When did you meet Gabby?"

"April auto show. I stand next to car look pretty; Gabby come from car very beautiful."

"You worked together?"

"Work, bed; two nights. She tell me about you; ask me to visit."

I felt like Orlando, confused; so I asked, "Gabby is beautiful?"

"Yes."

"Gabby is smart and kind?"

"Yes."

"Gabby is loving and generous?"

"Yes, she say all same for you."

I smiled, "Gabby is my friend, I love her."

"One week . ."

"Last week?"

"Yes. No. I sorry."

"It's okay, Suki." I shrugged and gestured; "Go on."

"Japanese man bring package tell me; key, money, plane, car to Gabby house in package and message; "Wait in house for Joseph."

"Suki, hug?" We both stood and hugged a good hug.

"You are a very brave and beautiful woman and I think you are very smart."

Suki was crying and I swept her off her feet, carried her to the sofa and held her while she cried it all out.

"You okay?"

"I sorry."

"No sorry Suki, you are a very daring girl to fly half way across the world; you trusted Gabby, and now you can trust me."

"Joseph, come to bed?"

"No, I have to read and study; you go, get rest and I will come up in a while."

Suki kissed me on my lips, "See you," She said and went upstairs; I watched.

I read and studied for a few hours along with a bourbon on the rocks and then I went upstairs. As I brushed my teeth everything in me, everything, wanted to get in bed with Suki; even to just sleep with her, but I couldn't, I didn't dare.

"You insult me," Suki said, waking me in the guest room the next morning. She was pissed.

"I'm sorry Suki, I wanted you to sleep; I care about you."

"You love me?"

"I like you Suki, big like you."

"Please, tonight Joseph, even sleep only; bed together?"

"Yes," the word escaped my senses.

"Promise?"

"Promise."

"We make Gabby happy."

"Really?"

"She not want hurt you."

That night I enjoyed a delicious Japanese plum.

THE KISS

CHAPTER 10

PETE'S GYM

I was suited up, had on my high-tops, my gloves and my face-guard sitting on a stool in a corner of the ring at Pete's Gym.

"You've got the dance, you've got the balance, you've got the footwork, you've got the punches and the punch combinations, you have the strength and the stamina and the focus; now it's time for actual fight conditions. This, Kid, is going up the ladder."

Pete was in my face as he delivered that message; he wanted me to not just hear it but to feel it. He wanted me to know that he and the guys feel I am ready.

"Here's how it works: you are going to fight each one of us for two minutes, with two minutes between rounds. When you're fighting me, Boozer, Jim and Art will be in your corner; they will tell you all about me, what my strengths are and my weaknesses. They will tell it to you straight and you put it in your head so your natural talent can focus on the fight. When you're fighting Boozer; Artie, Jimmy, and I will be in your corner and we will tell you all about Boozer. You get the picture. It will be the same against each of us. Who do you want to fight first?"

"Art first, Jimmy next, then Boozer and you last. I'm ready."

Art went to the far corner and sat alone. I looked at him as Pete told me that Art wants me to think he's kind of sleepy and slow, inviting you closer, but he's dangerous with body punches. Jimmy added, "Art drops his hands a lot but it's a ploy to bring you closer. He backs up, wants you coming at him but when he stops, watch out."

Boozer offered some final advise, "This is your first fight; keep breathing and save some energy for the last thirty seconds."

"One last thing," Pete said, "We are not trying to hurt anyone, so you don't go one hundred percent. But your not just waving "hello" either."

The bell rang and I was on my feet but I wasn't in the ring; I could see Art but my mind was eating Jello in a meat packing plant and my feet were kind of shuffling in place. Art actually came and addressed me with a punch to the face. I felt it, nothing serious but an awakening none-the-less. I got moving and I focused on Art; I hit him in the forehead area of his faceguard.

"Too hard," he said.

"Sorry," I mumbled through my mouthpiece.

Art punched me in the stomach with a quick left-right combination that pissed me off and got me into the fight. I stalked him, aware of his sleepy pretension, crouched, fended off his body punches and made a discovery, I was faster, much faster than Art, and finished the round: pop, pop, pop.

The bell rang and we touched gloves.

I sat down in Art's corner and he led me to mine where I sat as Jimmy, my next opponent crossed to the other side of the ring.

"Nice work after a weird start," said Art, now wrapped in a towel that Pete gave him.

"What happened," Pete asked. "You know, at the start."

"Mind cramp? I don't know; I was lost."

"Okay, we only have a minute," said Boozer. "Jimmy is quick and he's cocky and that's his weakness. Stay on him and the openings will show."

Pete hadn't said a word when the bell rang and I was on my feet. I dogged Jimmy and I was as fast or faster than he and I kept jabbing with my left. At one point he switched and started leading with his right but that left him more open to my right. The bell rang and we touched gloves and Jimmy surprised me with a hug. "Good work, Kid."

"Thanks, Jimmy."

I went to my corner and sat; I was tired.

"Okay Boozer is a wise older fox." Pete continued, "so be careful and calm down; you're spending too much energy and you're going to need some for me."

The bell rang and boxing with Boozer was a waltz with some jitterbug mixed in. Boozer was smooth, very calm and very focused. I followed his lead with some surprises of my own. I loved boxing with Boozer; I learned from Boozer. The bell rang and we touched gloves. "Thank you, Boozer, I like you a lot."

I went to my corner and Boozer followed telling me about Pete before I sat down.

"It's his ego, that's the weakness."

"What does that mean in boxing terms," I asked.

"Let him do all the work, all the razzle-dazzle and wait for an opening and take it and the softer you hit him the more pissed off he will get. You will do fine, I know it."

The bell rang and we touched gloves at the start. I focused on Pete like he was a god and waited. Of course I was jabbing but I was really waiting. And there it was, a clear quick shot to the head with my right; I made it a tap and Boozer was right, Pete was pissed.

"That was just a "hello," Pete said.

"Pete, mine was just luck or it would have had more."

I got another clear shot, this time to his jaw with my left and I made it gentle. Pete, this time, didn't say a word but we both knew I got him.

The bell rang and Pete said, "Damn good, Kid."

"Thanks Pete." I pumped my gloves trying to applaud my thanks.

"Thank you guys, all you guys. Months ago you let me in; Pete you let me in and today will forever be one of the happiest days of my life. I'm learning and you guys have shared yourselves with me, thank you."

"I didn't know you were going to get all gooey on us."

"Well, Pete, I'm a gooey kind of guy."

For the rest of the summer I was, Kid Gooey and that was okay with me.

THE KISS

CHAPTER 11

GABBY, SUKI AND ME

"Joseph, Gabby home!"

"Here we go!"

"Go where?"

"Into a whole new world."

I had moved in for the summer and what I wanted, more than anything, was harmony and friendship; Gabby and I had been friends and lovers for almost nine amazing months and I wanted our friendship to last forever.

I opened the door and a very tired Gabby said, "I am so glad to be home."

"It's universal." I gave Gabby a hug, "I'll get your bag and take it up." I wanted to give Gabby time with Suki.

"I'll be up in a minute or two; I have missed you, Joseph."

"Me too, you. Welcome home beautiful woman," and I started upstairs.

Suki and Gabby hugged, "You like Joseph?"

"I love him. So glad you home safe."

"And you?"

"Happy."

"I'm going upstairs; we'll be down in a little while."

Upstairs Gabby and I hugged hard and we kissed.

"You kissed Suki?"

"Yes, you?"

"Yes. You slept with her?"

"Yes, you?"

"Yes."

We sat on the bed.

"Joseph, I will love you forever; and Suki . ."

"I understand, she's beautiful and smart and we both knew this was a possibility. What I want is for us to remain friends; you are an important part of my life."

"We are friends, we will remain friends and for three months we can make this work."

"I will do whatever is appropriate and I can move out if needed."

"No, I want you here, I want you in my bed."

I was dizzy with the craziness of living, the three of us, together. "I am sure we can work this out."

"I'm going to take a quick shower; be down in a few."

"Are you hungry?"

"Starving."

Downstairs I asked Suki to help me put out some cheese, sliced ham, lettuce, tomato and French bread so we could all snack and talk. While we were setting up I asked Suki,"Do you want to stay in America or just visit?"

"I want stay.""

"What about your brothers?"

"With uncle."

"English; you want to learn to read and speak English?"

"Gabby say school, she help."

"Good for you; you are very smart, school good and Gabby very smart and good teacher."

"You smart, Joseph."

"Thank you Suki; Gabby helped me, that's how we met."

"I was his tutor," Gabby said, entering the kitchen.

"How do you go from looking exhausted to looking great," I asked.

'Hot water, the only thing missing was you, Joseph."

"What is tutor?"

"Teacher," Gabby and I said together. "One special tutor, very smart, gives you pleasure of learning," I finished.

"You both tutor for me."

We all sat, munching; a little awkward.

"I'm going to have a beer, I got some Japanese beer, Saporo, very good." I headed for the fridge..

"I am going to sleep with Joseph, Suki. He will be here for three months going to school, special classes, and you and I will have plenty of time together. I am so glad you are here, I want us all to be comfortable and happy."

"Suki happy."

"Joseph is happy; the beer is good, the women are smart and beautiful and you, Gabby, my closest and dearest friend, are home safe and sound." I raised my beer, "Here's to the three of us."

What a summer; my first time going to summer school and taking three courses at that, and living with two women and sleeping with one of them.

Gabby read my course books as usual and we continued to talk and argue our way through them all summer.

Every day Gabby was up early with me for a thirty-minute workout before showering together, brushing teeth included. Then, down for break-fast. Suki would join us and I would get two kisses as I set off for class.

During the day Gabby was working with Suki on her English; organizing nouns, pronouns, adverbs and verbs and she was learning to read; good teacher, good student.

We had a pleasant balance, we three. We most often had dinner together, talking throughout and cleaning up together before the girls chased me away to study or Suki would go off and Gabby and I would talk through one of my classes. I would sometimes go upstairs to study and they would listen to music and dance together.

It was a summer I will never forget; especially two incidents. One weekend, when Gabby was in St. Louis for a Lincoln car event, I asked Suki if she had ever been to the beach.

"What is beach?"

"The ocean, where it comes to the shore; that's the beach. The ocean makes big waves and special noises and it's very beautiful and lots of people go to the beach for the day and they swim in the ocean. Do you have a swim-suit?"

"Yes."

Let's go to the beach, Suki."

"Okay, I get swim-suit."

We both went upstairs where I finally found and put on my trunks and a T-shirt. Downstairs I found Suki in a very tiny two-piece suit.

"Wow, Suki, you are beautiful."

"Thank you, Joseph," and she did a full fashion turn.

"Suki, you have to put on a top, you know over your suit."

"Why?"

"Because we may go into a restaurant for lunch; you need a shirt."

When she came down she was wearing sunglasses, a baseball cap and a button up shirt.

"Perfect, you will be the most beautiful and cutest girl at the beach."

"Your girl, Joseph."

"Lucky me. Let's go."

We drove down to the Jersey shore, Asbury Park maybe, I don't remember. We found a place to park, had a couple of cheeseburgers and beer, good burgers, and then put our shirts and shoes in the trunk and walked to the beach, just a hundred yards away.

Suki loved the beach and the roar of the ocean.` We went down to the water's edge and walked and talked along the shore. We were holding hands and enjoying each other and everything about the day.

"Hey buddy, white girls not good enough," asked the biggest of the three late teenaged guys that were circling us.

"What's your problem?"

"My problem is my dead older brother, killed by some Jap bastard on Iwo?"

"That was more than ten years ago, you idiot."

"Maybe killed by the dad or older brother of this juicy, little Jap girl."

Suki let go of my hand and kicked the shortest of the three squarely in the nuts and he went down in pain. I planted my feet in the sand and punched the middle guy in the stomach; he folded up like a two day old pancake while the biggest kid swung at my face with what looked like a rock in his hand; it glanced off my cheek and I caught him with a right hand punch that broke his nose.

We were mostly at one end of a stretch of public beach that was pretty deserted but I saw a lifeguard running toward us,

"I saw the whole thing, I have to admit I was watching your girlfriend on my binoculars. These punks are out here every day looking for trouble."

"We slowed them down a little. What's your name?"

"Jeff."

"I'm Joe and this is Suki; thanks for looking after us.

I think we'll be heading home now."

"I'm going to report those boys to the police; this is a good town with a nice beach and we hope you come back."

"Thanks Jeff."

When we got to the car I opened the trunk so we could get our stuff.

"Suki, you were, you are, fantastic!"

"Angry at idiots, Joseph. We great team. I love you."

I had one sneaker on when Suki kissed me in a way that could not be denied. "I love you too, Suki."

We drove home with the windows open and the radio on high with the two of us singing along at the top of our lungs; some English and some Japanese and a lot of love.

Later that summer, in August, Gabby and Suki gave me a birthday party. We had caviar and Roederer Crystal and after dinner we cranked up some show tunes for dancing. I danced with Suki, I danced with Gabby and we all danced together. Soon Gabby took my hand and led me upstairs and made love to me wonderfully, like we used to.

September arrived; time to move on; It was not going to be easy.

"I am going to miss our showers, Joseph."

We were in bed together for the very last time and we were doing what we always did; touching, holding hands and hugging. We were experiencing bittersweet to the max.

"Brushing our teeth in the shower," I said, "frothing at the mouth, kissing and laughing and making faces."

"And pretending to be frightened," said Gabby.

"Maybe we were frightened, scared that this day might come?"

"You promised, no reminiscing."

"You started it."

"Because I'm going to miss you. I liked the drying and the crazy, wild hair. That was scary."

"I liked reading your course books; I was going to college with you."

"You changed my life, Gabby; you believed in me and predicted the WHAM. Thank you."

"We danced together," Gabby squeezed my hand.

"To Chopin."

"The Charleston and we waltzed and did the Lindy to the big bands."

"How about the kisses," I asked.

"The most exquisite thing we did was share our truths."

"Experiences, strengths and hopes; we trust each other."

Gabby was crying and I held her very close.

"You give so much and ask for so little."

"I hurt you, Joseph, I am so sorry."

"You didn't hurt me; life hurt me years ago, you too, and it caught up to us. It's okay."

I held Gabby in my arms until her breathing settled into the sweet rhythm of sleep.

The next day, my last day, the three of us put on our happy faces; we were courageous.

Gabby insisted we continue our Saturdays on the third Saturday of each month; eight o'clock for breakfast and continue the day learning and sharing. My Christmas gift book,, "Architecture Since Man," would remain at Gabby's, safe until I go off to grad school and I had packed my stuff in my car early in the morning to muffle my departure.

Gabby, Suki and I shared a farewell dinner prepared by the girls: soup, salad, sea bass and Sapporo beer. Suki was influencing the menu and there was a surprise dessert; big as your fist, Japanese fortune cookies; we each got one. Gabby's read, "LOVE LIVES IN YOUR HEART AND YOUR HOME."

Suki's read, "I AM SAFELY SURROUNDED BY LOVE."

And mine read, "WE LOVE YOU, JOSEPH."

After a little while it was time to go; I kissed them both and left with my heart pounding and my head filled with cherished memories.

THE KISS

CHAPTER 12

LIQUIDITY

"I see all your stuff; does this suggest I have a full time roommate?"

"Yes, sir, full time, right here at number four Mine Street."

"What happened?"

"It's very complicated. No, that's wrong, it's simple; Gabby and I are friends, forever, I hope. We are going to spend the third Saturday of each month together for breakfast. She is a great woman and we are moving on."

"Moving on," Richard mused.

"How was your summer," I asked.

"Family, pleasant, no surprises. You?"

"Aced my three courses; thrilled about that."

"You continue to amaze," Richard was shaking his head, "How is Gabby?"

"She's good; no, she's amazing. She believed in me and then I believed in me and I got the WHAM."

"An acronym?"

"A happening."

"Can you bottle it?"

"It's more like a bug; I got it and I yearn to learn, I want to excel. I think I may graduate by the end of this year."

"Seriously?"

"Yes."

"Wow. What's next?"

"A quick visit with my mom; she doesn't believe I'm alive."

I hadn't seen my mom since the beginning of summer; I felt guilty. She was in terrible shape; the Florida boyfriend situation lasted four months and she refuses to talk about it. So she's living alone in that big house, no social life, afraid to sell the house, afraid of living in the city; The Widow Anne, lost in sorrow and self-pity. God, it was awful and I didn't know what to do.

My sisters had visited during the summer and "begged" her to visit them; Mom always had an excuse and we all agreed, she wants to die in that house as the long suffering widow after the horrible tragedy that took her husband's life.

I was helpless and promised to visit her soon.

On the way back to Rutgers I stopped to see my sister in the city. She and Al had set a date in June of the coming year for their wedding; Sylvia asked me to walk her down the aisle and I was thrilled.

We talked about mom and I said I would come up with a plan.

I went to see Hopkins, my Rutgers counselor, trusting she could help.

"You look good, Joseph, healthy and happy, content, perhaps."

"Thank you, Caroline Hopkins, PhD, you look good, too.

"I hear you are doing well."

"Hear?"

"I ask around."

"It's hard to believe it has been a year," I said.

"Perhaps the most important year of your life."

"So many people believed in me: you, Dean of Men, Ed, my roommate at Phi Ep, my almost father-in-law and my calculus tutor; she's the one who helped the most, we have become dear friends."

"Gabby is a wonderful woman."

"You know Gabby?"

"Yes."

"How?"

"For two years she rebuilt her home and herself."

"Oh," I said, "I get it; small world."

"You have quite a few wonderful people in your life."

"I do and I am very worried about one of them, my mom."

Caroline Hopkins had a hint of a smile and a bit of a frown as she waited for me to continue.

"I made peace with my mother, actually peace with myself about my mother. At any rate she is shutting down, isolating, living alone in our family house filled with difficult memories. My sisters agree; she wants to die there."

"How old is she?"

"I think she's fifty, maybe fifty five."

"I suggest you get your mom out of the house; you pick her up for a short visit, just a couple of hours, with one of your sisters."

"I think I know where this is going. It would have to be Gloria, the oldest, she lives in a house, has the room and has an infant son."

"Perfect. This is covert ops all the way. Your mom has to think this is a visit for a few hours and Gloria has to be in on a visit of three days or a week. Gloria has to tell you what clothes to bring for your mom and where to look for them. When you are in the car, before you leave for your sister's, you say, "Almost forgot, got to grab some stuff from my room.""

Leave mom in the car, you need a small bag, you get your mom's stuff, throw the bag in the trunk and off you go.

"You visit your sister, leave and Gloria takes your mom home whenever."

"Covert ops. I like it, good idea."

"It's a start, a change of place and pace and your mom will feel the love and the caring."

"Thank you, Caroline."

"Joseph, use my phone, call your sister."

Everything was set for the second Sunday of the following month.

"Thank you, it's a good idea."

"You are welcome; just one other thing, a hug."

"Oh, my God, a hug with Caroline Hopkins."

We hugged, tentatively, and then we made it a Gabby hug.

"Joseph, it's tine you call me Caroline."

"Thelma," I said to the Dean of Men, Ed's secretary, "these are for you," and I presented a basket of fresh flowers that I was hiding behind my back.

"Oh, they are beautiful, thank you."

"You are very welcome."

"Do not, however, think this will push me to forgiving you for showing up only once a year."

"It has only been ten months, but we should not quibble over time, we should enjoy the moment."

"Oh, you are good, very good," Thelma said, standing. "In that case I'll take a hug."

Thelma hugged me and it was quite refreshing.

"Thank you, Thelma, if we just traded gifts, I got the better part of the deal."

As we parted Dean of Men, Ed came out of his office.

"Shame on you both; misconduct in the Dean of Men's office; outrageous! I'll take one of those," and Dean of Men, Ed, put a bear hug on me, "Come on in, Joe, I have a few minutes."

"You should come in as well, Thelma, we need someone who can add and subtract."

We all trooped into the office.

"Here's what I'm trying to figure out; can I graduate at the end of this, my junior year?"

"Are you serious?"

"Yes, I took those two junior year finals last year and just aced three summer classes; I think I'm there, or close?"

Thelma had pulled a file from a huge filing cabinet in the Dean's office and after looking through it, "You're short one course of graduating as a Civil Engineer."

"What course?"

"Liquidity."

"Seriously?"

"I'm afraid so."

"That's Bardlow's class, I think," said Dean of men, Ed.

"It is, said Thelma, "He's tough."

"Liquidity; I'll get the book, I'll study and I'll ask him if he will give me an oral. What do you think?"

"I don't think you have a chance," said Dean of Men, Ed, "but you could ask Thelma to ask Professor Bardlow?"

"Thelma?"

"He's my husband."

"Your husband? I don't know what to say. Wait, yes I do; give him a hug for me."

"I will and I will lobby on your behalf."

THE KISS

CHAPTER 13

BREAKFAST OR LUNCH-OOPS!

I called Jerry Brown at "41" and told him I wanted to catch up; nothing urgent.

"I'll be working this Saturday after ten; we can talk and nibble on something."

"That would be fine, I'll bring bagels."

"Sounds good. Downstairs, side door, see you Saturday."

"It's a date."

"Gabby, I am going to see Jerry Brown on Saturday morning; I'm sorry, it was going to be our first third Saturday of the month."

"It's okay, can you be here for lunch?"

"Yeah, around noon. Thanks, Gabby."

"I miss you, Joseph."

"Me too, you."

"I was hoping you would say exactly that."

"I love you, Gabby, I always will."

"See you around noon."

Jerry and I were in the kitchen at "41" as Ernest, a chef's assistant, sliced us some smoked salmon for the bagels I had brought along with some cream cheese. We took our breakfast in to the bar room and, under the work-lights and the hundreds of model cars, boats and planes that hang from the ceiling, we shared news and played catch-up.

"Mmmmm! Good bagels, Joe."

"Wonderful smoked salmon and thanks for seeing me. How is Celeste?"

"She's wonderful; engaged to a young neurosurgeon out of Boston who plans to move down here after Celeste graduates."

"Congratulations and best wishes to Celeste; I am happy for her."

"And you, Joe, how are you?"

"I'm good. I am on this side of what turned out to be the best year of my life. I am clear-headed and grateful. A lot of people believed in me, including you, when I didn't even know who I was or what I wanted or needed. I became a bit of a scholar, switched my major, I'm leading my class and have a good chance at graduating a year early. I plan on going to Pratt in Brooklyn for architecture; I'm excited."

"I'm excited with and for you."

"Thank you but that's not why I'm here. Four years ago, when I was dating your daughter, you opened your heart and your home to me after my father's death; I was so upside down and didn't realize that the sense and sensibility you shared kept me afloat, kept me in the game. I am here to thank you for being the man you are; you set the bar high. I am very grateful to you, Jerry."

"I am at a loss for words and as you know that's not often."

"I brought the bagels as a memory gift for the Sunday brunches at your home, back when Celeste and I were dating; but this was more fun, raiding the kitchen at "41"."

Jerry stood up, "We will do this again, the door is always open."

When I left Jerry I thought I would make it by noon; traffic had other ideas.

"You're late, Joseph."

For half a second I felt bad, but in the next half second I was in a hug with Gabby; with Suki waiting in line. When the hugging ended I was exhausted; wonderfully exhausted and hungry.

"I don't smell the bacon?"

"Special treat," said Suki, "Smoked salmon and bagels and Sapporo beer."

"We were putting a new spin on breakfast and now it's lunch," Gabby announced.

There was no way I would tell them, no way.

"Perfect, I said, "absolutely perfect.""

We sat and managed the cream-cheese, the sliced smoked salmon and got everything assembled on our bagels.

"Orlando say, Joseph no like."

"Orlando wrong; Joseph yes like."

And we were off and running; talking about Rutgers, Suki learning better English, Gabby getting a boost from a few weeks off, Jerry; everything, including our love for each other and Gabby's and Suki's love for each other, the two of them for me and my love for them. We talked about my mother and Suki's brothers and the New York Giants, and, of course, while we talked we touched; a tap on the arm, a finger on my nose and when we stood to clean up there was more hugging. I would never be tired of hugging, ever since Gabby introduced me to its magic. We listened to music and Suki made me dance with her, we talked about my classes and then I dropped the bomb; this, I was fairly certain, would be my last year.

"What mean, last year?"

"I am going to graduate early; a year early."

"You smart."

"Yes, and it is Gabby's fault."

"Fault?"

"Gabby made it happen."

"No, Suki, I did not; I told him it was all in there waiting to happen."

"WHAM! Gabby told me to wait for the WHAM!"

Suki was giggling and then laughing, "She tell me same thing; wait for WHAM, you walk in."

"Joseph, really," Gabby asked, "This year?"

"I'm pretty sure but that doesn't mean I will disappear; I want to go to the Pratt Institute, it's in Brooklyn, not that far away."

"Brooklyn too far," Suki said and we all felt sad.

THE KISS

PART THREE

THE BEAUTY

THE KISS

CHAPTER 14

MRS. BRAND; EILEEN AND THE NEIGHBORS

I'm a pretty good sleeper but every now and then I have one of those nights when I can't fall asleep and when I finally do, I can't stay asleep. On one of those nights, around three thirty, I left Richard snoring and went downstairs to raid the kitchen that was locked.

"Joseph," a voice hissed.

"Yikes! Damn, Mrs. Brand, you scared me."

"Well you scared me, I wondered who was sneaking around; it's four in the morning."

"I couldn't sleep. I was going to raid the fridge but I forgot the kitchen is locked."

"I have peanut butter and crackers."

"Oh, you are the prettiest girl on the block."

"Don't go away."

"I'm all yours."

Mrs. Brand returned, as promised, and she had a spoon, too.

"How come you and I end up eating together in the dark," I wanted to know.

"I remember, you brought cheeseburgers and asked me if I could keep a secret."

"This is good peanut butter. You said you had amassed hundreds, if not thousands of secrets over the years."

"A closet full."

"A trove."

"A nest."

"A treasure chest."

"A sea."

"An ocean. Can you keep a secret, Mrs. Brand?"

"Perhaps."

"I don't have a date for Homecoming."

"That is not a secret, it's common knowledge."

"Oh. Do you always keep the spoon on your side of the table?"

"You are fresh."

"You are beautiful."

"Here's the spoon. Keep it up, you know, the beautiful thing."

"Any suggestions, gorgeous?"

"Eileen Kelly; she's Catholic, smart, very pretty and she's waiting for your call."

"You are messing with me, Mrs. Brand."

"Here's her number," handing me a slip of paper.

"You just happen to have her number on a slip of paper at four in the morning?"

"I have been carrying it for a month. Pass me the spoon."

"You are ravishing early in the morning, Mrs. Brand."

"Goodnight, Mr. Gordon."

I called Eileen Kelly the next afternoon; she answered the phone.

"Eileen, this is Joe Gordon."

"Oh, hi, Joe."

"I feel like we have already been introduced, but I would like to get a drink or a bite to eat during which we can decide on spending Homecoming weekend together?"

"I would like that; sort of a face to face decision making process."

"And we can test Mrs. Brand's intuitive prowess. How about tonight?"

"Perfect, six thirty, 129 Victoria Lane; it's a house, super casual." She hung up.

Victoria Lane was a lovely tree lined street a few minutes from Phi Ep. I pulled up in front of a small Victorian style house where, Sitting on the front porch was a lovely young woman with jet black hair and amazing green eyes.

"Eileen?"

"Joe, come sit with me."

I sat, "Your eyes, I have to say this, so I am not staring at you, your eyes are stunning."

"They are green."

"They are. Hello, Eileen Kelly."

"Hello, Joe. You have questions."

"I do. This house?"

"My parents."

"Mrs. Brand?"

"A long time friend of my parents; she has watched me grow up."

"Your parents?"

"Living in Spain for a year."

"Siblings?"

"Only child. You?"

"Youngest of three, two older sisters. Mom alive, dad died in an accident almost four years ago. I like you."

"I like you, too."

"I am going to stare at your eyes a lot."

"You will get past my eyes and into my mind."

"What are you studying?"

"I am on my way to becoming a doctor. You?"

"Architect."

"Drink?"

"Bourbon, rocks."

"Be right back."

Eileen returned with our drinks, identical.

"Thank you." We touched glasses, "Here's to Mrs. Brand and Home-coming."

We sipped and never lost eye contact.

"Mrs. Brand told me that I would enjoy spending time with you, Joe, and I thought, what does that mean? You know, usually you hear, "He's a really nice guy"; and then you wonder, is that until he wants to get in my pants; or is he a nerd and really is a nice guy."

"Eileen, I haven't even gone beyond your eyes."

Eileen put her drink on the railing, rose and sat on my lap. She put her arms around my neck and kissed me slow and easy and warm and wet and hot. Several neighbors across the street applauded and we laughed.

"You," Eileen whispered, "are a wonderful kisser. I didn't want to wait hours and hours to find that out."

"Well then, let's talk about your pants!"

She tried to slap me but I knew what was coming, I grabbed her wrist.

"Eileen, I want you to know I was kidding; your eyes and your lips are enough to keep me busy. Friends?"

"Yes, friends, and you are quick."

"Boxing."

"Seriously?"

"Yes, for about a year now; a physical challenge and learning something new."

"And how to defend yourself against an Irish girl with a temper; I'm sorry."

"It's okay, apology accepted."

"I'm glad. Are you hungry?"

"I am; Sally's?"

"Sure. I'll just be a minute."

Eileen grabbed our empty glasses and disappeared into the house.

Sally's was busy but not packed; we got seated pretty quickly.

"My treat," I said, "and you changed something when you went into your house?"

I did two things: I called one of my neighbors and said if I'm not home in a couple of hours something has gone wrong and I gave them your name; the other thing was I put on lipstick."

"You did, I didn't notice because."

"Of my eyes," Eileen finished for me.

"Yes, and I'm getting used to being with you; you're very beautiful."

"I am going to help you get past that."

"A magical spell or some time together will work."

"Do you believe that?"

"Of course. I am no stranger to beauty, Eileen, it's just your . . ."

"I know."

"Did something happen in your past that made you cautious, you know, calling the neighbor?"

"When I was fifteen I looked like I was twenty and older guys wanted to date me. My dad was very protective, especially in this college town, and it became the norm. Even now, especially with my parents away, our neighbors are looking after me."

"Even after our kiss?"

"Especially after that kiss."

"I am going to take that as a compliment."

"You should, we kiss well."

Our food arrived and we were eating and sipping our beers and I was enjoying this woman.

"Doctor Kelly; when did you decide on that?"

"In high school I knew I didn't want to "just" go to college; I wanted a career and I wanted a challenge, I like to excel. I like to feel good about myself and help others."

"I applaud you and wish you well."

"Thanks. What about you, Mr. Boxer? That surprised me."

"The short version is I had two dreams as a kid: one was to work with my dad who had built a very successful motion picture distribution company in

New York or become an architect; fate made my decision for me when my dad died in an accident."

"I'm sorry for your loss, I hear a lot of love in your story."

"Yeah, he was quite a guy."

"I like you, Joe; I am very comfortable with you."

"I know, we both felt it on your porch."

"Kiss?" Eileen was sort of standing and leaning toward me and I leaned in to share a kiss that was more than a peck but not over the top in public.

"I am all for going forward with our Homecoming plans," I said, "and I know you are too."

"Mind reader."

I signaled for the check and in the car we chatted on.

"Come in for a nightcap?"

"Your neighbors?"

"They will be shocked and pleased."

"Your invitation is the signal of approval."

"The earlier kiss on the porch was just a hint; this is "I'm a big girl who knows what she's doing."

"Okay, Eileen, a nightcap it is."

Inside the phone rang, "Hello. Everything is fine. Yes, thanks, I've got it from here.""

While Eileen was on the phone I took a seat on the sofa.

"Bourbon, right?" I nodded.

"I love bourbon," Eileen said as she poured our drinks, "It's warm all the way down to, you know. Scotch, yick! I don't get scotch, but bourbon clears the way for fun; it pushes aside all the stuff that goes on in your head."

"Eileen, I like your house, it's lovely."

"Oh, yeah, I grew up in this house. Do you want to go upstairs?"

"Another time, Eileen. I want to spend some time with you."

"That's what we would do upstairs, Joe."

Eileen sat next to me on the sofa, took a good swig of her drink and tried to set her glass down, almost missing the coffee table.

"Oops, got it just in time."

And then, like a little girl having a revelation, "You don't want to go to bed with me."

"Eileen, earlier, sitting on the front porch, you told me that you would help me get past your beautiful green eyes and into your mind. That's what I want for both of us; to find that moment in each of our hearts and minds that sleeping together would be bliss. If that is what's waiting for us we don't need bourbon, we need time and trust."

"I don't know what to say, I feel foolish."

"No need, just one of life's little moments. It doesn't change my feelings for you."

"Friends?"

"Absolutely."

"Homecoming?"

"Definitely."

"Kiss?"

"Endlessly."

God, she was a good kisser. During our kiss we ended up stretched out on the sofa in each other's arms.

"I've got to go."

"I know."

"I will call you, Eileen Kelly."

"I know."

THE KISS

CHAPTER 15

MY MOM IS A MESS!

"Mom?"

"Who is there?"

"Mom, it's your son; we are going to Gloria's for lunch."

"I'll be right down."

"Okay."

I had called my mom a couple of hours ago to let her know I would be picking her up at eleven; I was a little late but we could still be at Gloria's by noon.

My mother came downstairs in her nightgown and robe.

"Mom, what's going on? You're not dressed; we have to go."

"I'm not going."

I was sitting on the sofa and I patted the cushion next to me; "Come sit with me, Mom."

She heaved a huge, sad sigh as she sat.

"What's going on, I called you, I gave you plenty of time? We're going to see Gloria and your grandson; he's three months old and you have only seen him once. I thought you would be excited."

"I'm not leaving this house; if I do they are going to take it away from me."

"No one is taking away your house, no one. Please get dressed, we have to go."

"I'll get dressed," she was moving toward the stairs, "It's in the letters."

I rushed to the stairs, "What letters? Where are the letters?"

"In the dining room, it's all on the table."

A quick scan of the mess of opened and unopened mail and mom's big, business style check book revealed that my mother had not been taking care of business; nothing that couldn't be taken care of through immediate attention. So much for my plan to leave mom at my sister's; I would have, or one of us kids, would have to get on mom's bank account and get everything up to date. I called Sylvia and gave her a quick advisory and called Gloria and told her we were coming a little late and I would explain "Plan B" when we got there. Then I left a message for Dean of Men, Ed, to cover for me as I would have to miss classes on Monday.

"Why are you going to miss classes on Monday, Joseph?"

Mom could be pretty covert when she wants to and she had dressed and come down the stairs in time to overhear me.

"Two things, Mom, one is that no one is taking away your house and I'll explain number two when we get to Gloria's. Let's go, kid, you look great."

"Three months old, are you kidding, he looks like he's six months, at least," I said while holding my nephew.

"What do you think, Mom?"

"I think he's beautiful." She was crying and I put my arm around her, "So are you, Mom, so are you."

Sunday night with my mom was the pits; not much food in the fridge and not much to do; I was waiting to go over the mail, bank statements and correspondence after mom went to bed. I made some tuna salad sandwiches and "forced" my mom to have a half of a sandwich. She went to bed early and I called Eileen Kelly; I was glad to hear her voice.

"Eileen Kelly, it's Joe Gordon."

"I was hoping you would call."

"I was hoping you would be home. I miss you."

"I feel like you became my dearest friend in the last ten minutes we spent together."

"You touched me, Eileen; something inside said, "Speak your truth, she wants to hear you."

"I am grateful for your words."

"I'll bet your neighbors miss me?"

"I'll bet they do, but not as much as I do. Where are you?"

"I'm in Rockville Centre, out on Long Island, in the house I grew up in, visiting my mom. The original plan for the day, which was supposed to be for a day, was scuttled when I realized my mom needed my help; I won't be back to New Brunswick 'til Monday night. Tell your neighbors the coast is clear."

"I'm sorry everything got turned upside down."

"Yeah, thanks, me too. It's all fixable but I am worried about my mom."

"Tell her that an Irish lass wishes her well."

"I will, thanks. I love/like you, Eileen Kelly."

"This is crazy; my spine is tingling. I love/like you Joe Gordon."

"Goodnight, Eileen.

"Goodnight, Joe."

I went through the books; I wrote seventeen checks for my mother to sign that would bring everything up to date.

On Monday mom and I went to the bank, cleaned up the mess, and added me to the account; no, I did not need a separate checkbook. Then we went to the savings and loan, the holders of mom's mortgage, where I got them to waive the late fees when I gave them a cashier's check for the three months past due and the upcoming payment two weeks early.

"I love you, Mom, and I will visit you once a month and we will write checks together. Okay?"

"Yes, okay, and thank you."

"You are welcome. We filled up your fridge, so you have plenty to eat and you have cash, so no checks 'til we sit down together next month.

"Okay, we will do it together. I like that."

"Me, too, I'm happy to help. Mom, you have friends in this town, they miss you; reach out to them, you don't have to isolate."

"I don't understand."

"I know you miss Dad but it's time to move on."

My mother stood there, she had no words.

I hugged her, "I have to get on the road, goodbye, Mom."

I backed out of the driveway and headed for Rutgers; I had gone too far, I should not have said anything; she has to figure it out on her own.

CHAPTER 16
HOME COMING AND COMING HOME

I picked up Eileen Kelly at five for the first event of Homecoming; a cocktail reception at the Phi Ep fraternity house. Eileen wasn't sitting on the porch so I knocked.

"Come on in, I'll be down in a minute or two."

"Okay."

I made myself at home and when Eileen came downstairs I wasn't sure I could stand; Eileen, in a black dress, cut above the knee with a plunging neckline, was breathtaking.

"Eileen Kelly, you are stunning."

"Thank you, Joe, I think we make a very handsome couple."

"No argument from me, it's good to see you again." I reached out and took Eileen into my arms; it felt so good to hold her.

"I have missed you, Eileen."

"I have missed you Joe, and it has been a warm, loving feeling."

"Everyone is going to want to meet you, be ready."

"Stay close to me and I will be fine."

"My intention is to stay very close to you."

"I like the sound of that."

"Let's go get 'em."

Phi Ep was crowded, actually tumbling out to the front landing and yard: current members, their dates and any number of alumni, the very reason for Homecoming, and their dates or wives. It was all very lively and fun and, indeed, everyone wanted to meet Eileen.

"This is Max, this is Noel, this is Richard, my roommate; it was tedious but we managed to get a drink for me at the bar; Eileen begged off.

"Let's find Mrs. Brand, after all she's responsible for "us."

I led the way and knocked on her door.

"Welcome, welcome, whoever you are."

When we entered I watched Mrs. Brand's face light up.

"Oh, my goodness, Eileen Kelly, you are such a beautiful woman. I am so glad to see you," and they hugged.

"Is this young man taking good care of you?"

"He is. Don't tell him, but I like him a lot."

"Keeping secrets is what I do best, not to worry."

"I can attest to that," I added, "That and you have the best peanut butter stash in town."

"I am so glad you came to say hello, it's grand to see you, Eileen. Go have fun."

"Come with us," I prompted.

"I was out there earlier, now it's overwhelming."

"Get you anything?"

"No, Joseph, thank you. Off with you."

We found Richard and I left Eileen with him while I refreshed my drink.

"Is he a good roommate," Eileen asked.

"He is and he has great taste in women."

"He dates a lot?"

"On the contrary, I was referring to you, you are beautiful."

"Thank you, Richard; no date for you?"

"No, but that's not a bad thing; this way I get a few minutes with you."

"That's sweet."

"Joe told me two things about you; he said you are going to be a doctor and that he likes you."

"That, Richard, is one thing about me and one thing about Joe."

"He said you are very smart and something about your eyes. I don't know why?"

"Yes you do." I said, returning with my drink.

"I'm staying out of this; this is between you two," Richard said.

"Oh, come on," I said, "I am going to need some protection from this woman."

At that very moment Eileen kissed me, a very profound kiss.

"I deserved that, I'm going to keep doing my best for more."

"Eileen, that's my cue," Richard said, "I look forward to seeing you at the game."

"You will, see you tomorrow."

Richard moved off.

"He's a good man, dedicated to becoming a dentist and he is confident that the right woman will come along at the right time."

Eileen agreed to mingle for a while longer and she was spot on; cordial, friendly, warm and fun as she met Alan, Charlie, Art, Mal, Bob and others until it was time to go.

On the way to the car Eileen suggested, "Out to dinner, then home to my place to enjoy each other for dessert?"

"Deal."

After dinner we pulled up to Eileen's and were inside in a heartbeat. We kissed in the kitchen, couldn't keep our hands off each other. Upstairs we went to bed and held each other as we enjoyed the dessert we longed for; we were enthralled.

"I think I am falling in love with you, Joe."

"Think?"

"Think, yes, because I have never been in love. I have been hiding behind bourbon since ninth grade; I heard what you said a couple of weeks ago and I admit, I have a problem; I am getting help.

We huddled under the covers, each of us off in our own thoughts.

"This is bliss," I said.

"I feel it, too."

"I have an idea, Eileen, I want you to be my girl. I like you, I love you as much as I can."

"Explain, please."

"You are smart, I like the way you think and speak, you are beautiful in so many ways and you are brave and honest. I trust you and we each have goals and dreams that can separate us as we pursue them."

"I am listening."

"We have today and it is heaven; lets go forward together; talk together, reason things out together, be there for each other in good times and bad."

"And?"

"And always understand that life, our goals, something unknown, can pull us apart."

"I love us, Joe, and we will have challenges but I agree that together we will find answers."

"Will you be my girl?"

"I am your girl; I'm all in."

"I am the happiest man in the world."

Eileen Kelly brought her body firmly against mine, "I have some happiness for you, Joe."

We slept long and late and woke up staring at each other; and then we laughed and hugged.

"My God, you are beautiful."

"There are no words that can express my happiness."

"I woke a minute or two before you and was tempted to kiss you awake."

"You could have."

"I was enjoying watching you sleep."

"I have never awakened to a man in my bed."

"Neither have I."

Eileen kissed me and we didn't care that it was an early morning kiss.

"You started this, Eileen, on the porch; in front of the neighbors.""

"Mrs. Brand started this while you two were sharing peanut butter and crackers at four in the morning. An older woman, shame on you."

"Hold me, Eileen, I will confess my sins, all of them."

"We don't have enough time for that, besides Jews don't confess, I don't think?"

"We don't but I don't think beautiful, young Irish girls do either."

"Some of us do and one of us wrote her parents and said she had fallen in love with a Jew."

"Really?"

"Really, after you and I talked on the phone."

"Really?"

"My parents will love you. I'm going to shower and then you and while you shower I'll make us breakfast."

"I am going to watch."

Eileen was already gone; she called out, "Fine, but you can't touch, we don't have time."

On the way to the stadium we stopped at Phi Ep so I could get into some warm clothes; it was cold and raw, a perfectly ominous day for Rutgers who had lost the first three games of the season. Eileen was wrapped up in a stylish coat; a large Rutgers scarf and she had gloves, smart girl.

Each of the fraternities had "stations" that provided food and drink; thousands of students and alumni were scattered across a huge grassy field outside the stadium and lively marching band music filled the air and stirred the crowd.

Eileen and I found a place to park and we set off through the throng to find the Phi Ep gang. We were holding hands, filled with the warmth and love that we had shared the night before; we had "happy" written all over us. We found our group, probably sixty or so, and blended in with Richard, Noel, Charlie, Max and their dates. There were the usual tailgate burgers, hot dogs and brats but everyone was saying, "Get some of the chowder, it's delicious!"

I led the way through the crowd with Eileen holding on to my hand. We reached the food area where someone was walking away with a cup of chowder.

"Mister Joe!" Orlando Sideri dropped the chowder ladle and wrapped me in his arms.

"Orlando, my God it's good to see you."

"And you, Mr. Joe, I miss you; you don't come by the store."

"I miss you, too. This is a great surprise. Every one is raving about the chowder and you made it."

"The chowder, yes, but who is this beautiful woman?"

"This is the love of my life. Eileen Kelly, I would like you to meet Orlando Sideri."

"Miss Kelly, you call me Orlando, I call you Eileen. Okay?"

"Yes, Orlando, it's a pleasure."

"Watch out," I warned, "He's going to hug you."

Orlando hugged Eileen and I beamed.

"Eileen, Orlando said, "You got a good man and he got the best in this whole crowd." Orlando's arms spread wide; "Now you have my chowder, you get from the bottom."

Orlando ladled two big cups, bigger than we had seen.

"Mr. Joe, you come to my store?"

"Yes, I promise."

"You bring Miss Eileen?"

"Yes, he will, Orlando, I promise," Eileen asserted.

"Orlando, I said, "this is delicious, thank you. We will see you soon."

"Goodbye, Orlando, Mmmm, great chowder," Eileen said, and we turned to see the crowd was emptying into the stadium. As we walked Eileen asked, "Who is Orlando?"

"He owns a food store, probably the best in New Brunswick; over near Ninth."

"He greeted you like you are his son."

"That's because you were with me."

"Nice try, Mr. Joe, there's more to it than that."

"You're right, I used to shop at his store but it has been months. You and I, we will go see him; we'll do some shopping."

"I would like that."

I could tell that Eileen sensed there was more to the story but she didn't push it.

"I love you, Joe."

We put our arms around each other's waist and kissed as we walked into the stadium. I spotted Richard, he was waving; he saved us two seats.

Up in the stands Eileen sat between Richard and me as we all got into game mode, cheering for the Rutgers' eleven and huddling together for warmth. Rutgers opponent for this Homecoming game was Temple University from Pennsylvania. The visitors were very gracious; they failed to score a touchdown while we, the Scarlet Knights of Rutgers, scored four touchdowns and missed three extra points. Final score: Rutgers,25, Temple,0. Hurrah!!

Back at the fraternity house there was more chowder along with cheese, salami, French bread, chips, booze and beer; all spread out for everyone to enjoy as we celebrated Rutgers' victory. Eileen and I were nestled on a sofa; I was nursing a bourbon on the rocks and Eileen had a sip to shake the chill. Music was playing: big bands mostly and an occasional show tune. There was plenty of conversation and overall good times as we enjoyed the second wind of a long day. Occasionally I got up to get us some food or drink and each time a fraternity brother sat down with Eileen and it went something like this:

"Hi, I'm Alan."

"Hello, Alan, I'm Eileen."

"Eileen, has Joe told you about Barbara?"

"Um, Barbara? Oh, yes. Yes he did."

The next time I got up; "Eileen, Hi, I'm Jack and I want to be sure Joe told you about Nancy. Just wanted you to know."

"Jack, tell me about Nancy."

But there I was, back with food and Jack moved on.

"Eileen, did Joe tell you about Elizabeth?"

"He did, he told me that he and Elizabeth, Nancy and Barbara all went skinny dipping one night this past summer."

And then I was back. "Are you having a good time," I asked.

"Yes, I'm learning about your supposed past girlfriends."

"Oh, for God's sake, we have not done that in years; they make the freshman pledges hover near the prettiest girl at the party."

"Now they know you went skinny dipping with them all."

"Good job, Eileen. Are you as hungry for me as I am for you?"

"Two things, I thought you would never ask."

"And the second thing?"

"Are you going to tell me about Barbara and Elizabeth and Nancy?"

"Not until I kiss you in the car."

"How about kissing me now?"

"It will get noisy."

Eileen gently put her lips on mine and the chant started instantly; "Eileen. Eileen. Eileen. Eileen."

That was our cue; we said goodbye to our sofa mates and headed for the door. Alan, Phi Ep's current president, stopped us at the door, "Eileen Kelly, thank you for being a good sport; we are just a bunch of guys acting, occasionally, like little boys."

Eileen smiled and surprised Alan and me: she kissed him for a couple of seconds and Alan turned beet red.

We waved to everyone and left. We kissed in the car and I turned toward Victoria Lane.

When we walked into the house we were giddy with lust.

"Hi, kids."

"Neighbors," I asked, shocked.

"No, it's us, the Kellys."

"Mom, Dad, what the . .?"

"Joe, I'm Bob Kelly and this is my wife, Edna."

I smiled at Edna and, still in shock, shook hands with Bob Kelly.

"What an incredible surprise; it's a pleasure to meet you both."

Eileen gave her mom a big hug and then her dad the same.

"You're here, are you okay?"

"We're fine, we will explain, but let's all sit."

Eileen and I sat on the sofa with a thousand thoughts racing through our minds; we held hands.

"Joe, you look like you could use a drink?"

"I am startled, but I'm fine, thanks."

"Your dad and I loved your letter, Eileen."

"And we missed you," Bob continued, "and we had some papers we needed to sign," he shrugged, "So why not come home and see our daughter and scare the heck out of both of you."

"You did that, Dad."

"We're going back on Monday," said Edna.

"Dad and I changed the sheets and made the bed."

"So, if it's okay with you two, your mom and I will sleep in our own bed and you two can sleep in Eileen's double bed."

Eileen was laughing, "You rehearsed that whole spiel, huh?"

"That was a rough draft," Edna said.

"Spain agrees with you, you both look great; you're taking care of each other."

"Before we get to Spain let's get to Joe. You, sir, have stolen my daughter's heart with your sense and sensibility. Thank you for that."

"And you're handsome," Edna said, "and smart; Eileen wants a challenge, you are it, Joe."

"Your daughter stole my heart with her truth, trust, bravery and beauty; I love your daughter. We each have goals and dreams; we have a long way to go and we are here for each other."

"We noticed that, you know, upstairs."

"I offer you both a sincere apology and my gratitude," I said.

Bob stood, "We are exhausted, we are going to bed and I expect that you two are as well. Keep the noise down and tomorrow we will have brunch and talk about Spain and goals."

Edna stood, "I want hugs with both of you."

We all hugged, even Bob and I, "Are you still in shock", he asked me.

"With Eileen I will always be in shock; she keeps me on my toes."

They were on their way upstairs when Eileen put her arm around my waist, "I love them." She reached up and kissed my cheek, "That's all your getting tonight, Mr. Joe."

"Bet you!"

We were having brunch at Gauchos, a favorite of Edna's. Huevos rancheros, breakfast burritos; stuff like that.

We had just ordered and our chat was pretty broad.

"Joe, are you Jewish," Edna asked.

"Yes, I am," I answered.

"I was born Jewish," Edna said, looking directly at Eileen.

"What!"

"Edna Greenberg."

"You never told me," Eileen bristled.

"Your dad and I have wrestled with this for years; when do we tell our daughter she's Jewish, you know, the mother's religion dictates the child's. But technically I was Catholic when you were born."

"Your mom and I fell in love in the early 1930's when any kind of mixed marriage was more than frowned upon. Edna's family refused to attend a Catholic wedding and the rift was deep; your mom converted because she loved me but a profound sadness haunted us for years."

"The longer we waited to tell you the more embarrassed we became," Edna continued, "and now you are in love with this wonderful Jewish man and the door opened; we are sorry we never told you."

"It's okay but there is sadness still and it gives Joe and me something to chew on."

"It does and there are other hurdles that lie ahead; which takes us to our goals," I said.

"My goal is to become a doctor," Eileen raised an eyebrow, "Pretty simple."

"Joe," Bob asked.

"Architect, husband and father; pretty challengingly simple, if there is such a word."

"Are you proposing to me?"

"Yes, but I don't expect a response; we have work to do."

"What about your dreams," Edna wanted to know.

"My dream is to live and work in Manhattan; I want to create urban apartments and Brownstone conversions. And, especially, I want to design suburban homes, country estates. I'm all about buildings people live in not buildings where people work. Also, I want us to have a summer home on the beach. Pretty simple!"

"I accept," Eileen said and she kissed me on the cheek, "I love you and I love your/our dreams."

"What about your dream, Eileen," her dad asked.

"I'll be a doctor in Manhattan."

"Now you have a plan," Bob said, "and I think you can do it."

"But what about that child; a Catholic or a Jew," Edna posed.

"I don't care," I said, "as long as he's circumcised."

"In that case my answer to your proposal is a big, "yes"," and Eileen kissed me on the lips.

Bob looked at Edna, "I am so glad we made this trip."

"And," Edna added, "and that we know that you know there will be hurdles."

"We know, Mom, Joe and I have discussed the separation we will have to deal with while we are at different grad schools and the challenges that lie ahead; our eyes are open."

"This is Mrs. Brand's fault," I said.

"How is Mrs. Brand," Bob wanted to know.

"She's fine. I bumped into her a couple of months ago; we chatted and I asked her if she knew a guy that could handle a headstrong, Irish, Catholic girl. She said she had the guy and I gave her a slip of paper with my phone number; this is what I got."

"You got good, Eileen, and fast," said her mom.

"You and I fell in love in two weeks Bob, and Joe is Jewish, like I was! Oh, boy, you two are in for a hell-of-a ride and I know you can do it."

At noon the next day, after morning classes, Eileen and I drove her folks to the airport for their flight back to Spain. Hugs and kisses were abundant and Edna was crying when they went out to the tarmac to board their flight.

"Hold me."

I held that beautiful Jewish/Catholic, headstrong girl/woman close to my chest, "I love you, Eileen."

"Are we moving too fast?"

"There is no fast, we have all the time in the world."

We slept together that night in her parents' big bed. There was a note on one of the pillows, "Trust yourselves, trust each other and trust God. We love you both," Edna and Bob.

CHAPTER 17

THE MERRY GO ROUND

As I jumped rope I wondered if Eileen knew how; it would not surprise me. Would she come to Pete's Gym and mix it up with the guys? Would the guys behave? Maybe? Who am I kidding?

I was sweating and it felt good, I hadn't been to the gym in a couple of weeks. When I got there the guys were in the ring doing the Merry-Go-Round and wanted me to join them.

"A quick warm up and I'm in."

I stepped through the ropes, caught the cadence and got in the circle. Balance, focus, footwork; five guys in a tight circle, all within arms reach: punches can come from anywhere. They must have set it up and when Pete coughed they all punched me at once. I pretended not to take notice and got Pete on the chin. These punches are cup cakes, you know, not wedding cakes, but even so, a punch is a punch.

"Nice work guys, thanks a lot; a sign of love."

"We don't see much of you, Kid."

"Pete, I'm carrying a full load at school; I'm graduating a year early."

Art got it right away, "When is that?"

"Next June."

"That'll be it, you will be gone?"

"Yes, Boozer."

Jimmy caught me on the chin, "That is unacceptable," he said.

The four of them surrounded me and pummeled me with cup cakes.

"Enough," Pete ordered.

"I am taking that as a shower of love. I'll be around."

"I don't see your car at the Evers' place," Boozer kind of, sort of, gently wanted to know.

"Gabby Evers is my friend, a very special friend forever."

"No offence."

"None taken."

We were all standing in the ring; "Come on, Pete, a little sparring?"

"Sure, Kid," and he punched me in the stomach. Boozer said, "I better ref this." We stayed in one corner so Art and Jimmy could spar in the other corner.

"You still seeing her, you know, sort of when you want her?"

"No, Pete, we were going to spend the third Saturday of each month hanging out but stuff gets in the way."

We were trading punches, clinching, and talking; "So, you're going solo," Pete wanted to know.

"No, I have a girlfriend, well actually we are engaged."

Everything stopped, no one moved, there was silence for a minute at least.

"Hey, fantastic," Jimmy spoke up.

"Engaged? You just had, you know," gesturing like, right over there, "just like that, somebody else," Pete was shocked.

Boozer said, "She must be special. Congrats."

"Yeah, she's amazing. Thanks Boozer."

"Jewish girl," Arthur wanted to know.

"Eileen Kelly, not exactly Jewish."

"Bring her around, we all would love to meet her."

"I will, you can bank on it." With that I punched Pete in the stomach.

"Low blow," called Boozer, the referee.

"No, it was fair but it was a little bit more than a cup cake."

CHAPTER 18

LIVING TOGETHER

Eileen and I decided to sit at the kitchen table and spend some time "figuring us out." We had classes and studying and questions.

"I want you to meet my mom and my two sisters; oh, boy."

"What, oh, boy?"

"My sisters are okay; one, Gloria, is married with an infant son, they live in Glen Cove on Long Island and Sylvia, working for CBS, engaged to Al, a numbers guy, working for a real estate developer; they are living in New York City on the upper West side."

"That leaves your mom."

"My mom is a little unpredictable; she can be very lovely but she's in a weird place and I am worried about her."

"Do you think she'll accept me?"

"She will be dazzled by you, Eileen, no question." I shrugged, "It isn't you, it's my mom; you never know who is going to show up."

"Oh, boy."

"Your parents, I like them; what did your dad do, I'm guessing he's retired?"

"I'm going to have to keep you after school; he is not retired, he created a reference book, something about car values, updated annually; they, we, are very comfortable. My mom worked as a seamstress and dress designer until three years ago."

"When will they return from Spain?"

"In time for graduation in June."

"That's eight months; we'd be crazy not to live together." "I'm all for it," Eileen asserted, highlighting her vote with a warm kiss.

"Me too," I assured Eileen, even though I knew in my gut it would be excruciating going off to separate grad schools next September. "I want all of our time together to be special; we have Thanksgiving, Christmas and Spring break that we can plan."

"Listen to you, Mister Architect, planning and building. I love you, Joe."

"And I you, Eileen Kelly, and we can rent a place at the beach for the summer, or part of the summer."

"I would love that."

"I have a couple of thoughts: I'll need a key to the house, we will have to tell the neighbors and I am concerned about your fear of our moving too fast."

"I'll be okay, I'm sure."

"If you are sure that's good enough for me."

"Zero to sixty, one of my dad's favorites; we are going sixty and it is scary, spine tingling, good scary."

"I'm excited too, I get to love you for the rest of my life."

We both got lost in that thought for a moment until I broke the spell. "As to moving, I don't have that much stuff to be moved right away, so that can happen over time. Richard will miss me."

"Yes, but he won't be surprised."

"Unlike your neighbors."

"We can have them over for drinks. I want them to meet you."

"Eileen, drinks, really?"

Eileen took a deep breath and took my hand, "To the sofa."

We settled on the sofa, which was to become, along with our bed, her parents' bed, our talking ground.

"You woke me here," Eileen patted the sofa, "startled me, bewildered me when you sucked the bourbon from my dizzy mind, touched my heart and led me to want to be the best me I can be. Then on the phone, you were visiting your mom, we talked and hearing each other's voice was stirring and we both wanted more. I fell in love with you and this last week has been the happiest of my life."

I wanted to speak but Eileen silenced me with her lips.

"Hush. I am seeing a counselor, we are looking into Alcoholics Anonymous and I can drink a soda while our neighbors drink booze."

"I'm a beer and bourbon guy but I will not have them in the house."

"You can; I can do without. Let's see what happens?"

"My turn." I stood, offered Eileen my hand and led her outside to the porch; I sat and took Eileen on to my lap.

"It was here that you gave me two marvelous gifts: a kiss I will never forget and an invitation into your mind. You, my darling Eileen, are the gift bearer, thank you."

"My turn," Eileen was on her feet and led me upstairs, pushed me on to the bed and had her wonderful way with me and I with her.

Gabby and I juggled Saturdays; her schedule was hectic and mine was unpredictable with my mom and then Homecoming and now Eileen, but we were able to find a Saturday that worked for lunch.

Suki opened the door and was instantly in my arms.

"Joseph, I miss you."

I hugged her tight, "I miss you too."

"Gabby down in few minutes. I have fire going."

Suki led me to the living room.

"You have kiss for Suki?"

"Just friends' kiss, sure."

I made sure it was brief and Suki took one step back, put her hands on her hips; "Joseph has woman, right?"

"Right. Yes, I do."

"Tell me."

"I will tell you and Gabby together."

"Sound like special."

"Yes, special."

"Gabby be happy for you."

"How is Gabby?"

"Gabby good. She happy. She tired; Lincoln very busy. I walk on back, she feel better."

"You walk on her back, seriously?"

Suki pointed to the floor and I lay down; she turned my head sideways, positioned my arms and stepped on my back.

"Let go, Joseph, breathe."

It took a few minutes for me to let Suki do her walk skill and then, heaven.

"I come downstairs, a few minutes late, and another woman is walking all over you. I can't hug you, I can't kiss you, and do you care? I think not."

"Go away," I managed in my stupor."

Suki stepped off and Gabby emoted, "Out, out of my house forever."

I was on my feet and said, "No hugs, no kisses and no food; you cast me out, you banish me? I will not go so gently unless a hug you might share to salve my despair. I beg thee!"

Suki, at first confused, realized we were being silly and was giggling; and I found myself in Gabby's arms.

"I love you, Gabby."

"Kiss?"

"Yes, a friends forever kiss."

Gabby knew; how do women know? We kissed briefly.

"Do you love her?"

"Yes, of course I love her; I wouldn't be here to tell you if I didn't. You are my dearest friend and I am here to tell you I love another woman and it shouldn't be so hard."

"I am happy for you and sad, that's what makes it so hard."

"Let's eat."

"Don't be such a man, let's talk about her."

"Let's compromise; let's eat and talk."

"Great, everything is all ready for lunch."

We moved into the kitchen where Suki served a very tasty shrimp salad and we talked.

"Joseph, Gabby started, "I'll give you a hint; Suki and I went shopping a few days ago and,"

"Orlando," I interrupted, "told you about."

"Eileen Kelly," Gabby interrupted, "and how beautiful she is and how happy you are, Mr. Joe."

"You knew! You knew and you let me suffer."

"We have good laugh," Suki said.

"I'm sorry, Gabby, I wanted to tell you; I wanted to be the one."

"I know. It stung when Orlando described Eileen, which is really crazy because we, Joseph, love each other and always will."

"How do you feel about all this loving stuff, Suki," I asked.

"I love you . . right word, both?"

"Yes."

"I love you both, for always."

Eileen and I enjoyed sex, sharing pleasure that often became pure bliss.

After sex we talked as we traced love maps with our fingertips, on each other's body.

Sharing, for us, was the icing; at times better than the cake.

One night I shared how I worked with the Rutgers' counselor to create peace within me about my mom and my dad's passing. That inspired me to change my major and get a calculus tutor who guided me to new thinking.

"Who," Eileen wanted to know, "was your tutor?"

"A teen age math prodigy who Dean of Men, Ed set me up with. I called her, went to her house one Saturday morning and learned she was no longer a teen; she is a thirty something, world famous model. Her name is Gabby Evers and we became dear friends; I want you to meet her."

"Are you saying it was Gabby Evers that brought you to me?"

"Mrs. Brand brought us together but Gabby opened my mind, changed my thinking; so, yes, she is "guilty.""

By then Eileen Kelly had left my arms and was in full battle mode. Within seconds we were fully engaged in crazy, outrageous sex.

When it was done I said, "Eileen, are you trying to tell me you love me?",

"I just did."

Eileen Kelly was ready to meet Gabby Evers anywhere, any time.

"Miss Eileen, you make my heart beat faster; welcome to my store."

"Thank you, Orlando, it's lovely."

Orlando leaned over the counter and Eileen kissed his cheek, right where he pointed. Orlando beamed.

"Mister Joe, you keep your promise; make me happy."

"Good to see you, glad to be back."

"A little shopping?"

"Our neighbors are coming for cocktails, ten of us."

"Miss Eileen, you like prosciutto?"

"Yes, with some cheese and bread, perfect."

"I slice prosciutto, you shop."

"Bravo," I said. Eileen and I picked up a basket and set off.

Eileen carried a basket of fresh flowers and I had bread and crackers; we were headed for the cheese when we bumped into Gabby.

"Joseph!"

"Gabby!! Eileen Kelly, this is Gabby Evers, my math tutor and my dear friend."

While the two women shared a visual smack down I added, "Eileen is my fiancé."

Gabby smiled, "It is a pleasure, Eileen."

"Thank you, I feel like I know you, Gabby, having grown up seeing your picture a thousand times."

"I wanted the two of you to meet, I never pictured twenty heads of lettuce looking on."

"Eileen," Gabby started, "I live two minutes from here, would you and Joseph come by, even for ten minutes, I want you to meet my partner?"

Eileen looked to me and I nodded, "Sure."

"We will do a pit stop visit, thank you."

"Okay, I'm leaving; when you're done here, come over."

Gabby walked in her front door and called upstairs, "Suki, change your clothes, Joseph and Eileen will be here in five minutes for a quick visit."

"Eileen coming?"

"Yes, Eileen coming. She is very beautiful."

We all sat near the fire, Eileen and me on the sofa; Gabby and Suki on chairs.

"Your home is lovely, Gabby. What I said in the store didn't come out right."

"It's fine, not to worry. I am so glad you are here because your future husband and I are special friends, hopefully forever. I want to share a confidence with you and ask that you honor my privacy."

"Of course," Eileen responded.

"Suki is my angel, my friend, my partner, my lover, my everything; I love you Suki. Joseph knows, and now you. I hope we all can spend time together on happy occasions. You are a beautiful woman and I am happy for both of you."

"I will honor your confidence and I look forward to our friendship, Gabby, thank you."

Gabby stood up, we all stood. "One other thing, Joseph knows this, we are huggers, serious huggers," Gabby opened her arms, "what do you say?"

Gabby hugged Eileen and Suki hugged me; we all hugged and Eileen's fear of the unknown was gone and a comfort zone was established.

The next day Eileen and I entertained the Rileys, the Crawfords, the Greens and the Rosens for cocktails and a delicious spread of cheeses, crackers, French bread and prosciutto ham. We talked for hours and I got to know them a little. They got to know me and shared Eileen growing up stories. Eileen nursed a coke, they were all lovely people and every one of the men gave me the same warning, "We'll be watching you, Joe."

If only they knew.

CHAPTER 19

EILEEN MEETS MY FAMILY. YIKES!!!

There was lots of traffic going to New York on Thanksgiving morning, lots. This was a family litmus test and Eileen was nervous.

"No one should have to go through this, especially on a day when we all give thanks."

"I know, your parents made it easy for me; we walked in on them when they actually walked in on us, scared me to death."

"You did very well."

"And so will you; Syl and Al are easy to be with and you'll get to know them on the way to Glen Cove. Glo and Hal are nice and we will all help you with our mother and I will help my mother with you."

"What does that mean, Joe?"

"That means I will let her know that I love you, love you, love you."

"I feel better, but a double bourbon on the rocks would help; not really, that's just illustrative."

"I will have a double bourbon on the rocks for both of us."

"Grrrr!"

"Okay then, we are here."

I had pulled up in front of Syl and Al's apartment building.

"I am going into the lobby to buzz them, I'll be right back. If a cop wants us to move the car, smile at him and he will melt and by the time he pulls himself together I will be back."

We were almost to Glen Cove and my sister, Al and Eileen were a happy, easygoing threesome and I was just the driver. Eileen leaned way over and kissed me to let me know she was fine.

The meal was great, Gloria takes no prisoners when it comes to putting a nice dinner together; and the conversation was gracious and welcoming. I realized I was more nervous than Eileen; I wanted my family to love and accept my girl and I hoped Eileen would be comfortable as well. As the day and the meal progressed I felt less and less stress; everything was going well. The star of the party was Steven, almost six months and adorable; he was passed around like a basketball and managed a smile for each of us.

Mom and I slipped away for fifteen minutes and took care of her banking that she had remembered to bring. Easy as pie; everything was on time and orderly, "Way to go, Mom."

"I am so glad you are helping me, thank you, Joseph."

"My pleasure, Mom."

"Do you love this girl?"

"I do, I hope to spend the rest of my life with her."

"She wants to be a doctor?"

"Yes, she will be a doctor; she's super smart and being a doctor is her dream."

"She is very beautiful."

"I hadn't noticed."

My mother smiled, "She's Catholic."

"I know, it's kind of interesting, her mom was Jewish."

"Was?"

"Yes, she converted and they have dealt with the repercussions ever since. Eileen's parents shared that with us when I met them; we know it's a hurdle and there's a lot of work between now and then. Mom, we have to get back inside, you're staying here tonight; I think that's great. It's time for us to leave."

Our plan was for Eileen and me to stay with Syl and Al in the city and spend Friday together, capped by going to Rockefeller Center for the lighting of the Christmas tree. Friday's lunch was at a Jewish deli where Eileen had no problem enjoying a kosher corned beef sandwich and she loved the big pickles.

The tree lighting was fabulous: we were there with about 50,000 of our closest friends as the switch was switched to much camera clicking, oohs, aahs, cheers and applause. It was Eileen's first time and she loved it. It was beautiful, we all agreed.

We shared hugs and kisses in front of their building; I wasn't sure Al was going to end his hug with Eileen, but he did. We made our way home to Victoria Lane, exhausted but not so tired that we couldn't share some "lighting" of our own.

"I love you, Eileen."

"I love you, Joe, thank you for introducing me to your family."

"They love you, Eileen, the hard part is over."

"No it's not, Joe, not tonight."

THE KISS

CHAPTER 20

HER BEAUTY

It's difficult to pick the right adjective as regards Eileen Kelly's beauty: Gracious, graceful, serene; all come to mind, as do startling, uncommon, rare (that's better), unique, pure; perhaps that is it, pure.

Eileen could wear a formal gown or jeans and a tee shirt and be equally beautiful; jewelry did not accent or advance her, in fact she wore little jewelry, nor did she employ much makeup. There was no taking note of her cheekbones, her eyes, her nose or her chin.

The simple truth was that Eileen woke up beautiful; she wears her beauty comfortably, she doesn't "bring" it, she just is. Why or how has this happened, I know not, but I do know the joy it brings, possibly a reflection of our appreciation. Perhaps it is a forced calm, afraid of the harm that might befall her? There is, within Eileen Kelly, a struggle, un-seen but to me.

One night while I was tracing a love map on Eileen's inner thigh we were talking about growing up.

"My dad was so proud of me, proud and protective and strict but never mean. I was a cute baby and as I became beautiful he sheltered me; it became over bearing; I hated him. He and my mom argued and I thought I was ruining their marriage. "She has to have a life," my mother advocated; "Not with those creeps."

"I guess it was paternal caring on steroids. He was keeping me for himself. I know that sounds terrible, and I don't mean it literally; he just couldn't let me be.

I started lying and going out; I was cheating on my father to get what I thought was normal. I started drinking and didn't experience anything; it was all a big blur. My mom, who had done her best for me, couldn't protect me from myself."

"We went to Palm Beach for a family vacation and that's when everything shifted. My dad saw me coming to join he and my mom poolside; he saw a young woman in a bikini, not his precious little girl."

"My dad is smart and he knew immediately that he had to let me go. As he put it that night at dinner, he had been an ass. He apologized to my mother and me."

"I didn't own up to the drinking until I wrote them in Spain, and told them about you and what you said. That's what brought them home; I am so grateful."

CHAPTER 21

LEARNING TO BOX. LEARNING TO DANCE

We, Eileen and I, were students, hard working "brainiacs" wanting to finish strong; this was our final year, Eileen, a senior, and I was ninety nine percent sure I would graduate a year early depending on the Liquidity exam. We were like a married couple: we each had a job, we went off to work and at the end of the day we talked about "work" and we helped each other. We put together our evening meal and "argued" our subjects and by that I mean, helped each other think things through. We were good partners, good school mates.

By accident we made another discovery we could share: we loved music and something was playing constantly; Big Bands were fading, the Lindy was still in, people were flirting with the Charleston again, Latin music was hot, trending toward Disco. One night I walked into the kitchen as Eileen, fingers snapping, was dancing alone and I caught her hand on a turn and we finished the number dancing together. Bam! We were hooked and every now and then we danced in the kitchen; great exercise, great fun.

I was still going to Pete's Gym and I finally convinced Eileen to come with and meet the guys. They loved her and not just for her beauty, they loved her spunk. They had her in the ring, teaching her basics and moves all built on one premise; "You want to beat him, don't you?"

When we were leaving, we were there for a long time, Eileen hugged Art, Jimmy, and Boozer; Pete she punched in the stomach, but like a cup cake. Eileen promised to come back and teach them a thing or two.

"Oh, yeah, and what could that be, Eileen?"

"I'm treating this like a title bout, so I am going to let you guess; it will give you something to worry about."

We heard a bunch of, "Oh, really"; "Big deal"; Sure you are!" But the bottom line was, "Come back soon."

We did go back and Eileen wanted to teach them something and she settled on a different kind of footwork, dancing. She danced with each of them. She taught them just plain dancing; how to move in a box in tune with the music, the Lindy, the ChaCha, and the waltz. When they weren't dancing with her Eileen had them dancing together. She danced with Pete for the goodnight dance, the waltz and I danced with Art, Boozer with Jimmy.

These guys, these boxers, all fell in love with this woman that I love and I loved her that much more for her gift to them. Of them all Boozer was the only one that had that quiet sense of moving with music; and now they all did and, in a small way, they are better boxers for it.

CHAPTER 22

CHRISTMAS GREETINGS AND
ESCAPE TO ACAPULCO

Eileen and I met in front of the Admin building on campus; I wanted to say hello to Thelma, maybe catch Dean of Men, Ed in his office and I wanted to see my counselor, Caroline Hopkins.

"Hopkins? She's my counselor."

"That's what I figured but didn't want to ask. This is so cool, if we get lucky we will see them all."

As we approached Thelma's desk she stood, "Joseph, You are not on my calendar."

"May we hug never-the-less?"

"Yes, but first," and she nodded toward Eileen.

"Thelma Bardlow, I would like you to meet Eileen Kelly."

A mixture of "It's nice to meet you," and "It's a pleasure," were uttered simultaneously.

"Eileen is my fiancé."

"Congratulations to you both."

"Thank you," I answered.

"And I have good news for you, Joseph, I spoke with Professor Bardlow and we would like you," looking at Eileen, "both for dinner shortly after Spring break."

"You are a good lobbyer, thank you."

"I promise you, it was my pleasure."

"I'll leave Joe to explain this mystery to you, Eileen."

"He has been very good at sharing everything with me. We brought you a Poinsettia and Holiday wishes."

"That's lovely, thank you."

"Is he," nodding toward the Dean's closed door.

"In a meeting that should end," as the door opened, "any second."

A scowling young man exited the Dean's office.

"I'll announce you," Thelma reached for her phone.

"Just send them in, please," Dean of Men, Ed said and Thelma gave us the go on in signal.

"Oh, my God, who are you," the Dean of Men, Ed asked, rising from his desk. "I was expecting that young man's parents." extending his hand.

"I'm Eileen Kelly and this is my fiancé, Joe Gordon, perhaps you've met?"

"Well, yes," waving me off, "please, Eileen, have a seat."

"Thank you, but first this poinsettia, along with our best Holiday wishes, are for you."

"Thank you, Eileen, My goodness you are a radiant messenger."

"I'll be outside with Thelma if you need me?"

"No, no, no! Fiancé? Congratulations to you both. I have five minutes."

"Ten," Thelma said as she closed the door.

Ed took hold of a spare chair, pulled it closer to us and sat with his head shaking from side to side, "I don't have words," He looked at us, smiling, "The two of you, together, are my Christmas present."

"That is very sweet," Eileen said, sitting back in her chair.

"Any plans for the break," asked the Dean.

"Nothing yet," Eileen said, looking at me.

"Well, we are thinking of Acapulco," I said.

"Seriously!" exclaimed Eileen.

"Si, como no."

The Dean of Men stood and opened his arms, "Hugs for the holidays, you two, I am thrilled for you both."

We all hugged and Eileen and I, holding hands, left after quick hugs with Thelma.

Caroline Hopkins was our next stop and we lucked out. I went in to her office first, "I promised I would stay in touch, so here I am, one year later."

"Joseph, fantastic, I needed a ray of light."

Caroline Hopkins got up from her desk and hugged me.

"How about two rays of light and a poinsettia along with Merry Christmas and Happy Holidays," said Eileen entering.

"Beauty enters the room, wait a second, you two; this is the guy?" "Yes," Eileen said.

"Together," I said.

"Wonderful," Caroline said, adding, "Thank you and best wishes to both of you. I am excited for you."

"Thank you."

"Plans for the break?"

"Maybe Acapulco," answered Eileen.

"Oh, my gosh; you two, Acapulco, wow!"

As we walked across campus toward the car Eileen asked, "You and Thelma, should I be worried?"

"A little; if I pass her husband's class I will graduate; she got him to agree for me to not attend class and take an oral final exam that we both learned will be over dinner at Professor Bardlow's house in the Spring."

"You are an architect, Joe. Amazing."

"You, my darling, are the amazing one."

We were in the car when Eileen grabbed me; "Let's go home and be amazing, together."

There are no words.

I made a few calls to Acapulco, exploring Christmas week; nada, nothing. This prompted a call to Jerry Brown who I had been meaning to call to extend season's greetings.

"Hello, Joe, how are you?"

"I'm good, family is good, school is great, no complaints. And you?"

"We are well, Celeste has set her wedding date, and business is good."

"Wonderful across the board; I am happy for you all."

"Thank you, Joe."

"Jerry, I am calling for advice."

"Regarding?"

"Acapulco, this coming Christmas week."

"Frank Stetter, he is the General Manager at Las Colinas; tell him you are my almost son-in-law and he will do everything he can to help you."

"Jerry, thank you, and Season's Greetings to you all. Almost son-in-law; makes me sad, like I have let you down; I don't want to ever do that."

"I am rooting for you and I expect you to excel."

"I will make you proud, Jerry. One other thing, how did you do that Frank Stetter thing just like that?"

"This is "41", Joe. I've got to run. Bye."

I hung up, stared at the phone, shook it off, asked the operator for long distance and thought of what this was going to cost the Kellys.

"Buenos Tardes, Las Colinas."

"Buenas Tardes, Frank Stetter, por favor."

"Please, who is calling?"

"I'm Joe Gordon, I am Jerry .'"

"Hold on, Senor Gordon," she interrupted, "momentito."

"Joe, this is Frank Stetter, how may I help you?"

"Your staff, they were expecting my call."

"Yes, we are at your service. When do you plan to arrive?"

"Friday, December 17th, departing on January 2nd."

"Joe, I look forward to your stay with us; I will personally look after you and Miss Kelly. Travel safely.

"Thank you."

"Adios."

"What will I need in Acapulco?"

"A bikini, no, make that two, shorts, a couple of tops, a simple dress, and a light sweater, just in case."

"Okay, and we will be there for New Year's Eve, so something for that," Eileen thought out loud.

"Dancing shoes. The hardest part will be winter clothes for the start and finish of the trip."

"I'm excited, Joe, what a great surprise."

"You have no idea."

"What does that mean?"

I told Eileen about my call to Jerry Brown and that kept us up half the night sharing my transformation from being Jerry's son-in-law to risking my own path, that led me to you, Eileen."

"You gave up every thing in order to find every thing. Brave, Joseph."

"I'm not sure I was brave; I could see the road ahead was paved with gold but I was concerned; would I be swept up by the bigness of "41"? Could I handle it and stay centered ?"

"I love taking this walk with you, Joe."

Eileen gave me a wonderful goodnight kiss to prove her point.

THE KISS

CHAPTER 23

A BUSY SPRING

Home from Acapulco, I went to visit Richard, my Phi Ep room mate.

"I thought you were dead," he declared, "or on safari in Africa or holed up behind locked doors with the most beautiful woman in the world. You are a very poor communicator and you look like you were in South America while we have been freezing in the Northern Hemisphere."

"Are you done having fun picking on your ex room mate?"

"Yes. You traveled somewhere?"

"You were close, we were in Acapulco for two weeks; fantastic time."

"Sleepy village on the coast, restless natives?"

"Not so sleepy, it is growing and the natives, many of them, are smart, talented and friendly. We stayed at Las Colinas, had our own casita at the top of the hill; we watched every sunset, I missed one, I think."

"Eileen had fun?"

"Richard, I have never seen her happier; her beauty commands attention and we will go back one day to visit friends, friends for life."

"Wow, tough to come home."

"Back to reality; and you?"

"Oh, Paris, London and Rome; a quick trip, good to be back."

"Richard, I am pretty sure I am going to graduate in June; it feels weird."

"You went from, "I don't care," to, "I'm out of here," I have never seen anything like it."

"I know, it's all because of calculus; calculus, Gabby, new thinking and a desire to excel. You are part of this, Richard; "Rutgers has a counselor, go see her." Remember?"

"I do, I am very proud of you."

"Thanks Richard. I have to get going."

"Give Eileen a hug from me."

"With pleasure."

It took Eileen and I a while to get back on track, we were exhausted; we gave everything we had to Acapulco: to the village, to the people, to each other; we left nothing on the table or in the pool.

In so many ways our trip rested on the shoulders of Jerry Brown, "Call Frank Stetter, he'll take care of you."

I wrote Jerry and Frank Stetter extending our thanks, that was all I could do and those letters helped get me back to reality, back to our studies for the sprint to graduation in six months. We settled in, we wanted to excel and we helped each other reason out some course conundrums.

We shopped at Orlando's; I thought he was going to jump over the counter when he first saw Eileen all tanned after winter break. It was good to be back.

I drove out to Rockville Centre to see my mom. It was crazy; I drove for four hours, there and back, to spend two hours with my mom. We went over her bills and bank statements and got her up to date and I brought mom up to speed about school, probable graduation; my mom cried with joy and pride.

"And Eileen," Mom asked.

"Eileen, I am still in love with her; she's beautiful and smart and we had a marvelous time in Acapulco. Mom, what about you, you should get away, go to Florida and visit cousin Birdy?"

"I'm okay here, just promise this girl won't take you away from me."

"I promise."

I called Syl and Al from mom's and we got together for dinner in the city.

"Eileen, I'm grabbing dinner with my sister and Al in the city, I'll be home around ten."

"Perfect, how about a corned beef sandwich for me and an appetite for dessert for you?"

"Sounds good; let's see, cheese cake or Eileen, hmmm?"

She hung up on me.

Eileen and I went to see the boxing boys, all of whom wanted to go a couple of rounds with her, but settled for Happy New Year wishes and hugs.

We danced in the kitchen, ate out once in a while, the neighbors dropped by, sometimes at very inopportune moments, we were either making love and/or having sex; we were married for the most part; we had jobs; we were hard working students coming up on Spring break.

No plans for Spring break other than one night in Manhattan to have dinner at "41". Jerry's response to my Acapulco thank you note was a phone call; "It's time for me to meet Eileen Kelly, Joe!"

"Good evening, Mr. Gordon and Miss Kelly," we were greeted by Monte and Jimmy inside the door at "41". We went into the bar for a drink where Henry, one of the bartenders, put a Birchbrook bourbon on the rocks in front of me.

"Miss Kelly, may I get you a drink?"

"Yes, thank you; Coke on the rocks."

Eileen was smitten with the atmosphere: the forty foot long bar, the red checkered tablecloths and napkins and the hundreds of model planes, ships, cars and trains hanging from the ceiling; the place reeked of success and the joint was jumping.

"Miss Kelly," Jerry startled Eileen, "May I steal you away from this man and see you to your table?"

Eileen looked at me, "Eileen Kelly I want you to meet Jerry Brown, my almost father-in-law."

Eileen hugged Jerry, startling him, "Thank you. Thank you for the many things you have done for Joe."

"Eileen, I had heard you are smart, lovely and beautiful and you are all of that and more, and, you are welcome. Come, both of you, we'll get you seated."

Jerry seated us in the premier first section of the bar and Vincent, our Captain, presented us with menus.

"My spine is tingling, Joe, this place is very special."

"I, my dear Eileen, I am thrilled to be here with you. I can feel the buzz."

Sheldon Cannon, an associate of Jerry's, came to our table to meet

Eileen; we were being treated like royalty. We ordered dinner and enjoyed a splendid meal and the excitement of this unique and famous restaurant.

Sheldon returned for a brief visit and I handed him an envelope to please give to Jerry. He said 'no problem' and suggested Eileen might enjoy seeing the wine cellar where the booze was hidden during prohibition in the 30's.

Ralph, keeper of the cellar, took us through the kitchen and downstairs to the wine cellar; we stopped in front of a brick wall and Eileen smiled, "I don't get it?"

Ralph produced a long, thin, steel rod that he pushed into an air bubble hole in the cement between some bricks and the entire wall swung open, revealing the cellar.

"Ralph, that is amazing," Eileen said, "Can we go in?"

"Step over these plumbing pipes, carefully." Ralph led the way and was thrilled to have Eileen there; she lit the place up with her beauty and excitement.

When it was time to go someone must have alerted Jerry because he caught us in the lobby, as we were about to leave.

"Joe, I got your envelope, thank you and Eileen, I hope you have had a wonderful evening. One other thing," Jerry pointed to his cheek and Eileen responded with the appropriate kiss, "Thank you, Jerry, may I call you Jerry? I just did, didn't I?"

"Yes, you did and yes, you may, Eileen, and bring him back any time you wish."

Jerry hugged me and whispered in my ear, "She's a keeper."

When we left "41" it was a beautiful evening, perfect for a window-shopping walk up Fifth Avenue. We held hands and strolled and talked.

"41" was your future and you walked away?"

"I did, it wasn't easy but it was the right decision."

"And his daughter, did you hurt her?"

"As gently as I could; it hurt us all, put us on a new path. Celeste is happy, engaged and getting married next year. And "41", God only knows, is doing fine without me."

We stopped in front of Van Cleef and Arpel.

"Yes, but Jerry misses you."

"I know, he's a very special man and I hope he will be in my life, forever."

"Mine too." Eileen said.

"Yours too, absolutely."

We shared a quick kiss before walking on.

"Joe, let's go home, I want us in bed together."

I called Jerry at "41"; I wanted to know if the two hundred dollars in the envelope was enough.

"It was more than enough, Joe, not to worry."

"We had a wonderful time; Eileen loves "41".

"We enjoyed your visit, in fact I am opening a charge account for you; I'll use your Rockville Centre address, okay?"

"Yes, that's fine; I really don't know what to say."

"Whenever you are here, sign your check, add an appropriate tip and we'll send you a statement at the end of the month."

"I don't know how often I'll. ."

"Joe," Jerry interrupted, "what I want you to know is that "41" will always be here for you, I will always be here for you, and I expect you to excel at Pratt and go on to be one hell-of-an architect in this town and we can help you."

"I'm speechless, I'm grateful, I love you, Jerry."

"And I you; keep up the good work."

And he was gone. I hung up the phone and was filled with a sense of security and peacefulness that I had never experienced before. Jerry Brown set the bar pretty high; I knew I would work very hard to meet his expectations.

I went to see Dean of Men, Ed, he and two of my professors had written letters of recommendation to accompany my applications for architectural grad schools. I was in at Pratt, my first choice.

"Thelma."

"Joseph."

"Hug?"

She was on her feet and we hugged. I loved hugging Thelma, there was no holding back; if we followed our hug with a hip shifting bottom bop we could have tried out for the Harlem Globe Trotters. She was fun.

"Joseph, perfect timing, Friday at six, casual attire, for a BBQ dinner and your final exam?"

"Friday?"

"Yes. Could be this Friday or the next, you choose."

"This Friday would be great; I've been studying."

"Eileen?"

"Eileen for sure. I want her to distract the professor."

"That's my job and I am very good at it."

"I would not bet against you, Thelma, the professor is a very lucky man. What can we bring?"

"You bring Eileen and your textbook and we will have fun."

"My graduation is on the line here."

"Then you had best bring your "A" game."

"Yes, Ma'am."

"Here's our address, directions and phone number and I need a number for you; there wasn't anyone at Phi Ep that thinks you are still alive."

"My apology, Thelma, Eileen's folks are in Spain and we have been living in sin at her house here in New Brunswick."

"Living in sin; lucky boy."

Thelma gave me another hug, just in time to be caught by Dean of Men, Ed, "That's disgraceful; I am going to tell Pete."

"Who's Pete?"

"My husband," said Thelma.

"Get in here," Dean of Men, Ed called to me, he had gone into his office.

"Shut the door."

I doubled back and shut the door.

"What is going on," I wanted to know.

"I haven't smoked a cigarette in almost three weeks."

"That's fantastic."

"I'm in love."

"It's in the air."

"It's been years."

"So, we meant nothing to you?"

"You didn't love me back, this guy does."

"As long as you give up cigarettes?"

"Yes."

"That's great, I am happy for you; happy and scared."

"Scared?"

"I don't want you to get hurt. What's his name?"

"Frederic."

"Frederic. I hope this works out for both of you."

"Thank you, I had to tell someone; I trust you."

"I'm honored and I am grateful; you have helped me big time and I am about to take a giant step toward fulfilling my dream that you told me to go after. Thank you, Dean of Men, Ed."

"You're welcome. You know I want the best for you."

"I know."

"How is Eileen other than stunning?"

"She's wonderful and I'm scared; I am going to be direct, she's got a little bit of you in her."

"Cigarettes?"

"Bourbon. She likes bourbon; too much. She's fighting and I keep telling her, I am not the boss of her, it's her fight, but I'm scared. I don't want to lose her."

"Let's take it one day at a time and pray a lot."

"Sounds good for both of us. I have to go."

I was on my feet headed for the door.

"No hug?"

"Not since you have Frederic."

I got to the door, made a U-turn and hugged the Dean of Men.

It was just past six on Friday when Eileen and I arrived at Peter and

Thelma Bardlow's home; Thelma opened the door, "Welcome, come on in, we're out in the back yard."

"We brought you some fresh flowers, Thelma," said Eileen.

"Oh, my goodness, they are beautiful; would you give them to Peter, he loves flowers, but I'll take a hug."

Thelma and Eileen hugged and I got a quick hug and Thelma led us through the house to the back yard.

"Peter, Joe and Eileen are here."

Peter was off in a corner of the yard, bent over some thing and didn't seem to hear which gave us a moment to take it all in: this wasn't your average back yard, this was a work of floral art, a yard of art that was a visual feast of shelves and trellises and old wheelbarrows that cradled and carried the many flowers and blended them together horizontally and vertically. It was an endless stream of color and varieties of plants and flowers. It was beautiful.

Peter, Professor Bardlow, stood and headed our way, "I'm sorry, I had to get those two boards together. My goodness, you are beautiful, Eileen; Thelma told me but I figured, "nah."

"These flowers are for you, Professor, talk about coals to Newcastle; your home and your yard are very special," Eileen said.

"Thank you, it's a passion, we're a team; Thelma on the inside and me, out here. Eileen and Joe, I'm Pete, Peter to Thelma; so either one. Who wants a drink, we have water and sodas?"

"Coke for me," said Eileen and "water for me, Pete," I finished the sentence; "can I help?"

"Thanks, Joe, we're good. Why don't you all settle at that table over there; there are crackers and cheese and chips, I'll be right out with the drinks. Thank you for the flowers, perfect for the dining room table."

"Scotch on the rocks for me, Peter; that's code for root-beer."

"Coming up."

We sat and nibbled and chatted. We all shared little tidbits about ourselves and as couples. The Bardlows wanted children, but it was not meant to be so Thelma "adopted" a campus of students and Pete watches over young adults one class at a time. That and their shared passions, inside and outside, keep them content.

We shared about our first date "interview" and how Mrs. Brand put us together.

"Okay, before we put dinner on the table let's get this final exam out of the way," said the for-the-moment professor. "Two questions: first question; how many gallons of rainwater would it take to fill the storm drain at the base of a road with a six degree slope?"

I could hear the crickets as I mulled the question. "That was a trick question; there is no answer."

"Correct, you are batting five hundred,"

"No, no, no; I am batting a thousand."

"The student gets a star for paying attention."

"Hurrah," cheered Eileen and Thelma.

"Second question," announced the Professor, clearing his throat, "How many cubic inches are there in a U.S. liquid gallon?"

"Can I hug your wife for marrying you, when I answer this correctly?"

"Hmmmm? Eileen," Pete wondered, "what do you think of this blatant tom foolery."

"I think they should go for it because I am going to hug you for allowing Joe this opportunity."

"I like that; what is the answer, young man intent on stealing my wife away?"

"The answer, on your feet Thelma, is 231 cubic inches."

"That, fortunately for all of us, is correct."

We all started to scream, I hugged Thelma, Eileen hugged Pete and the neighbors, listening to the racket, figured the Bardlows had won the Publisher's Clearing House sweepstakes.

"Come on Eileen," Thelma said, "let's get the goodies that go with the burgers these two are going to cook."

"Lead the way."

Before following Thelma, Eileen kissed me in a way that made me forget I had locked up graduation.

"Pete," Eileen said, "sorry, I had to do that, I wanted to do that."

"I didn't see Joe protesting and I was looking the other way."

Eileen sashayed to the house.

Pete and I were doing the man thing, getting the charcoal going, fanning the flames and the smoke and talking.

"I'm six three, 200 pounds, and back then, years ago, I played lacrosse for Maryland. In my senior year, my parents and siblings had moved here, I came up to New Brunswick to watch my kid brother play football for the state championship. He played well, defensive end, they lost and what I watched mostly was a cheerleader for his team. Turned out she was a junior, five years younger than I, and she was cheering at me; kismet. We lied to our parents, we cheated, we did everything we had to in order to stay together. Finally we ran away, got married and Thelma and I worked my way through grad school so I could become a professor. It took years for our families to accept us. That's a long story just to say I hope you two hold on to each other."

"Thank you, I want that too. I love Eileen; she's smart, she's fun, and she's beautiful in every way, but our dreams are going to separate us; she's going to Johns Hopkins to become a doctor and I'll be at Pratt, in Brooklyn, to become an architect. It's going to be tough."

"Thelma and I will be cheering for you and ready to help, although I don't know what that would be."

"Did you and Thelma used to drink?"

"Like guppies. We were trying to make our fears disappear into a bottle of scotch. We drank hard."

Thelma and Eileen had come out of the house and put all the goodies on the table and brought six big hamburger patties to the chef; "How do you like these cooked?"

"Rare for me," Eileen spoke up.

"Same for me," I said."

"All four rare; makes my job easy," as Pete put all six on the grill, "This will only take a few minutes."

"We've been in the kitchen talking about scotch on the rocks being code for root-beer."

"We," I said, "have been talking about two special women and what it will take for us, Eileen, to hold on to each other while we chase our dreams."

Pete flipped the burgers. No one said a word; Eileen burst into tears. I reached out to her but she would have no part of that.

"No, no, I have to say it; I am scared: I am scared of Med school, scared of losing you, Joe, and you are scared of losing me in a bottle of bourbon, scared of scaring my parents. I'm sorry." Eileen was pulling herself together, Pete had lifted the burgers from the grill and Thelma handed Eileen a napkin.

"Oh, my God, I am so sorry."

Pete to the rescue, "You are not alone here; we are here with you and you said it yourself; "Oh, my God. God is here with you, with us. That's probably why I made a couple of extra burgers."

Eileen tried to laugh, "That was cute, Pete, thank you; I'm okay, I feel safe here. Can we eat?"

"You bet, I'll put these back on for a couple of seconds and we'll sit down to dinner."

There were buns and potato salad, coleslaw, pickles, lettuce, tomatoes, and sliced onions; it was a do it yourself burger fest, and it was damn good.

Pete turned on some outdoor lights and the gardens strutted their evening allure.

"Pete, Thelma told ne to bring the text, we did?"

"Oh, good, you remembered; I want to autograph it for you."

"Autograph it?"

"Not exactly a collector item, but I'm the author."

"You're Peter Ward?"

"Yup, that's me."

"Peter wasn't fond of a text called, "Hydraulics," too stuffy, so he wrote his own."

"I had fun with it, tried to keep it light, less stuffy and decided on the title, "Liquidity."

Thelma added, "The wonderful part was universities started to pick it up and it became the course standard."

"Which means that an autographed copy and fifty cents will get you to Staten Island."

"I love that you sat down and wrote it," Eileen said, "you didn't squander the idea."

"Thank you, Eileen, it's not a best seller but it is a steady stream, no pun intended, of cash flow. That one I said on purpose."

The professor inscribed in my text: "For Joe Gordon, A good student and a good friend; best wishes,

Peter Ward Bardlow."

"Thank you, Professor and thank you, Thelma and Pete, for a lovely evening."

"Eileen, before you go," Thelma said, "what can we do for you?"

Eileen took a moment, "You gave me a safe place to feel and express my fear; I am very grateful to you both and I am leaving with 231 cubic inches of courage and hope."

CHAPTER 24

REALITY HITS HARD

At home, in bed, I held Eileen close and she buried her face in my neck.

"My parents are coming home in six weeks," she whispered, "and I don't know what to do."

"In the morning we can reason this out together." I kissed Eileen's forehead; we fell asleep, leaving our tomorrows on the pillow.

I awakened first, remembering, as I stirred, we were expected at Gabby's for breakfast at eight thirty; we had forty five minutes.

"Eileen."

"Mmmmm."

I touched her belly, "Eileen."

"Go away."

"We are going to Gabby's for breakfast, you've got to get up."

Her eyes opened, "I'm not going. What happened to reasoning things out?"

"We will, after breakfast; I forgot about Gabby. Come on."

Eileen sat up, pulled the covers up to her waist; she was naked and gorgeous, "Joe, I'm not going. You go."

"Okay, I'll be home around noon, we'll talk. I love you."

I kissed Eileen and headed for the shower; I had to hurry.

I was only a few minutes late when Gabby opened the door.

"Where's Eileen?"

"She's not coming, she's home. I need a hug."

We hugged, maybe a little more than a hug as memories crashed around us.

"Where's Suki?"

"She'll be down in a minute. Come on, I'll get the bacon going."

"Gabby, you look great, everything okay?"

"Fine, busy; everything is okay. Your final, Joseph, what happened?"

"I passed, I'm graduating; Class of '55."

"Oh, my God, that is great. Congratulations!"

"I hear Joseph good news?"

"Suki, yes, good news, I passed my oral final, I'm graduating this year."

"Big hug for Joseph."

We shared a big hug but Suki, ever perceptive, "Something wrong?"

"Yes, Suki, something wrong."

"Where Eileen?"

"She is home, wouldn't come; I am worried about her."

During breakfast I learned that Gabby and Suki are happy, Suki's English is improving and Lincoln renewed Gabby's contract; good news.

"I am doing so much more than driving or getting in or out of a Lincoln; I am meeting with women's groups all over the world, spreading the good will of the Ford Motor Company and the Lincoln division; I'm an ambassador. It's exciting."

"Sometime gone for too long."

"True, some of these trips and or commercial shoots take weeks. It's good but it's hard on us both."

"I walk on Gabby back when she home."

"Suki, you are amazing," Gabby said.

"Suki amazing," she boasted, lifting her chin and tossing her head.

"You walked on my back once, I'll never forget it."

"Any time, Joseph, "you need now, can tell."

"We are here to help you, Joseph."

"I know, Gabby, I need advice; everything is happening at once."

"What happening, Joseph," Suki wanted to know.

"Graduation, leaving New Brunswick, wrapping up the two most important years of my life, leaving both of you, and Eileen's parents are coming home for graduation and I don't know if it will be comfortable living there."

"Live here, a day, a week, whatever you need," Gabby offered.

"Thank you, thank you both. What's weighing heaviest is that we are going off to grad schools, miles apart. Eileen is going to be a doctor, so that's a minimum of four years apart. Put all of that together and I am scared; scared for me, Eileen, and scared for us."

"Joseph, to keep love, you must give away."

"I know, Suki, and I knew this was coming; still, it hurts."

"I walk on your back, Joseph."

"I love you, too, Suki."

"You know," Gabby said, "there are parts of this puzzle you can not control and what I'm hearing is you and Eileen have not yet discussed this?"

"This afternoon."

"Let's talk about her parent's part in this," Gabby said, "together, along with them, you will reason this out."

"You're right. I love you both and thank you, you give me strength."

We hugged. I left and headed for Victoria Lane. In the house I called out for Eileen.

"I'm upstairs."

Eileen was still in bed; she hadn't moved.

"Do you love me, Joe?"

I sat on the edge of our bed, soon to be, once again, Eileen's parent's bed.

"Absolutely."

"Why?"

You're smart, beautiful, fun, helpful; we argue pretty well, travel well, dance well, we are partners, we shop and cook well, we make mistakes and fix them, we sleep well together and we make love well together."

"I love you, too."

"I know."

"I don't love me, Joe."

"Eileen, last night you were so open; scared from deep in your beautiful belly. That kind of pain can twist your mind, change your opinion of yourself."

"Last night I wanted a drink so bad and I recognized it was to take away the pain. I was glad they had no booze."

"How can you not love that, that insight?"

"Because that's just the tip of a very big iceberg; all together it's overwhelming."

Maybe it would help if I share my overwhelming list?"

"Maybe it would help if you took off your clothes?"

"It would only help for a while."

"I want you now, I waited all morning for you."

"Not 'til I give you my list."

"Bastard!"

"Your parents are coming home and there will be no space for me."

Eileen pulled the covers over her head, "I'm not listening."

"You will want time alone with your parents and they with you; I'll be in the way."

"Come on, Joe, get naked."

"After graduation will we have time together before we separate to go to grad schools, miles apart?"

"Of course we will; take your clothes off, damn it."

"I am afraid I am going to lose you, Eileen Kelly."

"I am afraid," said Eileen from under the covers, "I am too big a problem and I will lose you, Joseph Gordon."

I ripped the covers off Eileen, "We are scared," I was shouting, "both of us: we're kids, we're in love, we're crazy about sex, you're an alcoholic, we care about each other, you are outrageously beautiful, and that, oddly, is hard work, we are going to separate to fulfill our dreams; of course we are scared and we have to talk this all through."

"I want the covers back and I want you naked with me so we can love on each other and then we can talk about everything, I promise."

I have never had more intense fun in bed; we loved each other, we hated each other, we fought, we kissed, we turned our fears and pain into pleasure; pleasure that we refused to fulfill until Eileen screamed and I joined her seconds later.

We lay there together looking at each other, touching each other, laughing a little, kissing; sweet and gentle kisses, and Eileen cried. I found the covers, pulled then up and held her.

"When are your parents coming home?"

"Oh, For God's sake, Joe."

"This will take five minutes and then I will hold you for the rest of your life."

"They are coming home on the Thursday before graduation."

"Okay."

"They would like us to pick them up at the airport and they would like their bedroom back."

"I have an idea about that; fresh flowers on the bed with a note. "Welcome home and thanks."

"That's sweet. We have to clean the bathroom and put fresh linen on their bed."

"Okay, on that Wednesday we can clean the house, do laundry, do some shopping, "

"That reminds me," Eileen interrupted, "They want to host a graduation party for us, that's plural, inviting the neighbors and your family, Richard, Gabby and Suki, Jerry Brown, other Phi Ep guys, whoever you want."

"Did you get a letter?"

"They called while you were at Gabby's."

"You knew when I got home?"

"Yes."

"I am going to spank you."

"Don't start something you can't finish, Joe."

Eileen rolled over and pointed at a very lovely target.

"No spanking until you tell me; what else?"

Eileen sat up, "They will be exhausted Thursday night, so they want us to hold down the noise; Friday they are busy until we all have dinner, meaning the four of us; keeping the deep, heavy stuff until Sunday when the four of us will finally have time to, as my dad put it, dig into the stuff that matters."

"What time does their flight get in?"

"Six fifty five at night, TWA, at Idlewild. It's going to be a long day for all of us."

"Yeah, even if their plane is on time, with customs, and all that, we won't get home 'til close to midnight."

"You need to figure out who you want to invite to the graduation party."

"And you need to lean over and get that pillow off the floor."

"Roger that, Joe."

It was just one good spank and I was certain that Eileen was more upset that she allowed herself to be tricked than the solo spank, but she swore she was not going to talk to me for the rest of the day. That lasted two minutes; she threw a pillow to the floor on my side of the bed, "Aren't you going to get that, Joe?"

"I'll get it later, Eileen, right now let me hold you and love you."

Eileen folded herself into my arms; her warmth and the smell of her were intoxicating. She moved her head until she found comfort near my shoulder, "I am so scared."

"Me, too, Eileen; it's time for us to hold on to our love and let each other go, then what ever is meant to be will unfold."

"I don't know how to do that," Eileen admitted.

"I don't either but I believe we are learning."

"Don't you want to get that pillow?"

I didn't respond, I was processing at a hundred miles an hour: I had just learned something, something big; I didn't want to just have sex with Eileen; I wanted to love her and make love with her for the rest of my life. I leaned over and retrieved the pillow and the expected spank never came; Eileen must have been listening to my mind. Together, in the warmth of each other's arms, I fell in love, bigger and better.

CHAPTER 25

JUST ONE DRINK

We were in the kitchen, dance music blaring, when the phone rang; Eileen turned down the music, I picked up the phone.

"Hello."

"Hello, Joe, it's Jerry."

"Hi, Jerry, what's up?"

"I know it's late but I have two tickets, fourth row, on the aisle, for "The King and I", for tonight. Are you interested?"

"Eileen, do you want to see "The King and I" tonight?"

"Tonight?"

"Yes tonight, like leave here in an hour or so."

"Sure, we can do that. Great."

I was holding the phone up, "We would love that, I guess you heard?"

"Wonderful, Joe, the tickets will be at the St. James Theater box office in your name and, if you like, I'll call Vincent Sardi and you can go there after the show?"

"Awesome. Thank you, Jerry; regards to all."

"Have fun, Bye."

"He loves you," Eileen pronounced.

"He loves us, Eileen. Sardi's after the show, so put on something hot."

"Acapulco hot?"

"Too hot, too intimate."

"Okay, I'm going to shower and dress."

"Me too, right behind you."

By the time we left the house we had shared a sandwich to tide us over and we were dressed for a Saturday night on the town; Eileen was wearing a little blue dress with spaghetti straps and the back plunged down to "there." I was holding my own in a suit and tie.

After the show, which was exhilarating and romantic, we went to Sardis for a drink and dessert. Sardis was The after theater night spot in the city.

Vincent Sardi, the proprietor, with a heads-up from Jerry, was expecting us and we were seated immediately. We ordered two Crème Brule, a coke and a cognac; that brought a nudge from Eileen, "Make that two cognacs," I said.

"You are not the boss of me, Joseph, this is a once in a big while night for us; God knows when we will get to do this again."

"Let me tell you about the Hirschfelds," I said.

"Do you love me?"

"Completely."

"Who are the Hirschfelds?"

The two cognacs arrived in their snifters; we picked them up and I put the snifter under my nose, rocking it gently, breathing in the aroma.

"This is fine cognac." I took a sip, "Wow."

Eileen took a big sip and shut her eyes, "Mmmm."

"The Hirschfelds are all of the ink on paper caricatures hanging on the walls. Each one represents the star or stars of a Broadway show; there must be a hundred of them."

"The cognac is delicious," Eileen said after another sip.

The crème Brule was served.

"Eileen, you are delicious."

Eileen picked up her cognac, "You know what I want to do when we get home?"

I was afraid the couple sitting next to us was a little too interested in our conversation for a couple of reasons; Eileen was talking a little too loud and her beauty provoked attention.

"I do know," I whispered, "and I think that's a great idea."

Eileen had tasted her Crème Brule and had another sip of cognac, "Mmm, this is sooo yummy, but not as good as you know who."

I leaned in toward Eileen and whispered, "Eileen, please," and I rolled my eyes, "be here with ne, no more cognac."

It was a sobering request, presented indiscreetly, and Eileen took a moment to collect herself, "I'm fine, I'm okay," she said softly, looking straight ahead; she turned to me, "I love you, Joe, you know that, right?"

"I do and I love you back."

I purposely picked up Eileen's cognac and downed it. Eileen's gorgeous, green eyes were daggers that slowly softened, so close to tears.

The drive home was touchy.

"I liked the show," I said, "Yul Brynner was really powerful."

"Yes, but Anna, she was great; the King fell in love with her."

"But would not, could not show it."

"You were mean to me, Joe. You are not the King, you know?"

"Well, Anna got a little tipsy and there were a lot of people in the audience."

"The cognac was really something; I have never had that before."

"I've had you before and you are really something."

"You love me."

"Yes, I do."

"I'm sorry."

"Me too."

"I'll make it up to you."

"Way ahead of you, Eileen."

"Then step on it."

CHAPTER 26

EILEEN STANDS HER GROUND- IT'S OVER

On Wednesday Eileen and I did laundry, put fresh sheets on her parents bed, cleaned the house, top to bottom, and went shopping, where Orlando came around the counter for a hug with Eileen. We bought a variety of meats and salad stuff and cheese and bread. Orlando gave Eileen some vichyssoise soup to welcome home her parents.

"Orlando, we are graduating on Saturday and soon we'll be gone."

"Gone? Where?"

"I'm going to Johns Hopkins in Baltimore; I am going to be a doctor."

"And you, Mr. Joe?"

"To Pratt, in Brooklyn, to become an architect."

Orlando looked perplexed, "You will be apart? That's not good; you are perfect together."

"That's sweet, Orlando; we have dreams," Eileen shared.

"We all have dreams, Miss Eileen; you have love."

Eileen and I looked at each other, "We are," I said, "working to keep our love alive, Orlando. Thank you for everything."

Orlando came around and gave me a big hug, "I am going to miss you both."

On Thursday I knocked on Mrs. Brand's door and as usual the response was immediate, "Come in."

Good morning Mrs. Brand; I've come to say goodbye."

"It saddens me to think I may never see you again, Joseph. A lot of young men have come through that door but you are the only one I ever had an affair with."

"It is our little secret, is it not?"

"It is."

"Peanut butter sex."

"Joseph!!"

"It was good for me."

"And for me too."

"I wish you would come to the Kelly's."

"No, I have passed the baton to Eileen."

"You always make me smile, Mrs. Brand."

"As do you, for me."

"A sitting hug?"

"Of course."

I bent over and gently hugged Mrs. Brand, "I will miss you and I wish you well."

"Goodbye, Joseph."

I closed the door behind me and heard Mrs. Brand blow her nose.

Upstairs, in Richard's and my room, I gathered what little was left of my stuff; after one last look I turned and bumped into Richard.

"Oh, thank God, you are finally leaving."

"Yes, but you are coming to the Kelly's Saturday?"

"Wouldn't miss it."

"It's so weird, Douglass graduates the women at the exact same time as Rutgers does the men, but across town; what if you are parents of fraternal twins?"

"I know you don't expect me to answer."

"No."

"What's weird is you graduating a year early."

"Or at all, really, it's a miracle."

Richard nodded in agreement, "See you there."

We were in the middle of rush hour traffic trying to get to Idlewild Airport; by the time we got there and parked it was a little after seven. The International Terminal wasn't too busy and their flight had arrived a half hour early. The Kellys were exiting customs; our timing was perfect. Eileen inhaled deeply and ran to meet her parents, I smiled and waved and gave them time to hug; Eileen was wiping away tears and I was happy to see them home, safe and sound. I got hugs as well and I headed for the car to bring it around to pick them up; only one bag, the rest was being shipped.

"Good flight," I asked, steering us back towards New Brunswick.

"Great flight," said Bob, "wonderful year, damn near; Spain is a lovely country, good people."

"It was a terrific stay and we're glad to be home; there's just one thing, we are starving," Edna said.

"Tons of food in the fridge," said Eileen, "we went shopping yesterday." Eileen was on her knees, facing her folks in the back, "God, I am glad your home; you both look wonderful. I got a little teary back there."

"It's nice to be missed," Edna said, "and our little sojourn to check on you two seems like it was a decade ago, it's good to be home."

"How is this guy treating you, Eileen," Bob Kelly wanted to know.

"He's been much nicer, knowing you guys were coming home."

"Edna, help, it's the father daughter attack."

"Fear not, Joe, they are harmless."

"I never would have guessed. Thanks, Edna."

"Joe and I went to see "The King and I" last Saturday and ever since he thinks he's the king of me."

"We've been missing all the fun," Bob said to his wife.

"From the looks of things, you two are doing fine. Besides, we are not here to judge," Edna said, "we are here to love on you both and to eat; I'm starving."

"Almost home, Mom."

"We've been shopping at "Orlando's" and he made some killer welcome home vichyssoise."

"I'm in," said Bob.

"Mmmm, me too, love vichyssoise."

"Orlando is smitten with your daughter; Eileen walks in and she gets the A treatment."

"Mom, we'll go there tomorrow if you need stuff for the party."

I turned the corner onto Victoria Lane.

"We are home," exclaimed Eileen.

"You all go ahead, I'll get your bag."

We sat in the kitchen while the Kellys enjoyed the vichyssoise and extolled Madrid and the nine o'clock dinners. Their drooping eyelids forced them upstairs where they found the fresh flowers with a "Welcome Home" note.

"Beautiful, thank you." From Edna and "Hold down the noise." from Bob as he closed their door.

"Thank you, Joe, you are wonderful and I love you very big." Eileen sat next to me and I wiped away her tears.

Friday was very hectic: Bob had business to attend to and Edna had to put the finishing touches to the graduation celebration. Eileen went with her mom; I think they went to Orlando's, and I went to Gabby's; I lucked out, Suki and Gabby were home. They were invited to the graduation party but had declined.

"You will be missed, it's a small group, maybe twenty, and Eileen's folks are very nice."

"We stay home, better for everyone," Suki asserted.

"I don't agree."

"We are thrilled for you, you know that. We will be there in spirit," Gabby assured me.

"Okay. I do want a favor; your gift to me, 'Architecture Since Man,' it's under the coffee table; can I leave it here until I get settled at Pratt? Maybe not even then, until I'm sure it will be safe. Besides it's a great excuse for me to visit."

"Book safe here, Joseph," Suki was certain.

"Of course," Gabby added; "we look through it from time to time, my note is still at the Taj Mahal page."

"Thank you, two of my favorite women, I love you both."

"You know we are happy for you, we love you."

"I've got to go, I want to say goodbye to Pete and the guys at the gym."

"Hugs and kisses, Joseph; you can't just walk out of here."

We hugged and we kissed and my leaving pulled at each of our hearts, so many beautiful memories.

Down at Pete's Gym the guys were all there; Art, Jimmy, Boozer and, of course, Pete.

"Hey, hey, hey, look what the cat dragged in, it's the kid; how you doing Kid?"

"I'm doing good, Pete. How's everybody?"

Boozer was first up, "We're good. You just missed the Merry-go-round."

"I've been on a merry-go-round of my own: finals and a special oral final exam that put me in this year's graduating class; I'm graduating tomorrow."

"Hey, that's great, congratulations, Joe."

"Thank you, Jimmy." I shrugged, "I'm having a hard time believing it myself."

"Nice, very nice, you worked hard, you deserve it; way to go," Art said.

"How's Arlene?"

"It's Eileen, not Arlene, Pete, and, yeah, how is she?"

"Eileen is good, she's with her mom, shopping and stuff, so she couldn't come with me."

"You really like her, huh," asked Pete.

"I love her, I want to marry her, but we have some dreams to chase first."

"Dreams?"

"Eileen is going to be a doctor and me, an architect."

"Those are some big dreams. What's it take, five, maybe six years to become a Doc. How do you wait for that," Pete wanted to know.

"How do I wait for Eileen and/or she for me? We don't know. One day at a time, I guess."

"It's like going into the ring," Boozer was on his feet, gloves up, moving around, "one round at a time and you hang in there 'til the time is right and there's an open shot and you take it, bam."

Boozer took a swing and Pete ducked.

"Patience, patience and desire, that's what you're going to need; six years is a long time," Jimmy was shaking his head.

"I know, time will tell. I want to clean out my locker."

Pete walked with me, "I'm going to be at Pratt Institute in Brooklyn for three years, Pete, but if I'm in New Brunswick I'll check in on you guys."

I opened my locker, not much in there but I decided to keep my workout gloves and my jump rope and my shorts and stuff. "Pete, maybe one of the guys could use my boxing gloves?"

"Sure, Kid, that would be great."

We walked back to the guys, "Okay, time to say goodbye and thank you all for taking me in; I love you all, even you, Pete."

I hugged each one and then they were on me, like locusts: messing up my hair, pulling my shirt out of my pants and pulling my pants down a couple of inches.

"Thanks guys, it's been a great ride."

I walked out, determined to show Eileen what great friends I had.

When I walked into the kitchen Eileen jumped out of her chair, "Oh, my God, you've been in a fight."

"No, I'm fine, I went to Pete's Gym to clean out my locker and say goodbye and this," I held my arms out to the side, "is their way of showering me with love."

"You are an affectionate mess, Joe," Edna shared.

"I'm going to clean up. How was your day," I asked on my way upstairs. "I'll be right back." Upstairs the mirror revealed a raggedy mess that I pulled together and combed my hair. I was ready for dinner with the Kellys.

"Part of our day, Edna started, "was at Orlando's; the man is a charmer and his store a delight, and we bumped into Gabby and Suki."

"They said you, Joe, had laid a guilt trip on them and they might come tomorrow," said Eileen.

"I hope they do. Where's Bob?"

"Good question," Edna wondered.

"Edna, are you in the jet lag vortex?"

"Not yet, maybe I'll skip it or it will skip me."

"I'm sorry I'm late," Bob entered from the garage, "hello everyone, I ended up buying a new car," this as he kissed Edna and Eileen and patted me on the back.

"A new car, that's exciting; what kind of car," asked Edna.

Bob had moved to the bar in the living room, "Edna, a drink?"

"I already opened a Red wine, I'm good."

"Eileen? Joe?"

"Bourbon, rocks."

"Bourbon, same."

"An Oldsmobile convertible, light blue, it's in the driveway; the top is down."

Bob brought the drinks to the kitchen and we all settled around the table. "I almost forgot," Bob reached across the table and handed the keys to Eileen, "These are for you, from us, with love and congratulations for a job well done."

Bob raised his glass. We all did, "Congratulations."

Eileen took a sip and was out of her chair to hug, kiss and thank her mom and dad.

"The unfortunate part of being the boyfriend is you get gornisht! Surprised you, huh Joe; you marry a Jewish girl, you learn some Yiddish."

"But your daughter does not understand, Dad."

Edna was right there, "Gornisht means: nothing, nada, zilch."

"My gift from you, is your acceptance of me and, of course, what's her name," tilting my head toward Eileen.

"What's her name is going out to see her new car with her dad."

"One of the things I like about your daughter is you always know where she stands; there is no guess work with Eileen, and she knows how to argue; saves so much time."

Edna looked at me and smiled, "I hope this works out for the two of you; I would love you as my son-in-law."

I think I blushed, I'm not certain, but I expressed my gratitude.

Bob and Eileen returned with Eileen mumbling, "I'm sure that some people that can remember my name are going to enjoy riding with me in my new car."

"I am sure you're right, Miss Kelly."

We put the silliness aside and enjoyed a nice dinner; spaghetti with meat sauce and green salad. Eileen and I shared some, but not all, of our Acapulco experience and Edna and Bob told us tales of their time in Spain. When it was time for bed Eileen's parents went first and we followed shortly thereafter.

Eileen and I lay in bed and shared what almost amounted to disbelief; we were graduating from college at eleven the next morning and that a new, and even bigger chapter in our lives, lay ahead. Eileen shuddered and I held her very close until she settled into peaceful sleep. She was so very beautiful, and then I, too, accepted the joy of the day and the anticipation of tomorrow; I drifted off.

Excitement filled the air in the Kelly kitchen along with the delicious scent of eggs, toast and pancakes; Edna insisted we eat, "Next food 'up' would not be until two in the afternoon." In the middle of breakfast a messenger arrived with a large box and a note addressed to "Joe and Eileen. I read the note: "Dear Joe and Eileen, Congratulations and best wishes, Jerry, Martha and Celeste.

P.S. Congrats Bob and Edna."

I thought I was going to cry but I choked back the tears. In the box was a magnum of Louis Roederer champagne that Bob placed in the garage fridge. There was no time to explain the gift, nor did I want to intrude on the joy that was bubbling in the house at that moment.

We found our caps and gowns, Eileen and I shared a kiss, the three Kellys drove off to Douglass College, the Rutgers "sister" college, with Bob at the wheel of Eileen's new car and I set off for the stadium to line up with the other "G's" by ten o'clock. I was in time.

Lewis Webster Jones was the president of Rutgers and I know he spoke, as did the Provost,

Mason Gross; everything else was a big blur until my name was called and Dean of Men, Ed Draper, handed me my diploma and hugged me, no cigarette smell, way to go Frederic and Ed, and I was sure I heard Pete and Thelma chanting, "Joe, Joe, Joe!!"

"Joe," Bob Kelly was talking to me, "How about making a toast?"

I was holding a glass of champagne, Eileen was standing next to me and my mother was there along with a bunch of other people; "I would like to congratulate the future Doctor Kelly on the occasion of her graduation from Douglass College."

Everyone took a sip.

"I would like to propose a toast," it was Eileen's turn, "I have two men in my life; to my dad, thank you, thank you for everything, and to my guy, Joe, congratulations and thank you for being the amazing man you are."

Eileen and I were in a full eye-lock as everyone sipped and we stole a kiss.

"One more, one more, there are two moms here without whom we, Eileen and I, would not be; here's to Edna and Anne."

It was a wonderful party: lots of food, lots of good people, and lots of joy.

I made sure my mom met everyone and that my sister, Sylvia, and Al met Thelma and Pete because I knew they would hit it off. I realized that I had forgotten, maybe Eileen and I had forgotten, Caroline Hopkins, the Rutgers counselor who helped me so much. Richard, my roommate, was all over Gabby and Suki and the neighbors were all there; in fact they had gone to the Kelly's at noon and put the whole party together.

"Thank you Edna and Bob for including my friends and family."

"You're welcome, Joe," Edna said, "How many times are you going to graduate from college?"

"One more time, that should do it."

"Pratt?"

"Yes, Class of '58."

"I hope we are there."

"Can I give you a hug?"

"Sure."

"I hope you are there, too."

Right around five Syl and Al left with my mom; they had to take her home out on the island, they had a long trip ahead. Slowly the party stripped down to the neighbors, the Kellys and Eileen and I. A couple of times Eileen had whispered "upstairs, Joe," but I wouldn't; there was only one place for us and that was with her folks and the Rileys, the Crawfords, the Rosens and the Greens. After all, they had all warned me, "We'll be watching you!"

We were all out on the front porch enjoying a nightcap and a final toast to Eileen, followed by hugs goodnight and the neighbors drifted across the street.

"How about Eileen and I do a little cleaning up and you and Edna get some sleep?"

Bob looked at Edna who said, "It has ben a long and wonderful day and, yes, we are still on funny time, so thank you."

"Mom, our thanks to you and Dad; this was special. I love you both."

Eileen shared hugs and kisses with her folks and I got hugs. We all went into the house and then, as her parents started up the steps, Eileen and I did what we had practiced: simultaneously we said, "Hey kids, hold down the noise." We got smiles.

We gathered everything from the porch, the living room and dining room into the kitchen. We tossed any garbage, we put leftovers in the fridge, filled the dishwasher, started it and stacked everything else. During these simple tasks we managed kissing, holding, touching, unbuttoning, grabbing and small under garment removal. It was right about then that Edna screamed; we would never know if they were kidding; but we giggled.

Upstairs we brushed our teeth and very quietly celebrated each other.

Edna was up first and she emptied the dishwasher, refilled it, set the table and started some bacon. The aroma stirred the rest of us and we gathered for breakfast in the kitchen.

"Wonderful breakfast, Edna."

"Thanks, Joe. More pancakes, anyone?"

Bob was on his feet, "I can flip those, Edna. You sit and eat."

Edna joined us and within minutes Bob put a stack of pancakes at the center of the table.

"Joe, I want you to tell me about Jerry, Martha and Celeste?"

"Bob, these are really good pancakes," I said, stalling.

"I asked Eileen and she said you would have to tell me."

I finished the last bite and started,

"Jerry owns the "41" Club in New York, Martha is his wife and Celeste is their daughter who was my high school sweetheart."

"Jerry loves Joe like a son," Eileen added.

"Sending champagne was extremely thoughtful," Edna thought out loud.

"Eileen and I had dinner at "41", we were treated royally and when we were leaving,"

"He, Jerry," Eileen interrupted, "hugged me goodbye and told me I could bring Joe back any time I wanted."

"And then he hugged me and whispered, I never told you this Eileen, he whispered, "She's a keeper.""

"What happened to Celeste," Bob asked.

"That's none of our business," protested Edna.

"Thanks Edna, it's okay: I was sixteen, dating Celeste, my dad died suddenly in a railroad tragedy, I went upside down, drinking, angry, confused, my mother was in her own state of shock. Jerry and Martha welcomed me into their home whenever I wanted and it was a home, like this, filled with sense and sensibility that helped me get past the loss of my dad. Jerry's plan was, finish high school, graduate from college, marry Celeste, learn the restaurant business, join Jerry at "41", work hard and live happily ever after."

I stopped for a gulp of orange juice.

"Almost finished. Two years ago I called Celeste and then Jerry; I wasn't ready, I needed to "get my feet under me" and like and trust me. I switched my major to civil engineering, a doorway to becoming an architect, got a calculus tutor who changed the way I thought, I got my feet planted and I did three years of college in two years and one summer. Jerry and I stayed in touch, I became the son he never had and Celeste is engaged and getting married next year."

"Who," Edna wanted to know, "was your tutor."

"Gabby Evers."

"The model?"

"Yes, she was a child math prodigy and I credit her for helping me reset my thinking; intellectually and emotionally. Amazing woman."

"Now for the messy stuff; are you ready?"

"Bob, that was the messy stuff."

"I'm ready, Dad."

"Me too," I added.

"You are," began Edna, "asking each other to wait at least four years, maybe more, chasing your dreams, miles apart, while life moves full speed ahead around you."

"We have talked about that, Mom."

"And?" asked Bob.

"We talked about letting go and if we are meant to be, and I think we are, life will conspire to keep us together," I said.

"Have you thought about getting married, like now? Have you thought about changing your grad schools so you can live together and chase your dreams together, in the same city," asked Bob.

Eileen and I looked at each other; we had not discussed either option and told them.

"When your dad and I got married we knew this was it, for ever. I believe you love each other but I don't think either one of you is ready to marry."

"You're right," I said, "when you and Bob were here nine months ago we had just fallen in love and I was talking about being an architect in New York City and Eileen said, "okay, I'll be a doctor in New York." I can see that I have been sitting on the end result, not even thinking about the "we" of getting there. I love you Eileen but I have not thought beyond, "we'll be fine". Right now I am feeling a little immature."

"How about we take a break," suggested Edna.

"Good idea, come on outside, Joe, I'll show you the new car."

I waved to Eileen and Edna and followed Bob outside.

He put me behind the wheel and we talked about love and reality; he wanted me to know that he and Edna liked me, maybe even loved me and trusted me.

"That rests squarely on the shoulders of the letter Eileen wrote to us, about you declining sex with our daughter while she was drunk. We came home, met you, liked you and knew our daughter would be safe with you. We were right then and now we are scared for Eileen; she's going off on her own." Bob was shaking his head, "Do you think Eileen is an alcoholic?"

"I do, Eileen told me she uses alcohol to cover her fear. She is going off to Med school and she is afraid of dissapointing you and Edna."

"Damn, it's been hard for you?"

"I always told Eileen, "I am not the boss of you, this is your fight," but we have had our "too much booze" moments. I love your daughter, Bob, and I am scared for her and for us."

"Oh, boy!"

"That is exactly what we say in my family, Oh, boy."

"Joe, would you marry my daughter tomorrow if she was going to a med school in New York?"

"Yes."

"Knowing she is an alcoholic?"

"Yes."

"I don't know if that's the best thing for either of you? This is a conundrum."

"Bob, do you and Edna want, or need time alone with your daughter?"
"Lets go inside and put this all out on the table."

Edna and Eileen were sitting at the kitchen table; both had been crying.

"Eileen, will you marry me?"

"No."

"Will you switch med school to New York?"

"No."

"Do you love me?"

"Yes."

"What can I do to help you?"

"Come sit over here, next to me."

I did and Eileen took my hand and held it on her lap and kissed me on the cheek.

"You are breaking my heart." Edna was crying.

"Joseph," Eileen rarely called me Joseph, "I told my mom everything; everything that we are, everything we do together from dancing to loving to arguing to fixing us when we are broken, to your knowing "no" one step ahead of me and how my pride rules me and ruins us and how I fix the ruination with alcohol and escape from my own hell to heaven in your arms. Eileen burst into tears.

"It's me," I said, I pushed us too hard, too far, too soon; took us to places, real and almost imaginary, that most people don't dream of, I took us way past our emotional pay grade not to show off, but to be perfect for us. I forgot that we are just kids; kids with dreams."

"Together you have everything you need except life's experiences," Bob said.

"Edna, you said it, we are going to chase our dreams and life is going full speed ahead around us; but maybe, just maybe,"

Eileen pressed her finger against my lips, "No more."

"Are we giving up," I asked

"No, we are going to get our feet under us."

"Eileen, you talk in plural, yet you plan on singular paths," Bob observed, "and you, Eileen, face a challenge that calls for help from others."

"I know, Dad, not my strong suit. I am going to Johns Hopkins, I am going to become a doctor, I am going to seek help for my alcoholism, I am going to miss you, Mom and Dad, and I am going to miss you, Joe." Eileen was crying, almost sobbing and she was in my arms, her arms around my neck and our bodies pressed against each other.

Edna and Bob left the kitchen and Eileen managed, "I have to do this on my own, I want to grow up. I love you; I will always love you, Joe."

"I will always love you, Eileen; forever."

We kissed; so soft, so warm, so painful.

"I am going to go home and grieve and miss you, Eileen."

We let go of each other and, fighting my own tears, I managed to call out to Bob and Edna, "I am going to be leaving now. I have some stuff upstairs and a pile of things in the garage."

I came downstairs with a suitcase full of stuff and my cap and gown in my other hand; I lost it, tears streaming down my face.

"Put that stuff down, Joe, I'll take it to your car and I'll wait out there," Bob said.

Edna grabbed me and hugged me hard, "You are a great guy, Joe; I am rooting for both of you. Be well."

Eileen and I could not resist one last hug, each of us crying all over the other. We parted; there were no words.

Outside Bob helped me with a bunch of stuff stacked in the garage; we loaded up the car and we hugged.

"I have a favor to ask, Bob. When I get settled at Pratt I want to give you my phone number, I want to stay in touch."

"Absolutely, you are a member of this family until you're not."

"Thanks, that means everything to me."

"Edna will be very happy, Joe. Be safe and when you're ready for a new car, call me, I get them wholesale."

"Thanks. I love your daughter, Bob."

"I know."

I backed out onto Victoria Lane and waved goodbye to Bob and, I guessed, to Eileen Kelly.

THE KISS

PART FOUR

THE RUNNER

THE KISS

CHAPTER 27
HOME WITH MOM

On my way home to Rockville Centre I was filled with sadness; I would miss Eileen Kelly. I knew, however, if Eileen's folks had not been in Spain we would not have lived together for eight months and we would not have had the amazing intimacy that we shared. But we went far beyond intimacy; we were good together, happily 'married' in a fantasy kind of way. I was dizzy in my head with love and loss and my strong desire to become a responsible adult and an architect.

In a clear thinking moment I realized I had better call my mom and let her know I was coming home for a while. I stopped for gas and made a couple of calls while the service station guys filled the tank, added a quart of oil and cleaned the windows. I gave the attendant a twenty and asked him to move the car over to the phone booth where I would be.

Mom answered and she was surprised and excited that I was coming home; she wanted to know why and what was going on. I told her that we'd talk when I got home.

The attendant pulled my car over, gave me my change, I tipped him a buck, way too much, and I called Sylvia in the city. I wanted her to know that Eileen would not be at the wedding; Mom was going to be my date.

"Are you serious," my sister was shocked.

"Sad but true; we broke it off now instead of putting off the pain until September when we go off to grad school miles apart."

"I'm sorry to hear that, she's pretty special."

"Yeah, thanks. In two weeks you're going to be a married woman. Excited?"

"I am, I love Al."

"That's great. I'm at a gas station, I've got to get going."

"One last thing, I've been watching those want ads, like you asked, and there was one today."

"That's great; hold on while I get a pencil."

I had asked my sister to watch for anyone at Pratt looking for a room-mate.

"Okay, I'm ready."

"Rita Posinka and the phone is 565-5083."

"Thanks, Syl, I'll call her right mow. Hi to Al."

"Hello."

"Rita?"

"Yes?'

"My name is Joe Gordon and I would like to come and meet you about being room-mates?"

"You're a guy?"

"I am a guy."

"I wasn't thinking about a guy room-mate."

"I understand but I would like to meet so we might each consider the possibility."

"Hmmm, okay."

"Thanks, Rita, when is a good time for you?"

"Tomorrow."

"I'll be driving from Rockville Centre, how about eleven?"

"That's fine; this is a shift for me, so no promises."

"I understand, but if we do hit it off I have well placed people you can call for reference."

"Okay then, I'll see you at eleven."

She hung up and I called her back, "Rita, I need your address."

"Oh, yeah, sorry, it's 88 Bayview Place, Apartment 2B."

"Thanks, Rita, see you tomorrow."

Of course my mother was curious, she was at the Kelly's yesterday when

I was madly in love with Eileen; why was I coming home?

"Hi, Mom, where are you?"

"I'm upstairs, be down in about five minutes."

"Take your time, I have a ton of laundry to get going; I'll be in and out of the house."

I used the garage and created separate piles of laundry, stuff to go to the cleaners and a pile of question marks; keep or not. I had stuff in a suitcase that was clean and user friendly but I got a load of laundry going in the basement. When I came upstairs mom was in the kitchen and I hugged her hello.

"How are you doing, Mom; I haven't seen you since yesterday?"

"My son, the graduate, a year early; I am very proud of you."

"Thanks, Mom."

"The Kellys, nice people; Eileen, what's going on?"

"At a high level conference, over breakfast at the Kelly's this morning, since we are going off to separate schools in September, we decided to split up now, rather than prolong the pain. If Eileen and I are meant to be together, it will happen. Mom, I love Eileen, and I am in a world of hurt."

"I'm sorry and I'm a little relieved; she's Catholic after all."

"What she is, Mom, is smart, beautiful and, well, she's, um, Eileen; I love her, I am going to miss her and I'm going to get on with my life: next stop Pratt Institute; next goal, to be a certified architect."

"Joseph, you are becoming the man your father would be so proud of."

"Thanks, Mom, I'm working on it; I have had a lot of help from people who believed in me when I didn't. These past two years have been a hell-of-a ride."

Mom and I went out for dinner; we shared a club sandwich, I had a beer and mom a coffee. I told her I was looking for an apartment in Brooklyn near Pratt.

"Why not commute from home." Mom wanted to know.

"Two reasons: you're going to sell the house sooner or later and I don't want to influence the decision and because I want to be in the thick of things at Pratt; I want to know my classmates and be involved in every way. If I am commuting an hour each way that will never happen. Ideally I'll find someone to split the rent with; save some money and make a friend. I'm meeting someone tomorrow, you never know."

THE KISS

CHAPTER 28

AT PRATT I'VE GOT A ROOMMATE

I arrived at Bayview Place early enough to drive around the neighborhood; lovely tree lined streets, a mixture of single-family homes and small apartment buildings. 88 Bayview seemed to have two apartments on each of its three floors. I knocked at 2B.

"Whoa, six one!"

"No, Rita Posinka, six two."

"Sorry, you took me by surprise."

"That's okay, you must be Joe Gordon?"

"Yes, I'm Joe, thanks for being open to this possibility. Looks like a nice apartment."

"It is; two bedrooms, two baths, the kitchen and all this open living space. Pretty cool."

We walked together during the tour.

"One other thing, the owner is a really nice Jewish man."

"You could have two nice Jewish men in your life."

Rita cocked her head to one side, "Maybe, we'll see,

Let's sit."

Rita was tall, slender and attractive, brown hair in an easy to manage, over the ears cut. She was wearing sneakers, shorts and a T shirt; no pretensions there. I liked her easy- going manner.

"Rita, you're an athlete; volleyball, high jump?"

"I'm a runner. Every day."

"I just graduated from Rutgers and for the past two years I've been taking boxing lessons from four boxing crazy men who got me into running and jumping rope. Maybe we could end up running together."

"Boxing?"

"Yes, boxing, at Pete's Gym in New Brunswick, New Jersey."

"Why?"

"I was making some tough emotional decisions and wanted a physical release and I wanted to learn something new; I had no clue about boxing."

"I applaud you; my dad got me into running, he said it would sooth my mind but I think he was trying to get me out of the house."

"Out of the house?"

Rita hesitated and then, I think, she decided she could trust me.

"I've been tall for a very long time and when I was younger I was embarrassed; my peers called me, "Ears on spears" and other hurtful names."

"That was tough."

"Yeah, but by high school I could outrun everyone."

"I'm not going to run with you, no way."

"I'll bet you end up changing your mind."

"What made you change yours?"

"Not so fast; how do you see this going?"

"Separate bedrooms, separate bathrooms, respect privacy, no surprises and be there for each other when needed."

"I like you Joseph Gordon, I trust you; roommate?"

"Roommates, yes, I like you too."

We shook hands and I asked Rita, "How much?"

"Rent is three fifty, so one seventy five."

"Okay, starting July first. What about the phone, I won't be on it much but I need a number for my mom and I have two sisters."

"Okay."

"Two hundred a month, July first, share the phone. Can I buy you lunch?"

"No, but we can have lunch together. Come on, I'll introduce you to

Mel's."

Mel's had tables and a long counter; sandwiches and salads, milkshakes and Cokes and a griddle for burgers and bacon and eggs in the morning; open at six, close at six. Mel was okay, maybe a little cocky, and it was obvious, as she introduced us, he liked Rita.

"You be nice to her, Joe, or you'll answer to me."

"Rita is six two; you should be on my side, Mel."

"We'll see."

My ham and cheese sandwich was good and Rita let me taste her chocolate milk shake.

"Wow, that's really good."

"The best in town."

"Rita, how old are you?"

"You don't ask a girl her age, you goof-ball."

"I am not asking a girl, I am asking my roommate."

"Twenty six."

"Fill the gap?"

"After U. Mass, four years in the Army Corps of Engineers. I wanted to be a pilot and the Air Force declared me, Oversized."

"Yeah, but the Army Corps of Engineers; you built stuff."

"The first thing my platoon Sergeant said to me was, "Oh, good, we have someone to change light bulbs." After that I was called, The Bulb."

"I didn't know a woman was accepted for service."

"My dad was a big muckety muck and he pulled in some markers. I had a barrack to myself and some guys in my unit learned that I am very strong."

"Duly noted. Why Pratt?"

"We did build stuff, but it wasn't that; it was an overall sense that I acquired of design and planning and detail and sustainability and execution; that led to dreams of creating lasting buildings of value."

"I am impressed, Rita; that's got to be Architecture 101 in a nutshell."

"And you?"

"Almost a restaurateur. Almost joined the Army. Made some changes, switched my major from Arts to Civil Engineering and graduated two days ago, Rutgers, Class of '55. Now I am excited to become an architect at Pratt, Class of '58."

"Me too, but your story is in all of the "almosts" and what you said in my, our apartment; some tough emotional decisions."

"You listen, you pay attention."

"Well yes; a guy walks into my apartment who wants to do God knows what, so, yeah, I listen. Just so you know, it was when you talked about 'tough emotional decisions,' that I decided we were a go."

"Works all the time."

"Not funny, Joseph."

"I'm sorry."

"I want us to run together."

"I would like that as long as we both know I am not in your league."

"No sweat, you'll catch up."

I leaned over and took a quick look under the table, "I'm not so sure."

Back at the apartment I learned that I had a free parking place behind the building and I got a key to the apartment. I gave Rita a check payable to Jack Stein, dated July 1, 1955.

"I'll be bringing everything for my bedroom and I would like to add some furniture to the living space."

"Like?

"Like a sofa, an easy chair, a table, a lamp, stuff like that."

"Call Mr. Stein, he has a used furniture store about three or four blocks past Mel's, where we had lunch; it's a thought."

"I'll check it out, otherwise I will negotiate with my mother; she's going to sell our house, maybe, and move into Manhattan, maybe."

"Your dad?"

"He died in a railroad accident almost five years ago."

"I'm sorry, Joe."

"Yeah, me too."

We were quiet together, sitting at the kitchen table, looking at each other.

"Rita, I am excited about this; I am very comfortable with you."

"Me, too, with you."

"I've got to go but I want to tell you about Laura Duke; she took my hand and we walked into our first day of kindergarten together; she was the tallest kid in our class."

I went up the street to Mr. Stein's store and introduced myself; "I'm Rita's new roommate, Joe Gordon."

"Call me Jack, Joe. Nice girl, Rita, and she knows how to take care of herself; you two will figure out the roommate thing."

"I'm certain we will."

"How can I help you?"

"I'm looking for a table that I can use as a desk."

My eyes were scanning, "And that one," I said, pointing, "would be perfect if the price is right."

We had walked to the table, "Jack, you have a lot of nice stuff in your store."

"Young people like you come to Pratt, find a place to live, need furniture and then, three years later, they bring things back, usually in good condition, and I recycle stuff. The table is forty dollars."

"And I will need a chair like that one," once again pointing.

"Fifty dollars for both," he looked at me and winked, "such a deal."

I wrote a check to Jack Stein, used his phone and Rita was waiting downstairs to help me carry the table up to 2B. I brought up the chair, thanked my new roommate and took off for Rockville Centre. Lots of traffic, too much time to think and, of course, Eileen Kelly flooded my mind.

"Mom, I'm home."

"In the dining room; perfect timing."

Mom had her checkbook and bills and such spread out on the dining room table; talk about a big desk.

"Mom, you want some help with that?"

"Yes, I would like that, thank you."

I sat down next to my mother and found out what she really wanted.

"Did you find a nice place in Brooklyn?"

"I did, I am very fortunate, Mom; a nice apartment, near Pratt, and a very nice roommate."

"What's his name?"

"It's not a him, it's a her; Rita Posinka."

"How are you going to share an apartment for three years with a young woman that you just met?"

"She's five years older than I am, she was in the Army for four years, she's nice and there are two bedrooms and two bathrooms so privacy is assured."

"I don't know how you can spend a few minutes with someone and think everything is going to be fine?"

"Mom, a man named Jack Stein owns the apartment building, it's just six units, and if he accepted Rita as a tenant he did a lot of my homework. Relax, Mom, everything is going to be okay. What you can help me with is some furniture."

"That's not a problem, what do you need?"

"I figured the bed from the guest room with the pillows and sheets, blankets, the nightstand and lamp, that stuff and towels."

"Eileen called earlier."

"You're kidding."

"No she wanted you to know that her dad was driving her to Baltimore to find a place for her."

That just sucked the air out of my entire being; my getting settled was exciting, but hearing about Eileen was pure pain.

"Joseph, are you all right?"

"Yes. No, it hurts. I know she is getting on with her life; it just hurts. My mantra is, "If it's meant to be" and that's what keeps me going. Okay, where were we? Oh, yeah, an easy chair and a floor lamp. Oh, what about the small sofa in the den?"

"Whatever you need is fine."

"Mom, let's wrap up the banking and then we can walk around the house."

We did the statements and the bills; everything was to the penny. One of the bills was from Pratt and mom paid it out of her account; thank you Mom. Mom was wondering what to give Syl and Al as a wedding present; I suggested the same that she gave Gloria as a wedding gift.

"Yes, but I, we, are paying for Sylvia's wedding at the Pierre Hotel and Gloria's wedding was here, at the house, because of the accident, so I gave Gloria more. She shrugged and made out a check for a thousand.

There was a bill in the stack addressed to me; I had forgotten that I now had an account at "41". The bill, the statement really, showed a credit balance of two hundred dollars; Jerry gave me my two hundred back as a credit.

During the next few days I visited some high school friends including Celeste. It was good to see her and I met her fiancé, visiting from Boston. Her mom, Martha, hugged me and offered congratulations on my graduation.

"What graduation," Celeste inquired.

"I turned on my jets and graduated one year early as a civil engineer; I'm going to Pratt to become an architect."

"Oh, my God, Joe, that is fabulous, congratulations."

We hugged; this wonderful woman, who I had hugged a hundred times, was thrilled for me; that felt so good.

After I got home I went next door to say hello to John and Helen Miles who have known me since I was four.

I told them I had just graduated from Rutgers and was going to Pratt, in Brooklyn, to become an architect, so I'll be moving "stuff" to my apartment in Brooklyn.

"What kind of stuff, Joe?"

"A bed, a sofa, an easy chair, a floor lamp and some smaller stuff."

"How are you going to move your stuff," John wanted to know.

"Three or four trips with stuff tied down on the roof of my car."

John was smiling when he said, "I have a better idea."

"I love better ideas."

"Use my truck, I'll help you load it; I think you could do it in one trip."

I was in shock, "That would be awesome!"

"It's a graduation present."

"Thank you, and Helen, and for keeping an eye on my mom."

"You're welcome, Joe. You take the truck and I'll drive your car to my shop. At the end of the day we switch back and you can take whatever smaller stuff is left to Brooklyn in your car."

I called Rita for her help in Brooklyn and we set it up for Thursday. Everything was coming together.

Thursday, when I got back to Rockville Centre, my car was already parked in our driveway. I parked John's truck in his driveway and rang the doorbell.

"How did it go," asked John, coming down the outside steps.

"Everything went well. I filled the gas tank," I handed John his keys.

"High-test?"

"Yes, sir. I am very grateful, thank you, John."

"You are very welcome, I'm glad things went well. And these are your keys. Joe, your car drove like a brick so I tuned it and rotated the tires; you will feel the difference."

"I'll do better; thank you for everything."

"Goodnight, Joe."

"Goodnight."

I was fully moved into 2B before my sister's wedding and I was glad to have that out of the way. We now had a sofa, two easy chairs, a coffee table and a floor lamp in the living space. My bedroom was all set up and I put my table/desk and chair against the back wall of the living space. It all looked confortable and Rita, who helped get all the big items up the stairs, liked it a lot. When we were done we shared a beer and got a little silly; we sat in each chair and then tried the sofa and Rita suggested I pull my desk away from the wall so I could face the room. I did that and sat on the sofa. Rita sat right next to me and hugged me, "Roommates!"

"Roommates, yes and thank you for your help and for being you."

"It has been fun; we have created a little three year nest. I like it and I like you, Joe. The only thing left now is to get you running; we start after the wedding."

CHAPTER 29

MY SISTER'S WEDDING

"You are very handsome, Mr. Gordon."

"Thank you, Rita Posinka."

I was wearing a grey suit and tie; I had the honor of giving away the bride, my sister, to Alvin Myerson. I loved my sister and was thrilled for them.

"It is going to be a very long night, I may not be home until two or three in the morning."

"I'll be fine. Have fun, be safe."

"Thank you, Rita."

The wedding at the Pierre Hotel was lovely; the bride beautiful and the groom handsome. At the ceremony there were seventeen combined family members, the Rabbi, the Best Man and the Maid of Honor. A violinist played softly as I walked my sister down the short aisle. Before letting her go I kissed the bride to be on the cheek, probably the first time I ever kissed my sister. She gave me a big smile and I took my seat next to Mom. The service was short, as per the bride's wish. Al crushed the glass and the music swelled. Sylvia and Al kissed and we all stood and applauded. My Mom was crying and I whispered, "Dad is here in spirit, it's okay."

Everyone hugged and we retired to a larger room where twenty or so friends joined us for dinner and dancing. Syl and Al entered last as the violinist then played, "Here Comes the Bride."

What was neat, again, my sister's idea, the guests were lined up to receive the newlyweds instead of the other way around; it was quick and easy and different. Way to go Sylvia.

We were seated at five tables of eight, the food and service, excellent, champagne was cold, bubbly and delicious and the violinist low key and appropriate. The best man toasted the newlyweds who took to the dance floor. Al's dad was next to dance with the bride and then I did.

"You are a glowing and beautiful bride, my dear sister, I am very happy for you."

"Thank you, dear brother, I was very nervous and you were my rock."

"I thought I was the one that was shaking. I wish you years of good health and happiness."

I danced with my other sister, Gloria, who was pregnant with their second child; I walked her back to her hubby and danced with the Rabbi's wife; she was a terrific dancer and when the music stopped she curtsied her thanks and I bowed in appreciation.

The wedding cake was presented and Syl and Al shared the first piece and toasted each other. It was nice to see and hear them share their love for one another and then they danced into the evening and into life together.

The wedding couple departed to much applause and, suddenly, the evening was done.

People were leaving and I waited for Mom to call it a night, but she felt she was the hostess and we were there until the last.

While driving my mother home she was teary that Sam Gordon was not there. I agreed; I missed my Dad as well. At home Mom thought I should sleep there and go to Brooklyn in the morning. I begged off and kissed her goodnight.

Traffic was light for my trip to Brooklyn and I was content that my sister's wedding was, I believed, everything she had hoped for. They had deferred their honeymoon until the Fall and I wasn't sure if they spent the night at the Pierre or at their apartment; either way they were very happy newlyweds.

It was almost three in the morning when I unlocked the door at 2B and tiptoed to my bedroom; on the pillow was a note, "Welcome home"; I was flooded with memories of Eileen and her folks, but bottom line, I had a terrific roommate.

CHAPTER 30
THREE R'S: RITA, RUNNING AND RED SOX

"Tomorrow, Monday, we are up at six, dressed and stretched out, so we are ready to run by six fifteen, six twenty the latest." Rita's words, her early in the morning instructions, were loud and clear.

"Okay, Joe, let's go," and she was off. We had agreed Rita would set an easy pace and she would run in front.

"I want you to watch me run."

I was watching a graceful gazelle, every inch of her was effortlessly moving forward; she hardly touched the ground. I pulled up along side of her and she smiled, "You're my first, I've always run alone."

I nodded that I had heard her; "Run ahead of me, I want to watch you," Rita said, and I ran ahead. After a little while Rita ran next to me and it was a comfort to run together. By a little after seven we were back at Bayview.

"What did you think, Joe?"

"When I grow up I want to run like you."

Rita was stretching, she looked at me, smiled, and said, "Your growing up days are over, young man; there's no hope for you."

"Oh Great Gazelle, what am I to do?"

"Spend less time on your toes."

"Oh, really?"

"Yes, and that will move you along more horizontally; less up and down."

I must have looked pretty stupid because Rita spoke up,

"Pretend your foot is a hand pulling water while you are swimming. It's a game changer."

"Tomorrow at six I will be a champion," I offered.

"And a couple of days after that you will thank me."

"Yes, ma'am. How about breakfast?"

"Absolutely."

"You really are a beautiful runner."

"Thank you, and in just a few days you will be a very handsome one."

"Promise?"

"Yes."

By then we were upstairs and I was fumbling with the lock.

"Use your toes," Rita said as she took the key and hipped me aside, "Voila!"

"How about eggs and toast," I asked.

"How about Mel's after a quick shower?"

"Deal."

We closed our bedroom doors.

"Last one ready, buys," I heard through the door.

I didn't try to win; the hot water was heaven. I didn't take forever, either, and Rita was ready and waiting in her U. Mass sweatshirt and, as usual, shorts. Damn, she has nice, long legs. On the way to Mel's Rita announced, "I am going to order waffles, pancakes, eggs and bacon."

"Are you crowing because you can got ready in three minutes?"

"No, I am not crowing, I'm happy that we are going to run together."

"Yeah, I think I can get the hang of swimming while running."

"My high school track coach told me what I shared with you and, no pun intended, I thought he was pulling my leg."

"We'll see tomorrow."

"Good morning, Rita," said Mel from behind the counter.

"Mel, you remember Joe."

"Hi, Joe."

"Morning, Mel."

"What'll it be, Joe?"

"Eggs scrambled, bacon crisp, rye toast and orange juice. Thanks."

Rita's coffee and my orange juice were on the table seconds after we sat.

"Be nice to her," Mel said, smacking me on the back of my head.

"That's a one time thing, Mel."

"I certainly hope so," Mel said as he walked away.

"Are you paying him," I asked Rita.

"Her presence is payment enough, shot back Mel"

"Okay, enough is enough, Mel; Joe and I are roommates for crying out loud."

"That other guy, you kicked him out, Rita?"

"You're quick, that was a good one."

"This is Brooklyn, kid, get on the train."

And with that Mel brought us our breakfast.

"Joe, no more messing with you, I promise."

"Then I'll think I'm in the wrong joint."

"Enjoy, Kid, enjoy, breakfast is on me."

"Mel knew what you wanted for breakfast?"

"If it's breakfast I always have bacon, eggs over easy and coffee; any other meal I order what I want."

We were there for a long time; we had questions.

"Why no coffee?"

"I love the aroma but I don't like the taste. Everyone in my family drank coffee, but not me. I don't even like coffee ice cream."

"Tea?"

"Bourbon, beer, orange juice, champagne and water. My turn, your mom?"

"My mother? Hmmm, okay: very pretty, not very loving, left my dad when I was six, left a note and was gone. I have not seen her in twenty years."

"I'm sorry, I didn't mean to,"

"It's okay," Rita squeezed my arm, "we agreed, open book."

"Have you ever been married," I asked."

"It's not your turn, but the answer is, no, have you?"

"No, close, but smarter heads prevailed," I admitted.

"I get another," Rita said, "and we will be back on track. Are you currently in love?"

"Yes."

"Rita, When did you move into 2B?"

"May first. Where is she?"

"Johns Hopkins; becoming a doctor. What have you been doing since May one?"

"Running, getting to know Pratt and reading texts. Are you happy?"

By this time we were leaning into each other and whispering.

"Yes, I'm happy; I think we should go home and continue?"

"Absolutely."

I pulled out a ten to leave on the table; Rita put her hand over mine, "You will piss him off."

I put the ten away, "Bye Mel, thank you."

Mel was up to his elbows but managed a wave. Outside, on our way home, Rita took my hand, "Just pretend I'm Laura Duke." We squeezed hard, "Just to be sure you know, I am happy."

I was a good runner, according to Rita, and I was enjoying our early morning run. I was running easier, our pace was faster and we were up to five miles each morning; my roommate slash friend slash trainer promised we would settle in at ten miles; three weeks earlier I would have said, "No way," but we were getting there. We didn't talk much while we ran but the partnership was getting stronger each day. It was comfortable to run with Rita; there was nothing to prove. We both brought our best for a mutually rewarding experience.

Our friendship was deepening as well; we employed an "open book" policy that requires rigorous honesty that at times can cause uneasy moments but it was the way we both chose to be for each other.

I knew about Frank Collins, an on again, off again four year relationship that ended tragically; Frank died, a little over a year ago, in a small plane accident. Rita knew about Eileen Kelly and her parents' trust and ultimately their wisdom. I know that Rita's dad was twenty years older than her mom and they, Rita and her dad, don't enjoy a close relationship; barely managing to let each other know where they can be reached. Rita knows about my almost father-in-law and I know that Rita wants to learn how to fly and she knows that I do too. She also knows about Gabby, my calculus tutor and Rita pushed me through one of those "open book" uneasy moments when she asked, "Just your tutor?"

"We became friends."

"Just friends?"

"More than friends."

"How much more than friends?"

We were sitting on the sofa, "Do you want to share a beer?"

"Sure, I'll get it, you squirm."

Rita got the beer, took a swig; "Joseph?"

Rita handed me the bottle, I took a swig, "We became lovers."

"Gabby is a beautiful woman."

"So are you, Rita."

I gave the beer to her, she took a swig, "She's a world famous model, I'm an ex GI and an architect in the making."

"Rita, it's not what you do, it's who you are; you are a beautiful woman."

"Are you making a pass at me?"

Rita gave me the beer.

"Have you ever seen yourself run? Or stretch out? Or just out of the shower in your U Mass sweatshirt and shorts?"

"You are making me smile, pass or no pass."

"Gabby gave me a book for Christmas a year ago, "Architecture Since Man". I left it at her house for safekeeping but now I would like it to be here."

"Where does she live?"

"In New Brunswick, near Rutgers."

"I would have guessed New York."

"She lived in Paris for years but came home to New Brunswick and fixed up her family's old house."

"I shouldn't be surprised, it sounds like great therapy."

"She did a terrific job, the house is really nice. I'll get the book, I think we will have a grand time enjoying it together." I took a swig and passed the beer back to Rita.

"I would like that."

Rita took me to the Pratt campus and showed me around. We went a couple of times and being there became comfortable. The library is here, the bookstore is there, classes are here, here and here. There was a lab. I called it a lab, for putting things together and making models and such.

We were going to have the exact same schedule and Rita had all the texts but there were a few classes I felt, and Rita agreed, that having my own books would be best. We read and discussed every book and course; we wanted to be ready and we wanted to excel. We made a great study team.

We ran, we ate, we read and we talked. We talked not only about school but about everything, including sports. I was a New York Football Giants fan and Rita wasn't a football fan; she was a basketball junky, the Boston Celtics; really? We both liked baseball but I was a National League guy, the Brooklyn Dodgers, and Rita was an American League fan, the Boston Red Sox, of course.

We went to Nathan's for hotdogs and into the city one night for a couple of beers and a cheeseburger each, at P.J. Clarkes.

I drove East on 52nd Street so Rita could get a glimpse of the "41" Club: site of my almost job with my almost father-in-law.

We went to the beach; Coney Island a couple of times and Rita looked fantastic in her swimsuits; a snazzy one piece and a very small two piece that she filled out maddeningly well. We went all the way out on Long Island to Jones Beach. We both loved the ocean and we went during the week to avoid massive summer crowds. Rita liked Jones Beach with its endless white sandy ocean side, its very large pool and its various other entertainments; miniature golf, archery and shuffleboard. We staked out a spot on the beach to get some sunshine, talk and swim in the ocean. After lying in the sun for a while I started digging in the sand using my hands.

"Joe, what are you doing?"

"Almost done."

I did some more digging and reached out to help Rita get to her feet; she was puzzled until I asked her to stand in the hole I had dug.

"I'm not standing in there so you can satisfy your, 'I'm shorter than you complex.' No way."

"Come on, Rita, see what it's like for us little people."

"Okay, one time, Shorty."

We could actually see eye to eye and we started to laugh.

"You're not so tough now are you, Miss Posinka?"

"You know what's nice about this, Mr. Gordon?"

"What," I asked expecting some victory in this silliness.

"There's cool sand down here, you ought to try it."

"How tall are you down there?"

"Six foot three. There, the truth is out."

I helped Rita up and out, "I knew you were taller than six two; you are some kind of beautiful."

"Thank you, Joseph. How about a dip?"

We dove, side by side, into the first wave and when we came up we hugged; we each reached out for the other. In the ocean, soaking wet, it felt so good. We walked back to our towels holding hands. There were no words.

My mom and my sisters had my Brooklyn phone number and I had called the Kellys as well. I spoke to the office manager at "41" and gave them my Brooklyn address and phone number. Separately, I called Jerry to let him know about Eileen and that I had settled into a nice apartment, just minutes from Pratt, and the office had my address and phone number.

"Jerry, does "41" have any "juice" at Yankee stadium for a Yankee night game?"

"We have a box behind third base; you can have two seats for tomorrow night."

"That would be great."

"Ask Red, the outside doorman, to ask whoever is at the desk inside for an envelope with your name on it. Enjoy, Joe, and I am always here for you."

"I know, thank you. Bye, Jerry."

"You are wearing a big smile, Joseph."

"That's because I am about to ask you out to a baseball game at Yankee Stadium, tomorrow night."

"I would love to go to a game with you; who's playing?"

"I have no idea."

"Mel will know, he's a big Yankee fan; we'll go there for breakfast, my treat. How did you get the tickets?"

"I called my almost father-in-law to update him on what is going on in my life and asked if he had any juice at Yankee Stadium. The next thing I knew, we're going to the game tomorrow night."

"You know people, Joe."

"I do, I know you, Rita. How about a hug?"

"How about we talk about that?"

"Okay."

"Sit with me."

"Beer?"

"Sure; two."

I sat on the sofa with Rita; we tapped bottles and drank some Pabst Blue Ribbon.

"Joe, we are friends and roommates," Rita paused and swallowed some more Pabst.

"I know, Rita, I don't want to mess this up either; I'm guessing that's where you were going?"

I drank some Pabst; it was cold and good.

"Bull's eye, we've got a three year plan here; each of us wants to be an architect and I think we are an amazing team."

Rita had a swig of her beer.

"I agree, we are, and each day I appreciate you more, you are a beautiful person."

"You're room or mine?"

I finished my beer,

"You're messing with me, Rita."

"I am, but I'm not, we want each other, I'm sure of it, and it's straining our integrity," Rita said, and finished her beer.

"There are so many reasons to refrain."

"Do you think we can keep it to making out," asked Rita.

"Let's go to the Laundromat," I suggested, "we can't get into any trouble there."

"No, let's find out right here, right now," Rita insisted.

We kissed, big and long and great; an amazing Pabst Blue Ribbon kiss.

"WOW, Joe, how can you do that when you are in love with someone else?"

"How? Good question; how can I run with you and enjoy it as much as I do? How can we share the comfort that we enjoy in everything we do? How can I go to the beach without you, or to the game tomorrow night? Rita, we happened in the blink of an eye; we are in a unique three-year plan, we are attracted to each other and I am in love with Eileen! I want to wait for the phone call."

"You lost me?"

"Eileen is an alcoholic and if she's drinking she will call me one night, outrageously drunk; her headstrong, loving way of telling me she is losing her battle with alcohol and I will stop praying for this once in a lifetime woman and I will let go, weep and move on."

"I'm sorry; can I give you that hug?"

"I would like that."

"If we get a chance, what if we're not good in bed," Rita mused, while in my arms.

"Then we'll stick to kissing and running and reading and studying and,"

"So you're saying we'll be fine," Rita interrupted.

"No doubt about it."

That next morning we were up at six for our run; we hugged before leaving the apartment.

"Damn you're tall."

"Get used to it, Joseph."

Outside we stretched out and then had our best run ever; we were doing seven-minute miles, or eight miles in under an hour. We celebrated at Mel's.

"Morning Rita, morning Joe, one coffee and one orange juice coming up."

"Good morning, Mel," we managed in unison.

He arrived with our beverages a few moments after we were seated.

"Hey, Mel, who are the Yanks playing tonight," I asked.

"Are you kidding, the Red Sox; big game, the Yanks are hot!"

"The Red Sox, I can't believe it; Joe is taking me to the game."

"Tell Mel who you are rooting for, Rita."

"The Sox."

"Five bucks versus a kiss on the cheek, Rita, whadda you say?"

"Deal," Rita said.

"You're going to need a soap box to deliver that kiss, Mel."

"It's vice versa, smart aleck."

"Your breakfast, madam," Mel announced with a flair.

"What about me, " I asked.

"Oh, I'm sorry, I never heard you order," Mel said as he produced a plate he had momentarily placed on an adjoining table.

"Enjoy, just pulling your leg."

"Thanks, Mel."

We took the subway from Brooklyn to lower Manhattan and another subway up to seventh and forty-eighth. We walked east to "41" on 52nd Street. Red got my envelope and we walked to the east side for the subway to the Bronx and Yankee Stadium. It was an underground adventure; we asked a lot of questions and got a lot of help and made it to the stadium in time.

I suggested that we get seated; great seats close to the field by third base.

Rita was in heaven; she had never been to a major League game and this was Yankee Stadium for crying out loud!

"We will watch a couple of innings and then I'll get us a couple of beers and hot dogs. Rita was clutching my hand; we were in the middle of all the action.

"Joe, this is a night to remember, thank you."

Rita was wearing a dark blue, little summer dress; very short, revealing those long, lovely legs. A night to remember, indeed; it was exciting to be there together.

We were sitting in the "41" box for four and the two seats behind us were empty. In the bottom of the second inning a voice right behind me asked, "Are these seats taken?"

I turned around and there were Jerry and Martha Brown.

"Oh, my God, Martha, Jerry; I can't believe it!"

Rita, of course, turned around as well. Jerry and Martha each carried a cardboard tray with two beers and two hotdogs; Martha offered her tray to Rita, "These are for you."

"Rita I want you to meet my almost mother and father-in-law, Martha and Jerry Brown; this is Rita Posinka, my roommate. For two minutes the four of us had no idea that a baseball game was underway despite the cries of, "Down in front!"

Martha and I switched seats, leaving Martha and Rita sitting in front of Jerry and me.

"All these years and this is my first major league baseball game," Martha shared with Rita.

"Same for me," Rita said, "and I am a Red Sox fan. This is a treat, thank you."

Jerry handed me a hotdog and a beer, "Joe, Martha was in the city and I told her I had a surprise for her; it turned out to be a double header, you and the game."

"Jerry, this is a thrill, thank you for the tickets and for your being here. Rita gets a chance to meet you; she's quite a woman, a future architect, going to Pratt, who advertised for a roommate and we hit it off."

"I am happy for you. No word from Eileen?"

"No word. Jerry, she's an alcoholic; she admits it and her parents know as well. I am scared for her; she is very head strong and she is the only person that can take care of her disease."

"Rita?" Jerry looked at me.

"Fabulous woman: U. Mass, Army Corps of Engineers, for four years, six years older than me, very smart and she's a runner; we are up at six and running eight miles every morning.

"Living together?"

"Two bedrooms, two bathrooms, total privacy, total trust."

"Your hotdog is getting cold," Jerry picked up his beer, tapped Rita on the shoulder; Jerry raised his beer, "Joe says you are very special; here's to you, best wishes in all your pursuits."

"Thank you, Jerry; this woman was just saying nice things about you."

"Imagine that."

Jerry and Martha left at the end of the sixth inning and Rita and I huddled together and shared the joy that Jerry and Martha had brought during their four-inning visit.

"They love you, Joe."

"I know; they helped me to begin understanding love after my father's death. I went upside down, filled with pain, fear and loneliness and they took me into their hearts as if I was their own son."

"I think you are the son they never had."

"I am doing everything I can to deserve their love."

"This is an evening I will remember forever, Joe."

"I, as well."

"Thank you for pushing me into being roommates."

"Thank you, Rita, for pushing back."

The Yankees beat the Red Sox five to three and Rita kissed Mel on the cheek the next morning. All of us were winners.

CHAPTER 31

AN ARCHITECTURAL DESCRIPTION

"I'm going to New Brunswick to visit Gabby and get my book; do you want to come with?"

"Tempting, I was going to do laundry."

"Come on, we can do laundry any time."

"We?"

"Yes, as in you and me."

"I, Joe, you and I; I am going to do laundry."

"Okay, you know where my laundry bin is."

"Nice try, Joe. Be safe. When?"

"Three hours, four max. Bye."

"Bye."

I pulled into Gabby's driveway and sat in the car for a couple of minutes; I thought back to the first Saturday I arrived for breakfast a thousand memories ago. I could feel my head turning from side to side; it was almost impossible to imagine the past two years.

"You okay, Joseph?"

Suki startled me; she had come out to greet me.

"Yes! Yes I'm fine."

I got out of the car and into Suki's arms.

"Come, we share beer, Gabby home ten minutes."

Inside Suki said, "kiss?" and her lips were on mine before I could answer.

"You not okay, Joseph."

"I am. I am happy to see you; I'm a little melancholy, that's all."

"New word for Suki."

"Sad, not unhappy, emotionally tired; it's an in between place."

"Melon kolly, funny."

"Sad funny; that's what it is, sad funny."

We had been walking up the steps and into the house.

"You look strong, Joseph."

"I've been running every day, and look at you, pretty as ever."

"You make me blush, Joseph."

"And Gabby, how is she?"

"Gabby good," and on cue my calculus tutor was in the door, putting down groceries and coming into my arms; I hugged her tight.

"You haven't heard from Eileen, have you?"

"How do you know these things? Both of you."

"Your eyes," said Suki, putting food in the fridge, "Joseph melon kolly. New word for Suki."

"I'm okay, a little up in the air is all."

'Feet on ground, Joseph, head in clouds."

"Exactly, I want the clouds to go away, I want to know what is going on."

"What's going on with Eileen; you love her, she loves you but the demon is in the way. Not knowing, that's the crazy maker," Gabby laid it all out.

"She has my number and I'm certain she will call; I have to wait and see."

"Stay for dinner, then we can do some dancing?"

"Thank you, Gabby, but no, I want to beat the traffic and I have laundry to do."

"We miss you, Joseph."

"Make me mellon kolly," added Suki.

"Thank you, Suki."

"I put the book by the front door, Joseph, I hate to see it go; it's 'you' being here even when you are not."

"Book is not Joseph, Joseph here," Suki said, touching her chest.

"I love you both. Friends forever?"

"Yes," they both said.

It was almost six when I leaned the book against the coffee table.

"Rita," I called, "I'm home."

"Grab us a couple of beers, I'll be right out."

"Okay. I'm going to wash up."

On my bed was my laundry; clean and folded. I washed up and went to the kitchen for those two bottles of Pabst Blue Ribbon.

"Rita, thank you, the laundry, what a nice surprise."

I spoke loud enough for her to hear. Rita had quietly come into the kitchen and was almost next to me.

"You're welcome, it was fun; men's laundry is simple, buttons and zippers. Women's has shoulder pads, zippers, buttons, straps, hooks and snaps."

"My shirt, I think that's my shirt on your body; it only has buttons, none of which you have chosen to use."

"What are you trying to say, Joe?"

"Here's your beer."

"One of the buttons was missing; what was I supposed to do?"

"Let's put it this way, my shirt has never looked this good. Not ever."

"My pleasure."

"Mine as well; shall we sit on the sofa?"

"I'm not totally sure I can."

"I've never had a problem, Rita."

"Fine."

Rita crossed her legs and sat at the same time; mission accomplished.

"Here's to missing buttons and beautiful women."

"Thank you; this is fun."

We touched bottles and drank some Pabst. I could hardly swallow.

"I have a confession," Rita said and for the first time that I had ever noticed, she seemed unsure of herself.

"Number one, I hope you don't mind that I went into your room?"

"Not at all; open book, no secrets, no surprises."

"Number two, I saw Eileen's picture on your dresser and she is beyond beautiful. Number three, you were getting your book from Gabby Evers, the most beautiful woman in the world and I was thinking, because I like you very, very big, how do I even fit in?"

"Stop, Rita, stop. Drink some Pabst, and listen up; you are Rita Posinka, you are unique, you are smart, caring, a gifted runner, and you are a beautiful woman, all seventy-five inches of you. Now stand up and give me my shirt."

"Okay, you listen up, Joseph; this is not your shirt any more, it's my shirt and I am not taking it off. And thanks for the nice words; I'm sort of embarrassed."

"Are you hungry?"

"Starving."

"I stopped and got us a sandwich at Orlando's in New Brunswick; it's a special grocery store and he, Orlando Sideri, doesn't make sandwiches but he did me a favor; paper thin sliced prosciutto, Jarlsberg cheese, lettuce, tomato and Italian dressing on French bread."

"I'm in."

"I will serve you, my little laundress. Do we have any candles?"

"I do, I'll get one."

"Okay, kitchen table; you are not competing with anyone, Rita, you are perfect just the way you are."

During our candle light dinner, the sandwich, delicious by the way, I started thinking ahead; making do with making out was not going to be easy.

After dinner Rita led me into her bedroom, "I vote for looking at the book tomorrow."

"I agree, are we going to look for the missing button?"

"You have a way with words, Joe, but until the phone call we are going to do everything but!"

The next day we leaned the 17 inch by 20 inch book, "Architecture

Since Man", against the coffee table, turned on the floor lamp and took a trip through centuries of design and accomplishment:

Homes, from caves to "Falling Water", Frank Lloyd Wright's masterpiece, outside of Pittsburgh, churches including, Notre Dame in Paris, arenas, early Egyptian pyramids, mosques, and temples.

The book itself is a work of art and each page provoked, oohs and aahs and discussion.

We continued:

Castles, Greek and Roman phenomenon, the Parthenon, Temple of Athena in Greece, the Coliseum in Italy, Mayan temples, pyramids and buildings in Guatemala and Honduras, Aztec edifices in Mexico, museums, colleges, office buildings; The Empire State building in New York.

When we turned the page to the Taj Mahal in Agra, India, a note fluttered to the floor; Rita picked it up, "This is my favorite; "Serene beauty exerting max power."

Rita looked at me, "Gabby?"

"Yes, a note from Gabby. She was out of town and left notes everywhere for me to discover. It was sweet, like your note welcoming me home after my sister's wedding."

"Gabby's was more of a love note."

"Well, the Taj was a gift of love."

"I thought the sandwich you brought home for us was a gift of caring."

"And that was before I knew that my shirt was going to be more beautiful than the Taj Mahal."

"I am not the serene beauty type, Joe. What do you think Gabby meant;'Exerting max power'?"

"Being comfortable in your own skin; that's max power. Architecturally it is function, design, sustainability and execution; for example, I would never put starch in my/your shirt, it would inhibit its beauty and function."

"And I would never use the buttons as designed."

"Let's mark the page with that note and look for the missing button."

"Deal."

"I'll get the beer."

THE KISS

CHAPTER 32

LIFE IS MOVING ON

On the first day of classes it was drizzling so we walked to school under my large, colorful, golf umbrella and I held it aloft to accommodate my taller companion, "I've got you covered, Rita."

"That's good 'cause I'm a little nervous; it has been almost five years since U. Mass."

"Hold my hand and pretend you are Laura Duke, it will work like a charm for both of us."

Rita slipped her hand into mine; it was warm and comforting, we both smothered a giggle and climbed the steps to the Admin building where we would meet our classmates, a professor or two, listen to what was coming our way over the next three years and take a tour of the campus.

During that first week, as Pratt sorted out our class, Rita and I received a great opportunity; we were able to join the fifteen or so Class of '55 Bachelor of Arts in Architectural graduates who were proceeding in a two year Masters in Architecture program; Rita because of her accomplishments during her four year stint in the Army Corps of Engineers and I, because of my high grades and my Bachelor of Civil Engineering degree.

We could graduate in '57 and we would be able to be summer interns between our first and second year.

We were comfortable together, trusted each other and helped one another in our studies and in life. We continued to run together every day and we gave it everything needed to graduate with a Masters Degree in architecture, Class of 1957.

In our quest to be architects we amassed a huge amount of knowledge:

Environmental systems, architectural design, building science, and technology; we were off to a good start.

Eileen called early in October of the first year; it was awful, she was crying, breathless and drunk.

"Joe, gasp, Joe, I'mmm dr, druk. I'mmm sutcha whooore, gasp, love sex, gasp, I'msosorry, I'msosorry, sooo sorry." She hung up and I sat there with the phone in my lap, listening to the dial tone. I cried, I cried for Eileen, I cried for me, for the world; the world was losing a once in a lifetime woman to alcohol.

I called Edna in New Brunswick, Bob answered; at first I couldn't speak.

"Hello, hello?"

"Bob, I'm sorry, this is Joe Gordon, I just heard from Eileen and," I started to cry again.

"Joe. Joe, tell me, please."

"She was drunk, sad, sorry; very drunk, condemning herself and hung up. I'm sorry, Bob and Edna, oh, God, I don't know what to say."

"It's okay, we miss you. We will do everything we can; you can be sure of that."

"I know." I hung up.

"Joe, I'm sorry," Rita said.

"I know."

"I am here for you."

"I know."

Rita went into her room and gently closed the door.

I sat there feeling Eileen sitting on my lap, kissing me that first kiss she didn't want to wait for. I didn't know she was kissing me goodbye.

The year went on, life went on, school went on and Rita and I continued to run and learn and live together. It was strange in a way; we were a finite partnership, when school would end, we, most likely, would be done as well.

It was fitting; come on, we were going to be architects: you design a building, you watch it being built, you love it and when it is done you move on. Rita and I would move on, separately, as friends; we would each join a firm, perhaps where we intern.

Rita joined me, and my family for Thanksgiving at my sister Gloria's house in Glen Cove. It was nice for all of us to be together and Al, my sister Sylvia's husband, cornered Rita, "So, what's this roommate baloney all about?"

"Sex, 24/7 and we run 10 miles together every morning. Oh, yeah, one other thing; we study together."

"Is that so," more of a statement than a question.

"How about you and Sylvia, you getting much?"

"I can't answer that but it seems to me you were forewarned."

"Joe, being the good guy that he is, gave me a heads-up on everyone. Al, as you can well imagine, it isn't easy to walk into a room filled with family; and if you're six foot three, it's even harder."

"I like you, Rita, you've got, you know."

"I don't have those, but I have other assets."

Al smiled and shook his head, "I like you a lot."

Rita bonded with Steven, Gloria's son, who was now two and a half. Steven repeatedly took hold of Rita's pinky in order to lead her to his toy chest and take them, one at a time, to some other part of the house; they were Mutt and Jeff to the max! On the way home to Brooklyn Rita, who was exhausted, wanted to know, "Where does he get so much energy?"

When we got home Rita asked, "Share a Pabst?"

"Great idea. Sofa, two minutes." I went to my room, kicked off my shoes, brushed my teeth and splashed my face with cold water.

"My family likes you, Rita, even my mother," I said, sitting next to Rita on the sofa.

"I like them, even Al; he's tough."

"Thanks for going with me."

She took a good pull on the Pabst, "My pleasure, Joe. She gave me the bottle and said, "I want you to sleep with me tonight."

"Mind reader."

"Sleeping together will be good for both of us."

"I'm in."

"Give me a couple of minutes," Rita said.

We hadn't touched since Eileen's call and Rita was giving me all the time and room I needed.

After a while I turned off the lamp and followed the flickering candle light into Rita's room.

"Take your clothes off, Joe, I'm way ahead of you."

We held each other, we kissed and touched; then held hands and fell asleep.

In the morning it was pouring; there would be no running so we found a wonderful way to work out; we found the button, right where we both knew it would be, and we celebrated. Thank God for thunder and lightning.

At Christmas, actually the day after, we held a "Beer and Pizza" party for any of our classmates that were going to be "stuck" in Brooklyn and nine guys showed up; so it was ten guys and Rita. We shared a common denominator; architects all, but it was so interesting to learn how different our special interests were: from hospitals to armories to homes to office buildings to churches; we surprised one another with our diversity.

On New Year's Eve day I placed a call to Frank Stetter at Las Colinas in Acapulco, Mexico. The connection was superb; Frank sounded like he was around the corner.

"Joe, this is great, how are you?"

"I'm fine, Frank, and I could not let this day pass without my wishing you a Happy New Year."

"Thank you, I wish you the same. Joe, I hear singular wishes?"

"Yes, sadly, alcohol has come between us."

"I am so very sorry."

"Me too. Frank, a favor?"

"Anything."

"Be my envoy with best wishes to Edie, Sammy, Marti, Lumet, Claudio, Eduardo and Miki; I love and trust you all."

"Of course, and we will drink to you; we love and trust you, Joseph."

"Thank you, Frank." "Be well, my friend."

It was done; memories for a lifetime.

Rita and I enjoyed a Pabst Blue Ribbon New Year's eve. We listened to music and I learned Rita was not a dancer; "There were never enough tall guys to ask me to dance and the little guys were too embarrassed."

For a split second I drifted off to Acapulco and was dancing with Eileen.

'Where were you, Joe?"

"I'm sorry, but I'm here now, Miss Posinka, care to dance?"

"I would rather go for a run."

"We did that this morning; it's time to face the music. You taught me how to run, I will teach you how to dance."

"Fine."

"Fine, that's your give in word; you don't want to do something but you give in, "fine."

"Okay, Mr. Smarty, what's next?"

"I'm changing the record, I want something slow and sexy. Take off your sneakers."

"Seriously?"

"Yes, we want to glide, not scuff."

Sinatra was leaving his heart in San Francisco when I took Rita in my arms; we glided.

"I can go forward, backward for you, small steps in rhythm, or a small square; that's good for a crowded dance floor like it is tonight."

"I like this."

"If I was shorter I could rest my head on you breasts; if I was taller all our body parts would line up better."

"I think we're doing very well."

"I could hold you closer, like this."

"I like this."

"Wait 'til we do the Lindy, the Charleston, or the Cha Cha Cha."

"Who taught you, Joe?"

"My sister, some, but high school mostly. I used to say 'I'm not much of a dancer,' until I realized I was doing fine. You, Rita, are dancing very well."

Rita kissed me, a very serious kiss, "Happy New Year, Joe; I have never been to a big New Year's Eve party like this."

"That makes two of us and two is the perfect number for New Year's Eve."

"You're happy?"

"I am. To quote a good friend of mine, I like you very big."

In the morning we took our first run of '56; it was cold and wonderful; I loved running with this woman. Rita Posinka taught me how to run and I realized she was teaching me, or together we were learning, much more.

CHAPTER 33

THE TRUTH BE TOLD

Back to school and we were kicking ass; I'm not bragging, we were bringing everything we could to the party; reading, studying, talking, more studying and more talking, or arguing, as Gabby used to say.

Calculus was added to the course mix along with visualization,

Urban design and Creative design. We had poster boards all over the living room and rulers, T-squares and balsa wood, Xacto knives and glue; we were making models. On the sly I was making my own version of a Taj Mahal for Rita; more of a house than a palace.

I stayed in touch with my Rutgers roommate, Richard, and Gabby and Jerry at "41".

Early in each month I visited my mom to help around the house and look over her checkbook and help balance it or write checks if needed. On spring break in April, Rita came with me to my mom's.

Driving through Brooklyn I stopped at a florist's and picked up a vase of fresh flowers. When we arrived at my mother's she was surprised I had company.

"Rita, this is terrible, I'm not even dressed."

"You look fine, Mrs. Gordon, there's no reason to dress up for me. These are for you," Rita said, handing my Mom the vase.

"Thank you, Rita, they are beautiful. Joe, would you mow the back yard for your mother?"

"No, but I'll go over your books while you and Rita take a short walk and talk about me. We're going out to Montauk, so we can't stay."

"We'll walk to DeMott and back."

"Walk fast, this won't take very long."

"Rita, are you and Joe,"

"Joe and I," Rita interrupted, "are friends and room mates; we like each other, we trust one another and we study together. Joe is smart, he excels because he wants to be a topnotch architect. You should be very proud of him."

"I am. Is he over Eileen?"

"I believe so."

"Do you love him?"

"Of course."

"Does he love you?"

"Of course."

Rita saw that they had reached DeMott Avenue and turned my mother around.

"Mrs. Gordon, let me tell you about our love; we love to run every morning, ten miles; we love to study together, go to school together; we trust each other and we care for one another."

Almost back to the front door they stopped and Rita looked down at my mom, almost a foot shorter, "Tonight and most likely a lot of other nights, I am going to sleep with Joe and a year from June he and I will graduate from Pratt and you, I hope, will be there, after which Joe and I will separate, work apart, live apart and be friends forever."

"Really?"

"I am sure of it."

On the way to Montauk I asked Rita, "How did it go out there?"

"It went great, your Mom is sweet."

"What did you talk about?"

"The flowers."

"The flowers? Got it; thanks, Rita."

CHAPTER 34

HOORAY FOR THE CLASS OF 56

Early in May I called Gabby and asked for a big favor; Gabby assured me it would be her pleasure; thank you, Gabby. I sent her everything she needed.

Very early in June I convinced Rita to spend the next Saturday with me; no questions asked, dress super pretty casual and be prepared for a very long day.

"Good morning, Rita."

"Mmmm, morning, Joe."

We wrapped up tight, neither of us wanting to get out of bed.

"Come on, Rita, we have to get going." I slipped out of Rita's grasp and uttered the magic word; "Run, Rita, we need to run," I was in my room, pulling on my sneakers, "It's going to be a very long day."

"Last night was delicious."

"It was," I called out.

"And there are some mornings when you don't want to let go of the night before."

I was standing in her doorway, "I'm going to run without you."

"And I'm going to give you a five minute head start."

"Rita!"

"Okay, okay."

I watched Rita get out of bed, feet and long legs aiming for the floor.

"You're pretty."

"And you are a peeping Tom."

"I want to watch you get dressed."

"Go away."

"Fine, to quote a friend."

It was a marvelous morning; slight breeze, not too warm and we had a good run; more talky than usual and we laughed a lot as we verbally poked at one another.

Back at Bayview Rita said, "Good run."

"Not as good as last night."

"Braggart."

"I was thinking about you, Miss Posinka."

Rita was stretching and looked up at me and smiled, "You were pretty good, yourself, Joe."

We were in the Lincoln Tunnel when Rita asked, "What's up in Jersey, Mr. Gordon?"

"For starters," I took a quick glance at my watch, "we can see the guys at Pete's Gym; put you in the ring for a couple of rounds."

"Boxing?"

"Yes, ma'am."

Our timing was perfect; all four men were in the ring.

"What are they doing," Rita wanted to know. I put my finger on Rita's lips and whispered,

"They are doing what we call, the merry-go-round; any man can hit any other man, so you have to have good balance, good footwork and great vision. Someone can step on your toe just as someone else hits you or you are trying to hit someone else. It's intense even though the punches are what we call, "Cupcakes" or soft punches."

"You've done that," Rita whispered.

"I have," I whispered back, "many times, and it is that much harder when it's five guys."

"Stop!" It was Pete; he had seen us, "We have guests."

"We don't want to stop you," I said, taking Rita's hand and leading her toward the ring.

"It's Joe," Art said. "Hey, guys, we only have a few minutes but I wanted to say hello and I want Rita to meet the men she has only heard about."

Pete stepped through the ropes, all sweaty; they had been at it for quite some time; Pete pulled off his right glove and reached out to shake Rita's hand and punched me with his left. I was ready and stopped his punch.

"Welcome, Rita, Joe here couldn't have stopped my punch if he was never part of one of these."

"Rita Posinka, I want you to meet Pete and that's Art and Jimmy and Boozer."

"Joe, it has been a while," said Jimmy, still in the ring.

"So, Rita, are you Joe's personal trainer, he looks to be in great shape," Boozer inquired.

"We run ten miles every morning; we are friends and we are both going to be architects."

"Well, it's obvious Joe looks up to you, Rita," Pete said trying to be funny.

"Yes, but he doesn't have as far to look as you, Pete."

"You're quick, Rita," Pete acknowledged.

"Only when I want to be," Rita said, raising an eyebrow.

"Rita taught me how to run and that's what we have to do now."

"We are big kidders, Joe'll tell you. I'm glad you both stopped by," Pete said.

Jimmy, Art and Boozer shook my hand and said nice things to Rita.

"What happened to," Pete started, but before he could finish Boozer, from behind, put his hand over Pete's mouth and kept it there until the door closed behind us.

"What's with Pete," Rita wanted to know.

"You never know who you are going to get, but at his best Pete is okay."

"Today was not his best; he's jealous of you, Joe."

"I guess; but he knows boxing, that's for sure."

We drove to Rutgers Stadium for the graduation ceremony of the Class of 1956. My roommate, Richard, and friends Noel and Max were graduating; this was going to be my year as well until I accelerated. I was glad to be there and we were just in time. We listened to the tail end of the keynote speaker and then shouted and cheered for Richard, Max and Noel. Rita was a great partner; on her feet and cheering like crazy. We chose to exit before the mainstream to beat the traffic and because we were starving.

"What's next, Joe?"

"We are going to Gabby's by way of Orlando's; you get to meet the stars of my Rutgers past and I get to say my goodbyes.

"My goodness, Mr. Joe, you came to see me."

Orlando came around the counter and we hugged.

"Orlando, I want you to meet my dear friend, Rita Posinka."

Rita was immediately enveloped by Orlando, "It is my pleasure, Miss Posinka."

"Mine as well, Orlando and a chance to thank you for making a delicious prosciutto and cheese sandwich for us months ago."

"You remember!" Orlando stepped back and beamed, "Mr. Joe, she's got it." He tapped his head.

"We are going to Gabby's but not without stopping to see you, my friend."

"I turn off the stove, okay?"

"Sure."

Orlando disappeared into the back room and I picked up a basket of flowers; I put a ten-dollar bill on the counter.

When Orlando returned he asked,

"What is this," referring to the ten.

"For this basket of flowers I'm taking to Gabby."

Orlando instantly started waving his hands in front of his face, "No, no, no;" he gave me the ten, "the flowers are from me to Miss Rita, if she gives them to Miss Gabby," he shrugged, "so be it."

On our way to Gabby's I asked Rita, "Are you ready for this?"

"Joe, do we run together?"

"Yes, every morning."

"This is running together, Joe. The pace and the place are different, but this is running together."

There were no words.

The gathering at Gabby's was an emotional, spiritual and intellectual circus of the happiest and healthiest order. Hugging, inspired by Gabby, way back when, began with Suki hugging me when she came out to the car.

"Suki, this is my friend, Rita Posinka." It took Suki two seconds to embrace Rita and it took the two of them another two seconds to imagine what they looked like, Rita being a foot or more taller than Suki.

We went inside and Gabby and I hugged and kissed and then I was able to say, "Gabby Evers this is my very special friend, Rita Posinka; they hugged and out of the corner of my eye I saw Caroline Hopkins. I hugged my Rutgers counselor before introducing her to Rita.

"What a moment; I am here with four of the most important women in my life: Gabby, you believed in me when I did not; you helped me change my thinking, you opened my mind to learning; Suki you shower me with wisdom and love and then you walk all over me, explanation to follow; Caroline you counseled me when I was lost and put me on a path to wellness; and Rita, you have shared your wisdom and trust and we have run as partners, ten miles every morning and we have become solid friends. God gave me this moment with all of you and I am very grateful."

Richard, Noel and Max arrived and the graduates received a standing ovation.

Edna and Bob Kelly showed up; I wasn't sure they would. Bob and I managed a few minutes on the porch; Eileen was hanging on to her dream, barely.

"I believe Eileen will make it, Bob; she's a once in a lifetime woman."

"It's freaking scary, Joe; Edna cries daily."

"I wish you all a brighter tomorrow, you know what I mean, I don't know what to say."

"Rita?"

"Wonderful woman, good friend, running partner, and fellow aspiring architect. We are roommates 'til the end of school."

"Edna and I hope you stay in touch."

"I will, I want to."

"Don't forget, I am your car guy."

"I won't. Can I hug your wife?"

"She'll be pissed if you don't."

Thelma and Peter Bardlow came by and I introduced them to Edna and

Bob, hoping that Pete and Thelma might help the Kellys cope with Eileen's alcoholism.

All of the women put a group hug on Dean of Men, Ed; he turned beet red and loved it.

Each of the graduates made a short speech of thanks and of their intentions; one dentist and two salesmen.

We ate, we drank and we mixed it up; it was a lovely party.

"Thank you, Gabby and Suki, this is a special day."

"Sound like goodbye," Suki wanted to know.

"Not goodbye, Suki, more like saving memories."

"Tie with ribbon in your head."

"Exactly, tie with ribbon and no goodbye."

"Then, kiss, Joseph, for my ribbon."

In the car I realized the only one missing was Mrs. Brand and on the way home I confessed to my peanut butter affair.

CHAPTER 35

SUMMER INTERNS

We rode the subway into Manhattan every day for our summer internship. I interned at Reinhardt and Tufts and Rita at Green and Green. Both were successful and respected architectural firms and we got a "taste" of the big league.

At the end of each day we met at Jimmy's Bar and Grill, a couple of steps from the subway station to Brooklyn. Jimmy agreed to take our phone calls; I guess he got a kick out of us, "Hey, Shorty, the Tall One says, go ahead without her," or, "Hey, Tall One, Shorty'll be here in fifteen."

Our internships went well and toward the end of the summer I was invited to meet with Robert Reinhardt, the managing partner of Reinhardt and Tufts. He was a very pleasant man, maybe fifty, creative; based on the work that I knew he was responsible for, had a family and was straightforward. He expected creativity, hard work and wanted to be challenged. I had a rewarding summer at the firm; I had made a few friends and I learned quite a bit about architecture, problem solving and, perhaps more importantly, how the firm succeeds in the community; talent, reputation, social responsibility, connections and hard work.

"Joe," we were sitting in easy chairs in his office, "Three things: finish up strong at Pratt and you have a job waiting for you here at Reinhardt Tufts, I want you to work with me and lastly, call me Bob."

He stood up and I sprang to my feet; my heart was pounding.

"We are going to work hard, kick ass and have a little fun along the way. Figure the middle of June, call me after graduation."

"I will, I'm excited and I am grateful, Bob. That part was difficult."

"You'll be fine."

I was inspired, I was elated, I was in shock. I went down to Jimmy's, near the subway stop, and waited for Rita.

"Hey, Shorty, you look pretty excited."

"Hey, Jimmy, I am, I just got a job offer at the firm where I've been interning."

"That calls for a Pabst."

"Better make it two, Jimmy, I just got my job offer, as well."

I put a hug on Rita and we kissed. When we turned back to the bar there were two glasses of Pabst; one tall and one short.

"You kids figure it out, it's on the house!"

CHAPTER 36

THE WEDDING

We had a week before classes began so we started to study. There was a lot to learn and it was exciting that we had been exposed to quite a bit of this during our internships.

Creative design,

Function and safety, occupants' needs, problem solving, creative and alternative solutions.

We continued to run together and Rita was right, "You are going to love to run." We were easy together and we helped each other stay balanced; we were supportive. We just plain liked/loved each other and there were times we wondered, and we talked about it; what it would be like apart? It was like an undertow; it didn't feel good.

I asked Rita to accompany me at Celeste's wedding on Saturday, November 14th, "It will be fun, we will dance a little, eat a little, drink more than a little, be there to cheer the bride, and the groom, and congratulate Jerry and Martha."

"No. Thank you, but no."

"Waldorf Astoria, the Starlight Roof."

"No."

"Black tie, formal party dress for you."

"No."

I'm going to go alone, Rita. Come on."

"No."

"There will be 300 people there from all over the world."

"And I will be the tallest woman. No."

"That is not true, Celeste is six ten."

"That is not true. You have never lied to me, Joe."

"That was a form of groveling. I'm sorry."

"I will help you tie your bow tie and I will be here when you come home, and I will miss you while you are gone; that's the best I can do."

"Okay."

"You know what I like best about us?"

"I. . ."

"You don't have to guess, Joe; we have never, not once, asked, "Why?" We have always honored one another, trusted each other."

"I am sorry I pushed too hard. I pushed because there isn't anyone else I would rather be with."

"Okay, I'll go."

"Fantastic!"

"I already bought the dress, and it's not the 'I'll be the tallest woman there' thing either."

"I'm just glad you,"

"It's Eileen. You would rather go with Eileen, but you can't."

"I. . ."

"I'll keep talking, this is on me; I conjured up the Eileen is better than I and I made it into a negative narrative about you: your just living with me because, or we sleep together because; it's a long list that I've been working on so that when we part it won't hurt so much."

"Oh, my God, you're human. People do that. They put on emotional armor to prevent the pain. I like/love you Rita and you are the first woman I have ever loved intelligently; in my book we are wonderful together; we honor each other, we trust each other. I don't want to get married until I'm in my thirties and a practicing architect, I want to be a father, I think I could be a good dad. I'm getting off track; I want to be with you until it's time to part; I will miss you and I hope we remain friends forever."

"I have had a few men in my life, starting with my dad, which was not a good start, and then some other guys; it's been different with you, in a good way. We set the bar pretty high."

"Thank you for sharing your 'stuff' Rita Posinka, I am very grateful."

"I'm too tall for you."

"Are you saying I am too short for you?"

"No, I am not, you are perfect."

"Rita, that's my line; you are the perfect woman in my life."

"That would be me; right now I am your running partner and a couple of other perks, too. And, I have to admit, I love us."

Celeste's wedding was beautiful, followed by a wonderful party during which Rita and I danced a lot. Three inch heels, what was she thinking? Jerry was beaming and I was very happy for my almost wife and my almost father and mother-in-law.

THE KISS

CHAPTER 37

SWEET GOODBYES

Rita and I were headed into the home stretch; we had bolstered each other and we were proud to be leading the field as we loaded up on the remaining courses: Environmental systems, architectural design, and urban studies. In short we gathered what Rita shared with me the first day we met: a sense of design, planning, detail, sustainability, and execution, culminating in the creation of lasting buildings of value.

During that spring my Mom sold our house and she moved into the city; big stuff, lots of tears, but all for the best.

It turned into a family real estate circus; my sister Sylvia and Al purchased a home in Tenafly, New Jersey and I took over their apartment on the upper West side. I would be the "City Boy" and Rita was keeping the Brooklyn apartment and do the subway commute.

Rita helped me move my stuff into the city. I rented a truck and we were able to move everything in one day; Rita is some kind of strong!

I also was taking over Syl and Al's phone number and I alerted the office at "41" of my new address and phone number. I called Jerry, as well, and told him about my job.

"Bob Reinhardt is a customer at "41", he's a good man, you will do well with him. Best wishes, Joe; I look forward to seeing you here at "41".

Graduation was simple and straightforward; seventeen architects graduated from Pratt in the Class of 1957. Most of us went over to Dominic's to celebrate, drink beer and eat pizza. We had a good time and learned seven of us were going to scatter across the states and Juan was going home to Spain. After a few hours Rita and I went home.

We had one week before we started our new jobs, so we made the best of it. One day we drove to Tenafly, New Jersey to visit Syl and Al and see their new home; beautiful, on an acre with a tennis court, very nice.

Going home we took the George Washington Bridge and drove down the East River Drive to the 50's and went to P.J. Clarke's for dinner. Frankie got us a table in the back and we ordered a couple of beers.

"This is like a rehearsal," I said, "I am going to be a city dweller."

"I am not ready for you to do that, but I can handle it." Rita raised her beer, "To my friend, the big city runner."

I lifted my beer, "To my friend, the teacher. I love you, Rita."

We walked for a while in the city and then found the car and went home. We slept like puppies; waking if we weren't touching.

We ran every morning, we went to Coney Island and walked on the beach; it was warm but the ocean was too cold for a swim. We held hands a lot and we both felt the undertow; we were separating after two years of growing a very special friendship.

"Why is this so hard," Rita asked for both of us.

We both knew the answer.

Monday came and we had our last run, showered and had breakfast at Mel's, before we walked to the subway. In the city, in front of Jimmy's, we hugged and I watched Rita walk toward Green and Green; I turned and headed off to my new life.

PART FIVE

Four Years Later

THE THOROUGHBRED

THE KISS

CHAPTER 38

CLIMBING THE LADDER

In the four years I have been at Reinhardt-Tufts I have garnered lots of supervised practical experience and worked with five different architects on a variety of projects including apartments, office buildings, brownstone teardown redoes, a museum and homes in Westchester, and the Hamptons.

I am licensed and certified by the Architectural Board of the State of New York. I was the architect on a Brownstone redo in the East 70's that got a lot of press, mostly because of who it was for, and Architectural Digest did a shoot that's supposed to come out in a couple of months. Bob Reinhardt has directed my progress and I am grateful for his guidance and trust. I love being an architect.

My sisters have become little baby producers; Gloria now has three and Sylvia has a daughter, Shelly, three and Paul is one. My mom has adjusted to the city and is dating; marriage, who knows? Rita and I had lunch a couple of times, we phone each other occasionally, and we are friends.

I called Bob Kelly for advice on how to get rid of my car and he said to get it to his Manhattan office on the West side; he got me more than I expected, thank you Bob. Eileen managed to get through Med school and is interning and pregnant in Baltimore; conversation with their daughter is sparse and painful. The pain was there for me as well.

I'm still living on the upper West side, still running every morning, thank you Rita, and I like to get to my office at Reinhardt-Tufts, on 50th at Seventh Avenue, by eight thirty.

"Come on George, you have us tied up here and I'm just the architect, imagine what the construction guys are going through."

George Flores is the top dog of building permits in the city; he's a busy guy.

"Joe, we have never faced a situation like this; you want a driveway factored into the sidewalk; it's a safety issue."

"George, for God's sake, there are thousands of driveways crossing sidewalks; parking lots, ramps coming up from under office buildings, apartments; there's no difference."

"You're kidding, right; this is a residential area, the garage door looks like part of the front of the place, you would never know it's a garage door; no warning, nothing, and suddenly half of the house rises up and out comes, what? A Ferrari, a Rolls?"

"It depends on the day of the week. But look, we put up a warning bell; the bell goes off, pedestrians stop, they know something is happening, the garage door opens, the car is gone, the garage door closes, no harm, no foul."

"I dunno."

"I'll have Soloman call you; he's doing structural and he says this is a slam dunk."

"If Soloman calls and you do the bell, I'll give you a green light."

"That's great, I'll call Soloman right now. Thanks, George."

"One other thing, I'm curious?"

"Read the permit; we estimated 25 mil."

"A bottle of bourbon for you if it comes in under fifty? Over, one for me."

"Deal."

I hung up and was very relieved; this was my biggest architectural achievement, a new urban home I designed to replace a double, side-by-side, brownstone tear down. The client wanted a garage but not a conventional garage door. I designed, using hydraulics, what appears to be part of the front of the house, to move forward six inches, for clearance, and then slide straight up and, after a car has entered or departed, slide back down and in six inches to lock. It's ingenious and it works; thank you Bob Soloman , and now, by adding a warning bell, we will get the client (I can not tell you his or her name) permission to inhabit.

Quite some time ago, about a year before the sliding garage door, Bob Reinhardt called me into his office; he had a "gift" for me.

"These kids have a house in Easthampton, about a block from the beach; they purchased one hundred feet of beachfront and want to build their oceanfront dream house. I want you to do this one." He handed me a business card.

"Wow, Bob, my heart rate just doubled, thank you."

"He's a computer start up guy, systems management with IBM machines, I don't know."

Bob shrugged like this was a whole other world.

"Jeremy Mason, I read something about him a couple of weeks ago; a cutting edge kind of guy."

"You'll be looking him in the eye; Five O'clock, at the bar, at "41", his wife will be with him."

"I'll be there; I won't let you down."

"That's why you are going. Keep me posted."

"Yes, sir."

At Five I met Jeremy Mason and his wife, Marti; both tall, attractive and my age peers. They were there first and had drinks in hand; I ordered bourbon on the rocks and gestured to Henry, the bartender, this is my tab. When I turned back to the Masons I was hugged from behind and a familiar voice inquired, "Excuse me, is this man bothering you?"

I couldn't keep from smiling as I turned and hugged Jerry Brown.

"Jerry, do you know the Masons, Marti and Jeremy?"

Introductions were completed and the mystery of Jerry to the Masons lifted when Jerry asked, "Joe, are you planning on staying for dinner?"

"I'm not certain," looking to the Masons.

"We have children, five and three, and we like to get home before their bedtime."

"Another time; a pleasure meeting you," and Jerry moved on.

"He's the owner," asked Jeremy.

"He is and he's a wonderful man."

"He thinks the same of you," Marti said, "That's nice."

We had our drinks and I told them what I had done and what was currently on my plate, including a six thousand square foot single family, single story residence in a hilly stretch outside of Newport, Rhode Island that I wanted to nest into the terrain.

"What I want to know," I said, "is who you are, what you want, what your children might want or need. I believe any design starts with you."

We did stay for dinner; the Masons had a Nanny, and we agreed on my being their architect.

"I am going on a two week trip to South America, much of which will be fishing off the coast of Argentina, and when I return we can go to the beach, we have a house out there, and move forward."

"I wish you a good trip and success at sea."

I told Bob Reinhardt we had a new client and that we would commence upon Jeremy Mason's return.

Jeremy never returned from South America; he and his fishing party were lost at sea near the Falkland Islands, off the coast of Argentina. Not a single trace of the forty-foot fishing boat was found during a weeklong search requested by the United States Embassy in Buenos Aires. There was news coverage in the New York Times and on television; also rumors surfaced that British Naval maneuvers, taking place at that time, were responsible. The United States Government promised a probe.

It was awful and I was moved to hand write a note to Marti Mason on a simple sheet of paper:

Dear Marti,

I am deeply saddened for you and your children.

I wish you strength and peace.

My condolences,

Joe Gordon

I sent the letter to Jeremy's business address; that was all I had.

My design for the Newport house had been approved by the client and was working it's way through a maze of permits and a geologist's report; things were nice and quiet.

"Take a day off," suggested Liz, my secretary.

"Good idea, book me a flight to Acapulco."

"I will, but before you pack, Mr. Reinhardt wants to see you in the conference room."

"Seriously?"

"Seriously."

Bob Reinhardt was seated at the head of the table and the chair at the other end of the table was symbolically empty, as it always has been since Fred Tufts passed away during the first year I joined the firm. Seated to Bob's right was Jim Palmer who nodded and gestured to have a seat across from him.

"This, Joe, is the perfect moment,"

Winston Case and Leonard Fine came in and sat on opposite sides of the table; Bob resumed, "To acknowledge the fine work," Bob stopped again when Bob Anderson took a seat, "you have been doing," Liz entered with a tray of glasses and a bottle of Dom Perignon, "a marvelous job and you just made Junior Partner at Reinhardt-Tufts; congratulations."

Bob Reinhardt stood, as did I, he refused my extended hand and hugged me instead.

"We, the partners, are very proud of you, Joe, welcome aboard."

"I am speechless and grateful and very happy to be aboard."

Someone popped the cork and glasses of champagne were passed around;

"Cheers, Joe, you earned it."

I raised my glass and thanked them all. I had worked with each of these men and all of them were generous; they wanted me to learn, they wanted me to excel.

We all chatted for a bit and then, back in my office with Liz, "Take the day off, well done Elizabeth; you knew, huh?"

"I did, and I am very happy for you, Joe, you're a good guy and a terrific architect."

"Thank you, Liz, you are a huge help to me and I look forward to many more years together."

Inside I was bubbling; the only one missing was a spouse to share the joy.

THE KISS

CHAPTER 39

MARTI MASON

I dated: my sister, Sylvia, fixed me up, nope. Liz, my secretary was sure she had the right girl for me; nice, but no. I went to Temple and after the Friday night service I met Ellen Levine during Shabat, the coffee and cake social hour. Ellen was smart, socially upbeat, beautiful and an attorney; Ellen, in other words, was fabulous except for her dad, Dave. Dave's wife, Ellen's mom, passed away the same day Ellen passed the Bar; Dave was lost without his Connie and Ellen chose, still chooses, to tend to her dad. We lunched several times near her work; pro bono at ACLU, and I wished she would have "the talk" with Dave but I chose not to push. What a loss! For the time being my love affair is with my work.

One afternoon Liz announced, "Marti Mason, on line two,"

I told my sister I would call her back.

"Marti, how are you?"

"I wasn't sure you would remember."

"I'm an elephant, of course I remember."

"Your note touched me."

"Your loss touched me, Marti. How can I help you?"

"Meet me for a drink at our usual spot."

"Five O'clock."

"Thank you, Joe."

She hung up and I took a deep breath; the sound of her voice made me dizzy.

I walked over to "41" and was a little early; I decided to wait in the lobby.

Monte, on duty inside the front door, said he would watch for Mrs. Mason, who I described as tall, attractive, brunette and thirtyish. I settled into a comfortable chair and realized I was nervous; why was I nervous? I put it out of my mind and people watched. I saw Marti arrive, Monte smiled and pointed her in my direction. I was on my feet, "It's good to see you, Marti."

I reached out and took her hand in mine, "Let's get a drink," I said, and held her hand all the way to the bar.

"I am glad to see you, Joe." Marti gave me a sweet, short kiss on my lips and I swallowed hard, "What are you drinking?"

"You order for me."

I turned, Henry was waiting, "Hello, Henry, a bourbon rocks and a bourbon sour rocks, big tumbler."

"If you had said Scotch, I would have screamed."

"They would have thrown us out."

"Just me."

"No way, we are in this together."

Our drinks were waiting. "Bourbon sour rocks, Mrs. Mason and bourbon rocks for you, Joe."

"Thanks, Henry."

"How did he know my name," Marti wanted to know.

"First a toast, then we can connect the dots."

"My toast."

"Okay," I agreed.

"To you, to me, to us."

We locked eyes and drank.

"Mmmm, delicious."

"Agreed."

"The dots?"

"When I arrived I told Monte, at the door, I was expecting Marti Mason; tall, attractive, etc. Monte sent word to Jerry Brown that I was here, expecting you; then Jerry sent word to Henry and Gene, the two bartenders on duty that I was here and you, Marti Mason, would be here with me."

"No stone left unturned."

"One other possibility; when we were here a year ago Henry was our bartender, and it's very possible he remembered you."

"Fourteen months, one week, three days." Tears were welling.

"I'm sorry, Marti."

She took my hand and squeezed hard, "I'm okay, I promise."

"And I am here for you, I promise."

We sipped our drinks as the bar filled up with thirsty people around us. Marti moved closer to me and whispered, "We can not mess this up."

"If you are talking about the energy that is flowing between us, all we have to do is let it flow; we'll be fine."

"I needed to know."

We were whispering, just inches apart, "I have a thousand questions."

"Buy me another one of these and I'll tell you everything I want you to know."

"Very clever, Mrs. Mason."

I caught Henry's eye and he nodded.

"What's with you and Jerry Brown?"

"His daughter and I went to kindergarten together."

"Oh no, really?"

"We dated all through high school and into college."

"What happened?"

"We were going to get married until I realized I wasn't ready; so Jerry is my almost father-in-law and a great friend."

"I remember seeing the love you and Jerry share."

"My turn."

"I can't, I have to go; the kids. Joe, I'm sorry."

Henry looked at me and I signaled, Add ten.

"Marti, I'll walk you out."

In the lobby we took a moment and exchanged home phone numbers.

"Joe, I was scared to call you."

"I know. I'm glad you did."

We went outside together and hugged in front of "41".

"Call you later?"

"Absolutely," I said.

I watched Marti Mason walk toward Fifth Avenue and then I turned for home; I had a little skip in my step.

CHAPTER 40

THE MONARCH

I had been working with Jim Palmer for months on an apartment design for the Fisher Brothers, big property developers in town. The address would be 215 East 68th Street and they had put together a large property; we wanted to give them an exciting design.

The evening before the presentation I had a dream, a fantasy, a creative explosion; I didn't know what to call it but I knew it was exciting, provocative and it was, I was certain, beyond, in a good way, what the Fishers were expecting.

Early the next morning I closed Bob Reinhardt's office door and told him what I had. He loved it and I asked, "What do I do with Jim, I have to tell him."

"Leave Jim to me, this will work out fine; we'll make the presentation as planned and when you know the moment is right, take it from there."

"I'm worried about Jim."

"Joe, I have known and worked with Jim Palmer for almost three decades, he will see this instantly; you're not throwing the design away, your changing it in a very exciting way. Are you going to be okay?"

"I'll be fine; every experience I have had in my young life, and certainly my experiences here, have conspired to bring me to this moment. Yes, I'll be fine."

At two thirty that afternoon Bob Reinhardt, Jim Palmer and I shook hands with the three Fisher brothers; Larry, the oldest and the top dog, Frank and Jim. We had brought a large model of the building and a dozen artist's renderings of the lobby, apartment layouts, the awning cover out front and the roof. Jim talked them through all the latest "stuff" that would be a part of making every apartment desirable.

The Fisher brothers looked happy, they had some questions that Jim fielded. This was the moment, now or never, and I rose and approached the model of the building and Jim sat down.

"Or, you can create your legacy; the Dakota equivalent on the East side. Twin buildings," we had the model cut in half and hinged together at the front so I was able to grasp the two sides and bend them back, creating two buildings attached at the rear.

"Why two buildings?"

So that we can create a concierge station in each building that will service 250 tenants by name and satisfy their every whim: service; "Good morning, Mr. Fisher, how is the new grandson?" Our suggested name for these two buildings is, THE MONARCH, these are its two wings, like the butterfly. People getting in a cab won't say, 215 East 68th, they'll say, The Monarch; East Wing and West Wing. Between the two wings will be a Holiday Courtyard changing during the four seasons to reflect the holidays; pumpkins, Christmas tree, Easter Bunny, etc. We suggest a pool on the roof of the East Wing and planned recreation areas on top of the West wing; for example: a BBQ and picnic table, a sunning area with chaise lounges, a bar for a cocktail party area. Each area with different level platforms executed in cedar wood and separated by bushes, trees and flowerbeds. We also suggest a gym; more and more people are working out and underground parking for a limited number of automobiles because your tenants will be going to the Hamptons or the Berkshires. The Monarch is designed to provide recognition, attention to detail and service; The Monarch, the finest two apartment dwellings in Manhattan. The Monarch is your legacy."

I took a sip of water and heard Larry Fisher say, "I like it."

Bob Reinhardt addressed the brothers: "This idea surfaced yesterday and we at Reinhardt-Tufts decided to go ahead and shoot from the hip because The Monarch should be a Fisher Brothers achievement."

"I like it," Larry repeated.

"If we agree in principle we will need a little time to adjust everything to this concept."

"Boys?" Larry addressed his siblings; Frank and Jim were smiling, "Let's do it; The Monarch, that's a great name and it's a great idea; our legacy, I like it.

Whose idea was this?"

I spoke up, "Any idea comes from everything that surrounds us. One of the strongest, perhaps the strongest source of inspiration is: what does the tenant want? This is his home; Work backwards from there: he wants to belong, to be comfortable and safe, to be recognized, and he wants service. The Monarch, with its two wings, allows each staff to better serve 250 tenants than one staff overwhelmed by 500."

"I don't know when I was last this excited," uttered Larry, "We've got a deal."

There was much shaking of hands and back slapping as the messengers gathered up the model and the artwork; Bob, Jim and I headed down the corridor to the elevator.

"Hey, kid," Larry Fisher had stepped into the corridor,

"You have a second?"

Of the three Reinhardt men I was certainly the kid, "I'll be right down; I'll meet you in the lobby."

"What can I do for you, Mr. Fisher?"

"Larry."

"Okay, Larry, and I'm Joe, Joe Gordon."

"Joe, how did you know about my becoming a grandfather?"

"A couple of weeks ago I was at the bar at "41" when you were celebrating the happy event. Congratulations."

"Thank you. This was your idea, Joe, wasn't it?"

"Let's just say that you and I both know the answer to that."

"I need to know that you will watch over The Monarch?"

"You have my word, Larry."

We shook hands and I hurried downstairs.

"What was that all about," Jim Palmer wanted to know.

"Larry wanted to know if I would stay on the Monarch project; I assured him I would."

"That was great up there, Joe, good work."

"Thank you, I could not be happier."

"I think we should celebrate," Bob Reinhardt suggested.

"I think we just did," I said.

Back at the office Liz's expression asked the question and my smile earned me a hug, "I love working with you, Joe."

"It's mutual, Liz."

The phone rang, an interior line, Liz picked it up and listened, "Okay," she hung up, "The partners are gathering for drinks in the boardroom; that includes you, Joseph."

"Thank you, Elizabeth."

"Mrs. Mason called earlier, she wants you to go to Easthampton for the weekend, leaving tomorrow morning."

"What's tomorrow?"

"Friday."

"I meant, what's up tomorrow?"

"All clear."

"Would you respond, yes, and I'll call her tonight."

"Should I be doubly excited for you?"

"Yes," I said, over my shoulder, and headed to the boardroom.

CHAPTER 41

EAST HAMPTON WEEKEND

"Marti, it's Joe."

"Are you excited?"

"I am, of course, and I want to know the plan."

"The plan; good question. The kids are coming and Dawn, their Nanny, and you and I."

"My concern is the kids; who am I, in relation to you?"

"You are my friend."

"I am your friend and I had envisioned meeting your kids in the city; dropping in for a drink or even dinner."

"Joe, I'm sorry, I'm pushing. I get it. I got this idea, I've already told the kids: it's a big house, lots of bedrooms. I'm starting to feel foolish. I want you to know us; I'm a package."

"I understand. Maybe I'm the one with a deal breaker; every morning at six I run ten miles, takes a little more than an hour."

"I'm impressed but that's not a problem for me and the house is a block from the beach."

"I've never run near the ocean."

"We'll pick you up and you'll meet the gang: Dawn, the Nanny, is young, smart and pretty, Sara, no H, is six and Billy is four."

"And you, Marti, you are young and pretty and smart."

"I'm taking that as a yes."

I'm way over on the West Side."

"I know. I'm excited, see you at eight."

It took a little over three hours to get to Easthampton, pretty good time, probably because we were going against traffic. I sat on the back seat between Sara and Billy and made it clear that the three of us were the kids and those two up front were the adults. We talked and learned about one another and we shouted while playing word games and sang silly songs that they taught me. We had fun and would not let the adults sing along or play word games with us. I called Sara, Sara no H, and I called Billy, Wee Willy. It was us, against them, and we won. I was exhausted.

The house, on just under an acre, was a two story beauty; big kitchen, dining room with a great antique table for twelve, a den with a fireplace, a living room with a fireplace and a full bath on the main floor. Upstairs there were five bedrooms, the main suite with a fireplace and bath, and two other bathrooms. Marti gave me the tour while Dawn fixed lunch. Marti had not been to Easthampton since Jeremy's passing; she was excited and sad and I told her about Suki who described melancholy as, "sad funny," after I described it as, sad, not unhappy, emotionally tired; it's an in between place. Marti smiled and kissed me on the cheek. When we got to the Master bedroom Marti kissed me.

"Here," I asked.

"Yes, here."

We kissed again and began to experience the passion that had been building since Marti's phone call.

"Joe, I just read your wonderfully wicked mind."

"And you just revealed yours. Where do you plan to have me sleep?"

"I want us to sleep together."

"Isn't that . . ."

"I didn't," Marti interrupted, "plan on that until you bonded with Sara, no H, and Wee Willy; they like you. I would like to invite them into 'our' bedroom in the morning so there is no mystery; 'this is us and this is all of us'. What do you think?"

"On paper that sounds great; what happens when we are back in the city? Marti, we are moving at the speed of light."

"I feel it too and I am excited. Joe, there has been no man in my life these fifteen or so months and the only man in my dreams has been you."

"I don't know what to say. I have huge feelings for you that started the minute I heard your voice."

"We are sleeping together tonight, in this bed, and we are inviting the kids to join us after your run."

Marti sealed that with a kiss that melted my resolve.

"Lunch!" came the call from down below and we went down to satisfy that hunger.

"Okay, who is coming to the beach with me?"

After a chorus of, "I am," I asked, "Who has pails and shovels?" and both kids assured me they had them. "One last question, are you big kids coming with us?"

"Yes we are, you go ahead, we'll catch up."

"Sounds good. Let's go, gang, we have work to do."

"What kind of work," Wee Willy wanted to know.

"We are going to build a city."

By the water's edge we filled the pails with wet sand that we piled up far enough from the water but close enough so we could easily get more.

With my foot I dragged a line in the sand.

"This is Main Street and we can build whatever we want on either side of the street."

"What should I build," Wee Willy wanted to know.

"You can build what ever you want; a house, like this house, or a big apartment building, like in the city, and I can help if you want."

Sara, no H, declared she was building a castle for a princess.

"Great idea, Sara, no H. I'm building an office building, and Wee Willy is building a secret something that we don't understand yet and that is very cool."

We started construction.

"What do you do?"

"I'm an architect, Sara, no H."

"What's an architect?"

"An architect designs, creates, or," I couldn't decide what word they would understand.

"Like we are doing now," Sara, no H said.

"Exactly, thank you."

"Do you love my mom?"

Wee Willy caught me totally off guard.

"Well, I…"

I looked toward the house; was help coming?

"We think you do."

"Thank you, Wee Willy; your mom is special."

"Do you like Dawn," Sara, no H, wanted to know.

"Sure, I mean I just met her; she seems nice."

"She is nice. What do you think of my castle?"

"I like it but I think we all need more wet sand."

"Wet sand," shouted Wee Willy, and we hurried toward the water with our buckets.

Buckets full, we turned back to our creations where Marti was waiting.

"Mom," Wee Willy called, "do you like my house?""

"Yes, I like your house and I see a castle and something that is going to be very tall."

"And I see a beautiful Queen that might reside in the castle or, even, in the something that is going to be very tall."

"Thank you, my Lord, that is most kind of you." A lovely kiss punctuated Marti's remarks.

We dumped our fresh supply of wet sand and Sara, no H, said, "Build something, Mom, Joe's an architect, he'll help you."

Marti got right to it and asked Billy if she could help make his house a little bigger.

"Sure, Mom."

"We will make a big, beautiful house."

"Don't forget my castle, plenty of room for everyone."

"That's the joy of building," I said, "there's room for all of us."

"Good," Sara, no H, said, patting the wet sand.

"Joe and I are going out for dinner tonight; we'll probably take a nap before."

"Naps are for little people, Mom."

"And for grownups who have worked hard all week in the city," I added.

"Tomorrow night," Marti tacked on, "we are going to barbecue."

Wee Willy wanted to know, "Joe, are you doing the barbecue?"

"Yes."

"Can I help?"

"Absolutely."

"A nap," I asked Marti when we were upstairs..

"I'm sorry, I was selfish and my desire out ran my sensibility."

"Let's talk this through: you called me and I got dizzy from the sound of your voice, we met at "41" and we both experience some amazing energy that could be lust, or could be love, you arrange this weekend and I know it's ass backwards, we've kissed, we've hugged, now we are sleeping together based on emotional trust. Your kids asked if I love you, I could not say I don't know yet, I got away with not answering because Sara, no H, let me off the hook."

"It's my turn. My husband cheated on me before our first child, before our second child and before he went to Argentina to die, she was with him, I admired you and your relationship with Jerry at "41", your condolence note touched me deeply, I'm scared and pushed you into acting above the call of duty, I'm love lost and have been for years, I don't want to be a project, but I have two beautiful kids that are smart and, I think, are not messed up by what has surrounded them. I am exhausted and want us to lie together, share each other, and, I hope, love each other forever."

Marti stood up and took off her clothes; one shirt, one pair of jeans; I had no idea that Marti Mason was so incredibly beautiful. I got undressed and did not, could not, do anything other than take Marti in my arms and hold her close while she sobbed. The war was over for Marti and I had a woman in my life with a couple of recruits that I had not planned on. We had made love without making love. God, my God, your God, every God of the Universe was smiling and we, we were blessed.

We were showered and dressed for dinner when we went into the den where Dawn and the kids were watching television.

"Wow, check out the handsome couple."

"Thank you, Dawn; Marti could attract a crowd."

"Mommy," both of the kids wanted hugs, which they received, and then I was next; down on one knee I gathered Sara, no H, in one arm and Wee Willy in the other.

"I'll see you in the morning and tell you everything Mom had for dinner."

"Promise?"

"Promise."

"Have fun," Dawn said and we waved.

It was May, with enough of a chill for Marti to have a sweater wrapped around her shoulders and a lovely print, summer frock covering the rest of her.

In the car I said, "Marti, you are turning me on, I know exactly what you are not wearing."

"I assure you, it is my pleasure."

"Soon enough to be mine as well."

"Joseph, the car."

"Marti, the keys?"

"Oh."

Le Ponte was intimate with a kick, the music was soft, but upbeat and everyone was chatting; creating a nice hum. We ordered drinks and steamers to start.

"Joe, thank you, you did something so precious with the kids; 'I'll tell you everything Mom had for dinner.'"

"I did not say, your mom; I couldn't, I didn't want to; it would separate us."

"I love you, Joe."

"You say that now but when I leave our bed at six in the morning,"

"I will love you still, besides, I will be done with you, perhaps."

Perhaps was delivered perfectly with a toss of the head.

Dinner was good, very good; after the steamers we shared a roasted chicken breast and green beans. We skipped dessert; Marti promised there was ice cream in the freezer. I used my American Express card and we left for home.

"Food in the fridge; how does that work, Marti, you haven't been here in months?"

"We have a service that watches over the house; they check the place daily, they keep it clean and I alert them when we are coming and they shop for us."

"No stone left unturned."

"Exactly."

We tiptoed upstairs and I locked the door, Marti lit a few candles. I gently unwrapped Marti's sweater and turned her around to unbutton her dress and lift it from her body; I kissed her neck and we both shivered, she smelled so good.

Marti sat on the edge of the bed and lured me closer; she undid my belt, my pants button and my pants dropped to the floor. In bed we pressed ourselves together in passion, lust and love; all at a teasing, pleasing pace. When we gave up we did it together. We shared breathless kisses; joy was in bed with us and we held hands because we didn't want to let go.

"I love you, Joe."

"I love you, Marti."

At six my watch did what it was supposed to; it pulled me from the warmth of this exquisite woman who I kissed goodbye to go run on the beach; for a brief second I saw Rita running with me, she would always be running with me.

At seven fifteen I was back at the house where I thought, silly me, I could sneak back into bed and the kids would join us on cue.

"Where have you been, Joe," Sara, no H wanted to know. She and Wee Willy were in bed with Marti who was hiding behind a pillow.

"I was out running on the beach."

"Running?"

"Yes, you know," and I pantomimed running by lifting my feet and pumping my fists. "Where's Mom, I don't see her anywhere?"

The kids pointed to the pillow.

"Maybe, if you tickle her she will come out of hiding."

The tickle attack began.

"That is so unfair, using children that way."

Marti could hardly get out the words; the tickle attack was so severe.

"Keep tickling while I wash up. Then I'll get in bed and tell you what Mom had for dinner."

When I came back Marti had come out of hiding and there was room for me with the kids in he middle.

"Who wants to guess what Mom had for dinner?"

"I do," Wee Willy said.

"Okay."

"Pancakes?"

"Nope."

"Green beans,"

Sara, no H guessed.

"How did you know that," I asked.

"She loves green beans."

"Oh."

"Wee Willy and I know something else Mom loves."

"What is that?"

"It's who," Sara no H, said.

"Who," Wee Willy asked.

"You sound like a parliament of owls."

The kids were giggling; "W4ho is you, Joe. She loves you."

"I hope so?"

"She does," Marti said, "I know so."

"Does anyone know who I love?"

"We know, silly, you love Mom."

"You are very smart, both of you."

"I know."

"Smart enough to take your brother downstairs and tell Dawn that Mom and I will be down for breakfast in fifteen minutes."

"Okay. Come on Wee Willy."

Off they went and I feigned fatigue; I collapsed on the pillows.

"I know lots of ways to wake you up."

"We have twelve minutes."

Marti voted for brushing teeth, a long hug and a good morning kiss.

"Perfect."

Breakfast was first rate; eggs, bacon and pancakes.

"Thank you, Dawn, delicious."

"I helped with the pancakes," Wee Willy wanted me to know.

"No wonder they are so good."

"I can't believe you don't drink coffee, Joe," Dawn said.

"Love the smell but not the taste; I have tried and tried, no coffee for me."

"Joe, can I go back to being just plain Sara?"

"Of course, yesterday was spur of the moment fun."

"I like being Wee Willy with you, Joe."

"Okay, until further notice, Wee Willy."

Dawn asked, "Pancakes, anyone; last chance."

A chorus of, "groans, too full, no thanks," and breakfast was over.

"I would like to take a walk on the beach with you, Marti; are you up for that?"

"I am very up for a walk with you."

"We're off, see you all in a little while."

"We need to talk."

"We need to hold hands."

"You are a beautiful woman."

"I am happy."

"You are smart and caring."

"Do you have a 'but' ready to jump out at me?"

"I do not."

We had reached the beach and I stopped to take off my sneakers and roll up my jeans.

"Come on, you too."

"Mr. Bossy."

I watched Marti roll up her jeans and then we went to the water's edge.

"Whoa, cold!"

"This was your idea, Joe."

Marti gave me a playful shove.

"If I go, you are coming with me.""

"No! I'll scream; someone will come to my rescue."

"Someone already has; a total stranger who has fallen in love with a damsel in distress. My problem, no, I believe it's our problem; we don't know enough about each other. We need to put ourselves out there, we have to do the hard part, so we can understand what made yesterday and last night so special."

"And I'm supposed to go first?"

"Yes."

"Where do I start?"

"You start by leading me out of the cold water; bring me closer to you."

We moved away from the ocean and sat, cross-legged, inches apart.

"I am a runner, not like you; I'm smart and quick and pretty enough. Only child, both parents functioning alcoholics, a crazy, reckless, maybe fearless teenager, getting good grades with my eyes shut and doing drugs with older guys with my eyes open."

"Where?"

"Duluth. I wanted out, had SAT scores off the charts and I chose Berkley, English major, I stopped drinking, smoked weed, dropped acid twice, met Jeremy, super smart, married, moved to New York, he started his company, I plugged into Madison Avenue, three years started my own consulting firm, Jeremy extremely successful, Sara, we needed help, Jeremy's kid sister, Dawn, bought this house for summer fun, duplex on Fifth in the city, Billy, beachfront property, marriage hemorrhaging, architect at "41", death by fishing, fourteen months, one week, three days of personal evaluation, Dawn amazing, Joe Gordon amazinger."

Marti had been crying off and on; I thought I had a handkerchief but didn't so my shirtsleeves did their best.

Marti was done and leaned forward, gave me a brief kiss, stood and started toward the house.

"Marti, Marti, come back; your running days are done."

She stopped and turned, "I'm a mess, I'm scared shitless, Joseph. Dawn is a runner, you know, like you; she's smart and young and pretty, why don't you run with her? She thinks you are a great guy. That's what guys do, they run with the pretty young ones."

Marti had worked her way back and when she was done, she sat and grabbed my arm to wipe her nose on my sleeve.

"I wasn't thinking," I said, "I should have brought a towel."

"You are making fun of me."

"I was wondering how to reach Dawn, I guess I can call your home number?"

Marti swung at me pretty hard and I leaned back out of reach.

"That's enough, Marti, now you get to listen."

"Fine."

"Why do women say, 'fine' like they are surrendering?"

"Fine then, go ahead, or whatever."

"For the first sixteen years of my life I didn't know who I was. My mother had smothered me and made me into her little man, starting when I was a toddler. In school, year after year, I was smart enough, funny enough handsome and athletic enough to be popular but inside was a scared little boy. My future, my salvation rested on going to work with my dad, a very successful film distributer and early television pioneer. He would teach me how to be a man. When I was sixteen he and eighty five other commuters were killed in a Long Island Rail Road crash on Thanksgiving eve in 1950; my entire world flipped upside down; I was angry, a loose cannon, a scared little boy in a young man's body; posing every day, afraid. I was dating Jerry's daughter through high school and into college and working at "41" was an option for me once Celeste and I were married. I couldn't do it; I knew I had to find myself. I broke up with Celeste, changed my major and became an architect; along the way I became a man.

We are in different worlds; you are working, you have everything you could possibly want and need, I am on the threshold of self made success and will not give that away. Can we fit our lives together? Do we even want to try? There is only one way to succeed; honor each other with rigorous honesty and love, and see what happens.

Marti leaned forward and kissed me in a way that said she wanted us to try.

"I love you, Marti, I don't want you to have to guess."

I stood and extended a hand to Marti; on her feet she was in my arms instantly.

"I love you, Joseph. I want us both to do our best to make this work; we have two kids, three different residences, maybe four if we build our beach-front dream house, two jobs, three really, one maid, and Dawn."

We were walking, arms around each other's waist, picked up our shoes and continued on to the house.

"Let's smoke a joint," Marti said.

"Let's have a drink," I said.

"Let's run away from home," Marti said.

"You're the one that called me."

"You're right, smartest thing I ever did."

That afternoon Marti, Sara and Dawn went into town for some girl shopping and Wee Willy and I tried some kite flying on the beach. There wasn't much wind and our success was minimal, however we promised to try again.

"Wee Willy, we have an entire summer ahead of us, we are going to do lots of things together."

"Like tonight, we are barbecuing."

"Yes, right, I forgot all about that; let's find the barbecue and the tools."

We found the barbecue and the charcoal and the wood chips but could not find the long handled spatula and fork and we looked everywhere. Of course when the girls came home Dawn opened the pantry door and there they were, hanging on the inside of the door.

"Now you two know where the women hide the man tools."

"Thank you, Dawn."

"Joe, can I run with you in the morning?"

"Yeah, I guess, six A.M. stretch, seven minute miles, ten miles; back around seven fifteen."

"I would love that."

"Me too. Where's Miss Marti?"

"She went upstairs to rest."

"I am going to find her."

Upstairs Marti was on the bed and I joined her.

"So many people, residents and store owners, that I have not seen since, since Jeremy's disappearance; so many supportive and kind words; it was exhausting, I didn't expect it."

"Now it's over and I show up. This is part of what we talked about this morning; it's hard work on top of hard work. I'm not going into town with you."

"The hell you're not, I already added you to all the charge accounts."

"Okay, money, we have to figure out money."

"Joseph, I have millions and millions and millions, we don't have to figure out money."

"I do, I earn a lot of money, I have money and it's a guy thing; I'm the cave man, I bring home the kill."

"I want you to rethink that; why not begin saving your money for starting your own firm?"

"I don't know what to say; I mean you are right, that's my dream, my own firm."

"So we both work on that. We, you and I, have millions and we are smart shepherds of our money. We can work this out together, please."

"It's my ego, I think people will think I'm with you for the money; it's my problem, I'll work on it."

"I am here to help."

We had a wonderful barbecue outside on the back patio. Wee Willy and I set up the barbecue, following all the safety rules. The girls made a nice salad and they brought home a filet mignon that we cooked in addition to burgers and hot dogs. The filet, burnt on the outside and rare inside, was for Marti and Dawn; the kids and I had burgers and dogs and we all had salad.

"Job well done, Wee Willy; thank you for your help."

"It was fun, Joe, it got very hot."

"That's why we were super careful."

"I know."

"When everything cools down we can clean up and put everything away."

"Okay."

"Sara and Wee Willy, tomorrow morning, after my run, actually our run, Dawn is going to run as well, I want a chance to wash up and get back in bed with mom before you come upstairs to get in bed with us. Okay?"

"I'll see to it," said Dawn, "No invasion 'til everyone is ready; fear not."

"Thank you."

In the morning I learned that Dawn is a runner, no doubt about it, and we ran well together. Of course I was thinking of Rita; I had not run with a partner in years.

"That was fun, Joe, I would love to run with you when ever you are here."

"I'd like that Dawn; I ran with a partner every day for two years; something happens, you form a bond. It's nice."

"It's a date."

"For sure."

Upstairs I washed up and joined Marti in bed. Eyes open, eyes shut, Marti was a beautiful woman; I moved closer to her and she pushed her body against me. Only the impending invasion kept us modest.

"What time is it?"

"It's time for the troops."

"No, I want you."

"Well then you had better have Plan B."

"Lock the door."

"They will break it down."

"Do something, scare them away."

I turned and got a little closer.

"Joe, that's not fair."

"I hear them."

"What are you going to do with that?"

"Plan B, keep your eyes closed."

The door opened and I put my finger to my lips, "Shhh," I whispered, "Mom wants to sleep a little longer, we'll be downstairs in a little while."

God bless the troops, they put their little fingers to their lips and closed the door.

"Joseph, you are a very bad man."

"I am going to do everything I can to make sure you do not change your mind."

A little while later, when we were having breakfast, Sara asked, "Are we going back to the city today?"

Marti looked to me for an answer, "I have to be in the office tomorrow morning so, yes, back to the city, Sara."

"I have a great idea," Marti said, "If we leave around two we will be in the city in time for dinner; we can raid the fridge and show Joe our city apartment."

"Yes," said Wee Willy, "I'll show you my room, Joe."

"I would like that very much, Wee Willy."

"Dawn, work for you?"

"Sure, great idea."

"Okay, gang, we have a plan."

I remembered Marti mentioning, 'a duplex on Fifth,' but I was hardly prepared for this; five thousand square feet on the sixth and seventh floors, overlooking Central Park. I felt very small and worked hard to stay balanced and in the moment.

"Marti, this is amazing."

We were upstairs because the minute we arrived Wee Willy took my hand and led me up to his room; actually two rooms and a bath; all done in dark blues and tan it was very boyish/manly.

"I love my room and our city house."

"I can see why, Wee Willy, it is fabulous."

Marti continued from there: Sara's rooms and bath, Dawn's rooms and bath, two guest rooms sharing a bath and Marti's master suite with a den, huge bath, with walk-in shower, a sunken tub and Jacuzzi and the bedroom itself, with a custom oversized bed.

"I want us sleeping here, every night, forever."

"Right now I am a little overwhelmed. That doesn't mean I don't love you, because I do."

"I love you, Joseph Gordon; this is us."

"Let's go downstairs before I lose my balance.

Marti, this is a palace; it is stunning."

We took the in-house elevator down to the massive living room over-looking Central Park, the den, the home office, the dining room, the kitchen, pantry, and a peek at the maid's quarters where I met Alma, fiftyish and friendly.

What amazed me was that after the initial "shock", Marti's city house was welcoming, not intimidating. Yes, it's ambitious and dramatic, but because of the warm colors, the textures, the lighting, the custom oversized furniture, the layout and overall design, the place was inviting.

We all ended up in the kitchen where Dawn had put out sliced meats, cheese, bread, tomatoes and lettuce, mustard and mayo; all of which was a do it your self bonanza. I made a sandwich and cut it in half to share with Wee Willy. We were all tired and happy and we were all working at being not hungry. Under the table I had my hand on Marti's thigh and she had her hand on me.

After dinner the kids went off, assured that I would see them soon. Dawn insisted on cleaning up and Marti and I nested in the den.

"Joe, we all made it through an ass backwards weekend. I think you said that?"

"I said something like that; what I want to say now are words about your beauty, your intelligence, your tears and how brave you are. I love you, it's insane; I've known you for five minutes, or so, and your toast from Friday night is echoing in my head and my heart; 'To you, to me, to us'. Your us and my us could become our us; you even said, "This is us," and I want that; it's going to take time.

I closed the biggest deal of my life this past Thursday; my career is growing, I'm excited."

"Joe, that's fabulous,, congratulations; you never said a word."

"That's because we were having too much fun wiping our noses and opening up our hearts."

"You love me, I know you do."

"I do."

"And I do you."

"There it is, we are married; now all we have to do is take our time getting there."

Marti burst into tears and kissed me a snotty, teary joy filled mess. Then she wiped up her tears and cleaned my face with her sleeve.

"Come on, Joseph, I'll drive you home."

"I'll take a cab."

"Knock, knock,' it was Dawn, "I'll drive Joe home, you go up and talk with your children."

"Were you there for the whole time?"

"No, just most of it. Get your stuff, Joe, we'll find a place to park and I'll steal you from my sister-in-law."

Marti and I were standing, "I don't know where I put my bag."

"I know where it is," Dawn said, "give her a kiss and we'll get on to the big stuff."

We kissed, as instructed, "Marti, I don't have your office number."

"Dawn will give you my card. Goodnight, Joseph, I love you."

"Dawn, you are the prettiest cab driver ever; I thought we were going to park somewhere and I was going to get lucky?"

"Your full of it, Joe, you would never do that to Marti."

"What about you?"

"Marti and I already tried." "I meant you wouldn't get it on with me; you wouldn't do that to Marti."

"True."

"Back up a second to you and Marti."

"That was years ago when Marti and I found out that my brilliant brother was very busy outside his marriage."

"Marti told me."

"We smoked some incredible weed and slept together; Marti is not a woman's woman that way. We love each other and we love the kids and now we love you."

"That's nice and very complicated."

"It's simple, if it doesn't work out between you and Marti I'll be right there for you. I like you."

"Okay, three more things: I'm sorry for your loss, I like you and we both know I am going to be spending time at the indoor mansion; Central Park running partner?"

"Yes, if you give me a kiss goodnight."

"Seriously?"

"Yes, and make it a good one."

We kissed, Dawn was an excellent kisser, "Dawn, what the hell, I feel like a traitor."

"Me, too. Oh, almost forgot, here's Marti's card. Have a great tomorrow."

"Thank you, you too, be careful going home. I love your sister-in-law."

I had a ton of things, happy things, running around in my head; I focused on Marti and managed to shut down and sleep until six.

CHAPTER 42
THE FAMILY PACKAGE

"Good morning, Liz."

"Good morning, Joe, how was your weekend?"

"It was stellar; it was the beginning of something big."

"That sounds great, I am happy for you."

"In fact the number I phoned in on Friday, that's Marti Mason's Easthampton residence and this card is her business info and I wrote her Fifth Avenue address and phone number on the back."

"What happened?"

"I fell in love."

"Wow, Joe, I'm excited for you."

"Thank you, we'll see, one day at a time."

Liz gave me a hug, "You have had a full plate, Joe; the Monarch on Thursday and falling in love over the weekend."

"I need to talk with Mr. Reinhardt, see if he has five minutes for me?"

"Sure."

"What's up, Joe?"

Bob Reinhardt never sat behind his desk when we were together; there were two easy chairs and a small coffee table and that's where we were. I liked that; it was comfortable.

"Bob, I've entered into a personal relationship with a possible client and of course I'll keep you posted going forward."

"Who is the lucky woman?"

"About fifteen months ago you had me meet with a young couple interested in building their dream beachfront house in Easthampton."

"I remember, he went to Argentina and never came back."

"Yes, his name is Jeremy Mason; I'm dating his widow, Marti Mason. Of course she still has the property, it's beautiful, we were out there this weekend, but she's uncertain because of last March's storm that took roughly twenty houses from the Hampton's beaches out to sea."

"Understandably. I wish you both well; I'd like to meet her whenever it's comfortable."

"That would be a hoot, she's a wonderful woman."

"I am happy for you, Joe."

"Thank you. I am headed down the hall to sit with Jim; we have work to do on The Monarch."

For the rest of May and most of June Jim Palmer and I wrestled with The Monarch; changing its shape, especially at the rear of the building where the two wings join, affording us the opportunity to reposition some of the working parts, like the freight elevators and air conditioning units and to artfully use decorative baffles to muffle machinery noises. Everything was coming together, the Fisher brothers were happy and my relationship with Jim Palmer was solid.

Marti and I did not like being apart but I was unwilling to give up my Westside apartment; it was so tempting to move in with her, but for the moment I spent the middle of the week there; I even got 'home' in time for what was quickly becoming our family dinner.

At least one night a week we would go out on the town; usually drinks and dinner and the occasional movie or Broadway show. We were working hard and playing even harder.

One evening we planned to meet at "41" at six; I got there early and the Fisher brothers, seated at a table near the bar, invited me to have a drink.

"Love to, thanks; I'm good until my woman shows up."

Larry got all over me, "Listen to the kid, 'until my woman shows up.'"

"Larry, I'm single, I'm not dating my mother, or my sister, or a girl, what's left? My woman."

"I guess you got something there, Joe."

By then a waiter had delivered my drink and I raised my glass, "Here's to women and The Monarch."

We all drank and I realized they were all admiring someone or something behind me.

"This woman says she knows one of you gentlemen."

I turned around and Jerry Brown was standing there with his arm around Marti. Everyone volunteered but Marti put her hand on my shoulder, "Sorry, fellas, but this is my guy."

"Joe told us he was waiting for his woman and I gave him some flack; but now I can see what he meant."

I was on my feet, Jerry gave me a pat on the back and I got a kiss on the lips, "Gentlemen, I would like you to meet Marti Mason; Marti this is Larry, Frank and Jimmy Fisher. They all stood.

"Please," Marti gestured for them to sit, but they didn't.

"It is my pleasure to steal this man away from you, we have a long night ahead."

"You're traveling," Larry asked, ever the wise guy.

"No, we are grabbing a bite to eat, then to the theatre for Zero Mostel in, 'A Funny Thing Happened on the Way to the Forum', then we are going home where we'll think of something fun to do."

"Thanks for the drink, gentlemen."

We turned and walked away.

"You are fantastic, Marti, those were the Monarch guys and they all fell in love with you."

"That's sweet, however, what they really fell in love with is your idea, The Monarch. I was just the icing on the cake."

The first night Marti and I slept together in the city evolved from the insistence of the innocents. I had gone over to see the kids and stayed for dinner and then left. After several visits like that Sara and Wee Willy wanted to know why I wasn't sleeping with mom?

I told them I still had my own apartment and all my clothes and everything I need were there. And I get up at six every morning to run and that's a little disruptive. Of course I had to explain what disruptive meant and while I was doing that Marti interrupted, "We're still working it out, we love each other and we will be sleeping together, you can count on it."

We didn't tell them that it was because of fear: I was afraid of losing myself in the splendor of the place and the woman; Marti has that something, and that's it, she just has 'it'.

Marti was afraid of two things; first, my fear and I would run away and, second, she would do anything to keep me, Marti believed we were destiny's children; "Come on Joe, become part of my dream."

That first time in the custom, oversized bed we devoured each other; we were claiming that bed as 'ours' and with love and lust we erased every thought of anyone else having ever used that bed. When we were done we could not stop whispering and talking. We loved, loved, loved one another.

Over time I added more clothes and toiletries and shoes and running shoes to "my" closet, which, like Marti's, was an entire room. I slept at Fifth three or four nights a week.

We went to Easthampton at least one weekend a month and during the summer Marti, Dawn and the kids stayed out there, I took my two week vacation there.

There were times I commuted: Jeremy had purchased a Porsche convertible that he never got to drive, the odometer read twelve miles and we had the Porsche people freshen the car and make it perfect; it became my commuter vehicle when I couldn't get away 'til Saturday or if we had to run into the city during the summer.

My sister Sylvia and her husband Al invited the family to their home in Tenafly for a Sunday lunch barbecue so every one could meet Marti, Dawn, Sara and Billy.

My worst fears dissolved when Marti and my mom came back from a stroll to the tennis court and Marti winked at me; thank you, God. The kids had fun on the tennis court, my brother-in-law Al was a master barbecue chef and the menu satisfied the kids and adults. Dawn only grabbed my ass once and, of course, immediately apologized. Every one survived; actually everyone enjoyed the day and invites were extended to anyone who wanted to make the drive out to Easthampton.

Syl, Al and their kids visited us at the beach for a weekend; once again the kids had a great time as Dawn played camp counselor. The adults drank, ate, laughed a lot and Marti kissed me at least a dozen times over the weekend.. She and my sister took a long walk on the beach and found comfort in their differences and their mutual love of me. Marti is pretty mercurial and Sylvia somewhat sedate but I was common ground and loved them both and, lucky me, they loved me back. On Sunday, when they left, we were all outside to wave goodbye.

Marti would occasionally push me to leave Reinhardt and become a full time husband and dad. She was like an undertow and those were our most difficult times; I was shepherding The Monarch and I was in achieve mode, vital to me.

The Monarch was in the building stage and it was very, very exciting. After months of creating a building on paper Jim and I would see it become a reality. For me even watching them dig out the "big hole in the ground" was a thrill.

I had come up with an idea that made it much safer to build a beach house; less chance of it being swept away in a storm. It was an I- beam rectangle, at sand level, matching the size of the house (70x50), set on four I beams pile driven ten feet deep into the sand. From the sand level rectangle I beams, appropriately distributed, would rise ten feet to support a second matching rectangle upon which the house would be built. Ground level would be the garage, storage, stairway to the pantry and kitchen, heater and generator. Every thing at ground level, under dire circumstances, might be washed away but the house, ten feet above the beach, would survive.

Marti decided to go ahead and I was finishing the design; we hoped to start building in two months. I was thrilled and Marti saw the house as 'our' house and she yearned for us to marry. I wasn't ready; not for lack of love but for need of professional achievement: I was just getting started, a bundle of creative ideas, and I wanted to start my own firm as soon as my commitments at Reinhardt-Tufts were fulfilled. I loved being an architect and envisioned hard work and success. Marti's vision was more family oriented; work less, spend more time together.

On November 15th William Mason celebrated his birthday and Wee Willy had seen the light; he was giving up the Wee and the Willy. Billy would be okay but he preferred Bill. So, it was Bill now, after all he was in kindergarten and would likely end up being Bill or William. Happy Birthday, Bill.

We pretty much steamrolled through Thanksgiving and Christmas but had plans to go to the beach for New Year's. We had a commitment to attend the Reinhardt-Tufts Christmas Party and some of our clients, past and present, were in attendance.

Bob Reinhardt spoke briefly, conveying Holiday wishes to our guests. Larry Fisher spoke with enthusiasm about The Monarch project and their pleasure in working with us; he gave me a special nod, "This young man has created excitement for us; we've been around this town for a long time and you have given us the idea of creating a legacy. We are building that legacy and we thank all of you for your creativity and hard work. Merry Christmas to you all."

We all drank to a Merry Christmas.

"I am fortunate to be here in a dual role," Marti said, "I'm here with Joe because we are a couple and I'm here as a client because Reinhardt-Tufts has designed our dream beach house; who knew that sleeping with the architect would be such fun. Merry Christmas everyone."

Everyone sipped champagne, I gulped.

The beach in the winter; is stark and quiet, yet welcoming to those of us that don't mind bundling up; or actually enjoy bundling up to walk close to the angry ocean and listen to its harsh symphony. Marti and I love each other and together we especially love the beach in the winter; walking with our arms around each others' waist and looking ahead to a warm fire, soft music and being close. It's audacious but sitting in front of the fire we feel like the only humans within a hundred miles.

"Were we wrong to leave Dawn and the kids in the city?"

"No, I don't think so, do you miss them?"

"I do. I don't know."

"Marti, it's Saturday night; it's seven; we can drive to the city right now and stay there or drive back here tomorrow morning."

"You would do that?"

"Tuesday is New Year's Day; I don't have to be back to work 'til Wednesday or even Thursday."

"You would do that?"

"Yes, I would and, boy, would you owe me."

"Let's all start the New Year together; it's going to be a big year."

"Stay in the city or come back here?"

"Back here."

"We will need food."

"I'll call the service, tell them what we are doing,"

"Call Dawn first; tell her the plan."

"Okay. I love you."

"I love the idea of all of us being together."

I kissed Marti and went to the fireplace to damp down the logs.

"Marti, I had great plans for you."

I forgot she was on the phone with Dawn. Marti hung up.

"Every one is excited. I feel better. I'm calling the service; is there anything special you want?"

"No, but tell them we had a fire going and I damped it down; they may smell smoke."

We made the trip to New York in good time. Got goodnight kisses from Dawn.

"You are both nuts, you know that?"

"Marti wanted us all to be together for the New Year, me too."

We had an early breakfast, stowed every one's gear and hit the road.

"Why did you come back for us," Sara asked.

Marti and I answered at the same time, "Because we love you."

That moment alone made the trip worthwhile.

There were traces of snow when we pulled up to the house, a rarity at the beach. My first chore was to get the fire up and running; Dawn was making hot chocolate for the kids and I did something rare for me, it wasn't even noon; I poured some cognac into a snifter and took it up to share with Marti who was feeling "messy," her way of describing her monthly event. We sipped and napped, almost, until Sara and Billy found us and climbed on; shades of the very first weekend we ever spent together.

When we went down for lunch Marti stayed upstairs; she promised me she was okay, just a little melancholy.

We had a quiet lunch and then Dawn, Sara, Billy and I had a raucous game of Monopoly.

"You are so lucky,"Billy said to his sister.

"It isn't luck, Bill, it's skill."

"I keep going to jail." Bill was not happy.

"Can we take a break, I want to check on Mom."

Upstairs I slid under the covers and nested right up against Marti's backside; she was so warm.

"Are you okay," I whispered.

"Oh, Joseph, Joseph, I am going to lose you." She turned to me, teary eyed, "I am so sad."

"Marti, you will never lose me, not ever; you are the love of my life."

"You're afraid of me, Joe."

"That's not true, I adore you. We are here, all of us; we will always be together."

"Joseph, The Monarch, the new beach house; huge achievements, they are going to tear us apart."

I sat up, I was angry and emotionally confused, "Marti, I need your trust, I need your patience; we are going to do this big year together; here's to you, to me, to us, remember? We are fighters, you and I, we are a team, damn it. Yes, I need more time to establish myself, so we can win together. I'll be downstairs."

Dawn took one look at my face and went upstairs.

"Is mom okay," Bill wanted to know.

"She's okay, we are going to be building the new beach house and she's worried about it."

"Can I put a log on the fire?"

"Sure, Bill, I'll help you."

"I'm going upstairs to see mom," Sara said.

I helped Bill with the log; how to place it, not toss it, and which way the log should go so it wouldn't cause a flare up. We sat on the floor close enough to feel the heat.

"I love you, Joe."

"I love you, Bill."

Sara and Dawn descended together;

"Mom is fine," Sara told Billy.

"Marti is fine, Joe, she'll be down in a few minutes."

Marti came down and we hugged hard and didn't want to let go; we whispered, "I love you."

It was almost two and we were all starving. "Pancakes. Can we make pancakes?"

Dawn responded, "Of course we can. Great idea, Billy, would you help me?"

"Yes, Dawn, and mom gets the first one."

We had stacks of pancakes with butter and syrup and hot chocolate to drink. There was a little batter left, maybe two or three pancakes, and Dawn and I experimented, we added some bourbon to the mix and they were delicious; one for each of the adults, yummy! And a taste for the kids, Yick!

The next day, New Year's Eve day, was sunny and warmer, low 40's, so Dawn and I decided on a run, we would be back for lunch. We stretched and hit the beach. I had Marti on my mind.

"What is going on, Dawn?"

"I think she's scared."

"Of what?"

"This is my take, not her words."

"Okay."

"Jeremy screwed around, he was gone a lot, in fact he took his mistress to Argentina where they both died."

"Where is this going?"

"Your work is your mistress."

"Dawn, for God's sake, yes, I love my work, it's important to me."

"She's got two kids, a crazy sister-in-law, a gazillion dollars and you; she wants to be loved, she wants to be number one."

"She is number one."

"Marti wants to come first, all of the time."

"We've been together for seven months and I have never seen her act this way; I have loved her since day one."

"The Monarch changed everything; scared her."

My watch signaled for us to turn around.

"She thinks some woman is going to pop up while you are working on The Monarch, or you are going to design a new idea that will take you from her."

"Dawn, that is just plain crazy."

"Maybe she is having a moment."

"I'll pray for that."

Lunch was waiting for us; a platter of assorted sandwiches: ham and cheese, peanut butter and jelly, roast beef, lettuce and tomato. I opted for ham and cheese and a beer. I also opted to hug Marti; where was the woman I love?

There were no big plans for New Year's Eve; a simple dinner around seven and then endless cheese and French bread and a lemon cake. All of that was designed to compliment a magnum of Dom Perignon.

Sara and Bill had declared their intentions to stay up until midnight and we were all handsomely and comfortably dressed. The television was on but muted and we had show tune LP's playing softly.

Billy was the first to yawn himself upstairs to sleep; there were kisses and Happy New Year's wishes as he trudged upstairs.

Sara fell asleep on the sofa and I carried her upstairs and Dawn put her under the covers.

When Dawn came down stairs, I refreshed our champagne and toasted the ladies,

"Thank you, Marti, for being the most important woman in my life. I love you."

We drank and I looked at Dawn, "Dawn, you are a treasured friend; thank you for all that you do."

We drank and then Dawn asked me to dance; I looked to Marti who shrugged in a sort of 'why not' kind of way. Off came our shoes and we were dancing along with some nervous laughter; I had never held Dawn in my arms. When our dance tune ended I thanked Dawn and asked Marti to dance; off came her shoes and she was in my arms. Dancing with Marti was like floating on clouds; she was silk, effortless. Marti was a natural; we danced close and Marti let go of the angst that had haunted her. We danced in heaven for several tunes until Marti kissed me a Marti kiss of love and passion.

"I'm going to bed," Dawn declared.

"No you're not, Marti and I said in unison; the third 'in unison' of the weekend.

"We are in this together, the three of us," I said, "it's twenty minutes to the new year."

I put together some cheese and bread and filled our glasses, "Can I get anything for you or you?"

Everyone was content and I turned on the television sound; soon enough we were counting down with millions of other people.

At midnight Marti toasted me, "Happy New Year, my darling Joseph; To You. To Me, To Us; let's make this year our year. I love you."

We kissed and then remembered Dawn. Marti hugged and kissed Dawn and then I did also.

"Happy New Year, Dawn."

"Happy New Year to you both, to all of us; I am going to have lemon cake and Dom Perignon for breakfast," said Dawn, "Goodnight, you two, I'm going up to bed."

"Goodnight, Dawn."

"Marti, why don't you go upstairs; I'll close up down here."

"I'll wait for you, we'll go up together."

"Great, I have to be sure the fire is safe and put a few things in the fridge."

"I love you, Joe."

On the way upstairs I told Marti, "I am so glad everyone is here; the kids are a joy."

"They love you, Joe, you are an important part of their lives."

"I love them and I love their Mom."

We brushed, we undressed and we went to bed; physically tired and emotionally exhausted.

"Goodnight, Joe."

"Goodnight, Marti."

While the USC Trojans were beating the Wisconsin Badgers 42 to 37 in the Rose Bowl we drove back to the city and the start of the New Year.

THE KISS

CHAPTER 43

THE BEACH HOUSE BEGINS

A few weeks later Marti and I returned to Easthampton for the first phase of the beach house; pile driving the galvanized four corner I-beams and assembling the I-beam rectangle at sand level. The crane/pile driver was huge and there was a team of ten men including four ironworkers ready to tighten the oversized bolts and weld the joints at 90 degrees for posterity. It took two days and we stayed overnight. Late the first day sand was bulldozed to dress the site, leaving the 50x70 ground level I beam rectangle with eight, ten foot I-beams jutting toward the sky. The next day the I-beam rectangle was duplicated atop the vertical beams; upon which the house would be built. So far, so good; I thought.

Three weeks later an eight inch slab was poured from the street to the ocean side of the structure; on the west side for the driveway and the flooring of the garage and the storage and equipment area. This very thick reinforced slab would also cement in place the existing iron-work. The actual house construction could now begin.

By mid March The Monarch construction had risen almost to the top; two more to get to the 26th floor. Now I had four places to be at once: the office, the beach, The Monarch and home with Marti and the kids.

THE KISS

CHAPTER 44

THE INVISIBLE MAN

Easter was early, April seventh, and we drove to the beach Friday night. Traffic was awful but we kept things light all the way to the house. We never did, I don't think, correctly spell: supercalifragilisticexpialidocious.

We did have super nice weather and a well thought out Easter egg hunt: Painted on Saturday, hid on Saturday night by the Easter Bunny and searched for on Sunday, after breakfast; that was the plan.

Dawn and I ran on Saturday morning. She was shocked to learn that Marti and I had not enjoyed any love making over the past three months.

"You know where to find me, Joe."

"Knock it off, Dawn, I am seriously worried. I hate to see Marti so distant, so unhappy. I should not have told you."

"It's good that you did; I have not seen her like this since she learned my brother was cheating on her."

"Damn, that's encouraging."

"I'm sorry, Joe, I love you both; you belong together."

"It feels like she is waiting for the shoe to drop, so she can say, "I knew it." Meanwhile, she resents my workload. I don't know what to do to make her happy.""

We were almost done with our run and were going past the new beach house, "I love the design, Joe. It is going to be beautiful."

"Thank you, Dawn, I'm excited."

"Come on, Mr. Easter Bunny, let's get breakfast."

After breakfast we each got six eggs to color or paint or doodle, that's like scribble. We were all so different and Dawn was the judge, she got to pick "Favorite Egg" and she picked one of her own. Well, in that case, we decided we should each select our own favorite and then I decided that the invisible man, that I opened the front door for, would be the final judge.

"Well, sir, it's very nice of you to stop by to be the official Egg Judge."

He just said, "It's his pleasure."

"I can't see him, so this is not fair," Billy complained.

"Bill, I can't see him either; so it's not fair for all of us equally."

"I can see him," Marti said, "He's seven feet tall and wears glasses."

"I can see him; he has purple eyes."

"No one has purple eyes, Dawn. He does not have purple eyes."

"Oh, then you can see him?"

"No, I can't."

"He is wearing a green and orange suit," Marti said, "with a purple vest to match his eyes."

"I can see him," Bill said, "and he likes my egg the most. I win!"

I opened the front door, "Thanks for stopping by." I shut the door and when I sat down next to Marti she gave me a Marti kiss, something she had never done in front of the kids.

"Wow," Billy said.

"Holy smokers," Sara said.

"I'm not saying anything," Dawn said.

"I would like the man in the green and orange suit to stop by more often," I said.

After the kids went to sleep, Marti, Dawn and I took all the eggs outside and hid them. Inside we shared a nightcap. After a little while Dawn issued an ultimatum, "Okay, I am going to bed because you two haven't stopped touching each other. I'm just a kid and you are being inappropriate; it's kind of fun in a way that is also inappropriate, so, if you go to bed I can clean up down here."

"Are you admonishing us," I asked reaching for Marti's hand to lead her up to bed.

"Yes, that and telling you I love you both."

"Goodnight, Dawn, we both love you. Happy Easter."

We had brushed our teeth and were in bed kissing like we used to; hot, wet and soft and warm.

"Joseph, earlier, you created the invisible man, that's the you that I want, that's the you that makes this family complete."

"I am that man at work, I am that man with the kids, and I am that man when I am alone with you, like now.

"I'm messy."

"I'll become invisible and you won't even know I'm here."

"Don't be mean, I just can't."

"I didn't mean to be mean; I was disappointed."

"I just can't; I can't explain it."

"Marti, we are good together: we are good for Sara and Bill, we are good for our businesses and for each other but something is wrong and I don't understand it; I'm worried about you, I miss the Marti I fell in love with."

Marti was crying and turned to me for comfort; I held her close.

We had pancakes for breakfast because we had painted all the eggs. After the pancakes Sara and Billy, carrying baskets, set off on their egg hunt.

"Just a reminder," I said, "we each had six eggs and there are five of us, so that's how many eggs you are looking for. You have thirty minutes; good luck."

Thirty minutes later Sara had fifteen eggs and Billy had fourteen; however Billy said he saw the invisible man walking by eating an egg that was probably his.

"Sorry, pal, nice try but your sister is the winner."

When we left for the city I handed Sara a sheet of paper on which I had copied the word supercalifragilisticexpialidocious.

"Sara, if you read one letter at a time, out loud, by the time you get to the last letter we will be home."

Only one problem, she fell asleep half way there.

THE KISS

CHAPTER 45

A VERY LONG SUMMER

May was a big month, Marti and I got to celebrate her birthday for the first time; we had dinner at home, in the city, and dessert was a birthday cake with 29 candles and she was truly surprised. We sang Happy Birthday to Mommy/Marti; Sara and Bill helped blow out the candles while Dawn and I cheered.

"Oh, my God, thank you, thank you," Marti looked at me, "Now you know how old I am."

"If I counted the candles correctly, I am in love with an older woman."

"Oh, no."

"Oh, yes, three months to the day."

"Oh, no, there must be some mistake."

"Not cutting the cake and sharing would be a mistake."

Dawn had taken the cake and we were all getting a piece.

"Lemon with chocolate icing, my favorite."

There was a gift that Dawn handed to the birthday girl, Marti looked at me.

I held my hands up, palms facing her, "Don't look at me; I didn't know it was your birthday; I was told to be here, no matter what, by Miss Bossy over there."

Bill laughed, "Dawn isn't Miss Bossy, she's Dawn."

"You're right, I was being silly."

Everyone's attention was now focused on the two small pieces of black material coming out of the gift box; a new bikini for the summer.

"Put it on, Mom, let's see," Sara urged.

"Thank you all, it's nice but I'll try it on later; right now it's cake time."

Later, Marti modeled the bikini for Dawn and me.

"You are drop dead gorgeous."

"Joe's right. Wow."

"Do you think you can follow me up the stairs and give me a birthday present?"

"I'm certain of it."

"You are unconscionable, both of you."

"Goodnight, Dawn, thank you."

"Happy birthday, Marti, I love you."

"My clothes are over there, young man, why don't you get them and follow me."

"Yes, Ma'am. Goodnight, Dawn."

"Goodnight, Joe."

"Hurry up, Kid."

"I'm coming."

"Not yet, you're not."

On Wednesday, May 15th, I called Marti at work; I waited until she wrapped up another call.

"Hello, Joe."

"Marti, meet me for a drink at our favorite spot?"

"Five o'clock."

"See you there."

I was walking toward "41" and I saw Marti walking toward me wearing a short, deep purple dress; she was beautiful. At the top of the steps we kissed and walked into "41" together.

"Good afternoon," Henry greeted us at the bar, "Bourbon sour, large tumbler, Mrs. Mason?"

"Yes, please. Thank you, Henry."

"You are so beautiful, Marti, I watched you walking toward me thinking everyone was watching you wondering, who is that, where is she going, who is she meeting? And then you kissed me; lucky me."

Our drinks arrived and we touched glasses,

"Happy Anniversary, Marti. One year ago, right here."

"Joseph, you remembered;

Here's to you, here's to me, here's to us."

We sipped and kissed briefly.

"Good evening, Mrs. Mason."

"Jerry." Marti hugged my almost father-in-law and I think Jerry blushed. He and I hugged and he looked at us, "Dinner, when ever you are ready, we are holding table seven for you."

"Dinner, yes, thank you," Marti looked at me.

"That's the plan."

"Take your time," and Jerry moved off.

"I like him, Joe, he's a good man."

"He is and he just became a grandfather, again; this time a boy."

"How does that make you feel?"

"Happy for them all."

"Do you ever wonder, you know, what it might have been like?"

"No, not really, I walked away from a lovely woman and the incredible power of "41" to follow my dream, architecture, and, of course, I didn't know it, to find you. I am happy for them and thrilled for us."

We were seated and shared a steak tartar, no capers, that Vincent, our captain, mixed at the table and for dessert, a chocolate soufflé and two glasses of Louis Roederer champagne.

We talked endlessly and didn't get home until almost ten.

"Where have you been," Dawn demanded, "The little people missed their goodnight hugs and kisses."

"My bad, I lured this woman off the street and held her captive at "41".

"41", I've never been, I want to go."

"The kids are okay?"

"Yes, they are fine."

"Good, I'm going up to bed," Marti said, on her way up the steps, "I'm tired."

"I'll be up in a few, I'm thinking a nightcap would be good. What about you, Miss Dawn?"

"Are you going to put a move on me, Joseph?"

I had poured a short bourbon on ice.

"No, Dawn, I'm giving Marti time to go to sleep; if I was up there with her I would be disappointed."

"I'm sorry." Dawn took my drink and helped herself to a sip.

"It was our one year anniversary and all Marti talked about was my giving up architecture to run J's company; it would cement us as a family, we would have more time together and it would make Marti happy."

"Maybe it would make her happy,"

Dawn wasn't sure.

"It's not just sex, it's everything; she's a mystery, where is Marti Mason?"

Dawn had finished my drink and poured another; she handed me the glass and sat down right next to me.

"Dawn, are you going to put a move on me?"

"Thinking about it, you know I love you."

I took a big swig and Dawn drank the rest.

"I do know you love me and Marti and the kids, you are fabulous and all of us together are a once in a life time package. There is only one thing missing and it's on me."

"I would have put the burden on Marti."

"I can't accept Marti's failure to understand my need to succeed as an architect, to me it's so obvious and she refuses to see it. It will destroy us."

"You are right, she will not change. Would you kiss me?"

"No."

"Can I kiss you?"

"No."

Dawn kissed me anyway.

"I remember you, you're the prettiest cabbie in New York City."

Dawn kissed me again. `

"Stop!"

"No."

"Dawn, we have to stop; we are avoiding the reality of all of this coming to an end."

Dawn started to cry, "Marti is an ass."

"Yes, she is, and I love her.I'm going up to sleep with her. I am going to wait for the new beach house, and pray for a miracle. Goodnight, Dawn."

"Goodnight, Joe."

The following week Liz got me some time with Bob Reinhardt, my boss.

"What's up, Joe?"

"It's a long list; some of it is business, some of it is personal and some is just curiosity."

"Where ever you want to start."

"Personal, first, that will clear the way for everything else and also because it's the most painful. Marti Mason and I are not going to make it."

"Joe, I'm sorry."

"Yeah, me too. Short version, she wants me to give up architecture to run the company her husband started; we would be a tighter family unit, no outside distractions. I am not willing to do that and I doubt Marti will flip. I think, I hope we will remain friends; especially because of the children, I love them. Okay that's out of the way."

"You obviously love her?"

"I do, she's special, but my career is very important to me.

Next: The Monarch; I promised Larry Fisher that,"

"Joe, stop!"

"What?"

"Larry has an idea and he didn't want to cause any conflicts of interest."

"I am all ears."

"He wants you to manage the managers for a year while living there rent free."

"Are you serious?"

"That's what he said."

"What did you say?"

"I gave him a green light and if problems arise we would all sit down and work it out."

"I don't know what to say?"

"Think about it. When he mentioned it I frankly felt it wouldn't happen because of you and Marti."

"If only! Okay, business; what was it like starting your own firm?"

"Scary, courageous, determined and the thrill of a lifetime. Are you thinking?"

"Sure, thinking, but that's it. I love working for you; you have been generous and paternal, I am grateful, very grateful."

"It's mutual, Joe, you are a swizzle stick, you have stirred the firm up in a healthy, helpful way. You scared some folks but you never intended that, you were excited and enthusiastic. Swizzle stick."

"What are you planning re: partners and Tufts passing?"

"No decision at this time."

"Understood. Thank you for trusting me and guiding me, I am very grateful. Lastly, my secretary, Elizabeth, is first rate, I cherish her; I would like to give her a raise?""

"I'll look into it."

"Thank you."

"Anything new on your horizon, any new business?"

"No, but the Newport house is calling to me, I want to go up and see it."

"Sounds like the right thing to me."

"It will be an overnight, okay?"

"It's your call, Joe, I trust you completely. Lastly, I am very sorry about Marti; I'm here if I can help in any way."

"Thank you, Bob. Am I going to hear from Larry Fisher?"

"You heard it here, now it's up to you."

"I'm on it."

I talked Marti into joining me when I went to Newport for a walk-through of the massive, single story residence that was about a month shy of occupancy.

We drove up in the Porsche, stayed at the Hilton and had a lobster dinner at Scales and Shells. After dinner we walked around Newport holding hands and talking about the kids and work. Marti was in good spirits and I was thrilled she had come along; I wanted her to see my creation.

"You're excited?"

"I am, especially because you are with me."

"You love me."

"I do and it matters to me that you see my work; that you feel the energy of what I do."

"I am so happy to be here with you. Newport is lovely, it's like being at the beach on the island; the air is so fresh."

"We'll sleep with the window open, we'll sleep like babies and in the morning we will have breakfast at Annie's."

"Sounds wonderful."

"We have to be at the "duck house" at ten, so breakfast at eight."

"No problem. The duck house?"

"The owner's name is Mallard, so I have always called it the duck house."

We got there a few minutes after ten, not a problem. Damn, the place looked great.

"I'm going to introduce you as my wife, okay?"

"Yes, very okay."

"Mr. Mallard, this is my wife, Marti, I hope you are comfortable with her walking with us; she wanted to see your home. And this is Jack Dougherty who did the construction."

Both men were pleased to meet Marti and we did the run through. To my eye the job looked first rate and Mr. Mallard was, indeed, very happy.

"When we started this two years ago, Marti, I wasn't sure about this young man, but his vision, his inspiration and his energy were contagious; I think some of that comes from being married to you."

"That is very sweet, Mr. Mallard; so I'm going to go along with you, I think your home is stunning."

We were a happy group of four as we finished the tour.

"Congratulations, Jack, construction is first rate."

"Thank you, Joe, and it was a pleasure having you along this morning, Mrs. Gordon."

"My pleasure as well, gentlemen, thank you."

"I would like to walk around outside, we did some innovative excavation; I'd like to check it out."

"I'm going to sit in the car; it was a pleasure meeting you both. Best wishes in your new home."

Marti went to the car and we three men circled the house and, again, well done.

"Joe and Jack, thank you both; this was pretty seamless all the way through and I know it doesn't always go that way."

I made my farewell and joined Marti for the ride home.

"I am glad I was here with you."

"Me, too. Mr. Mallard credits you as a source of my energy and I feel that way too."

"Mrs. Gordon, that startled me a little, not in a bad way; we are partners."

"Dear God, I hope so."

One Friday in June Marti and I left the city early for Easthampton. The contractor told me there was enough of the new house for Marti to walk through and get a feel for the place. We promised to be there around three. Our plan was to spend the night and return to the city on Saturday with special plans for a children's concert at Carnegie Hall on Sunday.

Driving to the beach we stopped for lobster rolls on Montauk Highway; delicious, and we bought more to take home, hoping they would be good the next day.

We parked at the house, put the lobster rolls in the fridge and walked to the new house just fifty yards away. The first thing I noticed was the build up to access the street-side front door. It was a half circle of three steps going up to a large landing and then three more steps to the landing outside the door; it was going to be perfect.

Steve Roberts, the contractor, saw us coming.

"Good to see you Mrs. Mason, good to see you, Joe."

"Happy to be here, Steve."

He led us to the beach side, out toward the ocean, so when we came around, there it was, already beautiful in rough form. It was obvious Marti was thrilled.

"Oh, Joe, it's beautiful." She threw her arms around me, "I love this house. Steve, lead the way."

"Mrs. Mason, we have to be careful in there, it's pretty rough still, but enough to see where everything fits."

"I will watch my step, I promise."

We entered by crossing the outdoor deck that was twenty feet deep. Inside we toured the pantry, the kitchen and great room with fireplace, dining room, den with fireplace, large bath and entry area at the front door with large closets for seasonal boots and coats. We went up stairs to the master suite with fireplace, and three other bedrooms, two baths and a mini-suite and bath. We went back downstairs, overwhelmed and exhausted.

"I felt it," Marti said, "It is going to be beautiful. Steve, this has been wonderful, thank you."

"My pleasure, I am glad you are pleased."

"Good work, Steve, any idea when?"

"By Labor Day we should be down to interior finishing; mid October."

I looked at Marti, "Any questions? Any changes?"

"No and no, although I'll probably think of something."

"You can call."

We had been walking down stairs and we took one more look at the kitchen and great room area.

"It's wonderful," Marti said, "I'm excited."

We shook hands with Steve and left as we entered; out to the beach and around the house to the street.

I took Marti's hand as we walked home.

"I'm glad we came out," I said.

"I am too." Marti stopped and hugged me, "Hold on to me, Joe, please hold on to me."

I squeezed Marti to me.

"What is it," I asked.

"I'm scared, I'm scared I am going to lose you."

"Marti," I gave her an extra squeeze, "you are not going to lose me."

Marti shook it off, "Let's go home, I'm hungry."

We made spaghetti and meatballs and had a couple of beers. We touched bottles; "Here's to us, Marti."

"To us," Marti responded, "and our new beach house; I love it, I can picture all of the furnishings." We ate and talked about the kids.

"We have the children's concert on Sunday afternoon."

"Oh, God, Joe, I would have forgotten."

"No problem, we are all going, Dawn, too."

"All piano, I think," Marti said, "and kids of all ages; should be fun."

"I'm looking forward to it", I said, "I never learned to play any instrument and I marvel at those that can."

"After the concert," Marti said, "we can go out for Chinese."

"Perfect, Billy loves the fortune cookies; we've got a plan."

After dinner we had a nightcap out on the front porch, while we listened to the ocean.

"That's a concert that never stops."

"I love it, too, it's hypnotic," Marti agreed.

"When Dawn and I run, the pounding of the waves is background music to our breathing; it's always there."

"You and Dawn are close."

"No, Marti, you and Dawn are close, Dawn and I are good friends; I think the world of her."

"She has a birthday coming up, July 18th."

"How old?"

"Twenty three."

"Can we figure out a way to surprise and take her to "41"?"

"Dawn, the kids and I will be at the beach all summer, I don't know how we can do that."

"You're right, and also celebrating her birthday should be with the kids."

"You better be there, Joe."

"I am going to spend a couple of weeks at the beach; I can split them up or lump them together. Do you have a preference?"

"Yes, I prefer going inside, going upstairs and discussing this in bed."

"I like your preference, I like it a lot."

In the morning, headed to the city, I had driven about a mile when I hit the brakes and made a U turn back to the house.

"Lobster rolls?"

"Yes, that was close."

"I forgot them as well, good work, Joseph. For a second I thought you were testing the brakes."

"The brakes are fine, it's the memory that is a little slow."

"Joe, I'll run in and get them."

"That would be great."

We had the almost forgotten lobster rolls for dinner; damn good.

On July 18th, I barbecued chicken breasts and hamburgers, so everyone had a choice. Marti made one of her amazing salads and we had fresh corn on the cob; dinner was enjoyed by us all.

The five of us cleaned up and loaded the dishwasher. All done until Marti appeared with a chocolate, chocolate cake with 23 candles and we all offered a terrible rendition of "Happy Birthday" to Dawn. The cake was delicious and Dawn's present was a black bikini, like Marti's.

"Are you two trying to drive me nuts?"

"Yes," was the answer, in unison, as I opened a bottle of champagne.

I took the first week of August as my second vacation week so I would be at the beach for my birthday. On Tuesday, August 6th, another chocolate, chocolate cake was served after dinner with 29 candles that everyone helped blow out and we all sang Happy Birthday to me. The real surprise came in a small box about the size of a wallet; inside was the key to the Porsche.

"No way, Marti!"

"Yes, way, Joseph, Happy Birthday, love of my life." Along with the good wishes came a kiss that, as usual, caused screams from the kids.

"Thank you, Marti, thank you each and everyone."

I opened a bottle of champagne and on the count of three Marti, Dawn and I turned to Sara and Bill, "Here's to you two, we love you so much."

After we enjoyed the cake and some bubbly we all went for a walk on the beach, the capper to a wonderful day.

Later that week Marti said, "I see the way you look at Dawn."

We were brushing our teeth before going to bed and it sounded something like: "ah ee thay ew ook a daw."

"What?"

"I see the way you look at Dawn."

"And?"

Marti rinsed and spit, "I don't like it."

"Because?"

We were headed to the bed, "You want her!"

"What!"

We were now in bed; "So I'm in bed with one of the smartest, prettiest, sexiest woman in my world; I love her and I am waiting for the Marti that I fell in love with to show up, but right now, this magnificent thoroughbred is accusing me of wanting to cheat on her, with her sister-in-law."

"She's young, she's beautiful, she has a perfect body, she loves you, she wants you and you want her."

"Marti,"

Marti stopped me, "She wears those short shorts and a bikini top and you . . ."

I put my hand over Marti's mouth and she bit me.

"Ow, damn it, Marti, listen to me; you wear short shorts and a bikini top and I get turned on because I know it's you, Marti, the woman, the mother of two kids that aren't mine but I feel like they are; Dawn is beautiful and I love her and she loves me but not that way."

"You're blind, Joseph, she's just waiting for you to fall; she'll be right there."

"Then go have this discussion with her, Marti, because I'm getting scared that you want us to fail, you have lost your way and it's getting worse."

Marti turned away from me.

"I hate it when you do that; you are busy in your own mind conjuring up strange behavior."

"Go away."

"Okay."

I went down stairs, poured a drink and took it out on the front porch. I honestly believed it was over; the best thing for me to do was walk away. I was in harm's way. We were sinking. I had told Marti that I would see a shrink together, oh, no!

I heard the screen door and Marti came out on the porch.

"I'm sorry, Joe. I'm very sorry."

"I'm scared, Marti."

"Come to bed, please."

"I'll be up in a little while."

Marti took my hand to lead me up stairs, "Please."

The next few days were walking on egg shell days; soft, gentle hand holding days; I felt like I was baby sitting a mentally ill version of the woman I loved. We made it through to Sunday when I reminded her I was not coming out the following weekend; I was visiting my sisters and was going to see my mom during the week.

"Fine, Joe, are you planning on coming out for Labor Day weekend?"

"Of course. I'm going to miss you, I'll call every day."

"You promise?"

"I love you and I promise. Where are the kids, I want to say goodbye."

Marti burst into tears, "You're not coming back!"

"I am. I have another idea, come with me to the city; I'll be working during the day, but otherwise, just the two of is. What do you say?"

"That's sweet. I'm going to stay here with the kids and the beach house is almost finished."

"Marti, they have about two months to go; they're getting close."

I found the kids; they were playing croquet in the back yard.

"Hey, you two, I want kisses; I'm going to be gone for two weeks."

"Gone where," Sara asked.

"I'll be in the city working and I am going to visit my sisters next weekend, that's why I won't be here."

"I'll miss you," Bill said giving me a big hug. Sara was next, "I'll miss you, too."

"I'll miss you both but I'll be back."

Marti was looking on and we went to the car together.

"Be careful."

"I will and I will call you every day."

"Leaving and no goodbye for Dawn? Remember me?"

"I'm sorry, I got all wrapped up with the kids."

"Be safe, we will miss you." Dawn delivered a quick kiss to my lips and went back in the house. Marti kissed me, "I love you, Joseph."

I started the car and looked at Marti; I ached for this beautiful woman, winked at her, and drove off.

CHAPTER 46

TWO WEEKS

I stayed at my apartment on the upper West side even though parking was a pain in the butt.

Everything in the refrigerator looked like a science lab project. Down the garbage chute and I went shopping for basics; two bags full, I felt like a city dweller again. In the elevator, going up was a cute little twenty something, "You still live here, I had given up on you; I'm Jane."

"I'm Joe, Jane, nice meeting you."

Jane exited at the 12th floor, "12B, Joe."

"Thank you, Jane."

I put everything in the fridge and looked for my running shoes and found a pair that I wore with Rita.

I called my mom and made a date for dinner on Thursday night. I called my sisters and confirmed Saturday with Gloria and Sunday with Syl and Al. I called Rita and learned she was moving to Boston in October and I shared that I had a sometime running partner and a maybe, very maybe, lifetime partner. I called Gabby who was traveling and Suki promised to send my love. "Joe, you sound like Suki walk on back."

"How do you know these things, Suki?"

"I woman love you; we know."

"I love you, too, Suki. I'll call you."

I called the Kellys; grandparents of a baby boy they were yet to meet as well as the father. Eileen had isolated herself but was somehow managing her medical goal. I wished them all good luck and they wished me well.

I called Marti, "Joe, I was getting worried."

"I'm fine; I'm at my place."

"Oh, I called Alma and told her you would be there for a couple of weeks. God, I'm going to miss you, Joseph."

"It's a good thing I came to my place; the refrigerator was going to explode."

"I don't understand."

"Everything in the fridge was green or purple or black; I had to throw everything out and clean the fridge. I went to the store and got some basics."

"Are you distancing yourself from me?"

"I am not; what I am doing is being a city guy for a couple of weeks."

"What does that mean?"

"It means meeting my mom for dinner, it means running overlooking the Hudson River, and I can't remember when I did that last, and it means having a corned beef sandwich at the Carnegie Deli and diving into my work, and that's important to me."

"You're my city guy."

"I am, for a couple of weeks. How are you and the kids?"

"We are good, it's very strange to know you are gone for a while; I don't like it."

"Maybe this is an opportunity for us both; we love each other, I know we do, but we have to trust each other; we have a couple of weeks to practice."

"I understand but I get scared and I go to a very dark place. I'm embarrassed, it's childish."

"I can't help you."

"I will do better, Joe."

"You can't do better until you understand why you go to the dark place."

"You think you have all the answers and that I don't."

"I should not have said that, I'm sorry."

"Oh, God, I want answers."

"I understand."

"I hate that."

"Okay, conversation is over, I love you and please tell Sara and Bill I love them."

"I will, goodnight."

I wanted to throw the phone through the window.

I ran the next morning; it was hot and muggy along the river and I loved it. I showered, dressed, and drove the Porsche over to the Fifth Avenue manse and parked it there so I wouldn't have to hassle with alternate side of the street parking. I took a cab to work and got a hug from Liz.

"I missed you, good time?"

"Yes, for the most part." Are we busy?"

"Yes, busy enough, and Larry Fisher is at the top of the list."

"Let's do it."

In just a few minutes Liz announced, "Mr. Fisher on line one."

"Larry, how are you?"

"I'm good, The Monarch is coming along nicely, we're very happy."

"I'm disappointed."

"What?"

"That means the world can get along nicely without me."

"That's true for most of us, Joe; it's funny how that works."

"Yes, sir."

"Have you an answer for me?"

"I want you to please hold on until right after Labor Day; I'll be back in the office that Wednesday."

"Make me your first call."

"I will for sure."

And he was gone. Liz came in with a list of calls and the weekly meetings schedule.

"Does your trusted servant, Elizabeth, that would be me, get to know why Larry Fisher is being so nice to you, he isn't nice to anyone."

"You let me know if he is ever rude to you, I will take him out."

"You are being clever and evasive, Joseph."

"Shut the door."

"Yes, sir."

"This can not get out to anyone in this firm; after I have told you only three people: you, Bob Reinhardt and I, will have this information. The Fisher brothers have offered me an apartment free for a year for me to manage their managers at The Monarch; to instill the service vision that I sold them during our presentation. Larry called Bob Reinhardt to discuss any conflict of interest since I would still be working here."

"I am thrilled for you, Joe."

"You can not tell anyone, including your husband."

"You have my word."

"I told you purposefully because Marti and I are having problems; if everything was fine I would move into Marti's Fifth Avenue place and say thanks but no thanks to Mr. Fisher, but they are not fine."

"I am so sorry, Joe."

"Yeah, me too; I love her and I love her kids, but there are issues."

"Marti loves you, but?"

"She wants me to give up architecture."

"No."

"Is it too early for bourbon?"

"Water, I'll get you some water?"

"Okay."

"Don't go away."

"I won't, and then we can call Mr. Sturner in Idaho; I may have a new client."

Liz handed me a large glass of water, "I'll make that call."

"I hear that you are the live wire in architecture these days, Mr. Gordon."

"That's a very nice compliment, Mr. Sturner."

"How about we do Chuck and Joe?"

"I would like that, just fine."

"Joe, I have three separate 10 acre properties on the Snake, here in Idaho. Have you ever been to Idaho?"

"No, Chuck, but I get the feeling I will soon."

"I'd like that; I'll show you what I've got and we could talk about designing three houses for my daughters."

"Sounds good and we could get to know each other; that's important to me."

"Do you like to fly?"

"I do."

"I'll pick you up at Teterboro; getting home to Idaho will be a bit longer than a commercial flight, but a hell-of-a lot more fun, spend a night or two while you and I figure each other out and discuss what's on my mind."

"I'm up for that, Chuck, I look forward to it."

"How about next Tuesday, be there at eight thirty and we'll be wheels up no later than nine."

"I have a must be home on Thursday afternoon."

"Works for me, Joe. Read up on the Snake, she's a lot of things, all of them beautiful."

"I am looking forward to it."

"Alright, Joe, see you Tuesday."

"Liz, we better look at what I'm supposed to be doing next week."

"I'll be right there."

We looked through my calendar and there wasn't anything that couldn't be pushed or massaged.

"Joe, are you sure you want to fly with this guy?"

"Yes, two reasons, both selfish; I want to learn how to fly and this could be a kind of hands on experience and I'm intrigued; this could be a game changer for my career. There's something about him; this could be big."

"All from a three minute phone call?"

"He's a do-it-yourself kind of guy and here he is, asking for help."

"I get it, and what I love is your excitement."

"I need your help, Liz, I need a map of Idaho and a book on the Snake River; all I know, I read about it somewhere, is that the Snake is over a thousand miles long; that's a lot of river. I wonder where Chuck Sturner fits in?"

I got a few minutes with Bob Reinhardt and told him about this possible new business.

"Are you sure you want to fly with this guy?"

"Liz asked the same question. Yes, I'm sure; I'll get to know him a little better."

"Okay, Joe. What else?"

"Since I am saving the company a fortune by putting my life at risk, I want a limo to Teterboro."

"I'll think about it."

"Thanks Bob, I'll have Liz find out who to call."

"You're pretty sure about this aren't you?"

"I am. One other thing, I would like to plan on not being in the office on that Friday; I may be in Idaho an extra day and I don't want to feel any pressure."

"Not a problem, I'll see you after Labor Day. Have a safe trip and good luck."

That night I had dinner with my Mom. She wanted to make dinner at home, her apartment, but I didn't want her to fuss so we dined at some little Italian place in the East 60's; it was nice, quiet and good food. Mom asked me about Marti and I side stepped the current situation; she's fine and the kids are great.

"How are you doing, Mom, and what about this Harry guy?"

"I like him, he's nice, we go places together."

"Is he good in bed?"

"Joseph," I thought she was going to scream, "I can't believe,"

"Mom, I'm sorry, I was just kidding around. I'm sorry.. What about the girls, do you get out of the city to see them?"

"Yes."

Things settled down and we talked about the good old days and her husband, my father, who she still misses every day. We walked back to her apartment and I kissed her goodnight.

When I got home I called Marti and we had a conversation that made me feel like we were strangers; the kids were fine, Dawn was fine and Marti was sad. I did not share about Chuck Sturner and the Snake River and Idaho, I didn't dare. We expressed our love and hung up. I felt so sad, it was like the last piece of a great apple pie had lost its flavor and you wished you could make it better and you can't.

My weekend was good: plenty to read in a book about the Snake River and maps to study; one of Idaho and one of the Pacific Northwest.

I ran both days; the heat was tough but the reward was greater. I visited my sister Gloria in Glen Cove, on the North shore of Long Island. Nice; the kids, three of them, were healthy and we all enjoyed playing in the back yard, I was one of the kids and it was fun. A drink before dinner lifted my spirits and dinner was delicious, but I wasn't much of a guest. My sister put her finger on the problem, "Things with Marti aren't going well?"

"No, the magic is gone, we have differences; I love her, she is amazing in so many ways, but she is unpredictable and very headstrong."

"Joe, it's okay, you're young, there's time."

I got home with enough time to call Marti.

"Hello," it was Dawn.

"Hey, Dawn, how are you?"

"Sad, we are all sad, the kids miss you, I miss you, Marti is a mess; we all know the sky is falling. Marti and I used to talk about everything and now we don't talk at all. Marti is at the new house, it's almost finished; I think she paid extra for more crew, I don't know; we are all out of sorts. Does that even make sense?"

"I think the whole eastern seaboard is drowning in thunder and lightning and rainstorms of sorrow."

"Fix it, Joe, please, fix it."

"I can't fix it, we are unfixable; the solution rests in our hands, Marti's and mine together and together is gone, maybe forever. It's a horrible waste and I am angry as hell."

"I love you, Joe."

"I am so glad you answered the phone; love to you and the kids and tell Marti I called."

"Will do."

Sunday morning I ran, I felt like I could run through a brick wall and the pain would smother the sadness. I tried making happy faces in the mirror while I was brushing my teeth; I could not do it.

At my sister's on Sunday, she and Al and I hit tennis balls for a while and then got into a round robin of two against one, hitting as hard as we could, until we were exhausted; the solution was a Bloody Mary, followed by a siesta, followed by a lite salad dinner. I went home early; I had a big week coming up.

Monday was a hoot; all I could think about was the Snake, Idaho and Chuck; I was on the cusp of a new adventure and I was ready.

Liz got me through to everyone I had to talk with or apologize to for changing an appointment and then I went over to see The Monarch. I was shocked at how quickly it was coming together; they were working on the interior finishing; I rode up to the tenth floor for a look-see and got goose bumps, The Monarch was a reality!

Monday night Marti answered the phone.

"You are coming to the beach next weekend?"

"Of course I am, I miss you and the kids."

"I have been busy with the new house; I love it, Joe, it is so beautiful. It's us, we built it together."

"Marti, I may not be able to call you Tuesday and Wednesday, I'll be out of town."

"Business?"

"I'll tell you all about it when I see you."

"Saturday, then?"

"Yes."

The gas crew at Teterboro Airport had topped off Chuck's twin engine Cessna 310I and he was leading me through the pre-flight walk around inspection: props, tires, wings, gas caps, fuselage and tail assembly; everything was thumbs up.

"Joe, just your shoulder bag?"

"Yes, sir."

"Okay, you can step up on the wing right here, open the door and settle in. I get in on the other side, we'll tighten up our safety harness, put on our head sets and I'll show you how we get this baby off the ground."

I was fascinated watching and listening as Chuck called out each step of starting the engines and activating communications and navigation 'tools'. With my headset on I was in on the progression from ground control to the proper runway and Teterboro tower control for permission to take off. It was exciting.

During our flight we were able to chat comfortably through our headsets.

"These two levers add power to the engines which has more to do with altitude than speed, these are the rudder pedals, this is the altimeter, etcetera;" in short I received an introductory lesson on aviation

After we had landed and locked the Cessna safely away in Chuck's private hanger we left the community airport and headed for Chuck's house where I was going to stay a couple of nights.

"I thought we could go out for a steak dinner; how does that sound?"

"Sounds good to me, I'm hungry."

"Me too, I think you are going to enjoy "Little Tommy's"; best steaks in Idaho!"

I am guessing Little Tommy weighs 400 pounds; he didn't take my hand when Chuck introduced us, he hugged me almost in half; but Chuck was right, the steaks were really delicious.

During dinner I told Chuck about Rutgers, calculus, Pratt and my wish to, one day, get my pilot's license. Chuck shared how he had taken the small trucking firm his father had started and turned it into the most trusted trucking firm in Idaho.

"Unfortunately my daughters are unavailable tomorrow but the rest of the plan is on; we will visit the three properties and Steve Thomson, the geologist, will join us for the day."

"I'm excited to see the properties, but the rest of my inspiration comes from the person, or the people, that will be living in the houses."

"I'm sorry, Joe. Actually my daughters are sorry as well. They are good for the last week of September."

"Perfect; let's plan on Monday of that week."

"Thank you, Joe, I'm glad you can work with us on this."

"We will be fine, but first, the properties."

Wednesday morning Chuck and I made breakfast together; eggs, bacon and toast and the bacon was exceptional.

"Joe, I wasn't sure you would eat bacon?"

"You mean the Jewish kid from New York thing?"

"Yeah."

"I love bacon, Chuck, just don't tell my mother!"

After breakfast I got three doses of "The Snake"; three breathtaking properties on the river.

"I'll cast my vote right now; if you will have me, I am coming back the last week in September."

I was right about Chuck Sturner; a fireball of energy, very direct, engaging, a hint of humor and a first-rate pilot.

We had wheels up at seven Thursday morning; ten New York time. Along the way Chuck gave me a gift.

"Okay, Joe, the sky is clear and there is no other traffic; you are going to do a three-sixty."

"What?"

"Take the yoke and follow my instructions. I'm right here so there's nothing to worry about"

"Okay."

"Lift the nose slightly above the horizon, move the rudder and the ailerons gently for a left turn, keep the nose above the horizon and . . . now gently turn back to the right out of the three-sixty, let the nose down to level and . . . you did it!"

"That, Chuck, was great fun; a full turn, in mid-air, ending up going in the same direction and altitude as when we started. Wow!"

CHAPTER 47

LETTING GO

Saturday, I got to Easthampton around two in the afternoon. As I was getting out of the car Sara and Billy were running toward me from the house. I dropped the fresh flowers I had brought for Marti and scooped the kids into my arms.

"I have missed you both so very, very much."

I was being smothered with kisses and besieged with questions;

"Are you staying?"

"Where have you been?"

"Mom called Liz who said you were in Idaho."

"Where is Idaho?"

"Who is Liz?"

"Who," I asked, "are you and you?"

"I'm Sara, your daughter."

"I'm Bill, why are you crying?"

"I'm crying because I love you both very big. Where is your, where is mom?"

"She's at the new house."

"She's always at the new house."

"Where is Dawn?"

"Inside."

"Let's go say hello to Dawn and I want to find a vase for these flowers."

Dawn emerged from the pantry with a vase for the flowers, she was crying, "I was at the door."

Dawn put the flowers in the vase, "They are beautiful."

"And they will be beautiful longer," I said, "with water in the vase."

I took care of that, "I'm taking these over to mom."

"Can we come," Sara asked.

"Sure. Dawn?"

"You guys go ahead."

"Sara, would you and Bill take the flowers outside and I will be right there."

The kids went outside and Dawn hugged me big, very big.

"Sara is your daughter," Dawn said, tears streaming down her cheeks, "How are you going to deal with that, Joseph?"

"I don't know; one minute at a time; we are all going to be together when the bell rings."

"What the hell does that mean?"

"I'm working on that, keep your chin up."

Dawn gave me a quick kiss and I joined the kids and went to see mom.

The beach house was beautiful; it had the look and feel of a weathered, old, clapboard Hamptons house; bracketed by two brick chimneys and capped by a four-angled roof leading up to a widow's walk. The ocean side is a whole other story; more like a huge beach cabana, with the kitchen spilling out onto the thousand square foot deck with a privacy outdoor shower and bath at the east end.

We approached the house from the beach side.

"Hello, Marti," I called, "anybody home?"

"I'm home," Marti said, coming out on the deck, wearing cut off jeans and a bikini top.

"We come bearing fresh flowers and, boy, do you look terrific."

"Joseph." And she was in my arms.

"Kiss him, so we can scream," Sara the troublemaker said; and she did, and they did.

"I was only gone for two weeks."

"You should come in and see what can happen in two weeks. How about a beer?"

"That would be great." "Hey, guys, I'm going to show Joe the house and then we will come over; would you tell Dawn, please."

"Okay, Mom," and the kids turned for home.

"The flowers are lovely, thank you."

"You are lovely, you're welcome."

Marti took my hand, "Come on, Joe, have a look at what we created."

All of the furnishings were in place; the house looked like it had been lived in for a year or more.

"How did you do this, Marti?"

"One room at a time, with us in mind, all the way."

"From the design plan and the measurements you were able to envision this?"

"Yes."

"You are incredible, Marti. I love you."

"Let's go upstairs."

We toured the entire upstairs, ending in the master suite.

"I want us to sleep here tonight and tomorrow night as well, okay with you?"

"Definitely."

"And a favor?"

"Okay."

"No running; not you and not me."

Marti hugged me.

"No running, I'm fine with that."

"And I thought Sara and Bill can come over Monday morning and we can tell them whatever it is we have decided."

"You have been busy in many ways; you are very brave."

"I have never been more afraid in my life."

"I will hold you close to me, Marti."

"Kiss me, Joe."

We kissed; we kissed in the way that used to make us each shiver with love and lust, and it happened again for me.

"And for me too, Joe."

"Mind reader."

"Let's lock up and turn on some lights so we can find our way back."

As we approached the house Marti said, "We are calling this the house and we are calling the new house, the beach house."

"Got it."

"Dinner is all planned for tonight at the house and tomorrow we will barbecue at the beach house."

"Sounds good, maybe Bill will assist?"

Marti stopped me.

"Sara and Bill love you, Joe, they missed you and I am afraid of how much they will miss you if we . . ."

My finger touched Marti's lips, "I will stay in their lives; I love them. Today, when I arrived, I got out of the car and said, "Who are you and you?" Sara said, "I'm Sara, your daughter." And I cried. Bill said, "I'm Bill and I love you; why are you crying?"

"What was your answer?"

"Because I love you very big."

"Let's go inside and love them very big."

"I'm making drinks; no alcohol for anyone under twenty five."

"Baloney, Mister Joe, I'll have whatever you're having," declared Dawn.

"I'm having water."

"Yeah, right."

Marti went upstairs to put on some warmer clothes, I gave Dawn her drink and I was lured outside for some croquet with the kids. They were getting pretty good and I helped them with strategy; if you do this, then you will be able to do that. They were catching on and Bill was getting better at handling his five-pound mallet. We were out there for at least an hour during which Dawn came out and refilled my drink; I even got a kiss on the lips and after a while we were called in for dinner.

During dinner, spaghetti and meatballs and a delicious green salad, Sara asked her mother, "So, what's going on with you and Joe?"

Marti hesitated before answering, "We aren't sure, but we love each other and promise to have an answer on Monday."

"Okay, Monday."

"Joe," Bill said, "We don't want you to leave. We love you."

"I know you do, and I think you know that I love you both; the important thing is that what mom and I decide is between us and it's not because of you."

Dawn's tears were falling on her spaghetti, Marti was mopping up with her napkin and I was blowing my nose.

"Grown ups are like little babies," Bill said, with more wisdom than he could possibly have imagined.

That, thank God and Billy, got us back to just being and the adult "thing" was put on the back burner and brought us all together and ready for dessert; blueberry pie and chocolate ice cream. Oh, boy!

"After dinner, can we play Monopoly," Sara wanted to know.

"After dinner Joe and I are going to the beach house. We won't see you guys until you come over for lunch tomorrow."

"What are you going to do," 'words of wisdom,' Bill, wanted to know.

"We are going to walk on the beach and then we are going to sleep together; no visitors 'til twelve thirty lunch."

"We," said Dawn, looking at Bill and Sara, "will have a superb breakfast without them." Dawn emphasized the last part by pointing at us.

In retaliation Marti and I enjoyed a terrific kiss, causing a great deal of screaming from the kids.

A little while later Marti and I kissed the kids goodnight and were headed for the door, "Hey, what about Dawn; I don't get kisses?"

"You do, I'm sorry," and Marti kissed Dawn and I did as well, "I love you, Dawn, see you all for lunch."

Marti and I held hands and crossed the street to the beach for our stroll. We went closer to the ocean that seemed upset with us; the tide was up and the waves were big and crashing.

"Those angry waves are not our song, Joseph, not tonight, not ever again; I love you and will love you forever. Let's go home and have a drink and then have each other."

I poured two bourbons on ice while Marti set the stereo for dancing, kicked off her shoes and dimmed the lights.

"To you, to me, to us," we drank and danced close until our passion drove us to bed. The moon was up and cast just the right amount of light.

We undressed each other; Marti, one sweater, one pair of jeans. I had one other item that disappeared with my jeans and we lay together our lips speaking the words silently, gently and lovingly. My mouth found the sweetest part of Marti and I had her in an instant. Everything else was in slow motion.

Marti didn't want us to talk; she wanted to be loved and to love in return.

Hours later Marti went downstairs and came back with a ham and cheese sandwich and a beer. Watching Marti move through the house naked was inspirational; there was great beauty in her nakedness. We ate, we drank and we touched and kissed each other everywhere. Aroused we loved each other again and at dawn we slept.

In the morning, I guess eleven was still morning, I was angry; it was us, but sort of a controlled us, not The us that I knew; this was a Marti us. A planned out us. I told Marti how I felt.

"It was the only way I could keep myself from breaking into a thousand pieces. I love you but I am capable of falling apart.

Marti started to cry, "Joe, please, I know we can do us; a different us that will keep us close forever. Get through today with love and tonight, just the two of us can put humpty dumpty together again."

"It's a deal."

"I called them and told them one o'clock; we have to shower together, you are going to love this shower." " I am going to love you in this shower."

Dawn and the kids came at one and we had made tuna salad and egg salad and put out sliced rye bread. We ate and drank milk and beer and went down to the ocean; it was still angry. We got the kite from the house and this time, with cheers of encouragement from the girls, Bill and I successfully flew it. Everything we did we all did; we were the fantastic five; we loved one another. We were going to be okay.

Bill and I christened the new barbecue; bacon cheeseburgers, with coleslaw and potato salad and the rest of the blueberry pie for dessert; we all had blueberry mustaches. The kids stayed at the beach house until nine; "Hugs and kisses, we will see you in the morning."

"Can we get in bed with you?"

"Yes, all five of us, somehow."

"Eight o'clock and we will make breakfast here."

"It was a good day," I thought out loud.

"It was wonderful, thank you."

"Drink?"

"Yes, please."

I poured a couple of bourbons and handed one to Marti, "Here's to us."

"To us." Marti took a sip, "I called Liz; I wanted to know where you were."

"The kids asked me about Idaho when I arrived."

"Joe, tell me about Idaho, please."

"A man in Idaho heard about me, called me, flew his own plane to Teterboro, picked me up, flew us to Idaho so I could see some property he owns on the Snake River. Fabulous guy, wants me to design houses for his three daughters; each on separate properties on the Snake River; absolutely stunning country. New opportunity, new challenge, new business; exciting."

"I'm happy for you and I want you to know that Idaho opened the door for me to see clearly how important your work is. I wouldn't let myself see your needs, I could only see and feel you being pulled away from me."

"Marti, it wouldn't have."

"Joe," Marti interrupted, "I have to finish. Now I can see both sides and I clearly know me, my own fear, insecurity, unpredictability, and I am not going to change, I can't."

Marti started to cry and she put her hands up signaling she had to continue. "I must let you go and find a way to deal with knowing that I will love you forever, a way to hold on to us and protect both of us from me, my behavior. I want you in my life and my kids life forever and I have to let you go."

I took Marti Mason into my arms; "I want you to listen to my heart and soul; I give you up and will keep you in my heart forever and in my life as well;

To you, to me, to us; Joe and Marti, Marti and Joe."

"Oh, my God, Joseph, you had made the same decision; can we do it?"

"We love each other, we want what's best for each other and I love the kids with all my heart. We can do this kind of love; we have to repeat our oath to God and another person; Dawn, if she's willing, not the kids, they wouldn't understand. We are going to have painful moments and we will survive and go on loving each other in this new, special way."

"I want you to have the house."

"I can't afford the house."

"I have already told my attorney to find a way for you to get the house as is; fully furnished, it's a gift and for the next five years I pay for the service and the taxes and I get the write off. I want you to have the house."

"We will be neighbors, I will be close to the kids. I'll be close to you; what if I'm here with another woman or a wife?"

"What if I am married, Joe? Can you handle that?"

"If we can remain us we can handle everything; starting with the kids."

"Will you visit us in the city?"

"Of course, pass up a free meal, are you kidding?"

'I'm serious."

"I will visit in the city, maybe we should set a day, like every Wednesday or every other day. We will make it work."

"Take me upstairs, Joe, I want us to celebrate; I am at peace."

Marti and I went to bed knowing we were parting, knowing we would never enjoy each other this way, not ever again. We started out holding hands and looking at each other; then we began touching and stroking until the first kiss led us to the passion; the 'this is the last time' passion and physical pleasure. Marti was crying, she tried pushing me away I refused to comply.

"Get off me."

"No running, Marti."

"You bastard."

Marti was strong, but not strong enough; I wouldn't stop. She grabbed my hair, I grabbed hers; that's when she joined the party; she wrapped her beautiful legs around me and we went to heaven together.

Marti was crying, "I can't help it; it feels like I will never stop."

I had my feet on the floor, "Pull on your pants, we'll walk down to the ocean."

"What, are you crazy?"

"That's why people live on the beach, Marti; come on."

"No, you go."

"Want anything when I come back up?"

"I'll meet you in the kitchen, I'm hungry."

I walked across the deck, down the walkway through the dunes, rolled up my pants and walked into the ocean. It felt so good; I wanted Marti with me but, oh no. I shouted at the ocean as loud as I had ever been, "I hate you, Marti Mason, I hate you!"

I expected the ocean to respond, "No you don't."

I yelled again, my throat hurt, "I hate you Marti." And there she was, next to me and we stood in the ocean together and let each other go.

"I let you go, Marti Mason, and I will love you forever."

"I let you go, Joe Gordon, and I will love you forever."

We were soaking wet, in the ocean up over our knees and getting pushed around by the waves; Marti got knocked over and I helped her up and out onto the beach.

"I fell for you, Joe, and I will never stop loving you."

"Come on, older woman, let's get something to eat."

Monday morning at eight o'clock Sara and Bill climbed onto Marti's bed and we did our best to explain "letting go" while remaining loving friends and, most important; being in their lives.

Sara was first, "You're not going to sleep together any more, are you?"

"No."

"Are you going to still love me and Sara?"

"Yes. I loved you yesterday, I love you right now and I will love you tomorrow and next week and next year."

"Joe is going to own the house, he's going to be right next door."

"What about the city," Sara asked, "will you come for dinner and do stuff with us?"

"Yes. Not as much, but yes."

"Can we eat now," Bill asked.

"Yes," Marti said, I'll bet we are all hungry."

Downstairs Dawn explained, "I couldn't come up, but I got breakfast started; eggs and pancakes, by request."

Dawn was crying and Marti took charge of breakfast while I took Dawn outside on the deck to hug her and explain what happened.

"The best thing, if there is a best thing, we both ended it; not like one of us wanted to hang in there. I will be around, I will be in your life, if you want, and the kids; I love you."

We all ate a lot of pancakes, probably because they were good, probably because we were hungry and definitely because we all needed something to do together.

Marti and I spent almost an hour going over the contents of several large manila envelopes: keys to the house, her attorney's name and phone, Yes, continue to park the Porsche at Fifth Avenue, the service that looks after the house, the beach house phone number and address; endless stuff. The house would be empty of everyone's things except mine by the coming weekend and they will be all settled in the beach house.

I planned to come down the next weekend and Marti was happy about that.

We were moving forward separately, but together forever.

CHAPTER 48

NEIGHBORS

Embrace loneliness; seriously? My memory bank was full and that was the problem: Moments of love and laughter and tears; pictures of Marti and Sara and Bill and Dawn. "I'm Sara, your daughter," "Adults are like little babies," "I'm sorry fellas, but this is my guy." "Are you going to put a move on me, Joe?"

I will continue to have these wonderful people in my life under a new set of rules; swim with them but wear a life preserver, love them and stay in the shallow end of the pool, celebrate with them but leave shortly after you help blow out the candles, avoid the beautiful young sister-in-law, and for God's sake, no that's wrong, for my own sake, don't smell Marti, don't touch Marti and don't kiss Marti for more than two seconds. In short, embrace loneliness.

I ran Tuesday morning and was in the office early. When Liz arrived my first call was to Larry Fisher.

"I'm in, Larry, I'm excited."

"November first, the place will be furnished as we will have shown that apartment to prospective tenants."

"I'm going to need parking."

"Your Lordship, what else can I provide?"

"I'll want to meet with your people in October or when ever you put the team together."

"We should have lunch, later this month. This is good, Joe, we are going to work fine together."

He was gone. I was looking out the window; it was raining.

"Liz, no later than the 23rd, lunch with Larry and I guess you should come in here, please."

"I'm here," Liz was standing in the doorway.

"I'm sorry, Joe, I thought about you all weekend."

"It's for the best and we both wanted it to be over, but it's not over, over."

"That's going to be harder than it's over, done."

"Why do women know these things?"

"We talk straight to the men we care about."

"I am going to stay in their lives; the kids, I love them. Marti, Dawn; we were a five-some."

"Joe, you were a twosome, now you will be a five-some."

"Yes, dinner once a week, birthdays, God only knows."

"Joe, one day at a time, you have told me that a million times; You've got this."

"Elizabeth, you could not have started my day any better, thank you."

"Any time."

"Oh, The Monarch, I'm moving in November first, I'll need a new phone number and, you are going to love this, the Easthampton phone number is now my Easthampton number and I have a new beach number for Marti."

"You are going to be neighbors at the beach, is that what you just told me?"

"Do you think that's crazy?"

"No, it sounds like you got a divorce and you each got a house."

"I told Marti, I couldn't afford it and she had already set it up; I have names, phone numbers and keys."

"She loves the beach house, I'll bet?"

"She does, it's all furnished; it is outstanding, she has great taste."

I had a brief meeting with Bob Reinhardt to bring him up to date on Chuck Sturner and The Monarch decision.

"Sounds like new business and sad news, I'm sorry, Joe."

"All for the best; I will stay in touch with Marti and her kids, they are special.

On Sturner, I'm going to Idaho at the end of the month to meet with his three daughters; I'm flying commercial and he's putting me up. I want to know what the daughters want and get to know them; for me that's the key to inspiration."

"Sounds good, Joe."

Saturday I drove to the beach early and the front door was locked; thankfully Liz had added that key to my key ring.

On the kitchen table was the vase with fresh flowers; there was a note:

Dearest Joseph,

Welcome to your new home, it is filled with love for you; love that you ignited in our lives. Enjoy in good health, forever.

Marti

P.S.

Lunch is at 12:30 and you are invited for dinner as well.

There was a separate envelope with a type written letter:

Everything you can possibly need is here; dishes, silverware, glassware, kitchen tools and towels, bath soaps, toothpaste, toothbrush, towels, bedding, all furnishings, etc. The croquet set is in the back yard shed.

There are fresh eggs, bread, butter, and beer in the fridge and Makers Mark bourbon at the bar. I could go on forever but you get the idea,

Isabelle

The Tankard Troupe

Your Home Care Service

I was stunned, appreciative and sad; it was all so bittersweet. I went upstairs and went through every room; three bedrooms, two bathrooms and the master suite with fireplace and large bath. I found my clothes in the dresser and one of the closets, including my running shoes.

I explored the downstairs; laundry room, pantry, kitchen, dining room, living room with a fireplace and den with a fireplace, and the large entryway. I was even more stunned, after all I had been a "visitor resident", but I had never taken in the scope of the place and the warm beauty of the furnishings. It was a beautiful home.

I had fifteen minutes before lunch so I sat on the back patio, closed my eyes and tried to prepare myself for whatever was next; Marti, the kids,

I didn't know, and then it came to me; it was like a message, "be in the moment".

The kids were on lookout,

"He's coming!"

I got hugs and kisses from Sara and Bill and then Marti hugged me too close and kissed me too long. Stay in the moment, be careful and then Dawn hugged me, just right.

"I was afraid you would not come, Joe," Marti said.

"Here I am and who are these two children?"

"That's not going to work, Joe, we know that you know who we are."

"If you are so smart would you please tell me which one of you is Jack?"

Sara and Bill looked at each other, "I'm not Jack," Bill said.

I looked at Sara, "Then you must be Jack."

"I am not Jack, Joe, you're just being silly because Mom is crying."

"Mom is crying because Jack isn't here," I said.

"She's crying because you don't love her any more," said Bill.

I picked up Bill and held him in my arms, face to face, "I love your mom with all my heart, and you and Sara too, and Dawn; I will not stop loving you, ever; not in a week or a month, not ever. The only thing that has changed is what we do or don't do together."

"They are not going to sleep together any more, Bill. That's all that's changed," Sara said to her brother.

"Well then why is everyone crying," Bill asked, looking at me.

"Because love is a feeling that's hard to describe; it's something that comes from way, way deep in your body and your heart and when the rules change, like we decided not to sleep together, it hurts from way, way in there and we cry."

"I don't understand," Billy shrugged.

"I'm sorry and I'm hungry," I said, "let's eat and figure this out after lunch."

"Those were good lobster rolls, Marti; great lunch, thanks."

Marti and I were walking on the beach; just a slight breeze, perfect weather.

"And thank you for the flowers and the house is beautiful. Are you sure about this?"

"Which this, our decision or the house?"

"I meant the house."

"Joe, I am sure about the house, I'm less sure about us; this is painful and confusing for the kids."

"I did the best I could."

"You did fine, it's hard; that's all."

"What we do or don't do; that's the game changer,

Then seeing you, seeing the kids, that's the pain maker."

We walked back to the beach house and Sara and Bill and I went to the house for an hour or so of croquet.

"If Mom loves you and you love her why don't you get married," Sara was the spokesperson.

"We don't want to get married, we don't want to live together; we just want to love each other as best we can and love you both, the best we can. What is super important is that you two terrific kids know that this change that we are making is not your fault, it's our decision and I can't explain it. It's not because of you."

At dinner things lightened up; we took turns describing things that we each thought were funny and we all got silly and laughed a lot. Nine o'clock was bedtime for the kids; Marti took them upstairs.

"This is hard, Joe," Dawn said, sitting down next to me.

"There are a ton of adjectives like; very, super, amazingly, impossibly; it's crazy making for me and it's confusing the kids."

Marti came down and said, "The kids want to know what is not their fault."

"Our decision to not live together, to not get married, that's what is not their fault."

"I told them that and they said, "Oh, we know that.""

"They get it, perfect, calls for a nightcap."

"Not for me, Joe," Marti said, " I'm going to bed."

"In that case, me too, I'm going home."

"How does that feel, saying that?"

Marti lingered on the steps for my reply, "Exciting, scary, sad."

Marti blew me a kiss and Dawn gave me a hug, "Goodnight."

"I knew you would be here, Joe, listening to the ocean."

Dawn sat beside me, took my drink and had some.

"It's peaceful," I said.

"You're excited about the house?"

"I am, it's a beautiful house. I'm worried about my neighbor."

"Marti is a big girl, she'll be all right."

"And the kids?"

"Sara and Bill heard everything they needed to hear today; now they will settle down, the worst is past."

"You are very smart for a pretty, young girl."

"I'm a woman, Joseph, it's time for you to find that out."

Dawn kissed me; I didn't want her to kiss me but I didn't want her to stop either.

"You and I have been here before, Dawn; avoiding the pain."

"I remember. Are you running in the morning?"

"Seven o'clock."

"Partner?"

"Absolutely."

"Goodnight, Joe, you are a wonderful man."

"And you are a beautiful young woman."

Walking away, Dawn mooned me and giggled.

When I got to the ocean side of the beach house Dawn was stretching at the end of the walkway that cuts through the dunes and Marti and the kids were up on the deck, waving.

"Morning, Dawn."

"Breakfast at eight thirty," Marti called out.

"Breakfast; great," I said, stretching out.

"Thanks for the nightcap, Joe."

"Thank you for the very pretty moon view. Ready?"

"You're welcome; yes."

With a wave to the deck and a push of a button on my watch we set off, headed east.

On the deck the kids were waving.

"I love Joe, Mom."

"I do, too," Sara added.

We were running on the damp, hard-pack by the ocean,

"It doesn't get much better than this," I said to God and anyone that was listening.

"I heard that; I agree."

We ran silently and I thought of Rita and the hundreds of runs we shared and the rigorous honesty that bonded us and then let us part friends. I liked running with a partner; I wondered what it would be like at The Monarch. My watch beeped; time to turn and Dawn saw me signal.

"Was that five miles of remembering some of the women you have run with?"

"I have only run with two women; a six foot three woman who taught me how to run, and you."

"What was her name?"

"Rita."

"Were you lovers?"

"Dawn Mason, that's like me asking you how many lovers you have had?"

"None."

"Come on."

"I am waiting for you."

"Dawn!"

"I can wait."

"I'm still in love with your sister-in-law."

"I know and the crazy thing is I was rooting for you; you two should be married, the perfect power couple; what is wrong with her?"

'We can't go there, Dawn."

"I love her; she hurts herself. I don't get it."

We ran past the last big dune and there it was, Marti's beach house; it was beautiful. We walked off the run and stretched and went up to the deck bath and washed up together.

We ate breakfast inside; eggs, pancakes and bacon.

"Good run," Marti asked.

"Great run, perfect weather and good company," Dawn said.

"And we were right on the money; ten miles in seventy minutes."

"Am I old enough to run?"

"Sure, Bill, but not ten miles. Next summer we'll mark off a quarter mile and in July you can work at running to the marker, and in August you'll work at running there and back; not too shabby for a six year old."

"Mom?"

"Sounds good to me."

"You're going to be here next summer?"

"Yes, Bill, I am going to be here for a lot of summers."

"Can I have another pancake?"

"Yes, Bill, you may," said Dawn, who winked at me and smiled a smile that said, "I told you the worst is past."

Back in town Marti's and my separation kicked in; she, they, stayed at the beach and even though I was busy, thoughts of Marti and visions of Marti clouded my mind and yet I was free of the intensity that Marti carried; loneliness had company, peace had come to ease the pain.

CHAPTER 49

SETTLING IN

Larry Fisher and I had lunch in his office; deli sandwiches that were first rate. A woman joined us; fifty, fit, looked forty and seemed smart. Larry had hired her to manage The Monarch, her name was Betty Grable, which threw me off track for at least fifteen minutes: "Really?"

"Yes."

"He didn't put you up to this," I asked, pointing at Larry.

"No. All my life I have held my ground and people always remembered me and my name."

"I think we share the same passion; I want every one that works at The Monarch to know our tenants by name."

"Certainly."

"Betty, may I call you Betty?"

"Yes, Joe, of course."

"May I call you Betty Grable just once?"

"Get it over with."

"Betty Grable, I believe every tenant of The Monarch wants to feel safe, wants to belong, wants to be recognized by name and, when needed, will receive prompt and professional help. I want The Monarch to be the most sought after residential dwelling on the East side. How can I help?"

"Joe, you are a tenant, by the way you are our first tenant, congratulations! You are not staff, but all staff will be told you are; that way you are not a spy and all of your observations should come to me: so and so is a jerk, so and so is excellent, the Smiths in 2B just became grandparents; every thing comes to me."

"How?"

"Good question."

"Something you should know: weather permitting, I run ten miles every morning at six; about an hour and fifteen minutes and I am at my office by 8:30 or 8:45. I could slip a sealed envelope under your locked office door? We'll come up with something; maybe a phone call?"

"We have to wrap this up," Larry said, "you two will work it out."

We exchanged business cards and shook hands.

"Larry, thank you and Betty, a pleasure."

"Thank you, Joe, my compliments on The Monarch design, it's a beauty."

"Thank you, Betty, I am looking forward to living there."

Chuck Sturner called to confirm my visit with his three daughters.

"Chuck, I'm coming out on Sunday, hopefully staying with you that night so we will have all of Monday with your three daughters."

"I am coming to get you at the airport and of course you can stay with me; we might even have to go to Tommy's for a steak."

"My turn."

"Not in Idaho, Joe."

"Okay, I'll have Liz send you my travel info."

"See you then. Travel safe."

"Will do. Bye."

"Liz, would you please send my travel info to Chuck."

"I just did."

"Do you listen to all my calls?"

"Just the business ones."

CHAPTER 50

THE HEALING

I returned from Idaho having met Chuck's three daughters; all of them lovely, each unique, yet they shared their chosen calling, they were in the process of studying to become nuns with the idea that they would live on their own while serving the needs of their community. All in their thirtyish, they were smart, fun, funny, determined, accepting, loving of their dad and their faith; I was knocked out and thrilled to be with them.

The oldest, Sister Valerie, was wheelchair bound, Sister Joan was blind and extraordinary, I felt like she could see better than I. Sister Susan, the youngest, was breathtakingly beautiful; if she was not a nun she could have been a movie star or a model.

They worked me over about my faith; I was the Jewish guy from New York whose God doled out lots of guilt; Oy Vey!

"I get a dozen holidays and you get Gornisht."

"What is that?"

"Gornisht is a Yiddish word that means, 'nothing.'"

"Nothing?"

"Yes, nothing or pretty close to nothing. Easter and Christmas, big deal."

"Christmas and Easter; that is a big deal."

"See, now we disagree and it's going to turn into a big mishigas."

"A what?"

"A mishigas; a period of craziness or emotional frenzy."

"I like that one; a little problem at church, and no one can agree, it becomes a mishigas!"

Chuck got a glimpse of each of his daughters that he had never seen before.

We were enjoying one another and I felt comfortable enough to ask a few questions. Chuck got it right away; I wanted to know what they wanted.

"Sister Valerie, can I call you sister even though you haven't taken your final vows yet?"

"Sure. You can call all of us Sisters. God won't mind."

"Thank you. Sister Valerie, your strongest desire?"

"To walk with God."

"A walkway with handrails on both sides that you can hold onto and walk; God is always with you."

"Joseph, may I touch your face," Sister Joan asked.

"Of course," I responded, a little surprised, as Joan's fingers gently caressed my face.

"You're cute, I want to see again."

"We will create a grand deck overlooking the Snake River as it bends north, where God will speak the view to you."

"I love it, thank you."

"Sister Susan, your greatest desire?"

"To share the beauty of this valley of God's creation. Give me that perch, Joseph, and come sit with me forever."

"Are you flirting with me?"

"Oh, darn, you're on to me!"

We lunched together sharing childhood stories that revealed middle child challenges, Joan; youngest child with two bossy sisters. I wondered about growing up in the suburbs of New York or a small town in Idaho. As we shared I listened, learned and was inspired.

"When will you live in your homes; what do your duties permit?"

Their response was universal; as soon as possible, as often as possible and with friends, to share the glory of the valley.

The next day Chuck drove me to the airport in Boise and walked me to my gate.

"Three years ago my wife and the girls were driving home after an evening of drinking and dancing; there was an accident and my wife, Dana, died and I blamed the girls. We were all distraught and they distanced themselves from me and chose the church. Slowly we have been coming together and yesterday you touched us all and relit our family fire; I am very grateful, Joe."

"It wasn't me, Chuck, it was the girls and you and God; you were all ready and I got to watch; I'm the one that's grateful and sad for your loss."

"I know you wanted to, but by your not asking me about my wife; everything got to play itself out. You're pretty wise for a youngster."

"Thank you, there is a question I have to ask; do you want to build some houses?"

"Most definitely, Joe, those girls will beat me up if I don't get you back to Idaho."

"You and I are going to build three fine homes together and God is going to give us a sharp shovel."

Chuck gave me a hug that I never saw coming; "Fly safe now, you hear."

"Roger that."

CHAPTER 51

KEEPING MY PROMISE

Marti asked Sara if she wanted a school friends' birthday party or a family birthday party?

"A family party, Mom, and at the beach, unless it's raining."

The forecast for Saturday, October 1st, was for clear skies, with temps in the 50's; so, at five o'clock, at the beach house, the family would celebrate Sara's eighth birthday.

I arrived at my house around noon and brought ham and cheese slices for a lunch sandwich. I figured that and a beer and a fire in the den would be perfect for getting some work done.

I also began a list of things I wanted to have at the house; split up some of my music, the table/desk that I bought in Brooklyn would be perfect for work here in the den. I realized I had an apartment full of furniture and lamps that I had to either move to here or the new apartment or give away. I better get on the ball!

The doorbell rang and Dawn let herself in; she hugged me and kissed me.

"I have missed you, we all have missed you, Joe, where have you been?"

"I've been working and I just returned from Idaho where I spent a day with three almost nuns."

"Really?"

"Yes, I was in Idaho with the land owner and I spent a day with his three daughters, all of whom are nuns or probationary nuns."

"You are coming over at five, right?"

"Yes, that's why I'm here and I have a present for Sara."

"Sara loves you, you are her present."

"That's very sweet, Dawn."

"Running in the morning?"

"Seven?"

"Perfect."

"You look good in jeans, Dawn."

"Thank you. I look good without them; think about that, Mister Gordon."

I did.

Marti's hug was full of suspicion and her kiss was a peck, "Good to see you, Joseph."

"Good to see you as well."

"Hi, Joe."

"Hi, birthday girl," and we shared hugs and kisses.

"Hey, Bill." I picked him up and held him tight, "I love you, Mr. Bill."

"Drink," Marti asked.

"Yes please, bourbon and I'll be right back."

"What?"

"Forgot something."

When I walked into my house there was a woman standing in the den where I had forgotten Sara's gift.

"Who the heck are you?"

"I'm Isabelle, tell me your first name."

"Joe. Isabelle, I just put it together; the Tankard Troupe?"

We shook hands, "Joe, you are supposed to call us when you are coming to the beach."

"I'm sorry, I thought it was when, or if, we needed something. Lesson learned; glad to meet you, I forgot this," picking up Sara's gift.

"You're the architect?"

"Yes."

"She's a beauty, we all love it."

"Thanks, Isabelle, gotta go, I'll remember, don't lock me out."

"Goodnight, Joe."

"Sorry, I didn't think I'd be gone so long."

"What happened?"

"Tell you in a minute."

I handed Sara the gift wrapped box, "Happy Birthday, Sara no H."

"Thank you, Joe, I'll open it after dinner. No H, that's a long time ago."

"I had a memory flashback; we had fun. I love you, Sara."

"What happened," Bill wanted to know.

"When I ran into the house there was a woman in the den; it took us a few minutes to figure out that she was Isabelle and I was Joe and she is with the Tankard Troupe, the house care people."

"All these years and I have yet to meet any of them. She was nice," Marti asked.

"Yes, and now I know to call them whenever I'm coming to the beach. Who stole my drink?"

Dawn confessed and handed it over. I raised my glass and looked at Marti, "Here's to the birthday girl," and I turned to look at Sara, "best wishes for a wonderful year."

The discomfort level was at an all time high and Marti wasn't doing anything to help. Dinner remained pretty solemn and I got the feeling that I was supposed to liven things up; not my job. Thank God there were presents to open after dinner.

A very lovely scarf from Bill; "Thank you, silly Billy, it's a beautiful scarf," and Sara gave her brother a big kiss on the cheek.

"Good one, Bill, well done," I said. "What do you think of that scarf, Marti?"

Marti responded with a torrent of tears, a rain forest of moisture and I called time out and walked Marti out on the deck. It was chilly and I held her close.

"Marti, every one in that room loves one another and that includes my loving you and you loving me; look at me Marti Mason and tell me I'm right."

"You are, you're right."

"I love you so much I could almost explode but I am holding myself together for two reasons; one is because we have chosen a new path and the other is because I love everyone in that room. Look at me; you have to do the same. I get it that you're sad, I get it that you want me to disappear like I never came into your life in the first place. I get that because that's the way I feel; the pain is enormous. We have to go back in there and be brave for each other and for them."

"I want to kiss you, I want to tremble in your arms."

"Marti, that will get you past the pain but it won't get you back in that room."

"You went away; I didn't hear from you for almost three weeks."

"I am sorry and I will never do that to you again, but you can't take that out on your daughter, that's not who you are, that's not what this family is all about."

"What do I do next?"

"We go inside together and you tell your daughter, our daughter, exactly what's going on with you; that will be your birthday gift to her."

"One little kiss?"

"No, but if you tell Sara your truth we will share a kiss that will make them scream."

I took her hand and Marti stepped up to the plate and shared her anger, sadness and loneliness. It didn't matter if the kids understood any of it; they could feel their mother and she put trust back into her relationship with those of us that love her. I apologized for not staying in touch with Mom, which put her on edge; boy, did we make the kids scream with a colossal kiss. After the screaming, Sara opened her other presents: some socks, two pairs of shoes, a dress and a beautiful sweater from me, and I got a hugemongus kiss of love and thanks from my 'daughter'.

A birthday cake with eight candles appeared miraculously and we ate cake and talked and laughed until bedtime for the kids. Marti kissed me goodnight, she was going to stay upstairs after putting the kids to bed.

"Are you running?"

"Yes."

"Breakfast?"

"Yes, breakfast; how is eight thirtyish?"

"Perfect."

"See you then Marti, I love you."

All of a sudden, loving Marti was going to be okay.

"Goodnight, Dawn, I love you too."

At home I poured myself a nightcap and sat on the front porch and listened to the ocean; it was quiet and peaceful, perfect for us all.

Marti was staying at the beach as long as the weather was fair; she ran her business by phone and she and Dawn kept Sara and Bill up on their studies.

I was busy fitting in with The Monarch staff and getting ready to move into Apartment 16B. Chuck Sturner was excited with some preliminary designs while we waited for the geologist's reports. The more I talk with Chuck the more I learn and the more I like him. Bob Reinhardt is happy; we are going to design three homes on the Snake River in Idaho.

Marti brought her gang back to the city and I had dinner with them at the Fifth Avenue apartment two weeks in a row and I was put on notice that Friday, November 15th would be Bill Mason's sixth birthday; nothing would keep me away.

Marti, Dawn and the kids visited me at my new apartment and The Monarch got kudos as did 16B. Time was flying and Marti was planning Thanksgiving at the beach and wanted me there; I told my first lie to her, saying I was going to my sister's. I wanted to be alone; I didn't know why but I choose to honor my feeling.

I was delighted to be at Bill's birthday celebration. I had ordered a custom three pound croquet mallet with his name on the handle; it arrived on the 12th, just in time.

On Friday November 22, Bob Reinhardt and I had lunch in the bar room at "41". At a little after one, the room full of patrons was silenced by the loud clanging of one of the railroad locomotive bells perched between sections of the room. Jerry Brown delivered a sad and chilling report; President John F. Kennedy had been assassinated while riding in a motorcade in Dallas, Texas.

"Politics aside, this is a stunning blow to our country and to the world," Bob shared with me.

"I am deeply saddened, Bob, shocked actually, I want to reach out to my family and Marti. Lyndon Johnson is going to be our new president; he's a crafty politician. Oh, boy."

"Joe, I am going back to the office, sign our check and I'll see you later."

"No problem, I got it."

I asked a waiter to bring me a phone, there were plug ins around the room, and I was able to get through to Marti, "You've heard?"

"Yes, a minute ago. Joe, this is crazy."

"Marti, I would like to come over around dinner time to be with you and the kids."

"Oh, Joe, Yes, please, I would love that."

"I'll see you later."

I went back to the office and gave Liz a hug, she was deeply moved by this tragedy.

"Joe, who would do this; someone planned this, knew the route, it's awful."

"I don't know if we will ever know the answer, Liz."

In the Reinhardt-Tufts boardroom it appeared the company was pretty much split down the middle politically, but the shock and sadness was universal. The pragmatist, Jim Palmer, said, "The country, actually the world, will shrug its' shoulders and move on; that's the way life is."

That evening, at Marti's, we talked with Sara and Bill about President Kennedy and what had happened; it was sad, shocking and death, especially, was a difficult topic since their dad had never returned from Argentina.

"We have a new president and we will continue on; you will go to school, we will go to work and we will all help each other get through the tough times, because we love and trust each other," I said, trying to keep it simple.

"We're going to the beach tomorrow," Sara said, "and Mom said you are not coming for Thanksgiving. Why not?"

"I'm going to be at my sister's."

"I'll miss you, Joe," Bill gave me a big hug.

"I wish you all a wonderful week and a special Thanksgiving."

Marti walked me to the elevator, "Thank you, Joseph, the kids and," Marti was crying, "I love you and miss you and want you and I'm sorry; I'm trying to be better."

"We are all doing our best, Marti."

The elevator arrived for the second time and I stepped in.

PART SIX

One Year Later

THE CHRISTMAS TREE

CHAPTER 52

CAN IT BE KATE?

It has been a little more than a year since Marti and I broke up and what a year it has been: Rinehart-Tufts is thriving, I have a new client whose wife admired the "Duck house" in Newport, the Monarch is a huge success, I have the first of three homes under construction in Idaho, Marti and I are friends and I visit the kids at least once a month and at their birthday parties.

All-in-all, a wonderful year capped by celebrating Thanksgiving with my sister; family, football, fun and lots of delicious food. At the end of the day, after thanks and hugs, I received a care package that included a piece of apple pie.

I ran Friday morning; it was a good run and I convinced myself that I deserved, no, I had earned that piece of apple pie.

Late in the afternoon I went to Rockefeller Center to hang out with 50,000 of my closest friends for the lighting of the 85 foot tall Christmas tree.

There were oohs and aahs and thousands of flash bulbs and a sense of well being that eclipsed the sorrow that still lingered from President Kennedy's assassination a year ago.

Slowly our focus turned from the beauty of the tree to finding a way out to Fifth Avenue where the sidewalks were jammed with people gawking at the seasonal window displays from Saks to Tiffany.

I had made it to the sidewalk, no easy task, when I saw the face, a face I knew but couldn't place.

A face across Fifth Avenue, lost in the crowd; no, there she is again, in front of Saks. I stepped off the curb, weaving through traffic while keeping an eye on the face and enduring a cacophony of honking and cries of "Idiot". Don't lose sight of that face, now disappearing into Saks. Hurry, Joe, there they are, she and her husband, maybe, walking deeper into the crowded store; she's going into the Lady's Room, the man waiting.

"Excuse me; your wife, I know her." "My sister, but what's your point?"

"I went to school with her years ago, that's Kate, I know it."

"Who are you?"

"My name is Joseph Gordon, I knew your sister at Rutgers and she disappeared."

"I need you to quickly understand; she was in an accident, in a coma for three months, she does not remember anything of her life before the accident. If she sees you it could def . . . "

"Joseph?"

"Yes, Kate, I am Joseph."

"Oh, my God, Joseph, you are a miracle."

"No, Kate, you are the miracle, more beautiful than ever."

"I'm Tom, her brother, I need to know what's going on."

"Tom, ten years ago I went to sleep in a coma and dreamed of Joseph waking me up."

"You're being serious?"

"Yes." Then, turning to me, "What took you so long?"

"I was busy."

"Doing what?"

"Getting ready for you."

"We were at Sally's," Kate said, "the place was packed, I kissed you, I invited you,"

"To walk with you," I continued, "talk with you, laugh with you," "And," Kate went on, "hold you with my entire being, forever."

"Kate, that night, that kiss, you touched me like no other."

"I fell in love with you when you were moving into your fraternity house."

"After the kiss I looked for you for weeks. I asked people at Sally's, and the bartender. I asked the professor of our classic music elective for your last name; he looked at me like I was crazy."

"I snuck into that class because you were there."

"You have been in love for almost a decade," Tom asked.

"When Kate kissed me everything went black, we were the only two people in the universe. When I went back to my table, my friends told me the lights had gone out for about a minute."

"Joseph, would you kiss me, I want to tell you something."

We kissed and Kate told me she would marry me if the lights went out at Saks.

The lights at Saks did not go out and it didn't matter; I was flush with joy as we kissed and Kate, I was certain, shared the joy as well. When our lips parted we held our embrace to erase the years that separated us.

"If I walk out of the Lady's Room can I have a kiss like that," asked an attractive, fortyish woman.

"I'm afraid you are a decade too late," I said.

"He's a wonderful kisser," Kate said, holding on to my arm.

"Tom," I said, "come on, let's go to "41" for a drink."

At the bar, with our drinks, Tom raised his glass, "As the kid brother who loves his sister dearly I drink to you both and pray that the door that you have opened to the past will bring understanding and closure and that your future will be filled with good health and joy."

We all touched glasses and drank.

"Tom, that is beautiful," Kate said, and she hugged her brother.

"I will do everything in my power to comfort you and love you as we unravel the past and go forward together; all of us, Tom."

"I'm in shock," Kate said, "not disruptive shock, sort of floating on clouds of joy shock. I'm a big girl but I'm counting on both of you."

"I'm in," I said.

"I'm in as well," Tom added.

"Dinner? I'm starving," I announced.

"Mmmm, yes," Kate agreed.

"I'm going to pass so you two can talk about me and start to fill in the past lost years. Joe, we should share phone numbers."

We exchanged business cards and Tom hugged his sister and hugged me, "Sunday brunch," he asked.

"Sure," I said looking at Kate who nodded in agreement.

"Call me," and Tom was gone.

I caught Walter's attention, one of the captains, and signaled for a table, holding up two fingers. Shortly we were seated, sitting side by side at table number 23 in the center section of the bar.

"Walter, I would like you to meet Kate Lawrence, we are going to be married in the spring."

Walter beamed, "Congratulations to you both; that's wonderful."

Walter took our order and left.

"You used that nice man to propose to me, Joseph."

"Only after you proposed to me outside of the Lady's Room in front of your brother and at least fifty strangers."

"We're even."

"You know what I am feeling right now?"

"What, Joseph?"

"The warmth of your leg pressed against mine under the table."

"May I invite you to spend the evening with me at my apartment?"

"The answer is yes even though I am supposed to seductively lure you to my man cave."

"Joe, I want my own comfort zone tonight."

"Understood."

"Kate, your apartment is lovely."

"Thank you; I moved in a few months ago. I like the building, I like the location and I like the people."

"Two bedrooms, two baths, living room, a nice kitchen and a small laundry room."

"Are you a realtor?"

"I'm an architect, Kate, I designed this building."

"The Monarch?"

"Yes, I live in the east wing."

"Why didn't you say something on the way or when we got here?"

"I'm in shock; we have been living about a hundred yards from each other and yet it took mingling with 50,000 people to find you."

I reached out to Kate and took her in my arms; she started to cry. I swept her off her feet and settled us on the sofa.

"Am I dreaming?"

"We are dreaming, Kate, we are living the dreams we have held onto. We are blessed."

"Oh, my God," Kate said, wiping away her tears, "You are a miracle."

"We are a miracle."

Kate kissed me, a short, happy, wonderful kiss; "I'm going to change my clothes while you take off whatever you don't want to be wearing and find the bourbon, it's over there somewhere, and pour us a big, very big, drink we can share. I'll be right back."

I took off my jacket and tie, kicked off my shoes, found the bourbon and a big tumbler and ice and heard soft music coming from the living room. Kate was wearing a button up the front, blue sweater that was sort of buttoned. She was fresh and beautiful.

"Tell me who you are, Joseph, and kiss me and touch me while I go crazy with love for you."

I started with when I was a little tot and finished with walking away from Marti Mason. Along the way we kissed and touched and I discovered how beautiful Kate is.

"At Saks, it already feels like years ago, you said, when I asked 'what took you so long', you said, 'you were getting ready for me'. Tell me about that part. "I'll keep it simple; I broke up with Celeste, I wasn't ready; Gabby exploded my curiosity, thinking and maturity; Eileen wasn't ready, alcohol; Rita, the ethics of running and parting; and Marti, the big one, independence in a relationship.

My intention today is to bring the best me I can be to you every day for the rest of forever."

Kate took my hand and led me to her bedroom for the sweetest, most loving night of my life.

We woke at eleven and Kate shared her toothbrush.

"Where did you learn all of that," I asked, my mouth full of toothpaste.

"I read a lot and dream and it's always with you."

Back in bed we hugged and kissed and laughed and talked.

"I'm a runner," I shared.

"You mean this is it?"

"No, Kate, I mean up at six and run ten miles unless it's raining, snowing or icy."

"I am an up at seven, do pilates, shower, breakfast and I am at Saks by nine."

"Saks?"

"Yes, I am in charge of buying all things woman."

"I am impressed and not surprised; you are all things woman."

"Mmmm," Kate purred, and we kissed.

"I am an architect with Reinhardt and Tufts; I like getting to the office before nine. I have a very good relationship with Bob Reinhardt and my secretary's name is Liz; she is going to love you."

"Because?"

"Because I love you."

Kate was lying comfortably in my arms as we put our separate lives together, we were painting a new canvas; filling in the background.

"I have a house in Easthampton close to the ocean. I designed an ocean front house for Marti Mason and she gave me her old house when she moved into the new one."

"I love the beach," Kate mused and she started to cry.

"Oh, my God, my mind is overflowing with memories; memories that have been tucked away for years."

Kate was sitting up, pulling at the covers, trying to hide.

"Kate, you don't have to."

"I do have to . ."

"Do you want me to call your brother?"

"No, Joseph, please, I want to spill this out, it's buckets and buckets, it's my turn and some of this isn't pretty."

"Hold on."

I found Kate's sweater and my shirt that we pulled on for warmth and correctness of the moment.

"Kate, this is day one of forever and you are the miracle of my life. Go for it."

"When you said beach house it unleashed a torrent of memories and emotions. We had a beach house on the Jersey shore and we spent summers there. I had lots of beach girl friends, the same families every summer, and we all grew up together from the time we were five and into our teens. We were all into volleyball, swimming in the ocean, getting tan, gossiping and then, as we got into our teens, boys. Boys and dating and making out and becoming a pretty teenager. I wasn't conceited; I just loved blossoming physically into a young woman. Even then, Joseph, I knew I would fall in love with "you," I didn't know it would be you!"

"I'm your guy, Kate."

"My brother, Tom, had his growing up at the beach guy friends and he was, and is, a natural athlete on top of being smart; my girlfriends loved him, teased him and taught him a lot about girls. He's a numbers guy that, I guess, he got from my dad who had a seat on the New York Stock Exchange and was a great provider.

My mom was first rate; she was beautiful, smart, an avid reader that she passed on to my brother and me.

Another thing my mother did, a very strong thing that few women have the courage to do; she protected us from our alcoholic father. My dad was a great guy and a scary drunk. Mom didn't hover over us, or my dad, but when the situation called for her to step in, she didn't hesitate.

Unfortunately there were times, when I was a teen- ager, my dad's arms went too far around my body so he could touch my breast or his eyes would devour me. Our relationship became predator and prey; it was horrible but I didn't want to burden my mom."

Kate was crying and she was balled up, her arms wrapped around her knees; she was a living fortress.

"One afternoon at the beach, I had just showered, my dad opened my bedroom door, I was naked. Startled, I grabbed a pillow to cover my body.

'My God,' he said.

'Get out,' I hissed in disgust. He left and I cried for hours. For me my dad was dead, he no longer existed. I never told my mom but she knew something had happened and as a family we shifted and shuddered, like a painful death."

Kate uncoiled and threw herself on me, holding me so tight it hurt.

"That Friday night," Kate started, "at Sally's, when I kissed you and the lights went out, I slept and dreamed of us. The next morning my folks picked me up, Tom was along as well, for our last weekend at the beach house until the following spring. We all cleaned things, scrubbed, covered and put things away; it was hard work that we had done a hundred times. When we were done we locked up and left for home, traveling on a busy highway.

My dad, who had been drinking, insisted he was fine and would not let my mom drive. He fell asleep at dusk and we drifted into oncoming traffic; taking my parents to their grave."

Kate looked at me, stared at me really, and whispered, "I didn't know what had happened until three months later but I must have had a few seconds before blacking out, when I saw my father was dead and I was glad."

Kate began to sob and I held her close. Her whispered confession was like a voice from her soul and I understood she could never tell her brother.

Kate's sobbing subsided and this beautiful survivor began to breathe serenely as if a mighty boulder had been lifted from her being; the very being that would hold us close for the rest of our lives.

I kissed her awake with the softest kiss I could produce.

"I love you, Kate."

She purred.

Kate showered and packed a small bag for her overnight at my apartment. Upon entering my place Kate grabbed my arm, "Two bedrooms, two baths, a living room, kitchen and laundry room except this place is not you."

I explained my deal with Larry Fisher; "Rent free, for a year and now it's month to month at half rate while I continue to instill the welcoming spirit of The Monarch to all of the employees that make you feel cared for in your home."

"You should move in with me, Joe."

"Mind reader. I'm going to shower."

"I'm going to watch."

Kate insisted on towel drying my body that caused a bit of an interruption before heading to P.J. Clarkes for dinner.

It was clear and not too cold so we walked down Third Avenue laughing like kids who had misbehaved in grade school.

After dinner we took a cab back to The Monarch where the doorman helped us out of the cab.

"Good evening, Mr. Gordon and Miss Lawrence, welcome to the East wing."

"Thank you, David, see you tomorrow."

The next day, Sunday, we met Tom at eleven for brunch at Tavern on the Green. Tom waved to us from the bar.

"Fear not," Tom said, hugging us, "I got here early, I'm one Bloody Mary ahead of you and our table will be available in about ten minutes."

Three Bloody Marys magically appeared on the bar.

"You, Tom, my soon to be B-I-L are, I have learned from a beautiful and reliable source, a wonderful brother and a very special man." "Thank you, reliable source."

We picked up our drinks and simultaneously Tom and I said, "To Kate."

Lobster bisque followed by mac and cheese were perfect as Kate, who loves us both, led the way for Tom and me getting to know each other.

Tom, it turns out, graduated from high school at 16 and graduated from Harvard and Harvard Law School; took over his father's seat on the New York Stock Exchange that he leases out, is a Certified Public Accountant and a deal maker of mergers and acquisitions.

"Tom has a great reputation; he wants every deal to be win-win," Kate wanted me to know.

"I'm busy, I'm happy and comfortable in my own little house in the Village. The only thing, no, the only one missing, is this empty chair. I date, came close once, but I didn't; well, you know, I'm young and "she" is out there somewhere."

"Somewhere? I will be right back; Lady's Room."

In a way it felt like Kate was giving Tom room to talk about the accident.

"By the time I was ten," Tom said, "I had a sense of responsibility; I don't know why, maybe I got that from my dad. I knew if an emergency came along I would know what to do; so, when the accident happened, the last Sunday in September, and I was miraculously unhurt, I called my mom's brother, Uncle Buddy, who arrived the next day. Together we reasoned things out: Kate and I had become instant orphans; with houses, a business to protect, parents to bury and I had a sister to look after, Kate was in a coma. During October, November and December I lived at the hospital and talked to my sister, read books to her and prayed for her. On January 11th Kate awoke and three days later Uncle Buddy and I brought her home; she was petrified and remembered nothing of the accident and nothing of her life before the accident; she didn't know who she was.

During January, February and March she would not leave the house until one day in April she asked me if I played tennis.

"Sure, I play tennis."

"Would you teach me?"

"Of course."

We went outside and what I prayed for happened; her body remembered how to play and we hit balls for ten minutes when Kate announced, "I'm exhausted, let's have lunch."

Her body's muscle recall opened the door for her brain to slowly remember some of the good that she had tucked away. Enough for her to go back to school, graduate, take a job opportunity at Saks and, over time, become the beautiful Kate that we both love so much.

Back from the Lady's Room Kate announced, "Tom, Joe has a house in Easthampton."

"And," I said, "I have a car that will get us there. It's a Porsche and it might be a little crowded but it will be worth it. I have a suggestion I hope we can make happen; Christmas and New Years at the beach? And the week between?"

"I'm in. I'll get a date, I'll rent a car," Tom was excited.

"I am ninety nine percent certain I can take the week off," Kate said.

"Me, too, Kate, but New Year's for sure?"

"For sure," Kate responded.

"Tom, Do not get a date, trust me on this and bring sneakers or running shoes."

"No hints?"

"No hints. Can you run ten miles?"

"I guess, I've never tried, but I have played five set tennis matches that lasted for hours."

"You will be fine."

"I," Kate said emphatically, "am not running any miles."

"Will you welcome me back to our bed after the run, I'll only be gone a little more than an hour?"

"Of course, I think," Kate said, shivering and hugging herself, "If I didn't love you this would start to be overwhelming."

"I know, we are just getting started: there's the Reinhardt partners Christmas party, meeting my crazy mother and my two sisters, move me into your apartment, and plan a wedding."

"My sister is getting married and 72 hours ago we were warming our hearts at the lighting of the Christmas tree at Rock Center. This, Kate and Joe, is wonderful."

"Good morning, Joe, you're late; you are usually here before me."

"I have had a very unusual Thanksgiving weekend."

"Unusual?"

"Yes. You know how sometime things happen to us and sometime things happen for us. This weekend had it all."

"All? What happened?"

"It's complicated, sort of a miracle."

"A complicated miracle, I'm hooked, tell me."

"Okay, Elizabeth, you are going to say, 'Oh, come on Joe, you've got to be kidding!', but here goes. Friday I went to Rock Center for the tree lighting; thousands of people and I saw her face, I remembered her face, she was across Fifth in front of Saks, I ran through traffic but she was gone, inside of Saks, I saw her go into the Lady's Room and I waited, when she came out she uttered my name and kissed me."

"She?"

"Yes, Kate. A decade ago, when we were kids at Rutgers, she kissed me like no other and then disappeared, vanished, gone for almost a decade."

"Kate?"

"Katherine Lawrence, she lives at The Monarch, West wing; I am moving into her apartment, she will be here for the Reinhardt Christmas party, you will meet her."

"Can I be candid?"

"That's exactly why you are my secretary."

"You are moving at the speed of light?"

"Moving at the speed of a lost decade."

"People are going to think you have lost your way, Joe."

"Is that what you are thinking?"

"A little."

"Liz, do we have time for this?"

"Yes, you're good 'til lunch with Larry Fisher."

As if on cue the phone rang; Liz picked up.

"Joe Gordon's office,"

Liz listened and looked at her watch, "Sure, no problem." She hung up, "You now have twenty minutes; Mr. Reinhardt wants to see you at ten thirty."

"Perfect, I want to see him."

"I'm ready, Joe."

"We saw each other the first day I got to Rutgers; she was across the street, very pretty, the following week we introduced ourselves after a class we shared, The following Friday I was at Sally's, the local burger and beer hangout, and she was there with some girls; I said hello and was going back to my guys when she said, "There's a Sally's tradition, a goodnight kiss: it was the purest, warmest kiss that became a conversation about life and love and when I rejoined my friends they said the lights had gone out for about a minute. I never saw her again, she disappeared, I looked for her and asked about her, but she was gone."

"I have goose-bumps and you have ten minutes, Joe."

"She was in an accident; her parents died, Kate was in a coma for three months. Her younger brother was unhurt and lived at the hospital reading to her, praying for her. When she woke she remembered nothing of the accident or her life before until she walked out of the Lady's Room at Saks and saw me and whispered, Joseph."

"My God, Joe."

"She was at Saks with Tom, her brother, the three of us celebrated our miracle with a drink at "41". The rest is self explanatory; we spent the weekend, each of us filling in the blanks."

"Time's up, I am thrilled for you."

"Thanks, Liz, there is not anyone I would rather have told," I was leaving the office, "my family doesn't even know!"

"Joe," Bob Reinhardt gestured for me to sit, "Joe, Larry Fisher is excited, The Monarch has a waiting list; he wants your apartment."

"I'm having lunch with him, I'll take care of it."

"He told me you rejuvenated their spirit, they are putting together another piece of property."

"There you go, it's going to be an exciting year."

Bob Reinhardt stood, signaling our meeting was over.

"Bob, I want to go to the beach for Christmas, New Year and the week between, it's important."

"You'll be at the Partner's party on Friday, the 20th?"

"Absolutely, and back on the sixth."

I knew I was pushing pretty hard.

"You have earned it, Joe, but I would like to keep this between us; no one need know that you are taking the vacation we would all like to have."

Bob Reinhardt gave me a hug, "I am very proud of you, Joe."

"Thank you."

"I have a solution to your problem, Joe."

"I didn't know I have a problem, Liz."

"The Kate story; you can't tell everyone the whole saga and that you are getting married, it's too much."

"And the solution is?"

"Kate is Kate; she's awesome and you love her. That's all anyone needs to know right now; keep it simple."

"I love you, Liz. I wonder what Larry Fisher is going to say; there is a waiting list for The Monarch, he wants my apartment and he has no idea I am moving to the West Wing."

"What do you mean," Larry Fisher started, "you will give up your apartment and continue to supervise The Monarch staff if I give you a parking place in the West Wing; what's wrong with your parking place at the east wing?"

"Convenience."

"Convenience," Larry paused, "You've got to be kidding; you're moving in with some broad in the West Wing?"

"Larry," I said with a wink, "I'm trying to help you here."

"Yeah, yeah, okay parking in the West Wing. Who is this woman?"

"Just someone I met over the weekend."

"That'll be the day. When do I get to meet her?"

"Right after the New Year, we'll have drinks at "41"."

"It's a deal, Joe. You're quite a guy; you were right about The Monarch, thank you."

"My pleasure, Larry. Happy holidays to all the Fishers, you mean a lot to me."

The Reinhardt Partners annual Christmas party is a lovely affair; lots of good food, good drinks, and good people.

This will be my seventh year, Christmas, 1964; celebrating with the architects and staff, all of whom I have worked with, learned from or assisted in one way or another.

I'm sure Bob Reinhardt will lift our spirits with a toast to a Merry Christmas and a Happy New Year.

"There is a very beautiful woman at the front desk asking for you, Joe," Liz announced.

"I asked Kate to come a little early so the three of us will have a few minutes together. I'll be right back."

At the lobby I collected Kate and a kiss and led her to my office.

"Kate Lawrence, I would like you to meet Liz, my friend and my secretary, also known as Elizabeth Blanton."

"My pleasure, Liz," Kate expressed, "I look forward to getting to know you."

"Between the two of us we will keep an eye on this guy," Liz responded.

"Kate, why don't you sit at my desk, I'm going to get us a drink. Liz?"

"Bourbon, ice, thanks."

"I'll be right back."

"Kate, Joe told me your story; I got goose bumps. I am so happy for you both."

"Thank you, Liz, it's so hard, no, wait, strange would be a better word, to walk into Joe's world; his family and now his "work family". On my side I have my brother and my work environment at Saks isn't anything like what Joe has shared about you and Bob Reinhardt; you are a pretty tight knit group."

"True, Kate, but we are a family at heart and you are going to enjoy meeting the gang."

"I'm ready, I think."

"I'm sure you are; here's the scouting report: you are smart, caring and beautiful."

"Right on the nose," I said, handing out the drinks, "here's to the two smart, caring and beautiful women I am blessed to have in my life."

"I have met your Mom and two sisters and their families but I sense that this part of your life is tops."

"That's because Joe is Joe," Liz said to Kate.

"It's because I love being an architect, being creative, and everyone here helps me, trusts me and encourages me; how can you beat that?"

"By adding Kate to your life," Liz lifted her glass toward Kate.

They touched glasses and drank.

"I knew this would happen, I knew you two would click, which pleases me no end. Kate, you are the most important part of my life and, Liz, we have been at this together for six years; let's go celebrate."

"You two go ahead," Liz said, "I'll be along in a minute."

I introduced Kate to all the partners, the artists, the techies, secretaries; everyone. "This is indeed a family, Joe."

We filled our plates at the buffet and Bob Reinhardt invited us to join him and his wife Susan at their table.

"This is an honor, Bob, thank you," I said.

"I want you to know, Joe, that my husband," Susan Reinhardt said, "thinks very highly of you, but the reason you are sitting with us is, I want to get to know Kate."

"Thank you Susan," Kate said, "I think these two men love and respect each other in a very healthy way; I will very much like for us to become acquainted."

Dinner was splendid, during which Bob Reinhardt addressed us all with gratitude for everyone's contribution to a very successful year followed by best wishes for the holidays and the coming year.

When dinner was over, and Kate and I were leaving, Susan Reinhardt kissed me on the cheek and whispered, "Do not mess this up, Joe, Kate is a champ."

"It will be my pleasure to follow your advice."

I hugged Mrs. Reinhardt and she hugged me back.

"Thank you Bob, this has been a wonderful evening."

"You are an asset to this firm, Joe, keep it up," Bob said.

Mrs. Reinhardt winked at me as Kate and I went off to find Liz, to say goodnight.

"Mr. Reinhardt told me I will not see you until next year, Joe."

"I was about to wish you a Happy New Year and tell you myself. We are going to the beach and no one is supposed to know."''

"Happy holidays, Liz," Kate said as they hugged.

"Happy New Year," Liz said, "I'll see you both in the new year."

"Absolutely."

CHAPTER 53

LIVING THE "KISS"

Tom had come uptown from his house in the Village and we all had breakfast at Kate's.

"I'm excited," Kate said, "Two weeks at the beach with my favorite guys but it wasn't easy; Saks was reluctant but finally caved. I am ready."

"Me, too," Tom added, "I love the beach in the winter and add a mystery woman; this should be great."

"Thank you both for packing small bags, they fit perfectly in the front trunk; and I brought a pillow so you, Kate, can sit sideways in the back seat. Let's do it."

It was clear and chilly as we motored east on Montauk highway.

"How are you doing, Kate?"

"I'm good, I thought it would be noisy but it's not, and the pillow was a good idea; I'm very comfortable."

"I'm excited, I think you will love the house and we are going to have a good time but not without a few challenges for each of us. So, I want to share what amounts to a heads up."

"Great idea," said Tom, "maybe I'll get a hint about the runner."

"More than a hint, Tom, I promise."

"What do I get, Joseph?"

"You get one hundred percent of me for the rest of forever but I want to prepare you for your encounter with Marti."

"I am getting uncomfortable back here."

"Please don't, but it's important that I remind you that Marti Mason and I were lovers; I designed her beach house and she gave me her old house that is now my house, our house, Kate. Marti's house is only a few hundred feet away and we will be visiting her for several reasons; she and I are friends and I believe Kate, you and she will become more than neighbors, probably friends."

"Joe, I will be okay. Learning about her when you shared your story was one thing, becoming neighbors is, I don't know; intimidating?"

"I understand, I'm sorry, there's more; she has two terrific kids and I made a promise to stay in their lives."

"Can I cut in here," Tom interjected, "Kate, I think Joe is nervous, perhaps more nervous than you, for you."

"I'm okay, I promise," Kate assured us.

"The rest is simple, Sara is eight or nine, I can't remember, and Bill is two years younger; they are smart and fun."

"Are we coming to the hint part," Tom asked.

"Yes, the nanny. The nanny is Marti's sister-in-law, Dawn Mason. Dawn is the kid sister of Jeremy Mason, the deceased computer whiz, and she's the nanny because she loves the kids. I think you will hit it off."

"Dawn is the runner," Tom wanted to know.

"She is."

"Done," Kate asked.

"I saved the best for last, Isabelle and the Tankard Troupe."

"Joseph!"

"Isabelle takes care of our house, Kate. She, or one of her Troupe, goes in the house every day we are not there and when we are coming, like now, she prepares the house for our arrival with food, turns up the heat, anything and everything; all we have to do is let Isabelle know a day or two in advance."

"That's fantastic," Kate exclaimed.

"In about five minutes the proof will be in the pudding."

"Joe, this house, your house, is warm and inviting; it is quite wonderful," Tom said.

"Thank you, I'm so glad we are here together, I could not be happier."

We were in the kitchen where the tour had ended. Tom put his bag in one of the bedrooms and Kate joined me in the master suite.

"Joe, these flowers are fresh and beautiful, and there's an envelope under the vase."

"I saw them before we started the tour, would you read the note while I check the fridge."

"It's addressed to you."

"Well, my dear Kate, that means it is addressed to us."

"Dear Joe, You are a generous man; thank you very much. Remember, I am here to help when needed. And it's signed, Isabelle."

"Thanks, Kate, I sent her a check for Christmas and we got flowers and thanks. We also have, in the fridge, everything we need for all of our meals through the weekend and Monday we can go shopping."

"I'm ready for lunch, Joe, what can I do to help," Tom wanted to know.

"Your sister would love a Bloody Mary," Kate said.

"Great idea, me too," I added, "the bar is in the den; everything you need is there. Kate and I will make sandwiches."

Tom headed off and Kate and I immediately kissed.

"I know what you're doing in there," Tom called from the hallway.

"No sandwich for you, Mr. Nosey," Kate called back.

Lunch was good, the Bloody Marys were good, we cleaned up the kitchen and were in the den, fire going and football on the TV.

"They will be here any minute," I cautioned.

"They," Kate asked.

"The kids; I'm sure they saw the car, Marti and Dawn insisted they give us time to settle in, and now it's . ."

"Joe," Sara called, they had come in the kitchen door.

"In the den, whoever you are."

In a heartbeat I was on one knee hugging Sara and Bill.

"We've missed you," Bill said.

"And we have a message for you," Sara said.

"God, you kids look great."

"We are great, silly."

"Of course, I forgot. Okay, hold the message, I want you to meet my very special friends; this is Kate and her brother, Tom; I would like you to meet Sara and her brother, Bill.

They all said hello and then Bill said, "You're very pretty, Kate."

"Thank you, Bill, Joe has told Tom and me that you both are very special, I'm glad to meet you."

"Me, too," Tom said, "Who is delivering the message?"

"Oh, the message, almost forgot, you are invited for drinks," Bill said.

"At six," Sara added.

"We are supposed to go now," Bill said, "Mom said deliver the message and come home."

I looked at Kate and Tom and got the green light, "We will be over for drinks at six."

"That's great. Come on Bill."

"See you in a little while," Kate called after them.

"Okay," we heard just before the door shut.

At a few minutes past six we rang the front door bell.

"I designed this house and I have never entered the house this way."

"We were looking for you on the beach side," Sara said, opening the door.

We piled in to get out of the cold and left our winter jackets on the bench in the entryway.

"Oh, my goodness, what a beautiful home," Kate said.

"We love our house, Kate. Come on, I want you to meet Dawn."

We approached the living area where the fireplace was ablaze and Dawn and Bill were reading a book together. "The earth shook all around them and apples fell from the tree," Dawn finished reading and they stood.

"Hi, Joe and," Bill took a moment, "Kate and Tom."

"This is a huggy house, Kate, It's a pleasure to meet you and your brother." Dawn looked lovely in a red, Christmassy sweater and tight jeans.

"It's a pleasure meeting and hugging you, Dawn," Tom said.

I hugged Dawn and asked, "Marti?"

"Upstairs. Would you do the drinks, Joe?"

"Certainly, I'm pretty sure I know what everyone wants and maybe I can get help from Bill?"

"What do I do?"

"We'll figure it out." Bill and I went to the bar at the end of the counter that sweeps out from the kitchen.

"I'm going upstairs to check on Mom," Sara decided.

"And I'm going to wander, if that's okay," Kate asked Dawn.

"Of course; start at the far corner facing the beach and it's guest bedroom and bath, den with fireplace, guest bathroom and you're back to the front door."

Tom and Dawn settled on the sofa.

"Are you ever lonely here, Dawn?"

"Not really; there are the kids and Marti, my sister- in-law, who's my best friend. We have a duplex on Fifth in the city and the kids go to school there but we cone out here as often as possible. I love the beach in the winter. What about you, Thomas?"

"I have a seat on the New York Stock Exchange that I lease out and I'm a deal and merger guy. I bought a stable in the Village and converted it into my two bedroom, two bath home. I love the Village, the city and what I do."

"I would like to visit you in your stable, Tom."

"I'll take that as a stamp of approval, Dawn. It would be my pleasure."

"Drinks, everyone, my fellow bartender and I have a vodka on ice for Mr. Tom and Bourbon rocks for the rest of us."

"And Pepsi on the rocks for my sister and me. Where is my sister?"

"She's upstairs checking on Mom," Dawn said.

"Is Marti not well," I asked.

"I'm fine," Marti said, as she and Sara descended the stairs.

Kate was passing the stairs on her way back to the sofa and stopped, "Marti, I'm Kate Lawrence, thank you for inviting us for drinks."

"I'm so glad you are here, I am sorry I wasn't downstairs to greet you."

"No worries, Marti, your home is so inviting and it's nice that we are all together."

"Marti pictured every inch of the furnishings," I said, "from the floor plan; the day after construction ended the house looked like this! Bourbon?"

"Yes, please."

We were all settled on the huge, comfortable, U shaped sofa that surrounds an oak coffee table with books and newspapers and several platters of cheese, crackers, sliced salami, French bread and mustard.

Dawn and Tom sat side by side, Sara and Bill had me bracketed and Marti and Kate got right down to business; getting to know one another. I looked at them and was pleased Kate was comfortable.

"Here's to the two most important people here tonight," I said, "Here's to Sara and Bill."

We all raised our glasses, Sara and Bill included, and drank.

"Great toast, Joe, great kids," Dawn said.

The evening wore on as we nibbled, sipped and made new friends that would, I hoped, end up being fine neighbors for a long time. Before we left Marti insisted we join them for Christmas dinner. We sealed the deal with hugs goodnight and ran home to reignite our fire in the den.

"Dinner," I asked and was met with groans.

"Okay, it's everyone on their own; there's a ton of food in the fridge and the pantry."

The phone rang and I asked Tom to pick it up; I was sure it was Dawn. Five minutes later the four of us sipped our drinks and chatted until Kate and I said goodnight.

"See you in the morning," Dawn said.

"Bacon and eggs," and off we went.

"Your sister is lovely, Tom, she's beautiful and she's nice."

"I love Kate, we're close."

"And she loves Joe, that's obvious."

"I was with Kate at Rockefeller Center for the Christmas tree lighting and then inside Saks when it happened."

"After you kiss me, would you describe 'it' to me?"

Dawn and Tom kissed and then kissed again.

"I have waited a long time for you, Tom."

"And I for you. We have Joe to thank for this; he knew," Tom said.

"I'm ready for the 'it' description, Tom."

And Tom told her about Rutgers, the kiss, the accident, coma, Kate's new life, the tree lighting, Kate whispering 'Joseph', and their kissing again after a decade.

"That, Dawn, is the 'it' story."

"It's beautiful."

"I agree, you're crying."

"I am not crying and thank you for telling me," Dawn said, wiping her eyes, "Are you a runner, Tom?"

"No, not yet, but I'm a good athlete."

"You're a good kisser, Thomas."

"We are good kissers, are you spending the night, Miss 'see you in the morning'?"

"I don't want you to think I'm easy."

"Dawn, we have all the time in the world."

"I don't want the kids to wake up and wonder where I am."

"I respect that."

"Kiss me goodnight, Mr. Lawrence."

"I'll walk you home."

"No, Tom, I know my way blindfolded."

Tom kissed Dawn and they walked to the kitchen door.

"I'll see you in the morning," Dawn said and Tom watched her walk quickly toward the beach house.

In the morning I woke before Kate; I propped up on one elbow to watch her stir. One eye opened and she smiled.

"You are so beautiful," I whispered, "I love you, Kate."

"Mmmm."

"Let's brush and get back in bed, I want to talk."

"No way, Joseph, am I going to leave this bed."

"I'll be right back."

I brushed and returned and kissed Kate.

"Thank you," Kate said as she snuggled up close to me. "Do you want to know something wonderful," I asked.

"Of course."

"It's over, all the meeting of family and business associates and a previous lover; sure, there are still some friends to meet but the hard part is over. You are amazing, everyone loves you, likes you, and now we get to love each other, support each other and . ."

Kate's mouth shut me up; it was a wonderful Kate kiss, "Now, Joe, we get to love each other and do life together forever."

"I was getting to that and we have two weeks to relax our way into the New Year."

"This past month has been an oxymoron, Kate said, "it has drained me and rejuvenated me simultaneously."

"I know, I am very proud of you, Kate."

"Is this when you tell me the little people are coming?"

"No, Kate, this is when I tell you I'm starving."

"Me, too."

Downstairs we were surprised to see Tom and Dawn enjoying bacon, eggs and toast. My look must have begged the question; "No, Joseph, I did not spend the night."

"I didn't say anything, I'm glad you are here."

"Good morning Dawn and Tom," Kate said.

"Good morning, Sis, your breakfasts are in the micro, just punch start."

I retrieved the bacon and eggs while Kate got her coffee and we all settled in for breakfast.

"Thank you, Tom," I said.

"My pleasure."

"Marti has the kids?"

"Yes, Joe, Marti looked at me this morning and said, 'I know how to cook, go, go go'!"

"That's sweet," I mused aloud.

"Joe is taking me to Montauk Point, I've never been."

"And Dawn and I," said Tom, "are cooking lamb chops, asparagus and sweet potatoes for dinner; so, if you two are back by five we will have drinks and dinner at six; the four of us."

"I'll show Tom where the BBQ, charcoal and tools are," Dawn added.

"This is a great breakfast," I said as Kate's foot gently rubbed mine, "and we," I turned to Kate, "will be home no sooner than five."

"Wine with dinner," asked Tom.

"How about champagne," I suggested.

"We're having champagne with the surprise dessert."

"How about a Cabernet?"

"Perfect," Dawn said, as she leaned over to give me a kiss on my cheek.

We had winter jackets that we threw on the back seat of the Porsche; there was no wind and it wasn't that cold. I started the Porsche and let it idle for a minute.

"That was pretty cute, those two."

"They want time alone."

"I am one hundred percent in favor of Tom and Dawn getting together; that's why I wanted Tom to be here."

"Tom is a very good cook; I wonder what the surprise dessert will be?"

"I know what they're having for lunch."

"Joseph!"

With a fire going in the fireplace, soft music playing and Tom and Dawn glowing, the four of us enjoyed the warmth of the den, our drinks and the love in the room.

"Montauk is wonderful and the lighthouse and the blue ocean; I am having a perfect day."

"Kate is now a stick shift expert, took to it just like that," I said as I snapped my fingers.

"Not that quickly, but after some bucking and stalling I got a feel for it, and then, on the highway, I did have a nice, easy way of shifting through the gears; it's the letter H, I get it."

"Kate drove all the way home."

"Tom and I spent some time with Marti and the kids, it was nice."

"We spent some time here and that was very nice," Tom said, raising his drink toward Dawn, "To you Dawn Mason, "you are a beautiful woman."

We all drank to that.

"Have the kids ever been to Montauk," Kate asked Dawn.

"No, but they asked where you guys were and when we told them they immediately put in their bid."

"We need a bigger car," I said.

"Problem solved, Marti offered her car. Tuesday?"

"Dawn, Tuesday is Christmas Eve day."

"Joe, it will be fun," Kate said

"That would be a Christmas present for Tom and me," declared Dawn.

"We are being eased out of our own home, Kate."

"I know, and it feels good."

During dinner, which Tom and Dawn cooked to perfection, Kate and I cajoled Tom to reveal the surprise dessert; we threatened to not take the kids to Montauk thus depriving Tom and Dawn their private alone time, but Tom held out. After we consumed our meal I took a different approach.

"I was just starting to like you, Tom."

Dawn stood up, "Shoo, go away, go to the den, anywhere, until you are called back for dessert. Go, go," Dawn said, gesturing for us to leave.

"Come on, Joe, I am certain we can find something to do."

Kate led me to the den, pushed me down on the sofa and kissed me.

"This is dessert, Joseph.

I promised to close my eyes and was led back to the dining room table.

"Eyes closed, Joe?"

"Yes."

"Okay," Tom said, I'm putting a big spoon in your hand."

"Got it."

"Okay, I'm guiding your spoon; now you can dig in and taste. Eyes closed."

Someone, I think it was Dawn, made sure I had "something" on my spoon and I tasted it.

"Oh, my God, it's a soufflé and it's delicious!"

I opened my eyes, "Tom, Dawn, thank you; this is my favorite dessert and this is a masterpiece."

"Any time, Joe."

Dawn poured champagne and we all enjoyed the soufflé and each other.

"Here's to a great day and to my brother and Dawn. Hurrah!"

Monday morning Dawn phoned Tom and lured him out for a practice run; "Temps are going up to the low 50's," she assured him. Kate and I went into town to shop for food and gifts for Sara and Bill. Gifts for Marti, Dawn and Tom were ready to go under the tree at the beach house thanks to Kate's shopping prowess at Saks. We, Kate and I, agreed on no gifts under the tree but we would shop for an engagement ring at Fabricant's in the city.

Home from shopping we put everything away and prepped the beef filet for dinner. Tom called, "Joe, Dawn, Marti and I are talking business, can you guys cook dinner?"

"Of course, dinner at six and bring the gang, there's plenty of food."

"Thanks, Joe, if I don't call you back it'll be all of us."

I set up the BBQ and Kate put potatoes in the oven. We tossed a salad and I figured I would cook at a quarter of six.

"Kate, would you please pour us a bourbon to share while I make a few holiday calls to friends that are important to me; to us really, you will meet them all, sooner or later."

"Coming up."

I got lucky and reached Chuck Sturner in Idaho, Jerry Brown at "41", Gabby Evers in New Brunswick, Rita Posinka in Boston and Frank Stetter in Acapulco.

"Done, Kate, here's to you," and I got a delicious Kate kiss.

"I have never been more relaxed," Kate said, "or happier. I am living my dream, Joseph. Here's to us." Kate took a sip, gave me the glass and curled up in my arms.

During dinner Sara and Bill reminded us of the planned excursion to Montauk and the lighthouse the next day, Christmas Eve day.

"Absolutely, and Mom has to loan us her car," I said.

"Keys will be on the counter," Marti assured us, "Bill will bring them down to the garage."

"Okay," Bill said.

"We'll leave at ten and be home no later than five."

"I have an idea," Dawn said, "Let's have a light dinner at the beach house and we can open presents on Christmas Eve."

"We are having Christmas dinner with you the next day," Kate said.

Marti spoke up, "Reflecting on our business talk this afternoon and Dawn and Tom's feelings for each other we are on the threshold of lots of dinners together; here, there," Marti shrugged, "It's one big happy family."

"Does that mean," Sara started, looking at Dawn, "You and Tom are going to sleep together?"

"Yes. No! It's, complicated, Sara, yes, I think."

"Adults are complicated," Bill said.

Sara responded, "They will figure it out, they always do."

On the way to Montauk Point and the lighthouse we had lunch in Amagansett where Sara and Bill began the process of asking Kate a "thousand" questions that lasted throughout the day; they are expert interrogators: where did you meet Joe and when; how old is Tom; do you like your brother; do you think he loves Dawn, and so on. During the day they attached themselves to Kate; often one on each hand as she answered each question open and honestly, even the accident and Tom being at her bedside for three months.

Later in the day, at Hither Hills State Park, we stopped briefly for a quick look at the beautiful beach.

"We love Joe, you know," Sara said to Kate.

"I know," Kate said, "I do too."

"For three months sleeping; that's a long time," Bill mused.

"I know, Bill, and then many more months until I had the courage to move on with my life; Tom helped with that, too."

"Where was Joe," Bill wanted to know.

All of this was going on as if I wasn't with them.

"Joe didn't know about the accident; he thought I had disappeared."

"Wow," Bill said, "so that's how Joe fell in love with my Mom."

"Yes, Bill, in a way."

"She missed the boat," Sara said, "but we love you, Kate."

We all looked at each other for a short while and then we all laughed; it was as if we had signed a contract and we were all pleased.

"I'm freezing," Sara said, and we ran to the car and piled in. My heart was dancing with joy.

Christmas eve was a hoot. Dawn and Tom had put all the presents under the tree and there were sandwiches and hot cocoa for the kids and Sara and Bill told us how much they enjoyed their day with Kate and me. We ate, we drank and we warmed ourselves at the fireplace and we all settled in on the sofa.

Marti was crying, dabbing at her eyes.

"Marti?" I was concerned.

"Tears of joy, I guess. There is so much love in this house, in this family; that's why I'm crying, we are one big happy family!"

"We are always going to be a big, happy family,"

I assured Marti.

"Mom, can I hand out the presents," Bill asked.

"That would be wonderful, Bill, you be Santa."

"I am Santa," Bill said and handed his mother a handsomely wrapped box.

"You first, Mom."

Marti opened her present and revealed seven T- shirts, each a different color and each labeled the days of the week.

"Stunning; I love them, who are they from?"

"They are from all of us," we all said, "we love you."

"I will wear them every day this summer," and Marti burst into tears.

Sara and Bill wedged in next to their mom, one on each side, and Marti, this amazing and beautiful woman, managed a smile, "This is the best Christmas ever."

Marti was right, we all had a grand Christmas and realized we are each other's gifts.

Wearing new shirts, sweaters and running shoes, or playing Backgammon on Bill's new board, Kate's and my gift to Bill, we managed to eat, drink and play in both houses and find private time as well. Tom shifted to the beach house to be with Dawn and he and Marti finalized plans for Tom to bring his financial expertise and contacts to MasonCo in a six-month trial that worked both ways.

On Monday morning, the thirtieth, I called The Monarch, spoke with the manager, and had them move everything from my apartment, other than the furniture, to Apartment 18B in the West wing; I had forgotten to take care of the move.

"No problem, Joe, we will take care of that today. By the way, your new parking stall is number one, in the West garage. "That's great; thanks for your help and Happy New Year."

"And to you."

CHAPTER 54

A KISS GOODNIGHT

Kate and I promised to have a day just for us; with the phone call out of the way, this is the day.

"Where are we going," Kate wanted to know as I let the Porsche warm up.

"We are going west to Riverhead and doubling back on the north fork to Orient Point."

"Of course we are," Kate asserted as a question.

"You are a hot Jersey shore girl who doesn't know squat about Long Island."

"Joseph!"

"My apology, Katherine, I guess I was looking foe a way to tell you, I think you're hot."

"I know that you think that and I love that you do. What about Long Island?"

I made a vee with my left hand, held it out horizontally and touched the tip of the index finger with my right hand, "South fork, Montauk Point," then I touched the tip of my forefinger, "North fork, Orient Point"

"Got it, and where your fingers meet your palm is Riverhead."

"You are an excellent student, Kate."

"And you, Joe, are going to get a lesson tonight on the ecstasy of the Jersey Shore you will never forget."

"I love being threatened by you. Let's stay home."

"Oh, no; we are going for a drive to the tip of your finger."

"Orient Point."

"Exactly, and we are going to talk about our wedding, having children, where we want to live, do you travel much for work, are you going to start your own firm, and we are going to stop for lunch during which I want to discuss how much I love you, Joseph; my love for you is endless."

I smiled and Kate turned on the radio and found a station she liked and played it softly.

At Riverhead I followed the signs to route 25 – 48 to Orient Point. Along the way, on route 48, we stopped for lunch in Greenport.

"Two bowls of broccoli cheddar, some bread or rolls and a Pabst beer, please."

"City folk?"

"How could you tell?"

"You said, please."

"This is Kate, I'm Joe, and who are you?"

"I'm Betty."

"Local?"

"My whole life."

"Betty, we are cold, hungry and in love."

"Hot soup coming up, Joe."

"Thank you."

Betty was headed to the kitchen, "I knew you are in love!"

Kate took my face between her cold hands and kissed me, "I love you, city boy."

"We, Kate, are locals; we live near by."

"Oh, my God, I would love to live out here."

"What about the schools and business; we would starve," I said

"Be careful," Betty said, "The soup is very hot, the bread is warm, the beer is cold, the schools are good and I don't know your business but I would recommend you. Enjoy."

Betty wandered off and I took a quick taste.

"The soup is delicious," I called out.

"Thank you," Betty called back.

"City girl," I called out to Betty and we heard her chuckle.

After a few spoons full Kate and I settled into our meal and each other.

"This is a wonderful day, Joe, we needed a break from the gang. I like Marti and the kids are smart and fun."

"But?"

Kate shook her head, "It's the amazing lifestyle, I mean, wow."

"Kate, I know it's heady stuff. You've been wonderful and your brother has thrust himself in the middle of it; especially with his relationship with Dawn. I think they are perfect and I think he is going to end up running MassonCo."

"No doubt, he's super smart and he has the company's best interests at heart."

"Kate, are you overwhelmed?"

"Well you and Marti; almost, huh?"

"Almost, but you and I are not an almost, we are a forever. We have a wedding to plan."

"Can we have a small wedding, Joseph, I only have my brother and my Uncle Buddy."

"Just family, works for me; my mom, two sisters and maybe the Reinhardts; like fifteen max. We can have it upstairs at "41", they have a private party room that's like a living room; it would be perfect. When?"

"I don't know, soon. I want us to have two children, one of each."

"That would be wonderful, Kate, we're going to need a bigger car."

"You look shocked, Joe."

"No, not at all, I was just thinking out loud, this is exciting. Books, Kate, lots of books; I want our kids to be readers."

"Me too, and travel all over the 50 states when they are old enough and before sixteen so they can enjoy summers with their friends."

"Sounds good, we can visit all the National Parks."

"Fine, but tonight it's the Jersey shore."

"I have not forgotten, but first we are going to Orient Point."

"I'm ready."

"Betty," I called.

"Coming, Joe."

"We had a wonderful lunch, thank you."

"Thank you both for coming, it's twenty five."

I put two twenties on the counter.

"That's too much, Joe."

"We came in cold and hungry and we're leaving warm and full. Happpy New Year, Betty."

"Bye, Kate, best wishes to you both."

In the car I let the engine warm up for a minute; Kate was staring at me.

"What," I asked,

"You are amazing."

"Thank you, my almost pregnant future wife."

I put the Porsche in gear and turned toward Orient Point.

"It's beautiful here, Joe, I like the North fork."

"I like it too."

"You've never been to that restaurant before, have you," Kate asked.

"No."

"And yet, within minutes, you made a friend who will always remember you."

"Betty will remember us, Kate."

We motored along for a bit with Kate's knees up in front of her face and her arms wrapped around her legs; I recognized she was deep in thought.

"Joseph, at the Reinhardt Christmas party, Susan Reinhardt told me Bob thinks you will leave to start Gordon and Associates. It sounded like she was predicting it."

"That's a tall order, Kate, a new family and my own firm."

"You can do it. We are partners for life and I want you to have your dream along the way."

"You are my dream, Kate."

"Your dream, Joe, your "guy" dream, and I want to help you get it!"

"For the moment why don't we concentrate on getting pregnant."

"We are doing really well in that department, Joe. We've been together for five weeks."

"Oh!"

"Nothing to report yet."

"We have room in the apartment and our house at the beach for the Spring, Summer and Fall and right now I love you very big for your understanding and support and for luring me into your nest."

"My pleasure, Joseph."

"My pleasure as well and we are at Orient Point."

"How fitting for us."

I brought in a few logs and got a fire going in the den. I poured a bourbom on the rocks, put on a stack of L.P.'s, mostly vocals and show tunes and headed to the kitchen where I threw a half of Brie cheese into the micro for thirty seconds and cut some slices of French bread.

Kate was waiting for me, wearing a short robe loosely tied at the waist and as she leaned over toward the warmth of the fire I was warmed with a view of the "Jersey shore."

"I know you are enjoying the view, Joseph."

"True enough, Katherine, and I come bearing gifts."

I barely had time to put down the tray before Kate was in my arms.

"We are each others gifts, Joseph."

I then received a Kate kiss that probably ignited every fireplace on the north fork. We danced, we talked, we sipped, we touched, we nibbled, we kissed and we went to bed where we gifted each other with pleasure and joy.

Tuesday evening, New Years Eve, we celebrated at the beach house, twice. Tom and I bartended, cooked and served a candlelight, filet mignon dinner for seven that Tom capped off with two soufflés; one vanilla and the other chocolate. Delicious! Prior to dinner we had oysters and shrimp and music and dancing that included Sara and Bill. Tom is six two, handsome, agile and a good dancer and he and I and Bill enjoyed dancing with Sara, Dawn, Marti and Kate. At ten we celebrated "1965" with a count down from five, four, three, two, one; and a sip of champagne, even the kids, and hugs and kisses goodnight. Marti took the kids up to bed and the four of us bunched together, arms around one another and swayed to the music.

"I know four, maybe five guys for Marti," Tom said, "they are smart, successful, athletic and nice."

"Oh, God, I would love to see Marti with a man in her life," Dawn said.

"I'll drink to that," I added.

"Drink to what, Joseph?"

Marti descended the staircase in a plunging, black, silk gown.

"To you, Marti, and the New Year," I said.

"Filled with Joy," Kate said.

"And success and fun," Tom added.

"Damn, Marti, you are some kind of beautiful," Dawn said.

"Where's my glass of champagne," Marti wanted to know. "I want to make a toast."

We all gathered our glasses of champagne and formed a circle of five;

"Here's to you," Marti said, looking at each of us in turn, "and to Sara and Bill," Marti gestured upstairs, and to me, too. Here's to us!"

We all drank and hugged and for a split second I thought of Marti's toast at "41", "To you, to me, to us," when Dawn tapped me on the shoulder, "Are you going to dance with me, old man?"

We all danced and talked and we went out on the deck for a few freezing cold seconds before coming inside to count down to officially enter into the New Year.

Tom stoked the fire and we sat on the sofa nibbling on little cakes and enjoying a nightcap.

At a little before one Kate and I bid Marti, Dawn and Tom goodnight and bundled up for the quick walk home.

Upstairs I turned on the gas fireplace in the bedroom.

"I'm exhausted and wide awake, Joseph."

"That's quite a problem and I have a solution."

"Oh?"

"I think if we sleep together we can solve your problem."

"This is a recurring problem that will last for decades."

"A lifetime together, born from a kiss a decade ago."

"We are a miracle," Kate said, just before she kissed me goodnight.

THE KISS

EPILOGUE

Joseph Gordon and Katherine Lawrence were married on Saturday, April 11th, at the "41" Club.

The Gordons announced the birth of their son, Zachary Samuel, August 18, 1965.

Gordon & Associates opened for business Monday, September 14, 1965.

Tom Lawrence and Dawn Mason live together in Greenwich Village and Tom is the C.E.O. of MasonCo.

Marti Mason is dating Albert Henderson, a Wall Street friend of Tom.

Rita Posinka lives in Manhattan and works at Gordon & Associates.

Eileen Kelly is now Doctor Eileen Naughton whose husband owns an alcohol and drug rehab center in Baltimore.

Gabby Evers continues to represent the Lincoln Motor Car Company and resides happily with Suki, her dear friend.

Jerry and Martha Brown are the proud grandparents of Celeste's three children.

The Monarch is the most desirable apartment building on the east side.

Richard, Joe's roommate at Rutgers, added a D.D.S. after his name as well as a lovely Mrs.

Joseph Gordon earned his Pilot's License; June, 1966.

THE END

ABOUT THE AUTHOR

Joe Goodson has experienced a prolific and varied career both as a restaurateur and an entertainment industry insider. He began his career in New York City as a restaurateur at the illustrious "21" Club for 13 years from 1955 – 1968. While there he met and worked with top celebrities of the day who frequented "21". As his career progressed, he took his chance in the entertainment industry, moving to Hollywood in the late 1960's. There, he became the Associate Producer for the popular TV sitcom, "I Dream of Jeannie". Goodson was a television writer, producer, director and studio executive; during this period he worked on "The Love Boat", "The Good Life", " On Our Own" and "Starman", as well as several movies for television. He served as Director of New Comedy Development for three years at Screen Gems. As a past member of the Writer's Guild and Director's Guild, this is Goodson's first novel. He resides in Riverside, CA with his wife, Susan, also a published author.

www.ingramcontent.com/pod-product-compliance
Lightning Source LLC
Chambersburg PA
CBHW070734190726
48292CB00002B/255